DEAD FAMOUS

Ben Elton

BLACK SWAN

DEAD FAMOUS
A BLACK SWAN BOOK : 0 552 99945 8

Originally published in Great Britain by Bantam Press,
a division of Transworld Publishers

PRINTING HISTORY
Bantam Press edition published 2001
Black Swan edition published 2002

9 10 8

Copyright © Bantam Press 2001

The right of Ben Elton to be identified as the author of
this work has been asserted in accordance with sections 77
and 78 of the Copyright Designs and Patents Act 1988.

Set in 11/12pt Melior by
Falcon Oast Graphic Art Ltd.

Black Swan Books are published by Transworld Publishers,
61–63 Uxbridge Road, London W5 5SA,
a division of The Random House Group Ltd,
in Australia by Random House Australia (Pty) Ltd,
20 Alfred Street, Milsons Point, Sydney, NSW 2061, Australia,
in New Zealand by Random House New Zealand Ltd,
18 Poland Road, Glenfield, Auckland 10, New Zealand
and in South Africa by Random House (Pty) Ltd,
Endulini, 5a Jubilee Road, Parktown 2193, South Africa.

Printed and bound in Great Britain by
Clays Ltd, St Ives plc.

With thanks to:

in the UK:
Andrew, Anna, Caroline, Claire, Craig, Darren, Mel,
Nichola, Nick, Sada and Tom
and
Amma, Brian, Dean, Elizabeth, Bubble, Helen, Josh,
Narinder, Penny, Paul and Stuart;

and in Australia:
Andy, Anita, Ben, Blair, Christina, Gordon, Jemma,
Johnnie, Lisa, Peter, Rachel, Sara-Marie, Sharna and Todd,

without whom this novel would not have been written.

David. Real job: actor. Star sign: Aries.

Jazz. Real job: trainee chef. Star sign: Leo (cusp of Cancer).

Kelly. Real job: sales consultant. Star sign: Libra.

Sally. Real job: female bouncer. Star sign: Aries.

Garry. Real job: van driver. Star sign: Cancer.

Moon. Real job: circus trapeze artiste and occasional lap dancer. Star sign: Capricorn.

Hamish. Real job: junior doctor. Star sign: Leo.

Woggle. Real job: anarchist. Star sign: claims to be all twelve.

Layla. Real job: fashion designer and retail supervisor. Star sign: Scorpio.

Dervla. Real job: trauma therapist. Star sign: Taurus.

The murder took place on day twenty-seven in the house.

Nomination

DAY TWENTY-NINE. 9.15 a.m.

'Television presenter, television presenter, television presenter, television presenter, train driver.'

Sergeant Hooper looked up. 'Train driver?'

'I'm sorry, my mistake. Television presenter.'

Chief Inspector Coleridge dumped the thick file of suspect profiles onto his desk and turned his attention once more to the big video screen that had been erected in the corner of the incident room. For the previous two hours he had been watching tapes at random.

Garry lounged on the green couch. The pause button was down and Garry's image was frozen. Had the tape been running, the picture would have been much the same, for Garry was in his customary position, legs spread wide, muscles flexed, left hand idly fondling his testicles.

A blurred blue eagle hovered above his right ankle. Coleridge hated that eagle. Just what the hell did this pointless lump of arrogance and ignorance think he had in common with an eagle? He pressed play and Garry spoke.

'Your basic English Premier League team consists of ten idiots and one big gorilla hanging about up at the front, usually a black geezer.'

Coleridge struggled to care. Already his mind was drifting. How much rubbish could these people talk?

Everybody talked rubbish, of course, but with most people it just disappeared into the ether; with this lot it was there for ever. What was more, it was evidence. He *had* to listen to it.

'. . . What the ten idiots have to do is keep kicking the ball up to the gorilla in the hope that he'll be unmarked and get a lucky shot in.'

The world had heard these sparkling observations before: they had been chosen for broadcast, the people at Peeping Tom Productions having been thrilled with them. The words 'black' and 'gorilla' in the same sentence would make a *terrific* reality TV moment.

' "Bold, provocative and controversial",' Coleridge muttered under his breath.

He was quoting from a newspaper article he had found inside the box of the video tape he was watching. All of the *House Arrest* tapes had arrived with the appropriate press clippings attached. The Peeping Tom media office were nothing if not thorough. When you asked for their archive, you got it.

The article Coleridge had read was a profile of Geraldine Hennessy, the celebrated producer behind *House Arrest*.

'We're not BBC TV,' Geraldine, known to the press as Geraldine the Gaoler, was quoted as saying. 'We're BPC TV: Bold, Provocative, Controversial, and allowing the world a window into Garry's casual, unconscious racism is just that.'

Coleridge sighed. Provocative? Controversial? What sort of ambitions were those for a grown-up woman? He turned his attention to the man sitting opposite Garry, the one on the orange couch: flashy Jason, known as Jazz, so cool, so hip, such strutting self-confidence, always grinning, except when he was sneering, which he was doing now.

'That's it, mate,' Garry continued, 'no skill, no finesse, no planning. The entire national game based on the strategy of the lucky break.' Once more he rearranged his genitals, the shape of which could clearly be made out beneath the lime-green satin of his sports shorts. The camera moved in closer. Peeping Tom clearly liked genitals; presumably they were BPC.

'Don't get me wrong about saying the big bloke's black, Jazz,' Garry added. 'Fact is, most League strikers are these days.'

Jazz fixed Garry with a gaze he clearly believed was both enigmatic and intimidating. Jazz's body was even better than Garry's and he too kept his muscles in a pretty continuous state of tension. They seemed almost to ripple up and down his arms as he idly fondled the thick gold chain that hung round his neck and lay heavy on his beautiful honed chest. 'Gorilla.'

'What?'

'You didn't say "bloke", you said "gorilla".'

'Did I? Well, what I mean is gorillas are big and strong, ain't they? Like your lot.'

Over by the kitchen units Layla, the blonde hippie supermodel in her own mind, tossed her fabulous beaded braids in disgust. Inspector Coleridge knew that Layla had tossed her lovely hair in disgust, because the video edit he was watching had cut abruptly to her. There was no way that Peeping Tom was going to miss that snooty little middle-class sneer. Coleridge was quickly coming to realize that Peeping Tom's editorial position was firmly anti intellectual pretension.

'We consider ourselves to be the People's Peeping Tom,' Geraldine was quoted as saying in the article. Clearly she also considered Layla to be a stuck-up, humourless, middle-class bitch, for that was how the edit was portraying her.

Coleridge cursed the screen. He had been watching Jazz, he wanted to watch Jazz, but one of the principal handicaps of his investigation was that he could only

15

watch whoever Peeping Tom had wanted to be watched at the time, and Inspector Coleridge had a very different agenda from that of Peeping Tom. Peeping Tom had been trying to make what they called 'great telly'. Coleridge was trying to catch a murderer.

Now the camera was back with Garry and his testicles.

Coleridge did not *think* that Garry was the murderer. He knew Garry, he had banged up twenty Garrys every Saturday night during his long years in uniform. Garry's type were all the same, so loud, so smug, so cocky. Coleridge thought back to how Garry had looked two nights before, in the aftermath of a murder, when they had faced each other over a police tape recorder. Garry hadn't looked so cocky then, he had looked scared.

But Coleridge *knew* Garry. Garrys got in fights, but they didn't murder people, unless they were very unlucky, or drunk and at the wheel of a car. Coleridge most certainly did not like this strutting, pumped-up, tattooed, cockney geezer, but he did not think that he was *evil*. He did not think that he was the sort of person to sneak up on a fellow human being, plunge a kitchen knife into their neck, pull it out again and then *bury it deep into their skull.*

Coleridge did not *think* that Garry would do something like that. But, then again, Coleridge had been wrong before, lots of times.

The nation didn't think that Garry was the murderer either. He was one of their favourites. Gazzer the Geezer had been amongst the early tabloid tips to win the game before it had turned into a real-life whodunit, and he rarely topped the poll when the media considered the identity of the killer.

Coleridge smiled to himself, a sad, rather superior smile. The only sort of smile he seemed able to muster these days. The nation did not really *know* Gazzer.

They thought they did, but they didn't. They had been given only his best bits, his chirpy one-liners, his unnerving ability to spot what he thought to be a snob or a clever dick, the relentless and gleeful way he wound up the snooty, self-important Layla. And the bold chunky penis end that had once been glimpsed peeping out from beneath his running shorts. An image that had immediately found its way onto T-shirts sold at Camden Lock market.

'Cyclops! In your bed!' Garry had shouted as if addressing a dog, before relocating the offending member. 'Sorry, girls, it's just I don't wear no pants, see. They make my love furniture sweaty.'

That was all the nation saw of Garry, just bite-sized chunks of honest, no-nonsense, common-sense geezer, and on the whole they liked him for it.

On the screen, Garry, like the video editor who had created the tape that Coleridge was watching, had noted Layla's doubtful response to his homily on racial characteristics and, sensing the reaction of a snob and a clever dick, had decided to press his point.

'It's true!' he protested, laughing at Layla's discomfort. 'I know you ain't supposed to say it, but bollocks to fucking political correctness. I'm paying Jazz a compliment. Blacks are faster and stronger and that's a proven fact. Look at boxing, look at the Olympics. Fuck me, the white blokes ought to get a medal for having the guts to compete at all! It's even worse with the birds. You seen them black birds run? Half a dozen bleeding ebony amazons charge past the finishing tape in a pack and then about ten minutes later a couple of bony-arsed gingers from Glasgow turn up.'

Bold stuff: bold, provocative and controversial.

'Yes, but that's because . . .' Layla stuttered, knowing she must refute these appalling sentiments.

'Because fucking what?'

'Well . . . because black people have to turn to sport

on account of the fact that other opportunities in society are closed off to them. That's why they're disproportionately over-represented in physical activities.'

Now Jazz chipped in, but not to support Layla. 'So what you're saying, right, is that in fact a load of white geezers could actually beat us blacks at running and boxing and stuff like that if only they wasn't so busy becoming doctors and prime ministers? Is that it, Layles?'

'No!'

'You're the fucking racist, girl, that is disgusting!'

Layla looked as if she was going to cry. Garry and Jazz laughed together. No wonder the nation preferred them to her. A large section of the viewing public saw Gazzer and Jazz as their representatives in the house. Jovial, no bullshit, down-to-earth blokes. Top lads, diamond geezers. But how would the nation feel, Coleridge wondered, if it had to suffer them twenty-four hours a day? Suffer them as the other inmates did? Day after day, week after week, with their unabashed arrogance bouncing off the walls and ceiling. How irritating would that be? How much might someone secretly hate them? Enough to attack either of them in some way? Enough to force one or both of them on to the defensive? Enough to provoke them to murder?

But people didn't murder each other because they found each other irritating, did they? Yes. As a matter of fact, in Coleridge's experience, they did. Irritation was the commonest motive of all. Sad, petty, human disputes blown up suddenly and unintentionally into lethal proportions. How many times had Coleridge sat opposite some distraught family member as they struggled to come to terms with what they'd done because of *irritation*?

'I couldn't stand him any more. I just snapped.'

'She drove me to it.'

Most murders took place in a domestic situation between people who knew each other. Well, you couldn't get a much more domestic situation than *House Arrest*, and by the time of the murder the inmates knew each other very well, or at least knew the bits of each other that were on show, which is all anybody ever knows about anyone. These people did virtually nothing but talk to and about each other every waking moment of the day and night.

Perhaps one of them really had simply become irritating enough to get themselves killed?

But they were *all* irritating. Or at least they were to Coleridge. Every single one of them, with their toned tummies and their bare buttocks, their biceps and their triceps, their tattoos and their nipple rings, their mutual interest in star signs, their *endless* hugging and touching, and above all their complete lack of genuine intellectual curiosity about one single thing on this planet that was not directly connected with themselves.

Inspector Coleridge would happily have killed them all.

'Your problem is you're a snob, sir,' said Sergeant Hooper, who had been watching Coleridge watch the video and had followed his train of thought as surely as if Coleridge had had a glass head. 'Why the hell would anybody want to be a train driver these days anyway? There *aren't* any train drivers as a matter of fact, just some bloke that pushes the start button and goes on strike every now and then. It's hardly a noble calling, is it? I'd much rather be a TV presenter. Frankly, I'd rather be a TV presenter than a copper.'

'Get on with your work, Hooper,' said Coleridge.

Coleridge knew that they all laughed at him. They laughed at him because they thought he was old fashioned. Old fashioned because he was interested in things other than astrology and celebrity. Was he the

19

last man on earth interested in anything other than astrology and celebrity? Things like books and trains? He was only fifty-four years old, for heaven's sake, but as far as most of his officers were concerned he might as well have been two hundred. To them Coleridge was just so *weird*. He was a member of the Folio Society, a lay minister, he never failed to visit a war memorial on Armistice Day, and he grew plants from seeds rather than buying them ready-made from a garden centre.

The fact that it had fallen to Coleridge to watch the *entire* available footage of *House Arrest*, to sit and watch a group of pointless twenty-somethings living in a house together and subjected to constant video surveillance, was a cruel joke indeed. It was safe to say that under normal circumstances there was no other show in the history of television that Coleridge would have been less inclined to watch than *House Arrest*.

Coleridge gripped the handle of the proper china mug he insisted on using despite the fact that it required washing up. 'When I want your opinion, Hooper, on train drivers or any other subject for that matter, I shall ask for it.'

'And I will always be happy to oblige, sir.'

Coleridge knew that the sergeant was right. Who could blame today's youth for its lack of sober ambition? In the days when little boys wanted to grow up to be train drivers they had wanted to grow up to be the master of a vast machine. A fabulous spitting, steaming, snarling, living beast, a monster in metal that required skill and daring to handle, care and understanding to maintain. Nowadays, of course, technology was so complex that nobody knew how anything worked at all except Bill Gates and Stephen Hawking. The human race was out of the loop, to employ a phrase he often heard Hooper using. No wonder all young people wanted was to be on television. What else was there to do? He stared wearily at the huge piles of video tapes and computer disks that seemed to fill most of the room.

'Well, let's go back to the beginning, shall we? Attack this thing in order.' He picked up a tape marked 'First broadcast edit' and put it into the machine.

One house. Ten contestants. Thirty cameras. Forty microphones. One survivor.

The words punched themselves onto the screen like fists slamming into a face.

Frantic, angry rock music accompanied the post-punk graphics and the grainy images supporting them.

A spinning hot-head camera.

A barbed wire fence.

A snarling guard dog.

A girl with her back to the camera removing her bra.

A close-up of a mouth, screaming and contorted with rage.

More big guitar noise. More jagged graphics.

Nobody watching could be in the slightest doubt that this was telly from the hip and for the hip. The message was clear: boring people should seek their entertainment elsewhere, but if you happened to be young, bigged up and mad for it, this was the show for you.

Nine weeks. No excuses. No escape.

House Arrest.

A final blast of swooping, feedback-laden guitar and the credits were over. For one last moment the Peeping Tom house was empty and all was calm. A big, bright friendly space, with a wide tiled living area, pleasant communal bedrooms, stainless steel washrooms and showers and a swimming pool in the garden.

The front door opened and ten young people spilled through it, spreading out into the large open plan living area. Ten people who, the pre-publicity had assured the nation, had never met before in their lives.

21

They whooped, they shrieked, they hugged, they said 'Wicked!' over and over again. Some went into the bedrooms and jumped up and down on the beds, others did chin-ups on the doorframes, one or two stood back a little and watched, but everybody seemed to be of the opinion that the adventure of a lifetime had just begun and they simply could not be starting off on it with a more wicked crew.

Having clearly established the fact that the viewing public were in the company of a party crowd, the camera began to introduce the housemates individually. The first to be picked out was an impossibly handsome young man with soft puppy eyes, boyish features and long shoulder-length hair. He wore a big black coat and carried a guitar. A graphic stamped itself across the man's face, letters made out of bricks, like prison walls.

David. Real job: actor. Star sign: Aries.

'Pause, please, constable.'

The image froze and the assembled officers studied the handsome face on the screen, a face disfigured by the angry graphic stamped across it.

'Real job: actor,' Coleridge said. 'When did he last work?'

Trisha, a young detective constable who had just finished pinning up the last of the seven suspect photographs, turned her attention to David's file. 'Panto, Prince Charming. Two Christmases ago.'

'Two years ago? Then it's hardly a real job, is it?'

'That's what Gazzer says later on in the show, sir,' Hooper chipped in. 'David gets quite arsey about it.'

'Arsey?'

'Annoyed.'

'Thank you, sergeant. It will speed matters up considerably in this incident room if we all speak the same language. Is there any evidence that this boy *can* actually act?'

'Oh yes, sir,' said Trisha. 'He had a very good start. RADA graduate and quite a lot of work at first, but recently it just hasn't been happening for him.'

Coleridge studied David's face frozen on the screen. 'Bit of a come-down, this, eh? I can't imagine that appearing on *House Arrest* was what he had in mind when he left drama college.'

'No, it does look a bit desperate, doesn't it?'

Coleridge looked once more at David. The face was flickering and jumping about because the police VCR was old and clapped out and did not like pausing. David's mouth was slightly open in a grin and the effect made him look like he was gnawing at the air.

'What does he live off while he's doing his real job of not acting?'

'Well, I wondered about that, sir,' said Hooper, 'and I have to admit it's a bit obscure. He doesn't sign on, but he seems to do pretty well for himself – nice flat, good clothes and all that. He told Peeping Tom that his parents helped him out.'

'Look into it, will you? If he's in debt or steals or sells drugs and one of the other people in the house had found out . . . Well, there might be something, the ghost of a motive . . .' But Coleridge did not sound convinced.

'The telly people would have heard it, wouldn't they, sir? I mean, if another inmate had found something out about him? Don't they hear everything?' Trisha asked. 'Not *absolutely* everything,' Hooper, who was a reality TV buff, replied. 'They *see* everything, but they don't *hear* everything – most but not all. Sometimes, when the inmates whisper, it's hard to make out what they're saying, and every now and then they leave their microphones off and have to be told to put them back on. And they sometimes tap them when they speak. The contestants in the first series worked that one out. Remember Wicked Willy? The bloke who

23

got chucked off for trying to manipulate the votes? That was his little trick.'

'Well, that would be worth watching out for, wouldn't it?' Trisha said. 'Microphone tapping – very conspiratorial.'

'Unfortunately most of the bits where you can't hear weren't stored on disk because they were useless for broadcast.'

'Oh, well,' said Coleridge. 'As my mother used to say, life wasn't meant to be easy. Next one, please. Move on.'

'Check it out, guys! A swimming pool!'

Jazz had opened the patio doors and spun round to announce his discovery. The graphic punched bricks into his handsome young face:

Jazz. Real job: trainee chef. Star sign: Leo (cusp of Cancer).

'This is better than Ibiza!' He performed a little acid-style dance on the edge of the pool while doing a convincing vocal impression of a drum and bass track. 'Duh! Boom! Chh chh boom! Chh chh boom! Chhh chhh BOOM!

Now a girl came running out to join Jazz. A pretty girl with a happy laughing face and a small jewel stud through one nostril.

Kelly. Real job: sales consultant. Star sign: Libra.

'Wicked!' shouted Kelly.

'Chh chh boom!' Jazz replied.

Kelly began to jump up and down, clapping her hands together with excitement. 'Wicked! Unreal! *Amped up!*' She shouted, and, kicking off her baggy hipsters, she jumped into the pool.

'Sales consultant?' Coleridge enquired. 'What does that mean?'

'Shop girl,' said Hooper. 'Miss Selfridge.'

Coleridge stared at Kelly's flickering image on the screen. 'Did you see those trousers she was wearing? They showed half her bottom.'

'I've got a pair exactly the same,' Trisha remarked.

'Well, frankly, Patricia, I'm surprised. You could see her knickers poking out of the top.'

'That's the point, sir.'

'It is?'

'Yes, sir, no sense paying for a CK G-string if people can't see it, is there?'

Coleridge did not ask what CK stood for. He wasn't falling into obvious traps like that. 'What sense of her own worth does that girl have if she chooses to *boast* about her underwear?'

Coleridge wondered if he was the only person in the world who felt so completely culturally disenfranchised. Or were there others like him? Living secret lives, skulking in the shadows, scared to open their mouths for fear of exposure. People who no longer understood the *adverts*, let alone the programmes.

On the TV screen Kelly burst back out of the water, and as she did so one of her breasts popped momentarily over the top of her sodden vest. By the time she surfaced for a second time she had got it covered up. 'Oh my God!' shouted Kelly. 'I'm wearing my microphone. Peeping Tom'll kill me.'

'She was wrong about that,' Hooper remarked. 'Kelly's famous boob. I remember it well. Definitely worth the cost of a mike. They used it in the trailers, all hazy in slow-motion, very cheeky, very nice. It was in the papers, too – "It's *House A-BREAST*!" Most amusing, I thought.'

'*Could* we get on, please?' Coleridge snapped testily.

Hooper bit his lip. He pressed play and a young woman with tattoos and a Mohican haircut strutted out of the house to look at the swimming pool.

Sally. Real job: female bouncer. Star sign: Aries.

'They should say "Real job: token lesbian",' said Trisha. 'She's the gay one. They have to have a gay or a dyke, I think it's part of the Broadcasting Standards Commission guidelines.'

Coleridge wanted to object to the word 'dyke' but he wondered whether perhaps it had become the officially accepted term without his noticing. Language changed so quickly these days. 'Do you think those tattoos mean anything?' he asked instead.

'Yeah, they mean keep clear 'cos I'm one scary hard bitch,' Hooper replied.

'I think they're Maori,' Trisha said. 'They certainly look Maori.'

Sally's arms were entirely covered in tattoos; there was not a single square inch of flesh left showing from her wrists to her shoulders. Great thick stripes of blue-black snaked and coiled across her skin.

'You know she's the number-one Internet choice for having done it,' Hooper noted, adding, 'She'd be strong enough. Look at the muscles on it.'

'That knife was very sharp,' Coleridge snapped. 'Any one of the people in that house would have been strong enough to pierce a skull with it if they felt strongly enough about the skull they were piercing. And would you kindly keep comments about the Internet to yourself? The fact that there are millions of bored idiots out there with nothing better to do than tap rubbish down telephone lines has absolutely nothing to do with this investigation.'

Silence reigned briefly in the incident room. Coleridge was so unabashed in the way he treated them all like schoolchildren; it was difficult to know how to react.

'This bouncer business,' Coleridge said, returning to the subject of Sally. 'Known to us?'

'Soho nick have talked to her occasionally,' said

Tricia, leafing through Sally's file. 'She's cracked a few heads, but only in self-defence.'

'Her mother must be very proud.'

'She also got into a bit of a fight at last year's Gay Pride march. Took on a couple of yobs who were jeering.'

'Why do these people feel the need to define themselves by their preferences in bed?'

'Well, if they didn't talk about it, sir, you wouldn't know, would you?'

'But why do I *need* to know?'

'Because otherwise you would presume they were straight.'

'If by that you mean heterosexual, I would not presume any such thing, constable. I would not think about it at all.'

But Trisha knew that Coleridge was deceiving himself. Trisha was quite certain that Coleridge presumed *she* was a heterosexual. It simply would not occur to him to think otherwise. How she longed to shock him to his foundations and prove her point by announcing that she was as entirely and absolutely a lesbian as the tattooed girl on the screen. *Actually, sir, all my lovers are women and what I particularly enjoy is when they bang me with a strap-on dildo.*

He would be *astonished*. He thought she was such a *nice* girl.

But Trisha didn't say anything. She kept quiet. That was why she secretly admired women like Sally, irritating and graceless though they might be. *They* did not keep quiet. They made people like Coleridge think.

'Let's move on,' said Coleridge.

'Nice knockers, girl!' Sally shouted at Kelly, who was just emerging from the pool.

Garry, all muscles and shaved head, was the next to emerge from the house. On seeing Kelly, soaking wet with her skimpy singlet clinging to her fit young body, he dropped to his knees in mock worship. 'Thank you, God!' he shouted to the skies. 'Something for the lads! *We like that!*'

Garry. Real job: van driver. Star sign: Cancer.

'Or the girls!' Sally shouted back. 'You never know, she might play for my team.'

'You a dyke, then?' Garry enquired, turning to her with interest.

'Derr!' said Sally, pointing to the front of her vest on which were written the words 'I eat pussy'.

'Oh, is that what it means? I thought it meant you'd just been to a Chinese restaurant!' Garry laughed hugely at his joke, which was to provoke a minor scandal when it was broadcast later that evening, being considered highly bold, provocative and controversial.

Inside the house a bald woman in a leopardskin-print mini-skirt was exploring the living area. 'Check it out, guys! There's a welcome basket! Wicked!'

Moon. Real job: circus trapeze artiste and occasional lap-dancer. Star sign: Capricorn.

'Fags, chocolate, champagne! Wicked!'

'Get stuck in!' shouted Garry from the patio doors.

The others quickly assembled around the basket and the four bottles of Sainsbury's own-brand champagne were immediately opened. They all collapsed onto the orange, green and purple couches on which they would lounge for so much of the long days to come.

'Right, since we're chilling out and kicking back, I might as well tell you now,' Moon shouted in her exaggerated Mancunian accent, 'because at the end of the day you're all going to find out anyways. First of all, I'm going to win this fookin' game, all fookin' right? So the rest of you bastards can just forget it! All right?' This exhibition of bravado was received with friendly cheers.

'Second, I've done lap-dancing, right? I took money

off sad blokes for letting them see me bits, I'm not proud of it, but at the end of the day I was fookin' good at it, right?'

This provoked more cheers and shouts of 'Good on you!'

'And third, I've had a boob job, right? I was dead unhappy with my self-image before, and my new tits have really empowered me as a person in my own right, right? Which at the end of the day is what it's all about, in't it? Quite frankly, at the end of the day, I feel that these are the boobs I was supposed to have.'

'Gi's a look, then, darling, and I'll tell you if you're right!' Gazzer shouted.

'Easy, tiger!' Moon shrieked, revelling in the attention. 'Take it easy. We've got nine fookin' weeks in here, don't want to peak too soon. Oh God, though, what have I said? I feel terrible. Me mum never knew 'bout me being a stripper, she thinks I'm dead proper, me. So-rry, Mum!'

'I've got nothing against a bit of cosmetic surgery,' Jazz reflected. 'I've never regretted my knob reduction, at least now it don't poke out the bottom of me trousers!'

The housemates laughed and shrieked and said 'Wicked!' but there were some who laughed more than others. A quiet-looking girl with raven-dark hair and green eyes only smiled. Sitting beside her was a rather straight-looking young man dressed in smart but casual Timberland.

Hamish. Real job: junior doctor. Star sign: Leo.

'He doesn't look happy,' Coleridge observed, staring at Hamish's handsome face, which was caught in a rather sullen expression.

'He's thinking about winning,' said Hooper. 'He went in with a strategy. Keep your head down, don't get noticed, that's his little motto. "Only the noticed get nominated." He went into the confession box every night and said that. It's a very complex game,' Hooper continued. 'They have to play their fellow housemates one way and the public another. Be unobtrusive enough not to get nominated but interesting enough not to get evicted if they do get nominated. I think that's why people find the programme so fascinating. It's a genuine psychological study. Like a human zoo.'

'Is it?' Coleridge snapped caustically. 'In that case I wonder why the producers never seem to miss a single opportunity to broadcast sex talk or to display breasts.'

'Well, breasts are fascinating too, aren't they, sir? People like looking at them. I know I do. Besides which, when people go to the *real* zoo, what do they like looking at most? Monkeys' bums and rumpo, that's what.'

'Don't be ridiculous.'

'I'm not being ridiculous at all, sir. If you had the choice of watching two elephants either having their tea or having it off, which would you choose? People are interested in sex. You might as well face it.'

'I think we're straying from the point.'

'Do you, sir?' said Trisha, who was looking at Hamish's face on the screen. 'I don't. This house was riddled with sexual tension and that's got to be relevant, hasn't it? For instance, just look who Hamish is staring at.'

'It's impossible to say.'

'You'll see in the wide shot, it's coming up next.' Trisha touched the play button on the ancient VCR and, sure enough, the picture cut to a wide shot of the laughing, slightly drunken group lolling about on the couches.

'He's looking at Kelly now, sir, and then he starts staring at Layla. He's checking them out. The psychologist on the show says that during the first hours in the house the group will be thinking principally about who they're attracted to.'

'Now that *is* a surprise, constable! And there was me imagining that they were thinking about the value of their immortal souls and the definition of God.' Coleridge regretted his outburst. He did not approve of sarcasm and he liked Trisha and valued her as an officer. He knew that she did not speculate idly. 'I'm sorry. I'm afraid I'm still having some difficulty getting over my exasperation with these people.'

'That's all right, sir. They certainly are a bunch of pains. But I do think it's important that we find out who fancies whom. I mean, in this unique murder environment jealousy has to be a fairly likely motive.'

'Who do you think fancies Woggle, then?' Hooper asked, laughing at the figure who had just appeared on the screen.

Woggle. Real job: anarchist. Star sign: claims to be all twelve.

'I mean, let's face it,' Hooper continued. 'If you were looking for a potential murder victim out of this lot, it would have to be Woggle, wouldn't it? I mean, that bloke is just asking for it.'

'Any white bloke with dreadlocks is asking for it in my opinion,' Trisha remarked, adding, 'Woggle was Geraldine the Gaoler's private little project, sir.'

'What do you mean by that, constable?'

Trisha was referring to one of the confidential internal policy briefings that she had secured from the Peeping Tom offices on the day of the murder. 'He was the only inmate of the house that Peeping Tom actually *approached*, rather than the other way round. In Geraldine Hennessy's opinion he was, and I quote, "guaranteed good telly. A natural irritant, like the grain of sand in the oyster shell around which a pearl will grow".'

'Very poetic,' Coleridge remarked. 'I must say, it's a

31

stretch of the imagination to think of Mr Woggle as a pearl, but it takes all sorts, I suppose.'

'She saw him on the lunchtime news on the day of the annual May Day riots, sir.'

'Ah. So he was arrested? Now that is interesting.'

'He wasn't arrested, sir, he was being interviewed by the BBC. It was Woggle's claim to fame.'

'I saw that interview you did 'bout anarchy and all that malarkey,' Moon was saying to Woggle, sensing a kindred-alternative spirit. 'You were fookin' magic, babe. Double wicked.'

'Thank you, sweet lady,' Woggle replied.

'But what was the story with the medieval jester's hat? Was it, like, making a point or what?'

'It was indeed making a point, O bald woman. When the so-called wise men have run out of answers it is time to talk to the fools.'

'So they talked to you, then,' said Jazz drily.

'Correctomundo, soul brother.' Woggle flashed what he believed was a smile of devilish subtlety but which, owing to his beard and the state of his teeth, looked like a few broken Polo mints buried in a hair-filled bathroom plug-hole.

'I couldn't get to work that day,' Kelly complained. 'They closed Oxford Street. How's stopping people doing their shopping going to help anybody?'

Woggle did his best to explain, but his politics were not overburdened with detail or analysis. He seemed to recognize something he called 'the system', and he disapproved of this system in its entirety. 'That's it, really,' he said.

'So what *is* the system, then?' Kelly asked.

'Well, it's all that capitalist, global, police, money, hamburger, American, fox-hunting, animal-testing, fascist-groove-thing, isn't it?' Woggle explained in his dull, nasal monotone.

'Oh, right. I see.' Kelly sounded unconvinced.

'What we need is macrobiotic organic communities interacting with their environments in an atmosphere of mutual respect,' Woggle added.

'What the *fahk* are you talking about?' Garry enquired.

'Basically it would be nice if things were nicer.'

Once more Inspector Coleridge pressed pause. 'I presume Woggle's antagonism to "the system" does not prevent him from living off it?'

'No, sir, that's right,' Trish replied. 'The one system he truly does understand is the social security system.'

'So the state can keep him fed and watered while he seeks to overthrow it? Very convenient, I must say.'

'Yes, sir, he thinks so too,' said Hooper. 'Later on he has a huge row with the rest of them about it because they refuse to celebrate the irony of the fact that the state is funding him, its most bitter enemy.'

'Presumably because they, like the rest of us, have to fund the state.'

'That's basically their point, yes.'

'Well, I'm delighted to discover that these people and I have at least one opinion in common. This Woggle, any history of fraudulent claims? False addresses? Double-drops, financial skulduggery, that sort of thing? Anything that might make him vulnerable to discovery?'

'No, sir, on that score he's completely clean.'

There was a brief pause and then, almost uniquely, all three of them laughed. If there was one thing that Woggle wasn't, it was clean.

'Shit, man,' Jazz observed, aghast. 'Haven't you ever heard of soap?'

Woggle had taken up what was to become his habitual position, crouching on the floor in the room's only corner, his bearded chin resting on bony knees which he hugged close to his chest, his great horned dirty toenails poking out from his sandals.

Woggle was dirty in a way that only a person who has just emerged from digging a tunnel can be dirty. He had come straight to join the *House Arrest* team from his previous home, a 200-metre tunnel under the site of the proposed fifth terminal at Heathrow Airport. Woggle had suggested to Geraldine the Gaoler that perhaps he should take a shower before joining the team, but Geraldine, ever watchful for the elements that could be said to make up 'good telly', assured him that he was fine as he was. 'Just be yourself,' she had said.

'Who's that?' Woggle had replied. 'For I am the sum of all my past lives and those I have yet to live.'

Woggle stank. Digging tunnels is hard physical work and every drop of sweat that he had sweated remained in the fabric of his filthy garments, a motley collection of old bits of combat gear and denim. If Woggle had worn a leather jacket (which, being an animal liberationist, of course he would never do) he would have looked like one of those disgusting old-style hell's angels who never washed their Levi's no matter how often they urinated on them.

'Guy, you are rank!' Jazz continued. 'You are high! Here, man, have a blow on my deodorant before we all get killed of asphyxiation and suffocate to death here!'

Woggle demurred. 'I consider all cosmetics to be humanoid affectations, yet one more example of our sad species' inability to accept its place as simply another animal on the planet.'

'Are you on drugs or what?'

'People think that they are superior to animals, and preening and scenting themselves is evidence of that,' Woggle droned with the moral self-assurance of a Buddha, 'but look at a cat's silky coat or a robin's joyful wings. Did any haughty supermodel ever look that good?'

'Too fucking right she did, guy,' said Jazz, who personally used two separate deodorants and anointed his skin daily with scented oils. 'I ain't never gone to sleep dreaming about shagging no cat, but Naomi and Kate are welcome any time.'

Layla spoke up from the kitchen area where she was preparing herbal tea. 'I have some cruelty-free organic cleansing lotions, Woggle, if you'd like to borrow them.'

Layla. Real job: fashion designer and retail supervisor. Star sign: Scorpio.

'They won't be cruelty-free after the plastic bottles end up in a landfill and a seagull gets its beak stuck in one,' Woggle replied.

'Don't be fooled by that fashion designer thing, sir,' said Hooper. 'She's another shop girl. It comes out later in the second week. Layla cannot believe it when Garry points out that she and Kelly do basically the same job. Layla thinks she's about a million miles above Kelly. There was quite a row.'

'Garry likes annoying them all, doesn't he?'

'Oh yes, anything for a reaction, that's Garry.'

'And this young lady Layla takes herself very seriously?'

'She does that, all right. Some of the biggest clashes in the first week are between her and David the actor, over who's the most sensitive.'

'They both reckon themselves poets,' Trisha chipped in.

'Yes, I can see that there's a lot of concealed anger there,' Coleridge remarked thoughtfully. 'A lot of failed ambition for both of them. It could be relevant.'

'Not for Layla, sir, surely? She got chucked out before the murder happened.'

'I am aware of that, sergeant, but seeing as how we don't know anything at all it behoves us to investigate everything.'

Hooper hated the fact that he worked under a man who used words like 'behoves'.

'This girl Layla's resentment and feelings of inadequacy could have found some resonance in the group. She may have been the catalyst for somebody else's self-doubt. Who knows, sometimes with murder it's entirely the wrong person that gets killed.'

'Eh?' said Hooper.

'Well, think about it,' Coleridge explained. 'Suppose a man is being taunted by his girlfriend about his powers in bed. Finally he storms out into the dark night and on his way home a stranger steps on his heel. The man spins round and kills the stranger, whereas really he wanted to kill his girlfriend.'

'Well, yes, sir, I can see that happening with a random act of anger, but the murder happened long after Layla left . . .'

'All right. Suppose you have a group of friends, and A has a dark, dark secret which B discovers. B then begins to spread the secret about and this gets back to A, but when A confronts B, B convincingly claims that the blabbermouth is in fact C. A then kills C, who actually knew nothing about it. *The wrong person gets killed.* In my experience there are usually a lot more people involved in a murder than the culprit and the victim.'

'So we keep Layla in the frame?'

'Well, not as an actual murder suspect, obviously. But before she left that house it is entirely possible that she sowed the seed that led to murder. Let's move on.'

Trisha pressed play and the camera panned across from Woggle to settle on the tenth and final housemate.

Dervla. Real job: trauma therapist. Star sign: Taurus.

She was the most beautiful, everybody agreed that, and the most mysterious. Quiet and extremely calm, it was never easy to work out what was going on behind those smiling green Irish eyes. Eyes that always seemed to be laughing at a different joke from the rest of the group. By the time of the murder Dervla had been the bookies' number-two favourite to win the game, and she would have been number one had Geraldine Hennessy not occasionally and jealously edited against her, making her look stuck-up when in fact she was merely abstracted.

'So what's a trauma therapist when it's at home, then?' Garry asked. He and Dervla were stretched out beside the pool in the pleasant aftermath of the morning's champagne.

'Well, I suppose my job is to understand how people react to stress, so that I can help them to deal with it.' Dervla replied in her gentle Dublin brogue. 'That's why I wanted to come on this show. I mean, the whole experience is really just a series of small traumas, isn't it? I think it'll be very interesting to be close to the people experiencing those traumas and also to experience them myself.'

'So it's got nothing to do with winning half a million big ones, then?'

Dervla was far too clever to deny the charge completely. She knew that the nation would almost certainly be scrutinizing her reply that very evening.

'Well, that would be nice, of course. But I'm sure I'll be evicted long before that. No, basically I'm here to learn. About myself and about stress.'

Coleridge was so exasperated that he had to make himself another mug of tea. Here was this beautiful, intelligent woman, to whom he was embarrassed to discover he found himself rather attracted, with eyes like emeralds and a voice like milk and honey, and yet she was talking utter and complete *rubbish*.

'Stress! *Stress!*' Coleridge said, in what for him was almost a shout. 'Not much more than two generations ago the entire population of this country stood in the shadow of imminent brutal occupation by a crowd of murdering Nazis! A generation before that we lost a *million* boys in the trenches. *A million innocent lads.* Now we have "therapists" studying the "trauma" of getting thrown off a television game show. Sometimes I despair, I really do, you know. I despair.'

'Yes, but, sir,' Trisha said, 'in the war and stuff people had something to stand up for, something to believe in. These days there isn't anything for us to believe in very much. Does that make our anxieties and pain any less relevant?'

'Yes, it does!' Coleridge stopped himself before he could say any more. Even he could occasionally tell when he was sounding like a bigoted, reactionary old idiot. He took a deep breath and returned to the subject of the young woman on the screen.

'So, this Dervla girl went into the house with the purely cerebral intention of observing case studies in stress?'

'Yes,' said Trisha, referring to her file on Dervla, 'she felt that the nomination process with its necessary winners and losers offered a perfect chance to study people's reactions to isolation and rejection.'

'Very laudable I must say.'

'And she also added that "she hopes one day to be a television presenter".'

'Now why does that not surprise me?' Coleridge sipped his tea and studied the screen. 'One house, ten contestants,' he said almost to himself. 'One victim.'

DAY THIRTY. 7.00 a.m.

It was now three days since the murder, and Coleridge felt as if his investigation had scarcely begun. No forensic evidence of any value had emerged from the search of the house, the suspect interviews had revealed nothing but apparent shock and confusion, the observers at Peeping Tom could not suggest even a hint of a motive, and Coleridge and his excellent team had been reduced to sitting about in front of a television making wild guesses.

Coleridge closed his eyes and breathed slowly. Focus, he had to focus, forget the storm that was raging around him and *focus*.

He tried to free his mind, rid it of all thoughts and preconceptions, make of it a blank page upon which some invisible hand might write an answer. *The murderer is* . . . But no answer came.

It just didn't seem credible that there had even *been* a murderer, and yet there had most definitely been a murder.

How could it be possible to get away with murder in an entirely sealed environment, every inch of which was covered by television cameras and microphones?

Eight people had been watching the screens in the monitoring bunker. Another had been even closer, standing behind the two-way mirrors in the camera runs that surrounded the house. Six others had been present in the room left by the killer to pursue his victim. They were still there when he or she returned shortly thereafter, having committed the murder. An estimated *47,000* more had been watching via the live Internet link, which Peeping Tom provided for its more obsessive viewers.

All these people saw the murder happen and yet somehow the killer had outwitted them all.

Coleridge felt fear rising in his stomach. Fear that his long and moderately distinguished career was about to end in a spectacular failure. A world-famous failure, for this was now the most notorious case on the planet. Everybody had a theory – every pub, office, and school, every noodle bar in downtown Tokyo, every

Turkish bath in Istanbul. Hour by hour Coleridge's office was bombarded with thousands of emails explaining who the killer was and why he or she had done it. Criminologists and Crackers were popping up all over the place – on the news, in the papers, on-line and in every language. The bookies were taking bets, the spiritualists were chatting to the victim and the Internet was about to collapse under the weight of traffic of webheads exchanging theories.

Indeed, the only person who seemed to have absolutely no idea whatsoever of the killer's identity was Inspector Stanley Spencer Coleridge, the police officer in charge of the investigation.

He walked through the house, trying to gain some sense of its secrets. Asking it to give him some clue. Not the real house, of course. The police forensics team had completed their business there in a day and had then been obliged to return it to its owners. This was a replica house that Peeping Tom Productions had been happy to lend to the police. The plasterboard and glue version that the producers had used during the months of camera rehearsal, during which they had ensured that every single angle was covered and that there truly was no place to hide. This replica house had no roof or plumbing and did not include the garden, but internally its colours and dimensions were precise. It gave Coleridge the *feel*.

He cursed himself. Standing in the imitation space, he felt that he had become like one of the actual housemates: he had no useful thoughts in his head whatsoever, only *feelings*.

'Feelings,' Coleridge thought. 'The *modus operandi* of an entire generation. You don't have to think anything, or even to believe anything. You only have to *feel*.'

Like the real house, the replica house, which stood on an empty sound stage at Shepperton Film Studios, consisted of two bedrooms, a shower room, a bathroom in which laundry could be done in a big steel trough, a toilet, an open-plan living, kitchen and dining area, a store room, and the room known as the confession box, where the inmates went to speak to Peeping Tom.

Three dark corridors ran along the edges of the house that did not open out on to the garden, and it was along these corridors that the manned cameras travelled, spying on the inmates through the huge two-way mirrors that took up most of the walls. These cameras, combined with the remote-controlled 'hot-head' ones situated inside the house, ensured that there was not a single square centimetre of space in which a person might avoid being observed. The only room that was not covered by the manual camera runs was the toilet. Even Peeping Tom's obsessive voyeurism had drawn a line at having cameramen standing 18 inches from the inmates while they evacuated their bowels. The duty editors had to watch, however, as the toilet contained a hot-head, which missed absolutely nothing. They had to listen, too, as the cubicle was also wired for sound.

Coleridge was reminded of the catchphrase that had adorned so many roadside posters in the run-up to broadcast. 'THERE IS NO ESCAPE' they had read. For one of the inmates that statement had proved horribly prophetic.

The house and garden complex was surrounded by a moat and twin lines of razorwire fencing patrolled by security guards. The monitoring bunker in which the production team worked was situated 50 yards beyond the fence and was connected to the camera runs via a tunnel under the moat. It was along this tunnel that Geraldine and the horrified Peeping Tom night crew had run on that dreadful night after they had witnessed a murder on their television monitors.

The murder.

It was eating Coleridge up.

For the umpteenth time he walked across the replica of the floor that the victim had crossed, to be followed moments later by the killer. Then he went and stood in the camera run, looking in on the room, just as the operator had done on the fatal night. He re-entered the living space and opened a drawer in the kitchen unit, the top one, the one the killer had opened. There were no knives in the drawer Coleridge opened; it was only a rehearsal space.

Coleridge spent almost three hours wandering around the strange, depressing replica, but it told him nothing more about what had happened during the few, brief moments of dreadful violence than he already knew. He asked himself how he would have carried out the murder had he been the killer. The answer was, in exactly the same way as the killer. It was the *only* way it could have been done with any chance of getting away with it. The killer had seen his or her one opportunity to kill with anonymity and had seized it.

Well, that was *something*, Coleridge told himself. The speed with which the killer had grasped his or her chance surely proved that he had been waiting and watching. He or she had *wanted to kill*.

What could possibly have happened to engender such hatred? Without any evidence to the contrary, Coleridge had to presume that these people had all been complete strangers to each other less than a month before. He and his team had been studying the background of all the housemates but had so far found not one shred of a suggestion that any of them had known each other prior to entering the house.

So why would a stranger plan to kill a stranger?

Because they were strangers no more. Something must have happened or been said in those three weeks that had made murder inevitable. But what? There had certainly been some dreadful goings-on in the house,

42

but nothing had been observed that looked remotely like a motive for the crime.

It could not be ruled out that two of the inmates had not been strangers. That some ancient enmity had been unwittingly introduced into the house? That some bleak and terrible coincidence in the selection process had led to murder?

Whatever the answer, Coleridge knew that he wouldn't find it there in that gloomy old hangar at Shepperton. It was inside the real house, it was inside the *people* inside the real house.

Wearily, he returned to his car, to which Hooper had retreated half an hour earlier, and together they began their drive back to Sussex, where the real Peeping Tom house was located, a journey of about twenty miles which if they were lucky would only take them the rest of the morning.

DAY THIRTY. 9.15 p.m.

While Coleridge and Hooper nosed their way along the M25, Trisha was interviewing Bob Fogarty, the editor-in-chief of *House Arrest*. After Geri the Gaoler, Fogarty was the most senior figure in the Peeping Tom hierarchy. Trisha wanted to know more about how the people she had been watching came to be presented in the way they were.

'*House Arrest* is basically fiction,' said Fogarty, handing her a styrofoam cup of watery froth and nearly missing her hand in the darkness of the monitoring bunker. 'Like all TV and film. It's built in the edit.'

'You manipulate the housemates' images?'

'Well, obviously. We're not scientists, we make television programmes. People are basically dull. We have to make them interesting, turn them into heroes and villains.'

43

'I thought you were supposed to be observers, that the whole thing was an experiment in social interaction?'

'Look, constable,' Fogarty explained patiently, 'in order to create a nightly half-hour of broadcasting we have at our disposal the accumulated images of thirty television cameras running for twenty-four hours. That's seven hundred and twenty hours of footage to make one *half-hour* of television. We couldn't avoid making subjective decisions even if we wanted to. The thing that amazes us is that the nation *believes* what we show them. They actually accept that what they are watching is real.'

'I don't suppose they think about it much. I mean, why should they?'

'That's true enough. As long as it's good telly they don't care, which is why as far as possible we try to shoot the script.'

'Shoot the script?'

'It's a term they use in news and features.'

'And it means?'

'Well, say you're making a short insert for the news, investigating heroin addiction on housing estates. If you simply went out to some urban hellhole with a camera and started nosing around, you could be looking for the story you want till Christmas. So you *script* your investigation before you leave your office. You say . . . all right, we need a couple of kids to say they can get smack at school, we need a girl to say she'd whore for a hit, we need a youth worker to say it's the government's fault . . . You write the whole thing. Then you send out a researcher to round up a few show-offs and basically tell them what to say.'

'But how could you do that on *House Arrest*? I mean, you can't tell the housemates what to say, can you?'

'No, but you can be pretty sure of the story you want to tell and then look for the shots that support it. It's

44

the only way to avoid getting into a complete mess. Look at this, for instance . . . This is Kelly's first trip to the confession box on the afternoon of day one.'

DAY ONE. 4.15 p.m.

'It's brilliant, wicked, outrageous. I feel just totally bigged-up and out there,' Kelly gushed breathlessly from the main monitor. She had come to the confession box to talk about how thrilling and exciting it all was.

'I mean, today has just been the wickedest day ever because I really, really love all these people and I just know we're all going to get along just brilliantly. I expect there'll be tension and I'll end up hating all of them for, like, just a moment at some point. But you could say that about any mates, couldn't you? Basically I *love* these guys. They're my posse. My crew.'

Deep in the darkness of the editing suite Geraldine glared at Fogarty. 'And that's what you want her to say, is it?'

Bob cowered behind his styrofoam cup. 'Well, it's what she did say, Geraldine.'

Geraldine's eyes flashed, her nostrils flared and she bared her colossal overbite. It was as if the Alien had just burst out of John Hurt's stomach.

'You stupid cunt! You stupid lazy cunt! I could get a monkey to broadcast what she actually said! I could get a work-experience school-leaver pain-in-the-arse spotty fucking waste-of-space teenager to broadcast what she *actually* said! What I pay you to do is to *look* at what she *actually* said and *find* what we *want her to say*, you *cunt*!'

Fogarty threw a commiserating glance at the younger, more impressionable members of staff.

'Who is Kelly, Bob?' Geraldine continued, throwing an arm towards the frozen image of the pretty young brunette on the screen. 'Who is that girl?'

Fogarty stared at the television. A sweet smile beamed back at him, an open, honest, naïve countenance. 'Well . . .'

'She's our bitch, Bob, she's our manipulator. She's one of our designated hate figures! Remember the audition interviews? All that pert ambition? All that artless knicker-flashing. All that *girl power bollocks*. Remember what I said, Bob?'

Fogarty did remember, but Geraldine told him anyway.

'I said, "Right, you arrogant little slapper, we'll see how far you get towards presenting your own pop, style and fashion show once the whole nation has decided you're a back-biting, knob-teasing fucking *dog*," didn't I?'

'Yes, Geraldine, but on the evidence of today she's turned out to be really quite nice. I mean, she's a bit of an airhead, and vain, certainly, but she's not really a bitch. I think we'll find it quite hard to make her look that nasty.'

'She'll *look* however we want her to look and *be* whatever we want her to be,' Geraldine sneered.

DAY THIRTY. 9.20 a.m.

'Does Geraldine normally talk to you like that?' Trisha asked.

'She talks to everybody like that.'

'So you get used to it, then?'

'It's not something you get used to, constable. I have an MSc in computing and media. I am *not* a stupid cunt.'

Trisha nodded. She had heard of Geraldine

46

Hennessy before her *House Arrest* fame. Most people had. Geraldine was a celebrity in her own right. A famously bold, provocative and controversial broadcaster, Trisha ventured.

'Rubbish!' said Bob Fogarty. 'She's a TV whore masquerading as an innovator and getting away with it because she knows a few popstars and wears Vivienne Westwood. What she does is steal tacky, dumbed-down tabloid telly ideas, usually from Europe or Japan, smear them with a bit of hip, clubby, druggy style, and flog them to the middle class as post-modern irony.'

'So you don't like her, then?'

'I loathe her, constable. People like Geraldine Hennessy have ruined television. She's a cultural vandal. She's a nasty, stupid, dangerous bitch.'

In the gloom Trisha could see that Fogarty's cup was shaking in his hand. She was taken aback. 'Calm down, Mr Fogarty,' she said.

'I am calm.'

'Good.'

Then Fogarty played Kelly's confession as it had been broadcast.

'I'll end up hating all of them.'

Seven words were all she said.

DAY ONE. 4.30 p.m.

Kelly left the confession box and went back into the living area of the house. Layla gave her a sympathetic little smile and stroked her arm as she walked by. Kelly turned back, smiled and then they had a little hug together.

'Love you,' said Layla.

'Love you big time,' Kelly replied.

'You stay strong, OK?' said Layla.

Kelly assured Layla that she would certainly attempt to stay strong.

Kelly was so pleased that Layla was hugging her. Earlier in the day they had had a small tiff over Layla's insistence on including walnut oil on the first group shopping list. Layla pointed out that since she ate mainly salad, dressings were very important to her and that walnut oil was an essential ingredient.

'Also it lubricates my chakras,' she'd said.

Kelly had suggested to Layla that with their limited food budget, walnut oil was surely rather an expensive luxury item.

'Well, I think that's an entirely subjective observation, babes,' Layla replied, relishing her own eloquence, 'and quite frankly depends on how much you value your chakras.'

David then weighed in, supporting Layla. He pointed out that as far as he was concerned the bacon that Kelly had suggested they order, because she cooked a wicked brekkie, was hardly an essential item . . . 'except perhaps to the pig that donated it', David observed piously from the unimpregnable fortress of his lotus position. 'Personally I would far rather order walnut oil than corpse.'

All the other boys leapt in and supported Kelly, but David and Layla's effortless occupation of the moral high ground had made Kelly feel rotten and for a minute she had thought she would cry. Instead she went into the confession box and told Peeping Tom how much she loved everybody.

Now she had re-emerged and Layla had rewarded her with a hug.

Kelly was wearing only a T-shirt and a tiny pair of shorts and Layla was dressed with similar minimalism in a little silk sarong and matching bikini top. Their tight little tummies touched and their breasts pushed against each other.

Across the room the hot-head camera clamped to the ceiling whizzed and whirred and zoomed towards them with unseemly haste.

DAY THIRTY. 9.45 a.m.

'You know that even though the weather was warm and sunny Geraldine insisted that the central heating be on at all times, don't you?' Fogarty said.

Trisha was astonished. 'You made it hot in order to get people to take their clothes off?'

'Of course we did. What do you think? Peeping Tom wanted bodies! Not baggy jumpers! Twenty-four degrees Centigrade is the optimum good telly temperature, warm but not sweaty. Geraldine always says that if she could make it twenty-five degrees in the room and minus five in the vicinity of the girls' nipples she'd have the perfect temperature.'

Trisha looked at Fogarty thoughtfully. He certainly was going out of his way to make his employer look bad. Why was that? she wondered.

'Anyway,' the man concluded, 'Miss High and Mighty, oh so brilliant, Machiavellian genius Geraldine Hennessy got it totally wrong with Kelly, although she has never admitted it. She thought that just because *she* didn't like Kelly nobody else would, but the public did like her and apart from Woggle she was the most popular one on the show. We had to change tack and from day two we edited in Kelly's favour.'

'So sometimes the subject does lead the programme?'

'Well, with a little help from me, I must admit. I gave Kelly plenty of cute angles. I was buggered if I was going to do Geraldine's dirty work.'

DAY THIRTY-ONE. 8.30 a.m.

After reading Trisha's report of her interview with Fogarty, Coleridge called a meeting of all his officers.

'Currently,' he said firmly, 'I am of a mind that we are pursuing the wrong seven suspects *and* the wrong victim.'

This comment, like so many that Coleridge made, was met with blank stares. He could almost hear the whoosh as it swept over their heads.

'How's that, then, boss?' said Hooper.

'Boss?'

'Inspector.'

'Thank you, sergeant.'

'How's that, then, inspector?' Hooper persevered wearily. 'How is it that we're pursuing the wrong suspects and the wrong victim?'

'Because we are looking at these people in the way that the producers and editors of Peeping Tom Productions want us to look at them, not as they *are*.' Coleridge paused for a moment, his attention drawn to an officer at the back of the room who was chewing gum, a *female* officer. He longed to tell her to find a scrap of paper and dispose of it, but he knew that the days when an inspector could treat his constables in that manner had long gone. He would not be at all surprised if there was a court in Brussels that could be cajoled into maintaining that the freedom to chew gum was a human right. He confined his reaction to a withering stare, which caused the girl's jaw to stop moving for all of three seconds.

'We must therefore be extremely cautious in our views, for apart from a brief interview with each of the surviving housemates after the murder, we know these people only through the deceiving eye of the television camera, that false friend, so convincing, so plausible, so *real* and yet, as we have already seen, so fickle and so false. We must therefore begin at the beginning with all of them and presume nothing. Nothing at all.'

And so the grim task of reviewing the *House Arrest* tape archive continued.

'*It's day three under* House Arrest *and Layla has gone to the refrigerator to get some cheese.*' This was the voice of Andy, *House Arrest's* narrator. '*Layla's vegan cheese is an important part of her diet, being her principal source of protein.*'

'You see how television pulls the wool over our eyes!' Coleridge exclaimed in exasperation. 'If we weren't concentrating, we might actually have formed the impression that something of interest had occurred! This man's talent for imbuing the most gut-wrenchingly boring observations with an air of significance normally reserved for matters of life and death is awe-inspiring.'

'I think it's the Scottish accent,' said Hooper. 'It sounds more sincere.'

'The man could have covered the Cuban Missile Crisis without altering his manner at all . . . It's midnight in the Oval Office and President Kennedy has yet to hear from Secretary Khrushchev.'

'Who was Khrushchev?' Hooper asked.

'Oh, for God's sake! He was General Secretary of the Soviet Union!'

'Never heard of it, sir. Is it affiliated to the TUC?'

Coleridge hoped that Hooper was joking but decided not to ask. Instead he pressed play again.

'*Layla has just discovered that some of her cheese has gone missing,*' said Andy.

'He says it as if she's just discovered penicillin,' Coleridge moaned.

DAY THREE. 3.25 p.m.

Layla slammed the fridge door angrily. 'Hey right, I mean, yeah, I mean, come on, OK? Who's been eating my cheese?'

'Oh yeah, right. That was me,' said David. 'Isn't that cool?' David always spoke to people in the sort of soft, faintly superior tone of a man who knows the meaning of life but thinks that it's probably above everybody else's head. Normally he talked to people from behind because he tended to be massaging their shoulders, but when he addressed them directly he liked to stare right into their eyes, fancying his own eyes to be hypnotic, limpid pools into which people would instinctively wish to dive.

'I mean, I thought it would be cool to have a little of your cheese,' he said.

'Oh, yeah,' Layla replied. 'Half of it, actually . . . But that's totally cool. I mean totally, except you will replace it, right?'

'Sure, yeah, absolutely, whatever,' said David, as if he was above such matters as worrying about whose cheese was whose.

'*Later*,' said Andy the narrator, '*in the girls' room, Layla confides in Dervla about how she feels about the incident involving the cheese.*'

Layla and Dervla lay on their beds.

'It's not about the cheese,' Layla whispered. 'It's so *not* about the cheese. It's just, you know, it was my cheese.'

DAY THIRTY-ONE. 8.40 a.m.

'I'm honestly not sure if I can continue with this investigation,' said Coleridge.

DAY THIRTY-ONE. 2.00 p.m.

'Actually it was Layla's cheese that gave Geraldine her first crisis.'

52

Trisha had returned to the monitoring bunker to speak once more with Bob Fogarty. She and Coleridge had agreed that Fogarty was the person who knew most about the housemates and also about the workings of Peeping Tom. 'Why was there a crisis over the cheese?' she asked Fogarty.

'Well, because the duty editor resigned and took both his assistants with him. I had to come in myself and cover. Don't you call that a crisis? I call it a crisis.'

'Why did he resign?'

'Because unlike me he still had some vestige of professional pride,' Fogarty reflected bitterly, dropping a square of milk chocolate into his cup of watery foam, something Trisha had never seen anyone do before. 'As a highly trained, grown-up adult, he simply could not continue to go home to his wife and children each evening and explain that he'd spent his entire working day minutely documenting a quarrel between two complete idiots about a piece of cheese.'

'And so he resigned?'

'Yes. He sent Geraldine an email saying that *House Arrest* was a disgrace to the British television industry, which, incidentally, it is.'

'And what did Geraldine do?'

'What do you think she did? She leaned out of her window and shouted, "Good riddance, you pompous cunt!" at him as he got into his car.'

'She didn't mind, then?'

'Well, it was very inconvenient certainly, particularly for me, but we soon got a replacement. People want to come to us. We make "cutting-edge television", you see.' Fogarty's voice was bitter with sarcasm. 'We're at the sharp end of the industry, we're hip, challenging and innovative. This is, of course, an industry where they thought it was challenging and innovative when the newsreaders started perching on the fronts of their desks instead of sitting behind them . . . Damn!'

Fogarty fished about in his cup with a teaspoon, searching for the square of chocolate. Trisha concluded that he had been intending only to soften the outside rather than melt it completely. People develop strange habits when they spend their working lives in dark rooms.

'God, I was jealous of that bloke who left,' Fogarty continued. 'I came into television to edit cup finals and Grand Nationals! Drama and comedy and science and music. What do I end up doing? I sit in the dark and stare at ten deluded fools sitting on couches. *All day*.'

Trisha was discovering one of the great secrets of *House Arrest*. The people who worked on it *loathed* the people they were charged with watching.

'It's all just so boring! *No one* is interesting enough to be looked at the way we look at these people, and particularly not the sort of person who would *wish* to be looked at. It's catch twenty-two, you see. Anyone who would *want* to be in that damn stupid house is by definition not an interesting enough person to be there.' Fogarty stared at his bank of television monitors. A long, sad, hollow silence ensued.

'It's the *hugging* I hate most, you know,' he said finally, 'and the *stroking* . . . And above all the endless *wittering on*.'

'You should meet my boss,' said Trisha. 'You two would really hit it off.'

Fogarty fell silent once more before resuming his theme.

'If that lot in the house had any idea of the contempt in which we hold them from our side of the mirrors, the cruel nicknames we give them . . . 'Nose-picker', 'Sad slap', 'the Farter' . . . If they knew the damning assessments we make as we chop up their comments to suit our needs, the complete lack of respect we have for any of their motives . . . well, they'd probably wish they'd *all* got murdered.'

DAY THIRTY-ONE. 3.00 p.m.

Coleridge and his team were becoming increasingly frustrated with Woggle. The problem was that he kept getting in the way of the other housemates. The people at Peeping Tom had thought him such good telly that large chunks of what footage remained from the early days of the show concerned his exploits and the other housemates' ever more frustrated reactions to them.

'If it had been Woggle that was murdered we could have made a circumstantial case against any of them,' Coleridge complained. 'I'm sick of the sight of him myself and I didn't have to live with the man.'

'You can't blame the producers for pushing him,' Hooper said. 'I mean, for a while there the country was obsessed. "Wogglemania", they called it.'

Coleridge remembered. Even he had been aware of the name popping up on the front pages of the tabloids and on page three or four of the broadsheets. At the time he had not had the faintest idea who they were talking about. He had thought it was probably a footballer or perhaps a celebrity violinist.

Hooper ejected the video tape that they had just finished and put it on the small 'watched' pile, then took another tape from the colossal 'have not yet watched' pile and put it into the VCR.

'You do know that the "have not yet watched" pile is just a satellite of a much bigger one, don't you, sir? Which we have in the cells.'

'Yes, I did know that, sergeant.'

Hooper pressed play and once more the sombre Scottish brogue of Andy the narrator drifted across the incident room.

'*It's day four in the house and Layla and Dervla have suggested that a rota be organized in order to more fairly allocate the domestic chores.*'

Coleridge sank a little further into his chair. He knew

that he couldn't allow himself another mug of tea for almost fifty minutes. One an hour, fourteen pint mugs a working day, that was his limit.

DAY FOUR. 2.10 p.m.

'I want to have a house meeting,' said Layla. 'So would it be cool if everybody just chilled? So we can all just have a natter maybe?'

Across the room Moon's bald head poked out from the book she was reading, a book entitled *You Are Gaia: Fourteen Steps to Becoming the Centre of Your Own Universe*.

'It's dead spiritual, this book,' Moon said. 'It's about self-growth and development and personal empowerment, which at the end of the day I'm really into, if you know what I mean, right?'

'Yeah, Moon, wicked. Look, um, have you seen the state of the toilet?'

'What about it?'

'Well, it's not very cool, right? And Dervla and I . . .'

'I'm not fookin' cleaning it,' said Moon. 'I've been here four days and I ain't even done a poo yet. I'm totally fookin' bunged up, me, because I'm not getting my colonic irrigation, and also I reckon the electrical fields from all the cameras are fookin' about with me yin and me yang.'

'Layla's not asking you to clean the toilet, Moon,' said Dervla gently. 'We just think it would be good to organize some of the jobs that have to be done around the house, that's all.'

'Oh. Right. Whatever. I'm chilled either way. But at the end of the day I'm just not scrubbing out other people's shite when I haven't even done one. I mean, that would be *too* fookin' ironic, that would.'

'Well, I don't mind doing heavy work, like lifting

and shifting,' said Gazzer the Geezer, pausing in the push-ups that he had been doing pretty continuously since arriving in the house, 'but I ain't cleaning the bog, on account of the fact that I don't mind a dirty bog anyway. Gives ya something to aim at when you're having a slash, don't it?'

The look of horror on Layla's delicate face filled the screen for nearly ten seconds.

'Well, never mind the toilet, Garry. What about the washing-up?' Dervla enquired. 'Or do you not mind eating off mouldy plates either?'

David, beautiful in his big shirt, did not even open his eyes when he spoke. 'Perhaps for the first week or so we should just do our own chores. I'm detoxing at the moment and am only eating boiled rice, which I imagine will be rather easier to clean off plates than whatever bowel-rotting garbage Garry, Jazz and Kelly choose to gorge themselves on.'

'Suits me,' said Gazzer. 'I always clean my plate with a bit of bread anyway.'

'Yes, Garry,' said Layla, 'and I'm not being heavy or anything, but perhaps you should remember that the bread is for *everyone*. I mean, I hope you think that's a chilled thing to say? I'm not trying to diss you or anything.'

Gazzer simply smirked and returned to his push-ups.

'Wouldn't doing our washing-up individually be a bit silly, David?' said Kelly.

'And why would that be, Kelly?' David opened his eyes and fixed Kelly with a soft, gentle, tolerant smile that was about as soft, gentle and tolerant as a rattle-snake.

'Well, because . . . Because . . .'

'Please don't get me wrong. I feel it's really important that you feel *able* to say to me that I'm stupid, but why?'

'I didn't mean . . . I mean, I didn't think . . .' Kelly said no more.

David closed his eyes once more and returned to the beauty of his inner thoughts.

Hamish, the junior doctor, the man who did not wish to be noticed, made one of his rare contributions to the conversation.

'I don't like house rotas,' he said. 'I had five years of communal living when I was a student. I know your sort, Layla. Next you'll be fining me an egg for not replacing the bogroll when I finish it.'

'Oh, so it's *you* that does that, is it?' said Dervla.

'I was giving an example,' said Hamish hastily.

'I'll tell you what's worse than a bogroll finisher,' Jazz shouted, leaping into the conversation with eager enthusiasm: 'a draper! The sort of bastard who finishes the roll, all except for a *single sheet*, which he then proceeds to *drape* over the empty tube!'

Jazz may have been a trainee chef, but that was just a job, not a vocation. It was not what he wanted to do with his life at all. Jazz wanted to be a comedian. *That* was why he had come into the house. He saw it as a platform for a career in comedy. He knew that he could make his friends laugh and dreamt of one day making a rich and glamorous living out of this ability. Not a stand-up, though; what he wanted to be was a *wit*. A raconteur, a clever bastard. He wanted to be on the panel of a hip game show and trade inspired insults with the other guys. He wanted to be a talking head on super-cool TV theme nights, cracking top put-downs about ex-celebrities. He wanted to host *an award ceremony*. That was Jazz's ambition, to be one of that élite band of good old boys who made their living out of just saying *brilliant* things *right off the cuff*. He wanted to be hip and funny and wear smart suits and be part of the *Zeitgeist* and just take the *piss* out of everything.

First, however, Jazz needed to get noticed. He needed people to see what a cracking good bloke and dead funny geezer he was. Since entering the house he had been looking for opportunities to work his ideas for material into the conversation. The mention of empty toilet rolls had been a gift.

'The draper is a toilet Nazi!' Jazz cried. 'He doesn't have to replace the roll, no, 'cos it ain't *finished* yet, is it? He's left just enough for the next bloke's fingers to go straight through and right up his arse!'

Jazz's outburst was met with a surprised silence, not least perhaps because he had chosen to deliver most of it directly into one of the remote cameras that hung from the ceiling.

'You don't even know if they'll broadcast it, Jazz,' said Dervla.

'Gotta keep trying, babes,' Jazz replied. 'Billy Connolly used to gig to *seagulls* when he was a Glasgow docker.'

'Look! Please!' Layla protested. 'Can we *please* just chill! We are trying to organize a rota.'

'Why don't we just take it easy and see what happens?' said Hamish. 'Things will get done, they always do.'

'Yes, Hamish, they will get done by people like me and Layla,' said Dervla, the soft poetry of her voice becoming just a little less soft and poetic, 'after which people like you will say, "See, look, I told you things would get done," but the point will be that *you* didn't do them.'

'Whatever,' Hamish replied, returning to his book. 'Make a rota if you want. I'm in.'

DAY THIRTY-ONE. 3.10 p.m.

'You see, sir,' said Hooper, pressing pause once more, 'Hamish backs off, he doesn't want to be noticed. Only the noticed get nominated.'

Coleridge was confused. 'Didn't Hamish go to the confession box and say that his ambition was to have sex before he left the house?'

'That's him – the doctor.'

'Well, wouldn't saying something like that get him noticed?'

Hooper sighed. 'That's different, sir, the confession box is for the *public*. Hamish needs to be a bit saucy in there so that if he does get nominated for eviction by the *housemates*, the public won't want to evict him because he says he's going to have sex on television.'

'But surely that would be an excellent reason *for* evicting him,' Coleridge protested.

'Not to most people, sir.'

DAY FOUR. 2.20 p.m.

The shrugs of the rest of the group indicated that Layla and Dervla had won the day, and since the inmates of the house were allowed neither pencil nor paper Jazz, drawing on his training as a chef, suggested that they make the rota grid out of spaghetti.

'Spag sticks to walls,' he said. 'That's how you check it's done. You chuck it at the wall and if it sticks it's done.'

'Well, that's fahkin' stupid, Jazz,' said Gazzer. 'I mean, then you'd have to scrape your dinner off the wall, wouldn't you?'

'You don't throw all of it, you arsehole, just a strand or two.'

'Oh, right.'

'*Jazz lightly boils some spaghetti*,' said Andy the narrator, '*and makes a rota grid on the wall*.'

'Bitching,' said Jazz, admiring his handiwork. 'Now each of us can be represented by grains of boiled rice. The starch will make them stick.'

'Wicked!' shouted Moon. 'We can each personalize our grains, like them weird fookers in India or wherever who do rice sculptures. I saw it on Discovery, they do all this incredible tiny detail and the really, really philosophical thing about it is, it's too fookin' small to see.'

'Well, that's just fahkin' stupid, isn't it?' Gazzer opined.

'It's not! It's a fookin' philosophical point, ain't it? Like if a tree falls in a forest but nobody hears it. Did it make a noise or whatever. These blokes don't do it for you or me. They decorate grains of rice for God.'

'You've lost me.'

'That's because at the end of the day you're dead thick, you are, Garry. You think you're not, but you are.'

They all began to discuss how they could individualize their grains of rice, and it was at this point that Woggle spoke up from his corner. 'People, I have yet to speak, and I think that this domestic fascism is totally divisive. The only appropriate and equitable method of hygiene control is to allow work patterns to develop via osmosis.'

They all looked at Woggle.

'Listen, guy, I have to tell you,' said Jazz. 'The only thing developing via osmosis on you is mould.'

Layla tried to be reasonable. 'Surely, Woggle, you're not saying that any type of group organization is fascism?'

'Yes, I am.'

There was a pause while the nine people who were trapped in a small house with this creature from the black latrine took in the significance of his answer. They were going to have to live with a man who considered organizing the washing-up tantamount to invading Poland.

Woggle took the opportunity of their stunned silence to press his advantage. 'All structures are self-corrupting.'

'What *are* you talking about, guy?' said Jazz. 'Because I have to tell you, man, you are sounding like a right twat.'

'Centrally planned and rigidly imposed labour in-itiatives rarely produce either efficient results or a relaxed and contented workforce. Look at the Soviet Union, look at the London Underground.'

'Woggle,' Layla was now sounding slightly shrill, 'there are ten of us here and all I'm saying is that in order that the house stays nice it would be a good idea to rotate the housework.'

'What you are saying, sweet lady,' Woggle replied in his irritating nasal tone, 'is that a person can only be trusted to act responsibly if he or she is ordered to do so.'

'I am *so* going to hate you,' said Jazz, speaking for the group.

'In the greater scheme of things,' Woggle said, 'within the positive and the negative energy of cre-ation, hate is merely the other half of love, for every season has its time. Therefore in terms of the universe as a whole, actually, you love me.'

'I fucking don't,' said Jazz.

'Yes, you do,' said Woggle.

'I fucking *don't*!' said Jazz.

'You do,' said Woggle.

Woggle never gave up.

DAY FIVE. 9.00 a.m.

Dervla pushed the bar of soap up under her T-shirt and washed her armpits. She was just beginning to get used to showering in her underwear; it had felt very uncomfortable on the first morning and rather silly, like being on a school trip and insisting on undressing under the covers. The alternative, however, meant exposing her naked body full frontal to the viewing millions, and Dervla had absolutely no intention of doing that. She had watched enough reality TV to know what the producers liked most and took great care as she lathered under her arms. It would be extremely easy to inadvertently pull up her vest and expose her breasts and she knew that behind the two-way mirrors in the shower cubicle wall a live cameraman was watching, waiting for her to do just that. One flash would be all that was required and her tits would be hanging around somewhere on the Internet till the end of time.

Having showered, Dervla went to brush her teeth, and it was while doing this that she noticed the letters on the mirror. For a moment she thought that they had been left in the condensation by the previous occupant of the shower room, but when more appeared she realized with a thrill that they were being written from the other side of the mirror.

Although Dervla had been incarcerated for only four days, already she had begun to feel as if she and her fellow inmates were the only people left on earth. That their little sealed bubble was all that was left in the world. It was quite a shock to be reminded that it wasn't. That outside, beyond the mirror, just inches away but in another world, someone was trying to talk to her.

'*Shhhhh!*'

That was the first word that had appeared. Written as Dervla watched, letter by letter appearing through the steam and condensation, right near the bottom of the mirror, just above the basin taps.

'*Don't stare,*' came next, and Dervla realized that she was standing bug-eyed, still holding her toothbrush in her mouth, looking at the letters. Quickly she re-adjusted her gaze, looking at her own reflection as toothbrushers are wont to do.

After a moment she allowed her eyes to flick down again.

'*I like you,*' said the words. '*I can help you. Bye now.*'

There was a pause and then the anonymous communicator's final letters. '*XXX.*'

Dervla finished brushing her teeth quickly, wrapped a towel around her, took off her wet knickers and vest, dressed as fast as she could and went outside to sit in the vegetable garden. She needed to think. She could not decide whether she was angry or excited about this un-sought-for development. On balance she reckoned that she was both. Angry because this man (she felt certain it was a man) had clearly singled her out for his special attention. He had been watching her and now he wanted to use the power he had over her to intrude on her space. That gave her rather an uncomfortable feeling. What were his motives? Was he attracted to her? Was he perving on her? What other reason could he have for risking his job in such a manner? On the other hand, perhaps he was doing it for a laugh? Perhaps he was just a wild and crazy guy who fancied the crack of manipulating Peeping Tom? Dervla was well aware of how much the media preferred scandals and skulduggery in the house to honest relationships. It was always the bad boys and girls who got the publicity. If this mysterious letter-writer managed to open up a dialogue with her, the story would certainly be worth more than a cameraman's wage.

That was a thought. Perhaps he was already in the pay of a newspaper? The press were always trying to drop leaflets and parachutists and hang-glider pilots into the house; it must have occurred to them to try to bribe a cameraman. Now another thought occurred to her: perhaps this person was no friend at all, but an *agent provocateur*! Seeking to tempt her into breaking the rules! Was this entrapment? A sting? Were Peeping Tom or the newspapers trying to catch her out? If so, then were they trying the same trick on the others?

Dervla imagined her exposure as a cheat, the earnest tones of the voiceover man revealing her shame. Revelling in it. '*We decided to test each of the inmates by offering them an illegal channel of communication with the outside world. Dervla was the only housemate to take the bait, the only willing cheat . . .*'

That would be it, expulsion in disgrace, for ever more to be labelled 'Devious Dervla,' 'Dastardly Dervla' . . . *Dirty Dervla*.

Her mind swam. She forced herself to focus her thoughts.

It simply couldn't be Peeping Tom doing this. Entrapment was immoral – she wasn't at all sure if it wasn't an actual crime. If a respectable production company did that, then nobody would ever trust them again. No, it couldn't be Peeping Tom.

What if it was the media? Well, so what? So far she had done nothing wrong and she would be careful to keep it that way. Besides, any paper that had bribed a cameraman could not publish anything about it without revealing their source, and they would certainly wait a while to do that. Dervla reckoned that at the very least she had time to sit back and see how the situation developed. And if it really was a friend, somebody who had taken a shine to her and wanted her to win . . . Who could tell? Perhaps it might give her the edge. It would certainly be nice to get a bit of outside information . . . And she hadn't actually *asked* for any help, so it wasn't really immoral. Not to look in the mirror, surely?

DAY THIRTY-TWO. 9.20 p.m.

One wall of the incident room had become known as 'the Map'. On it Trisha had affixed photographs of the ten housemates, which she had then connected by a great mass of criss-crossing lines of tape stuck to the plaster with Blu-Tack. On the strips of tape Trisha and her colleagues had written short descriptive sentences such as 'attracted to', 'loathes', 'had row about cheese', and 'spends too long in the toilet'.

Hooper had attempted to recreate Trisha's map on his computer, using his photo scanner and untold gigabytes of three-dimensional graphic-arts software programming. Sadly the project defeated him and a little bomb kept appearing and telling him to restart the computer. Soon Hooper was forced to slink back to the drawing pins and Blu-Tack along with everybody else.

Now Coleridge was standing in front of the map solemnly contemplating the ten housemates and the ever-growing web of interconnecting relationships. 'Somewhere,' he said, 'somewhere in this dense mass of human intercourse must lie our motive, our catalyst for a murder.' He spoke as if he were addressing a room full of people, but in fact only Hooper and Trisha were there, everybody else having long since gone home. They had decided that the evening's subjects for discussion would be Layla the beautiful 'hippie' and David the dedicated actor.

On one of the tapes that connected their two photographs Trisha had written: 'Friends for first day or two. Turned sour.'

'So what was this early friendship based on?' Coleridge asked. 'It can't have been much if it went sour so quickly.'

'Well, they have a lot in common,' Trisha replied. 'They're both vegans and obsessed with diets and dieting, which seems to have formed a bond between them. On the very first evening they had a long and rather exclusive conversation about food-combining and stomach acids. I've lined up the tape.'

Sure enough, when Trisha pressed play there on the screen were David and Layla, set slightly apart from the rest of the group, having the most terrific meeting of minds.

'That is *so* right,' said Layla.

'Isn't it?' David agreed.

'But it's amazing how many people still think that dairy is healthy.'

'Which it *so* isn't.'

'Did you know that eggs killed more people in the last century than Hitler?'

'Yes, I think I did know that, *and* wheat.'

'Ugh, wheat! Don't get me started on *wheat*!'

Now the sombre tones of Andy the narrator intruded briefly. *'David and Layla have discovered that they have a lot in common: they both miss their cats dreadfully.'*

'Pandora is the most beautiful and intelligent creature I have ever met,' David explained, 'and sadly I include human beings in that statement.'

'I *so* know what you mean,' Layla replied.

Trisha stopped the tape. 'Fogarty the editor told me they got very excited about David and Layla that night. They thought that they might even troll off to the nookie hut and have it off there and then, but all that happened was a shoulder massage.'

'But they were definitely friends?' Coleridge asked.

'I think it's more that they hated everybody else. Looking at the tapes, it's pretty obvious that they thought themselves a cut above the others. On the first day or two the cameras often caught them exchanging wry, superior little glances. Peeping Tom broadcast them, too. The public hated it. David and

Layla were the absolute least popular people in the house.'

'But of course they didn't know this.'

'Well, there's no way they could have done. They were sealed off. In fact, watching them you get the impression that they think people will love them as much as they love themselves. Particularly him.'

'Yes, David certainly is a cocky one,' Coleridge mused. 'Arrogant almost beyond belief, in fact, in his quiet, passive-aggressive sort of way.'

Hooper was surprised to hear Coleridge using a term as current and overused as passive-aggressive, but there was no doubt that the phrase summed up David exactly.

They looked at David on the screen and stared into his soft, puppy-dog eyes. All three were thinking the same thing.

'It would certainly take a very confident person to believe that they could get away with what our murderer got away with,' said Coleridge. 'No one with the slightest self-doubt would ever have attempted it.' He returned to the theme of friendship. 'So familiarity quickly took its toll on David and Layla's closeness. Like many a friendship too eagerly begun, it had no staying power.'

'That's right,' said Trisha. 'It started going wrong with the cheese and went downhill from there.'

'They were too alike, I reckon,' said Hooper. 'They got in each other's way. They wanted the same role in the house, to be the beautiful and sensitive one. It all fell irrevocably to pieces over Layla's poem.'

DAY FIVE. 9.00 p.m.

The row began with the best intentions. David had suggested, in an attempt to engineer a *rapprochement*

68

between himself and Layla (and hence avoid her nominating him), that since he was trained and practised in the art of recitation perhaps he should learn one of Layla's poems and recite it for her. Layla had been touched and flattered and because there were no papers or pens allowed in the house David had set to learning the poem orally directly from the author.

'Lactation,' said Layla.

'That's very, very beautiful,' said David.

'It's the title,' Layla explained.

'I understand,' said David, nodding gently, as if the fact that 'Lactation' was the title required a heightened level of perception to come to terms with.

'Shall we take it two lines at a time?' Layla asked.

By way of an answer David closed his eyes and put his hands together at the fingertips, his lips gently touching his index fingers.

Layla began. '"Woman. Womb-an. Fat, full, belly, rich with girl child. Vagina, two-way street to miracles."'

David breathed deeply and repeated the first two lines of Layla's poem. It was clear from his manner that he thought Layla would be amazed and thrilled to have her words lent wings by such a richly liquid and subtle voice.

If she was, she hid it well. 'Actually, that first line is meant to be very upbeat, joyful,' Layla said. 'You're being too sombre. I always say it with a huge smile, particularly the words "girl child". I mean, think about it, David, doesn't the thought of a strong, spiritual woman's belly engorged with a beautiful girl child just make you want to smile?'

David was clearly aghast. 'Are you giving me *direction*, Layla?' he asked.

'No, I just want you to know how to say it, that's all.'

'The whole point about getting an *actor* to work on a piece of writing, *Layla*, is in order to get another artist's interpretation of it. An actor will find things in a poem that the author did not even know were there.'

'But I don't want the things that aren't there, I want the things that are.'

David seemed to snap. 'Then you'd better recite it yourself,' he said, jumping angrily to his feet. 'Because quite frankly it stinks. Apart from the repulsive imagery of fat, engorged female stomachs, from, I might add, a woman with less flesh on her than a Chupa Chups stick, I am a *professional* actor and I simply will not take direction from an *amateur* poet! Particularly after I have paid her the *enormous* compliment of actually taking an interest in her pisspoor work!' And with that David headed outside for a dip in the hot spa.

DAY THIRTY-TWO. 10.15 p.m.

'Very short fuse, Master David,' Coleridge observed thoughtfully. 'Short enough for murder, do you think?'

Rewinding slightly and freezing on David's furious face, it did seem possible.

'He certainly looks like he wants to murder her,' said Hooper. 'But of course it wasn't Layla that ended up getting killed, was it?'

'As we have discussed endlessly, sergeant. If the motive were obvious our killer would be awaiting trial right now. All we can hope to find is the seed from which a murder will grow.'

Hooper informed Coleridge as briskly as he dared that he was aware of this.

DAY FIVE. 9.15 p.m

After David had left the room, Layla did indeed take his advice and recite the poem herself, grinning like a baboon with a banana wedged sideways in its mouth throughout.

Jazz, Kelly, Dervla and Moon listened respectfully, and when it was over, they all said that they thought it was very, very good.

Woggle opined from his corner that poetry was merely an effort to formalize language and as such indicated a totalitarian mindset. 'Words are anarchists. Let them run free,' he said. But the others ignored him, something that they had learned to do as much as possible, while counting the minutes to nomination day.

'That was the business, that poem, Layles. It was dead wicked, that, so fair play to yez,' Moon said in her Mancunian accent, which seemed to be getting thicker by the day.

'Did you notice my red lipstick?' Layla gushed.

They all had.

'Some anthropologists believe that women paint their lips red in order to make their mouths reminiscent of their vaginas.'

'Steady on, girl,' said Gazzer from over by the kettle. 'Just had my dinner.'

'They say that women do it to make themselves more attractive to men, but I do it as a celebration.'

'Of what?' Jazz asked innocently.

'Of my vagina.'

'Oh, right.'

'Any time you want someone to help you celebrate it, Layles,' said Garry.

'Sherrup, Garry,' said Moon. 'It's not about fookin' blokes, it's about bein' a strong and spiritual woman, in't it, Layles?'

'Yes, it is, Moon, that's exactly what it's about.'

Kelly was still a bit confused. 'Well, I don't get what these anthropologists are on about. Why would any girl want to have a face like a fanny?'

Layla had to think about this for a moment. She had never been asked before. People she knew just tended to nod wisely and ask if there was any more guacamole.

'I don't think they mean *exactly* like one. It's just an impression of genitalia in order to steer the male towards procreation.'

'Oh, right, I see,' said Kelly.

'It's why female monkeys turn their bottoms pink. If they didn't they would have died out as a species long ago. Trust the woman to find a way.'

Everybody nodded thoughtfully.

'Did you know that monkeys have star signs?' said Moon. 'Yeah. This mystic went to London Zoo and did horoscopes for all the advanced primates, and do you know what? She got them all bang on, their personalities and everything. It were fookin' weird.'

DAY SEVEN. 8.00 a.m.

For the previous day or two Dervla had made a point of always being the first up in the morning so that she might have the shower room to herself. On this occasion, however, she found Moon had beaten her to it, not because Moon had suddenly transformed herself into an early riser, but because she was only just on her way to bed.

'I've been sat up all night reading that Red Dragon book Sally brought in. You know, the first one with Hannibal Lecter in it. Fookin' amazing, I were fookin' terrified. I reckon that's the scariest kind of murder that, when there's no fookin' reason for it except that the bloke's fookin' mad for topping people, you know, a serial psycho.'

Dervla waited while Moon brushed her teeth and staggered off to bed.

'Wake me if I'm missing out on any food,' Moon said as she left the bathroom.

Now Dervla was alone, standing before the basin mirror in her underwear. She sensed movement behind the mirror. The housemates were occasionally aware of the people behind the mirrors: there were tiny noises and at night sometimes, when the lights in the bedrooms were off, shapes could vaguely be made out through the mirrors. Dervla knew that her friend had come to meet her.

'Mirror, mirror on the wall,' she said, as if having a private joke with herself, 'who'll be the winner of us all?' She pretended to laugh and put some toothpaste on her brush. None of the editors watching could have imagined that she was talking to anyone.

Soon the writing appeared, just as it did every morning. Ugly ungainly letters. The messenger was clearly having to write backwards and perhaps, Dervla thought, at arm's length.

'*Woggle number one with public,*' said the message.

She nearly blew it. She nearly blurted Woggle's name out loud she was so surprised to discover that he was in the lead. Fortunately she stayed cool, allowing her eyes to flick downwards only momentarily.

Her anonymous informant completed his message. '*Kelly 2. You 3,*' it said, and then, '*Good Luck XXX.*'

Dervla finished brushing her teeth and washed her face. So she was running third. Not bad out of ten. It was certainly a surprise that Woggle was so popular, but when she thought about it she supposed he must have a lot of novelty value. It would soon wear off.

Kelly was much more of a threat.

She was a lovely girl. Dervla liked her. Clearly the public did too. Never mind, Dervla thought to herself, there were eight weeks to go yet. A lot could happen in eight weeks and surely Kelly couldn't stay so happy and so sunny for ever.

Before leaving the bathroom Dervla wiped the words off the mirror and blew a little kiss at her reflection. She thought that her friend the cameraman might appreciate a small friendly gesture.

DAY THIRTY-TWO. 11.35 p.m.

Coleridge tiptoed from the kitchen into the living room with his second can of beer. Upstairs his wife was asleep. She had been asleep when he'd arrived home and would still be asleep when he left the house again at six the following morning. She had left Coleridge a note pointing out that although they lived in the same house she had not actually set eyes on him for three days.

Coleridge searched out a Biro and scribbled, 'I haven't changed,' beneath his wife's message.

The note would still be there the next night, only by then Mrs Coleridge would have added 'more's the pity'.

She didn't mean it, she liked him really, but, as she often remarked, it's easy to think fondly of somebody you never see.

Coleridge had brought home with him the Peeping Tom press pack relating to week one in the house. On the front was attached a photocopied memo written on Peeping Tom notepaper. It was headed 'Round-up of housemates' public/press profiles at day eight.' The writer had been admirably succinct.

Woggle is the nation's pet. Mega-popular.
David is the bastard. Hated.
Kelly has phwoar factor. Popular.
Dervla is an enigmatic beauty. Popular.
Layla is highly shaggable but a pain. Disliked.
Moon is a pain and not even very shaggable. Disliked.

*Gazzer and Jazz liked. (Not by feminists and intel-
lectuals.)*

*Sally, not registered much. When has, disliked.
(Note: gay community think S. an unhelpful stereo-
type. Would have preferred a fluffy poof or lipstick lez.)*

Hamish not registered.

Coleridge leafed through the clippings. Most of them
confirmed the Peeping Tom memo. There was, however, some discussion about the fact that *House Arrest
Three* was defying expectations and performing much
better than had been predicted.

'The saggy soufflé rises!' one headline said, referring
to its prediction of the previous week that soufflés do
not rise twice, let alone three times. This was news to
Coleridge, who had not realized that when the third
series of *House Arrest* had been announced there had
been much speculation that the reality show bubble
had already burst. Coleridge had presumed that this
sort of show was a guaranteed success, but he was
wrong. The press clippings revealed that many shows
conceived in the heady days when it seemed that any
show with a loud and irritating member of the public
in it was a guaranteed winner had failed to live up to
their promise. And at the start of week one the new
series of *House Arrest* was confidently expected to be
a big failure. But it had defied all the grim expectations, and after seven shows had been broadcast it
was already doing as well as its two predecessors.
Nobody was more surprised about this than Geraldine
herself, something that she freely admitted when she
appeared on *The Clinic*, a hip late-night chat show, in
order to promote week two.

Coleridge slipped the video into his home VCR and
instantly found himself struggling to reduce the volume as the screaming, blaring frenzy of the opening
credits filled his living room and no doubt shot straight
upstairs to where his wife was trying to sleep.

'Big up to yez,' said the hip late-night girl, welcoming Geraldine on to the programme. 'Cracking first week in the house. We like that.'

'Top telly that woman!' said the hip late-night guy. 'Respect. Fair play to yez.'

'Go, Woggle, yeah!' said the girl. 'We *so* like Woggle.'

'He da *man!*' said the guy. 'Who da man?'

'*He* da man,' said the girl. 'Woggle, he da man!'

There was much cheering at this. The public loved Woggle.

'Amazing,' said Geraldine when the cheering had died down. 'I mean, I thought he would be interesting and stir things up a bit, but I never realized he'd strike such a chord with the viewers.'

'Yeah, well, he's like a sort of pet, isn't he?' said the girl. 'Like Dennis the Menace, or Animal from the Muppets or whatever.'

'I mean, you wouldn't want to live with him yourself, but it's top fun watching other people do it, big time!'

'Woggle, he da man!'

'Da *top* man. Respect! But the whole show is totally wicked,' the guy added quickly, 'so fair play to all of the posse in the house!'

'Respect!'

'Kelly's my girl! Ooojah ooojah!'

'You would fancy Kelly!' said the girl, punching her partner in the ribs. 'Dervla's easily the most beautiful.'

'Dervla's beautiful, that is true, and she melts my ice cream big time, so fair play to her for that, but Kelly, well, Kelly has . . . something special.'

'Big knockers?'

'What can I tell you? It's a boy thing.'

The boys in the audience let it be known that they agreed with this sentiment.

'And don't we so *hate* David?' said the girl. 'We *so* do hate him.'

'We *so* do not, not hate him,' added the guy.

There was much booing at the mention of David's name, and the show's producer dropped in a shot taken directly from the live Internet link to the house. David was sitting crosslegged on the floor playing his guitar, clearly thinking himself rather beautiful. There was more booing and laughter at this.

'Sad *or what*?' shrieked the hip girl.

Sipping his beer and watching all of this, three and a half weeks after it had been recorded, Coleridge was struck by how astonishingly brutal it was. The man on the screen had absolutely no idea that he was being jeered and ridiculed. It was as if the country had turned into one vast school playground with the public as bully.

'All right, that's enough of that,' said the guy, clearly having an attack of conscience. 'I'm sure his mum likes him.'

'Yeah. Big up to David's mum! But can you *please* tell him to cut that *hair*?'

'And to stop playing that *guitar*!'

The interview passed on to the unexpected success of the third series so far.

'So you defied the snooties and the sneerers, and the show's a huuuuugge hit,' said the guy, 'which is quite a relief, Geri, am I right? Tell me I'm right.'

'You are so right,' said Geraldine, 'and if I wasn't a bird I'd say my balls were on the line with this one. I've sunk every penny I have into it. My savings and all of my severance pay from when I left the BBC. I'm the sole director of Peeping Tom Productions, mate, so if it fails I haven't got anybody to blame but me.'

'Gutsy lady!' the girl enthused. 'We like that! Respect!'

'Too right I'm a gutsy lady, girl,' said Geraldine. 'I gave up a cushy job as controller of BBC1 to do the *House Arrest* thing, and everybody expected this third series to fall on its arse.'

'Yeah, Geri, you really went out on a limb leaving the Beeb,' the hip late-night guy said. 'I know your name has often been mentioned as a possible future Director General.'

'Yes, I think they wanted to offer it to me,' she said, 'but stuff that, I'm a programme maker, I ain't spending my day kissing politicians like Billy here's arse. I ain't grown up yet.'

The camera pulled out to reveal Billy Jones, who was the other guest on *The Clinic*, and who was smiling indulgently. Billy was the Minister for Culture and had agreed to appear on *The Clinic* as part of the government's strategy to reach out to youth.

'I regret greatly that I shan't be having my arse kissed by a lady so charming as you, Geraldine,' Billy Jones said, and got a laugh.

'So, Billy,' said the girl, turning to him with a serious expression on her face. 'How do you rate *House Arrest*, then? Top telly or pile of poo?'

'Oh, *House Arrest* is *so* top telly,' said the Minister of Culture. 'No *way* is it a pile of poo.'

'And what about people who say that telly is dumbed down? That we need more, I don't know, history programmes and classic drama-type stuff?'

'Well, certainly there is a place for history-type stuff and all that classic drama malarkey, but at the end of the day politicians, teachers and social workers need to be *listening* to young people, because I don't think, right, that history and stuff is really very relevant to what young people are interested in today.'

'Big up to that,' said the hip late-night guy. 'We like that!'

'Because at the end of the day,' Billy continued, 'what politicians and teachers and stuff need to do is connect with what kids are really into, like the Internet. We think that the Internet and the web are terribly important, and of course these wicked experiments in reality TV like *House Arrest*.'

By the time the show was ending and the final band was being introduced, Coleridge had fallen asleep. He woke up to the vision of a sweating American skinhead wearing only board shorts and 90 per cent tattoo coverage shouting 'I'm just a shitty piece of human garbage,' at the screen.

He decided it was time to go to bed. Geraldine had had a lucky escape with her show, that was clear. By rights, it seems, it should have been a flop.

David, on the other hand, had not been so lucky. He was the fall guy, the national joke, and Geraldine had made him so. If David had known this, Coleridge reflected, he might have been tempted to take some kind of revenge on Peeping Tom, but of course he could not have known, could he?

DAY THIRTY-THREE. 10.15 a.m.

The picture of Woggle on the map on the incident room wall was almost completely obscured by the numerous tapes that terminated on it. Trisha had just completed the pattern by running a ribbon to him from Dervla, with the words 'pubic hair row' written on it.

Dervla had seemed so determined to be quiet and serene, so like the muse in an advert for Irish beer. But you couldn't maintain that if you followed Woggle into the bathroom.

DAY EIGHT. 9.30 a.m.

'*It's day eight in the house,*' said Andy the narrator, '*and Dervla has just had a shower.*'

'Woggle!' she shouted, emerging from the shower room, clutching a bar of soap.

'Yes, sweet lady.'

'Can you *please* remove your pubic hairs from the soap after you have finished showering?'

It was their own fault, of course. Woggle would have been quite happy not to shower at all, but the group had made a personal appeal to him to wash thoroughly at least once a day.

'That way in a month or two you might be clean,' Jazz had observed.

Now they were paying the price for their finickiness. Woggle's matted pubic mullet had never seen such regular action, and the unaccustomed pressure was causing it to moult liberally.

Dervla waved the hairy bar of soap in his face. She had thought hard before confronting Woggle. Quite apart from the fact that she did not like scenes, she also knew from her secret informant that Woggle was a very popular person outside the house. Would having a row with him alienate her from the public? she wondered. On the other hand, perhaps it would do the public good to get some idea of what she and the other house-mates were having to deal with. In the end, Dervla could not help herself: she just *had* to say something. Woggle tended to do his cursory ablutions in the middle of the night, and, being first up, it was always Dervla who encountered his residue.

'Each morning I have to gouge a small toupee off the soap, and the next morning there it is again, looking like a member of the Grateful Dead!'

'Confront your fear of the natural world, O she-woman. My knob hair can do you no harm. Unlike cars

80

of which you have admitted you own one.' In one single bound Woggle had got from his lack of social grace to her responsibility for the destruction of the entire planet. He was always doing that.

'It's got nothing to do with fucking cars!' Dervla was shocked to hear herself shout. She had not raised her voice in years. Hers was a calm, reflective spirit, that was her thing, and yet here she was shouting.

'Yes, it has, O Celtic lady, for your priorities are weirding me out, man, messing with my head zone. Cars are evil dragons that are eating our world! Whereas my hair is entirely benign, non-volatile dead-cell matter.'

'It is benign non-volatile dead-cell matter that grew out of your *scrotum*!' Dervla shouted. 'And it makes me want to puke! Sweet Virgin Mary Mother of Jesus Christ, where does it all come from! We could have stuffed a mattress by now! Are you using some kind of snake oil ointment down there?'

Unbeknown to Dervla, Woggle was actually a little hurt by her attack. Nobody ever credited Woggle with having feelings because he seemed so entirely oblivious to everybody else's. But Woggle actually liked Dervla, and he fancied her, too. He had even been to the confession box to confess his admiration.

'There is definitely a connection between us,' he said. 'I'm fairly certain that at some point in another life she was a great Princess of the Sacred Runes and that I was her Wizard.'

Confronted now by this attack from one he clearly rated so highly, Woggle attempted to assume an air of dignified distance. 'I remain unrepentant of my bollock hair,' he muttered. 'It has as much right to a place in this house as does every other item of human effluvia, such as, for instance, the pus from Moon's septic nipple ring, which I respect.'

It was a clever ploy. Moon had insisted that the

whole group look at her septic nipple the night before and had won herself no friends in the process.

'Hey! Leave my fookin' nipple out of it, Woggle!' Moon shouted now from where she sprawled on the purple couch. 'I've told you. How was I to know that dirty bastard in Brighton was using shite metal 'stead of gold, which he said it was. He said it were fookin' gold, didn't he? The bastard. Besides, I'm using Savlon on my nipple and I don't leave what comes out of it all over the fookin' soap.'

'Yes, don't try and change the subject,' Dervla insisted. 'Moon's doing what she can about her nipple infection and you should clean the soap after you use it. And not just the soap: clean out the plughole too. It looks like a St Bernard dog died there and rotted.'

'I shall clean up my hair,' Woggle said with what he assumed was an air of ancient and mighty dignity.

'Good,' said Dervla.

'*If*,' Woggle continued, 'you promise to renounce your car.'

DAY THIRTY-THREE. 2.30 p.m.

Every time the 'not yet watched' pile of tapes began to look a little smaller and less intimidating, somebody brought up more from the cells. They seemed to go on for ever.

'*It's day eight, and Jazz and Kelly are chatting in the garden.*'

DAY EIGHT. 3.00 p.m.

'What's the worst job you've ever had?' said Jazz.

He and Kelly were sitting by the pool revelling in the sunshine and the fact that they must look absolutely terrific on camera in their tiny swimming costumes.

'No doubt about that,' Kelly replied. 'Being a film extra. I hated it.'

'Why's that, then?' asked Jazz. 'It don't sound too bad to me.'

'Well, I think it's all right if you're not interested in being an actor. Then you just take the money and eat the lunch and try and spot a star, but it's really rough if you actually want to get into the profession properly like I do. Then being an extra makes you feel like you're just never going to get anywhere.'

'So you want to be an actress, then?'

'Oh God, I'd love it. That would be sooooo cool! Except you don't say actress any more, you know. They're all just actors nowadays, even the women, because of feminism. Like Emma Thompson or Judi Dench or Pamela Anderson or whatever. They're not actresses, they're actors.'

'Is that right? Sounds a bit weird to me.'

'Well, I think so too, actually. I mean, they're women, aren't they? But we've all got to get used to it, otherwise it's offensive, apparently. I'm not sure, but I *think* it goes back to a time when apparently all actresses were prostitutes, and I suppose Judi Dench doesn't want anyone thinking that she's a prostitute. Well, you wouldn't, would you?'

'No, not if you're a classy bird like her, certainly not,' Jazz conceded. 'So that's what you want to be then – a lady actor?'

'Absolutely, that's why I'm in here. I'm hoping I'll get noticed. I went in the confession box the other day and did a speech I'd learnt off *The Bill* about a girl doing cold turkey in the cells.'

'Fahkin' hell, girl, well pushy.'

'Yeah, I rolled around on the floor and cried and everything. Don't know if they'll show it, though. I'd do anything to get to be an actress. That's why I did the extra work. I thought I might learn something and even make a few contacts, but I hated it.'

David was swimming in the pool. Elegantly completing a series of gentle, desperately mannered laps in a perfectly unhurried breaststroke. A breaststroke which announced to the world that not only did David swim absolutely beautifully but that he had absolutely beautiful thoughts while he was doing it.

He had been listening to what Kelly was saying. 'I don't believe that anyone who would take extra work can truly want to be an actor, Kelly. I advise you to find a more realistic dream.'

'You what?' said Kelly.

'Fuck off, David,' said Jazz. 'Kelly can dream what she likes.'

'And I can offer her advice if I wish. Kelly's a big girl. She doesn't need you to protect her, Jason.'

'Jazz.'

'I keep forgetting.'

'Come on, then, David,' said Kelly. 'What do you mean, a more realistic dream?'

David hoisted himself up out of the water, quite clearly conscious as he did so of the splendid, glistening, dripping curves and tone of his muscular arms. He paused halfway out of the pool, arms stretched taut, taking his weight, shoulders rippling and strong, firm, shadowy clefts at his collar bone. His legs dangled in the pool and the hard, wavy plane of his stomach pressed against the terracotta edge. 'I meant exactly what I said.'

David emerged from the pool completely, in one single, graceful, uncluttered movement. 'Acting is the most demanding vocation imaginable. Harder, I think, perhaps, than any other.'

'Bomb-disposal expert?' said Jazz, but David ignored him.

'You have to believe in yourself utterly, and consider

your dream to be not a dream but a duty. If you're prepared at the very beginning to accept second best, then I suggest it is inevitable that you will never achieve your end. I personally would wash dishes, clean cars, wait on tables, rather than accept any job in the profession other than one I considered worthy of my dream. John Hurt resolved at the outset of his career to accept only leading roles, you know. I'm told he suffered thirteen years of unemployment as a result. But, ah, what triumph was to follow.'

'Well, what about all the actors who aren't John Hurt?' Jazz asked. 'The ones who suffered thirteen years of unemployment and then suffered another thirteen years of unemployment and then died of alcohol poisoning. What if that's what happened to you?'

'If that were my fate,' said David, 'then at least I would know that I had never compromised and that although my talent was not recognized I had never betrayed it. I would far rather be Van Gogh, tormented in life and dying unrecognized, than some comfortable portrait painter who prostitutes his talent for lack of faith in it. Winning is all. Consolation prizes are not worth having. I truly, truly believe that, Jason. I know you think me a pompous arrogant bastard . . .'

'Yes,' said Jazz.

'And perhaps I am. But I mean what I say. You have to have everything or nothing, and so you will never be an actor, Kelly, and I say that as a friend who has your best interests at heart. Do yourself a favour. Find another dream.'

DAY THIRTY-THREE. 2.35 p.m.

Hooper pressed stop. 'David knows what he's doing, he just doesn't know it isn't working.'

'You what?' asked Trisha.

85

'Well, he's not stupid. He must know he's coming across as arrogant and mean. I think it's his strategy. It's not always the nice people who stay the course in these shows. Sometimes it's the bastards. I reckon David wants to get noticed, noticed as someone great-looking, arrogant and uncompromising. In other words, a leading man, a star. I don't think that man cares what he does or what people think of him. He just wants to be a star.'

DAY EIGHT. 11.20 p.m.

The girls were lying on their beds drinking hot chocolate. The talk quickly turned to Woggle, as it had done on many previous evenings.

'He's a nutter,' Moon said. 'He should be in a loony bin. He's mad, he is.'

'He is strange,' said Kelly. 'I just worry that he might do himself some harm or something. We had a kid like him at our school, except he had a Mohican instead of dreadlocks. Always sitting on his own and swaying, he was, just like Woggle, and he ended up writing on his arms with a knife, there was blood everywhere, the school nurse fainted, it was gross.'

Then Sally spoke. After Woggle, Sally was the most isolated of the group, and had so far come to prominence only once, when she had insisted on raising her Rainbow Lesbian and Gay Alliance flag in the back garden. It had not been a major incident, however, because despite Sally's very best efforts nobody had objected.

Moon's comments about loony bins had touched a nerve.

'Woggle's not mad!' Sally snapped. 'He's just filthy and horrible and politically unfocused. That's all. He's not mad.'

86

'Well, he is a bit mad, Sally,' Kelly said. 'Did you see him trying to save that ant from the water that splashed out of the pool? I mean, how mad is that?'

The venom of Sally's reply took everybody aback. 'Listen, Kelly, you know absolutely nothing about it, all right?' she hissed. 'Nothing! People like you are so prejudiced and ignorant about mental illness. It's pathetic! Absolutely pathetic and also disableist!'

'I only said he was a bit mad, Sally.'

'I know what you said, and I find it totally offensive. Just because a person has mental health issues doesn't make them a disgusting anti-social pariah.'

'Yes, but he *is* disgusting, Sally,' Kelly protested. 'I mean, I feel sorry for him and everything, but . . .'

'And that's the point I'm making, you stupid ignorant cow! He's disgusting, he's not mad. The two are not the same thing. Everybody's so fucking prejudiced. Fucking grow up, why don't you?'

Kelly looked like she had been slapped in the face. Sally's anger had risen up so quickly that her fists were clenched and it almost seemed that she would lash out.

In the monitoring bunker they twiddled desperately at their controls to get the hot-head remotes to swivel and focus on the relevant faces. Geraldine ordered both operators in the camera runs to push their dollies round to the girls' bedroom immediately. That rarest of all events in reality television seemed to be developing: a moment of genuine, spontaneous drama.

'Hey, steady on, Sally,' said Dervla. 'Kelly's entitled to her opinion.'

'Not if it's oppressive of minorities, she isn't.'

'I haven't got an opinion,' wailed Kelly, tears springing up in her eyes. 'Honestly.'

'You do, you just don't recognize your own bigotry!'

Sally snapped. 'Everybody hates and stigmatizes the mentally ill and blames them for society's problems. They're denied treatment, ignored by the system and then when once in a blue moon something happens, like some poor schizo who never should have been returned to the community gets stuck inside their own dark box and sticks a knife in someone's head or whatever, suddenly every mild depressive in the country is a murderer and it's just ignorant fucking bollocks!'

Sally was getting more and more upset. The other girls had not seen this side of her before. The knuckles on her clenched fists had turned white; there were angry tears in her eyes.

Kelly appeared horrified to have been the cause of all this hurt, but also astonished at how emotional Sally had so quickly become. 'I'm sorry, Sally, all right?' Kelly said. 'If I've said something stupid I'm sorry. I didn't mean to, but really there's no need to cry about it.'

'I'm not fucking crying!' Sally shouted.

Moon had been lying on her bed listening to the conversation with a look of tolerant bemusement on her face. Now she raised herself up and joined in. 'Sally's right, but she's also wrong,' she said with a patronizing air of authority. 'Woggle ain't genuinely mad, he's just a twat with body odour, but on the other hand I wouldn't be too certain about how nice and cosy the average loony is, Sally . . .'

Sally tried to interrupt angrily but Moon continued.

'Or "people with mental health issues" as you choose to put it. I've seen nutters, real nutters, dangerous fookin' bastard nutters, and let me tell you, darling, society's right to be scared of them, I know I fookin' was.'

'That is just ignorant shit,' said Sally. 'What would you know about it? How would you know anything about the mentally ill?'

'Well, what would you know about it yourself, Sally?' said Dervla thoughtfully. Her face had a slightly troubled look about it.

But before Sally could answer Dervla's question, Moon pressed on. 'I know plenty about it, Sally!' she barked, seeming suddenly to be as upset as the other girl, 'and I'll tell you why: because I spent two years, did you hear me, love? Two fookin' years in a mental hospital. Have you got that? A hospital for the insane, a loony bin and that is why, Sally, I fookin' hate nutters.'

For a moment the room fell silent. The other girls were simply astonished at this sudden and unexpected bombshell.

'You never did,' said Kelly. 'You're having a laugh.'

But it appeared that Moon was not having a laugh.

'So don't tell me about people with mental health issues, Sally! I lived with them, I slept in their rooms, ate at their tables, walked the same corridors, stared at the same shitty walls for two years. So don't give me any of that *One Flew Over the Cuckoo's Nest* crap! Like *they*'re the bloody sane ones – the fookin' heroes.'

Sally clearly wanted to reply, but could find no words in the face of Moon's onslaught, which continued unabated: 'Oh yeah, I'm sure there's plenty of nice ones about the place, plenty of nice sweet little manic-depressives who don't hurt anybody but their mums and dads and themselves . . . but I'm talking about *nutters*. The ones that scream and tear at themselves in the night. All night! The ones that lash out when you pass them on the ward, trick you with their cunning, grab you, touch you, fookin' try and *eat you*.'

The other four young women sat on their beds and stared at Moon. Sally's passion had come as a surprise, but this was something more, much, much more. This was shocking. Moon had been so cheerful, so funny right from the first day, and now this.

'But why? Why were you there, Moon?' Dervla's voice was calm. Sweet and reassuring, like a doctor's or a priest's, but those who knew her would have heard the anxiety in it. They would have known that she was scared. 'Were you ill?'

'No, I wasn't ill,' said Moon bitterly. 'But my fookin' uncle was ill. My uncle is a sad sick ill bastard.' She stopped, and seemed to be considering whether to go on.

Layla asked if she wanted a hand to hold. Moon ignored her.

'He abused me, right? Not the full business, never rape, but plenty enough. A year it went on until one day I told my ma, that cow. I can say it now because she's dead. I never thought she'd believe her brother and not me, but he was a powerful man in the local community, I suppose, a doctor. And he had friends, counsellors, other doctors and the like, and between them they managed to make it all look my fault. I was a nasty lying little slut and a dangerous fantasist to boot. Maybe it woulda' been different if me dad had been around, but God knows where he is. God knows *who* he is.'

'They managed to get you committed?' Dervla asked, astonished.

'Yeah, you wouldn't have thought it could happen, would you? To a young teenage girl, in our day and age, but it did, and I got put away for trying to tell the world that I'd been touched up by my uncle.'

There was silence in the room. For the first time since they had all entered the house, nobody had anything to say.

The silence was echoed in the monitoring bunker, where Bob Fogarty, Pru, his assistant editor, various production managers and all their PAs were stunned.

'That is incredible,' said Fogarty.

'Yes, it is, isn't it?' said the voice of Geraldine Hennessy. 'An incredible load of bollocks.'

They turned round in surprise. Nobody had noticed Geraldine enter the bunker, but in fact she had been watching for some time. She had come on from dinner with her current boyfriend in tow, a beautiful nineteen-year-old dancer whom she had met backstage at the Virgin summer pop festival.

'I never thought Moon would be the one to go for the lying trick, I really didn't. I must say I'm impressed.'

'She's lying?' the various editors and PAs asked in astonishment.

'Of course she's lying, you stupid bunch of cunts. Do you really think I'd put an abused kid out of a loony hospital into my happy little game show? Bollocks! Woggle's as mad as I go. That bald bitch's mum and dad are alive and well and living in Rusholme. He's a tobacconist, she works in a dry cleaner's.'

There was great relief in the bunker at this and also excitement. It seemed that perhaps the game inside the house might turn out to be more interesting than they had feared.

'Look at her smirking to herself 'cos it's dark and the others can't see,' Geraldine said, pointing at one of the remote camera feeds. 'She knows *we* can see, though, oh yes! She's having a laugh, isn't she? She knows the public loves a stirrer. You get much more famous being naughty than nice. Get me a coffee, will you, Darren? Use the machine in my office, not the shite this lot drink.'

The impossibly beautiful nineteen-year-old boy grumpily stirred his perfect body and went off to do as he was bidden.

'Lucky you did your research, Geraldine,' Fogarty remarked. 'If you didn't know Moon was lying I imagine we'd all be pretty nervous now.'

'I'd have known anyway,' Geraldine replied

pompously. 'Those idiot proles in there might manage to manipulate each other, possibly even the public, but not me, mate.'

'You think you would have guessed she was lying even if you didn't know?'

'Of course I would. That woman's never been near a mental hospital in her life. She's watched too many films, that's all. People don't scream and shriek in those places. If they do they get sedated pretty fucking sharpish, let me tell you, and the only grabbing and touching that goes on is by the nurses. Mental hospitals are *quiet* at night. All you can hear is weeping, shuffling and wanking.'

For a moment Geraldine had a faraway look in her eye. To her assembled staff she seemed almost human. The next moment she was herself again. 'Right, package all that stuff up. I'm not using it now, I'm concentrating on Woggle. Besides, I'm not having some bald cunt like Moon influencing the public this early on. I influence the public, not the bloody inmates. Keep it, though. Could be useful later.'

'What, you mean put it in out of sequence?' Fogarty was taken aback.

'Maybe,' replied Geraldine. 'Who'd notice the difference?'

'But . . . but the time codes on the video . . . They'd be out of sequence. We couldn't adjust them.'

'Of course you can, you silly arse. They're just numbers on a screen, you can change them. Just go into the Apple menu and dig out the control panel.'

'I know *how* to do it, Geraldine,' Bob Fogarty replied coldly. 'I meant we couldn't do it morally, professionally.'

'Our moral and professional duty is to provide good telly to the public, who pay our wages. We are not fucking anthropologists, we are entertainers, mate. Turns. We work on the end of the pier along with the illusionists, the mystics, the magicians, the hypnotists and all the other cheating shysters who make up this great business we call show. Now stick the whole thing in a separate file and hide it somewhere.'

The team said no more, working on in silence, hoping that if Geraldine did want to do something as outrageous as broadcasting house events out of sequence it would not be them whom she instructed to do it. Back on the screens the attention of the editing team was drawn by a flurry of bras and knickers. The girls were getting ready for bed.

'Nipple-watch!' shouted Geraldine. 'Jump to it.'

They all had their styles. Sally got into bed in her T-shirt and knickers. Kelly allowed the occasional flash as she whipped off her shirt and dived into bed. Moon was happy to wander about in front of the infra-red cameras entirely naked. Layla and Dervla were the most coy: both put on long nighties before removing their underwear. When Geraldine saw this on the first night she had made a mental note to catch both of these prudes out at some point, in the showers, probably, or perhaps the pool, and put their nipples out in the Sunday night special compilation. She wasn't having hoity-toity little scrubbers like them holding back on the flesh. What did they think they were on telly for?

The atmosphere in the bedroom was sombre. On previous nights the girls had laughed and giggled as they got into their beds, but on this occasion there was silence. Moon's revelations had rocked them all. Not just because it had been such a sad and shocking tale, but also because her distress would so obviously appeal to the public's sympathy and give her the edge when eviction time came. It was very strange to have to remember all the time that every conversation was a conversation between rivals who were competing against each other for the affection of the public.

Then Moon spoke. 'Oh, by the way, girls,' she said. 'All that stuff I just told you. That were rubbish, by the way. Sorry.'

There was another moment's silence.

'*What!*' Layla, who rarely shouted, was furious.

'Don't worry about it, love,' Moon said in a calm, matter-of-fact voice. 'I were 'aving a laugh. Take me mind off me septic nipple.'

'You said you'd been *abused*!'

'Well, everybody says they've been abused these days, don't they?' Moon replied. 'Blimey, if you look at the posters them charities put out, apparently every fookin' kid in the country's getting touched up on a more or less continual basis.'

'What's your game, Moon?' said Dervla with barely controlled fury.

'Told you. Just thought I'd have a laugh,' Moon said. 'Plus, I thought our Sally was getting a bit too serious, hopping into Kelly a bit strong about fookin' loonies, that's all.'

'You rotten bitch,' said Layla.

'You cow,' said Kelly.

'That was a pretty low trick, Moon,' said Dervla. 'I don't think sexual abuse is a very funny subject.'

'Well, it passed the time, didn't it?' Moon said. ' 'Night.'

There was another long pause. Finally Kelly broke the silence. 'So were you telling the truth about your breast implants, then?' she asked.

'Oh, yeah, couldn't do without me kajungas, could I? I reckon they help me with me balance when I'm on the trapeze.'

As peace once more descended upon the room, Dervla thought she heard Sally sob.

It had been six days since the murder, and Sergeant Hooper and his team continued with the huge task of trawling through the vast archive of unseen Peeping Tom footage. Searching diligently for any hint of an incident that might have turned somebody's mind to murder. It was gruelling work even for Hooper, who was a big *House Arrest* fan, fitting their audience profile and advertiser expectations perfectly. Hooper was the opposite of Coleridge, a very modern copper, a hip, mad-for-it, bigged-up, twenty-first-century boy with baggy trousers, trainers, an earstud and a titanium Apple Mac Powerbook. Hooper and his mates never missed any of the various reality TV shows, but even he was being ground down by the task he now faced. Fortunately not *all* seven hundred and twenty hours a day of camera activity were available to the police, the vast bulk of it having been discarded on a daily basis by the Peeping Tom editors. But there were still hundreds of hours left, and watching it was like watching paint dry. Worse, at least paint *did* eventually dry. This lot seemed to stay wet for ever.

Hamish picking his nose again . . . Jazz scratching his bum.

The girls doing their yoga, *again*.

Garry doing more press-ups.

Garry doing chin-ups on the doorframes.

Garry running on the spot . . .

Hooper was beginning to despise the people in the house, and he did not want to. Quite apart from the fact that he did not think it would help him in his detection work, in a way these were his people. They had similar interests and ambitions, a similar honest conviction that they had a right to be happy. Hooper did not want to start thinking like Coleridge. What *was* that man like? Always *banging on* about the housemates having no sense of 'duty' or 'service' or 'community'. As if wanting to have it large made you an enemy of society.

Nonetheless, they were seriously beginning to wear him down. It was just that they never *did* anything, and, more irritatingly, they never *thought* anything. That most defining of all human characteristics, the capacity for abstract thought, was pressed solely into the service of . . . of . . . Nothing.

Hooper cursed inwardly. He was even beginning to *think* like Coleridge.

And of clues to a murder there were none.

Until Trisha spotted something.

Not much, but something.

'Have a look at this, sergeant,' she said. 'Arsey little moment between Kelly the slapper and David the ponce.'

'Arsey, constable? Slapper? Ponce?' Hooper replied, in Coleridge's schoolmasterly tone, and they both smiled grimly at the thought of the linguistic strictures under which they were obliged to work.

It was only a minor incident, just a whisper of a possibility, but then the police had long since given up any hope of happening upon the obvious.

'We are looking for a catalyst,' Hooper explained to the assembled officers. 'In chemistry, sometimes the tiniest element, if added to other compounds, can cause the most explosive results. That's what we're looking for: a tiny psychological catalyst.'

It had sounded good when Coleridge had said it to Hooper, and it sounded even better when Hooper showed off with it to his constables. Coleridge might have the lines, but Hooper felt that he knew how to deliver them.

The potential catalyst that Trisha had found was tiny indeed. It had not even been interesting enough for Peeping Tom to broadcast it, but Trisha found it interesting, and so did Hooper.

Kelly, Jazz and David were in the hot tub together. As usual, David was talking.

'It's interesting what you said yesterday about wanting to be an actress, Kelly. Because actually everybody in here is acting. You know that, don't you? This house is a stage and all the men and women merely players.'

'Not true,' Jazz replied, with his customary abundance of self-confidence. 'I'm being my true self, guy. What you see is what you get, because everything I got is too good to hide.'

'Oh, what nonsense. Nobody is ever truly themself.'

'And how do you know that, Mr Clever Arse Mind Games?'

'Because we don't completely know ourselves.'

'That's rubbish, that is.'

'Well, admit it, Jason.'

'Jazz.'

'Whatever. Haven't you ever surprised yourself, spotted some new and different personal angle that you've never seen before?'

'Well, I once squatted over a mirror. That was a bit of a shock, I can tell you,' said Jazz, and Kelly laughed loudly, a big, brash, irritating laugh.

Irritating to David, anyway.

'I was staring straight up my arse, man,' Jazz continued, grinning broadly, 'and even I was having trouble loving it!'

David was suddenly angry. He took himself very seriously and liked others to do the same.

'I can assure you, Jason, that we are all actors in life, presenting ourselves as we wish others to see us. That is why those of us who actually *are* actors, like myself, understand our world and the people in it more fully than ordinary folk do. We know the tricks, we read the signs. We recognize that we live in a world full of performers. Some of us are subtle, some are hams, but every one of us is *acting*. Seeing through your performance, *Jazz*, is my bread and butter.'

Jazz didn't reply for a moment. 'That's bollocks,' he said finally, which was sadly well below his usual natural wit.

David smiled.

Then Kelly leaned forward and whispered something in David's ear. It was hard to catch, but there was no doubt about what she said. What Kelly said to David was: 'I *know* you.'

Then she leaned back against the side of the tub and looked straight into David's eyes.

David returned her stare, his superior smirk undaunted. He seemed unruffled.

He was about to be ruffled. Very.

For Kelly leaned forward once more and whispered something else into David's ear.

DAY THIRTY-THREE. 5.30 p.m.

This time neither Sergeant Hooper nor Trisha could quite catch what Kelly said. None of the officers working in the room could work it out at all.

It sounded something like 'Far corgi in heaven.'

'That can't be right, surely,' said Hooper.

'It would seem unlikely,' Trisha agreed.

Whatever it was that Kelly whispered, David had understood it and had not liked it.

There on the screen his expression clearly changed, subtly – he was too good an actor for his face to give much away – but his expression changed. Suddenly the smug, superior smile had disappeared.

He looked scared.

DAY THIRTY-FOUR. 9.00 a.m.

Hooper showed Coleridge the tape the following morning.

'Whatever "Far corgi in heaven" means, sir, and that is certainly not quite what she said, it indicates to me that Kelly knew David before they entered the house.'

'It's possible,' conceded the inspector.

'I reckon probable, sir,' said Hooper, running the tape once more. 'When she says "I know you" I thought at first she meant she knew him psychologically, because that's what David was talking about.'

'Of course.'

'But then she says the other stuff, the corgi bit, and that's clearly something that only David understands, some secret or experience from the outside world that they share.'

'No doubt about that, sergeant,' Coleridge agreed, 'but it doesn't necessarily mean they'd met. Kelly may have recognized something in David that enabled her to work something out about him.'

'I don't count Kelly as the brightest apple in the barrel, sir. Working things out is not really her thing. I think they'd met.'

'Well, if they had then that is certainly a most significant discovery. Our whole catalyst theory is based on the presumption that they were all strangers. If two of them knew each other then that changes the dynamics across the whole group.'

For the first time the two detectives felt they might have a shred of a lead.

'So how do you read it, then, sergeant? Do you think that whatever Kelly recognized in David she recognized from the start?'

'Not unless she was as good an actress as she'd like to be. That first day was an absolute blank for her, I reckon. She just ran around shrieking, jumping in the pool and falling out of her top. Can't say I noticed a single reflective moment. No, I think that whatever it was that made the penny drop for Kelly happened later. At some point David gave himself away, and Kelly spotted something about him that she recognized.'

'In that case I imagine it would have occurred not too long before she revealed her knowledge to David.'

'For sure. Kelly does not strike me as the sort of girl to keep a juicy thing like that to herself. She couldn't wait to slap our Dave in the face with it, particularly after the way he put her down the previous day about her acting ambitions.'

'Well, if that's correct, then whatever she saw she must have seen between the conversation around the pool and the conversation in the hot tub. What were they doing on the evening of day eight?'

'Tattoos!' said Hooper. 'They were comparing tattoos! I've seen the tape.'

'Well, let's take another look at it.'

By the time Hooper had reloaded the video tape, Trisha had joined them, and together they sat down to study the faces of Kelly and David as the group discussed tattoos.

Supper was over and with the exception of Woggle the housemates were all sitting about on the couches. They had just completed a small task set by Peeping Tom in which each housemate was loaned a pencil and paper and had to write down their predictions of who they thought would be left in the house at the end of week seven. They were also encouraged to jot down any other thoughts they might have about how things would pan out. All the pieces of paper were then put in a big brown envelope marked 'Predictions', which was solemnly sealed and placed at the back of the kitchen unit.

It was after that that the conversation turned to

tattoos. They all had something to exhibit except Dervla and Jazz.

'I'm too black,' Jazz said, 'besides which my skin is too beautiful to be improved.'

'I don't have an explanation as to why I don't have any tattoos,' said Dervla. 'Except to say that it is extraordinary to me that these days when people talk about their tattoos it's the people who *don't* have them who have the explaining to do. Maybe that's why I don't want one.'

'Good for you,' said Coleridge, sipping from his china mug.

Hooper and Trisha said nothing. Hooper had the Everton football club badge tattooed on his shoulder and Trisha had a butterfly on her left buttock.

On the screen Garry was explaining that the eagle on his ankle stood for strength, honour and truth.

'What does the clenched fist on your shoulder stand for? Wanker?' Jazz enquired.

'No, it bleeding well doesn't,' Garry replied. 'Even though I am Olympic class in that particular sport.'

The girls groaned.

'My clenched fist also stands for strength, honour and truth. What's more, I'm going to get another one done across me back. I'm going to get "strength, honour and truth" written out in gothic script. It's my motto.'

The group indicated that they had rather gathered this.

Then Moon showed the floral arrangement that ran up her spine. 'The flowers are symbols of peace and inner strength. They're spiritual blooms, and I think Egyptian princesses used to get buried with them in a bouquet, although I might have got that wrong. It might be fookin' Norse women, but either way they're all dead significant and spiritual.'

Kelly showed the phoenix that was flying up from between her buttocks. Sally demonstrated the female warrior fighting a dragon that surrounded her belly button, and Layla showed the tiny butterfly on one of her buttocks.

'I've got one just like that,' said Trisha, outraged. 'The bloke who did it told me it was a unique one-off.'

Coleridge nearly choked on his tea. It had never even *occurred* to him that one of his officers, one of his *lady* officers, was tattooed. Particularly Patricia, whom he had thought such a steady girl.

Layla then proudly spread her legs and showed off the other butterfly she had, which was fluttering about right at the top of her perfectly lovely, smooth, groomed inner thigh.

'I keep it there,' Layla said, 'to remind my lovers of the importance and the beauty of delicacy and light-ness of touch.'

Coleridge groaned and looked away from the screen.

'Got one of those, Trish?' said Hooper.

'No *way*, not there. It's bad enough having a bikini wax without some hell's angel getting up you with his ink needle.'

'Be quiet, both of you!' barked Coleridge.

Now Layla was showing the little Eastern symbol on her shoulderblade. 'It's Tibetan,' she explained. 'A Buddhist symbol indicating a tranquil inner light.'

Everyone agreed that this was particularly lovely.

Except David.

'Tibetan?' he asked, a hint of indulgent surprise in his voice.

'Yes, Tibetan,' said Layla defensively.

'Oh . . . OK, right. Whatever.'

Layla wanted to kill him. 'What do you mean "Whatever"? It's fucking Tibetan!'

'Steady, Layla,' grinned Jazz. 'Hang on to your tran-quil inner light.'

'Look, Layla,' said David gently. 'It's very beautiful and it can and should mean whatever you want it to mean. It doesn't matter whether it's Tibetan or Thai, which is what it actually is: it's *your* tattoo, and it means whatever you want it to.'

Who would have thought that Layla's fabulous calm could have been shattered so easily. Her face was red with embarrassment and anger. 'It's Tibetan, you bastard,' she repeated. 'I know it's Tibetan.'

David gave an annoying little smile and shrug as if to say 'You're wrong, but it's beneath me to argue.'

'It is Tibetan! It means tranquil inner fucking light!' Layla shouted, and stormed off to get herself a soothing cup of herbal tea.

'I heard about this bloke, a gay bloke,' Garry said, 'who had this Chinese proverb put up his arm which meant "gentle seeker after truth". Anyway, one day he pulls this poofter Chinkie at a noodle bar in Soho, and his new boyfriend says, "Actually it means you are a stupid, gullible, round-eyed cunt." '

Garry, Jazz, Sally and Kelly laughed hugely at this. Hamish and Moon smiled. Layla, standing over by the kettle, bit her lip, red-faced with fury, and David closed his eyes for a moment as if gathering strength from his own stillness.

Then Hamish showed the Celtic Cross on his forearm, and finally it was David's turn. He had been waiting for it.

'I have only one tattoo,' he explained, as if this in itself was evidence of his exquisite taste and heightened perception. 'And it is very, very beautiful.'

With that David lifted the leg of his baggy silk trousers and revealed, inscribed upon his left ankle, wound three times around his leg, the first four lines of the 'to be or not to be' soliloquy from *Hamlet*.

'No butterflies, no Tibetan shopping lists, no fiery dragons. Simply the most perceptive investigation of the essential absurdity of man's existence ever committed to paper.'

'Or in this case skin,' Jazz pointed out, but David ignored him.

'Existentialism three hundred years before existentialism was invented. Humanism in a brutal and barbaric world. A tiny light that has illuminated every century since.'

'Yeah, all right, but why have it written on your leg?' asked Jazz, speaking for the nation.

'Because it saved my life,' said David with clear-eyed, unblinking sincerity. 'When I was in my dark time and saw no possibility of living in this world I fully intended to end my own life. Believe me, I had entirely resolved upon suicide.'

'Except you didn't do it, did you?' Garry said. 'Funny, that.'

'No, I didn't. Instead through one long night I read *Hamlet* three times from cover to cover.'

'Fuck me. I'd *rather* fucking kill myself,' Garry said, but David pressed on regardless.

'That sad prince also contemplated the terrible act of self-murder just as I was doing, but he rose above it, rose above it and achieved a grand and private nobility.'

'Is that why you didn't do it yourself, then, David?' asked Moon, obviously trying to be supportive of David's confessional. 'Because nothing that you were feeling could ever be as bad as *Hamlet*.'

'We did it at school,' said Garry. 'Believe me, nothing is as bad as *Hamlet*.'

'Oh, fookin' shurrup, Garry,' said Moon. 'David knows what I mean, don't you, David?'

'Yes, I do, Moon, and the answer is yes and no. Without doubt the sombre princeling's torment taught me much. But in fact I resolved against suicide because I realized reading that play that I did not wish to leave a world that could contain something as beautiful as

104

Shakespeare's verse, or indeed a flower, or a sunrise or the smell of fresh-baked bread.'

'Now you've lost me,' said Moon. 'What's fookin' bread got to do with it?'

'I believe, Moon, that once a person recognizes beauty they become alive to the possibility of beauty in all things. And so I decided to keep the words which the young Prince of Denmark spoke at his time of deepest sadness about me always. Just to remind me that the world is beautiful and to despair of it is an insult to God.'

Jazz wanted to tell David that he was a pretentious prat, but he didn't. There was something about David, something so handsome and compelling, something so utterly blatant about his colossal conceit that Jazz could not help but be a little bit moved.

None of them were sure about David. The obvious sincerity of David's self love was quite compelling. A love as true as the love David had for himself could not be simply dismissed, it was almost noble. They stared, unable to decide what to think about David.

Except Kelly.

The incident hadn't been noticed in the monitoring box on the night it happened because the editors were concentrating on the wide-angle shot, and Kelly's back had been to the camera, but the police had all the available video coverage of the scene: for once they got a little lucky. One of the live cameramen had been taking a reverse angle, and the disk had not been wiped. It was a three-shot of Kelly, Moon and Hamish on the orange couch.

Kelly was smiling, a big broad wicked smile. Hardly the reaction she would normally have had to David's tale of suicidal angst, no matter how absurdly pompous it might have sounded.

'She'd seen that tattoo before,' said Hooper.

'Yes, I rather think she had,' Coleridge agreed.

DAY THIRTY-FOUR. 10.00 a.m.

While various junior officers went off to run the phrase 'Far corgi in heaven' around the Internet and through various voice decoders, Coleridge and his inner team put David to one side for a moment and returned to the subject of Woggle.

'It seems to me that, for all that the public knew, there really *was* only one housemate in week two,' Coleridge said, glancing through the digest of the broadcast edits that Trisha and her team had prepared for him. 'Woggle, Woggle, Woggle and once more Woggle.'

'Yes, sir,' Trisha replied. 'Briefly he became a sort of mini national phenomenon. Half the country were talking about him and the other half were asking who was this Woggle bloke that everybody was talking about. Don't you remember it?'

'*Very* vaguely, constable.'

'The more revolting he got and the more he denied that he was revolting the more people loved him. It was a sort of craze.'

'I'll never forget when they showed him picking the fleas out of his dreadlocks,' remarked another constable. 'We were in the pub and it was on the telly; everybody just sort of gasped. It was soooo gross.'

'Gross if you were watching it. Pretty unbearable if you were living with it,' said Trisha. 'Those fleas nearly brought the whole thing to a halt there and then. Shame they didn't, really, then nobody would have got killed.'

'And we wouldn't have to watch this torturous drivel,' said Coleridge. 'Didn't those sadists at Peeping Tom offer them any flea powder?'

'Yes, they did, but Woggle refused to use it. He said that his fleas were living creatures, and while he

106

didn't much like the itching he had no intention of murdering them.'

'Good lord,' Coleridge observed. 'An abstract opinion! A moral point of view. I'd given up all hope.'

'Well, it wasn't abstract to the housemates, sir. And Woggle's flea debate gripped the nation.'

DAY TEN. 3.00 p.m.

Woggle was sitting in his corner ringed by the other housemates.

'My fleas are forcing you to address your double standards,' Woggle protested. 'Would you hunt a fox?'

'Yes, I fucking would,' said Garry, but the others had had to admit that they would not, David, Layla and Moon even to having been vaguely active in the most recent anti-hunting campaigns.

'Fox-hunting is an abomination,' David said with his usual air of quiet superiority.

'Yet you would hunt my fleas,' Woggle said. 'Explain to me the difference between a fox and a flea.'

Clearly nobody really knew where to start.

'Well . . .' said Kelly, slightly nervously, 'foxes are cute and fleas aren't.'

'Oh, don't be so silly, Kelly,' David snapped.

'She is not being silly,' said Woggle. 'She has articulated a universal truth, for it is the shame of humankind that we judge the value of a life in aesthetic terms. That which we find beautiful we nurture, that which we find ugly we destroy. Oh, cursed are we, the human virus that infects this perfect planet.'

David had clearly had enough of this. He wasn't having the moral high ground pulled from under him. 'Foxes do very little harm. Hunting them is a sport, not a necessity, that is what makes it despicable and utterly unacceptable to decent modern people living in twenty-first-century New Britain.'

'Fox-hunters say foxes do lots of harm. They say that foxes are vermin,' Woggle replied.

'I deny their claims.'

'Where'd you live, then, Dave?' asked Gazzer, who was always interested in a wind-up. 'On a farm?'

'I live in Battersea,' David replied angrily. 'But that's not the . . .'

Gazzer and Jazz laughed at David's discomfort, which made David furious. He loathed the way people pretended that you had to live in the country to understand anything about foxes.

'This is a serious debate,' he snapped. 'It is not about cheap point-scoring.'

Woggle agreed with him and pressed his advantage. 'The difference between foxes and my fleas, comrade, is that my fleas irritate you and foxes don't. But the fascist farmers and the Nazi hunters claim that foxes irritate them. They *claim* that foxes eat the chickens and terrorize the hedgerows.'

'I absolutely refute their claims,' David insisted, 'but the point is anyway—'

'The *point* is, O Adolf of the insect kingdom, the point is, *Herr Hitler*, that, whether foxes are rural terrorists or not, *I* would not kill them just as I would not kill my fleas, bite me though they will. This is because I am a morally developed individual, whilst *you*, on the other hand, are a vicious murdering bastard hypocrite scumbag member of the Gestapo who should be letterbombed.' Woggle's thin nasal voice had become firm; he obviously meant what he was saying. He actually leapt to his feet.

'Your concern for animal welfare,' Woggle shouted, the flesh around his bushy eyebrows suddenly glowing red, 'goes *exactly* as far as the point where your *own* interests are threatened, and no further. You are just like the tens of millions of vile scum in this country who would ban fox-hunting and seal-clubbing but happily gorge themselves on factory-bred fried chicken and mutated beefburgers! If you would hunt my fleas I suggest you do so with due self-knowledge. I suggest you wear a red coat, O *Genghis Khan*, and blow a bright horn. I suggest that you smear the blood of my dead fleas on the faces of your young after the kill and have a party to celebrate with stirrup cup served in beakers carved from the hooves of slaughtered stags! For you are no better than Lord Blood Sport of Bastardshire, David! You, who profess to care so much, are in fact the self-appointed Master of the Peeping Tom flea hunt!'

*

The curious thing was that when Woggle's flea rant was broadcast at the end of the first week of *House Arrest*, most people watching managed to find common ground with what he said. The anti-fox-hunters, of course, welcomed their most prominent ever national spokesman, while the country sports people hailed a man who forced urban animal activists to confront the selective nature of their agendas.

Woggle was like the Bible: everybody claimed he proved their point. And people just loved him. Suddenly it was as if Woggle was the nation's pet dog, dirty, smelly and intrusive, but somehow rather lovable.

If the nine other inmates of the house had had any idea of the extent of Woggle's popularity outside the house they would not have done what they did. But sealed off as they were from the outside world, they never dreamt that this flea-ridden crusty who could not sit down without leaving a stain was becoming a hero.

It wasn't fair, of course. Geraldine knew that it wasn't fair, but not surprisingly she didn't care.

Geraldine knew that nobody could have lived with Woggle and put up with it. The fact was that the other nine inmates had been incredibly tolerant; most people would probably have killed Woggle already. But, like life, television is not fair and Geraldine, having unwittingly created a national craze, was happy to edit towards it.

She therefore chose not to broadcast the patient and fairly considerate efforts that the housemates made to persuade Woggle to wash his clothes, clear up after himself and above all to deal with his fleas. She did not show how Kelly brought him blankets in the night and Dervla ensured that his dietary requirements were included on the house shopping lists. She showed only moments of the lengthy discussions that Garry, Jazz and Woggle had about football, a passion they all shared. No, Geraldine cut straight to the day when Garry, Jazz, David and Hamish leapt on Woggle as he lay in the garden and forcibly stripped him, burnt his clothes and covered his writhing, protesting form with flea powder.

DAY ELEVEN. 7.30 p.m.

The incident occurred on the second Thursday under *House Arrest*, the day of the first nominations.

The Peeping Tom rules were pretty much the same as all the similar shows that had gone before it. Each week, each of the housemates was asked to secretly nominate two people for eviction. The two most nominated people were then subjected to a public telephone vote to decide who should be thrown out of the house.

In order to allow people a chance to get to know each other there had been no voting in the first week and therefore day eleven was the first nomination day. The nominating took place in the afternoon, and in the evening the public got to see who had nominated whom, before the cameras cut live to the house to show the housemates being told who would be up for eviction on the following Sunday. Once this live moment of broadcasting was over, and everyone's face had been studied for traces of relief, glee, spite, etc., the rest of the evening's show returned to the usual round-up of the day's activities in the house.

The first thing that the public saw on that eleventh night of *House Arrest* was the nominations. All but one of the housemates voted for Woggle. The strange thing was that the housemate who did not vote for Woggle was not Woggle, because even Woggle voted for Woggle, which was a first for any reality TV show.

'I am voting for myself to be evicted from this house,' Woggle droned into the confession box camera, 'because I absolutely and entirely reject this highly divisive and gladiatorial system which is based on the inherently hierarchical principle that society must produce winners and losers, a principle aimed at the inevitable consequence of the emergence of a single oligarch, which is, let us be quite clear about this, nothing less than fascism. I therefore offer myself up as a sacrifice in protest against the transparently cynical deployment of a spurious democratic process in order to undermine genuine democracy. My other vote is for Jason, because his deodorants block my sinuses.'

After this astonishing display, which could only endear Woggle further to his adoring public, the other nominations seemed rather dull by comparison.

David voted for Woggle and also Layla, because he thought Layla was an irritating and pretentious pseud.

Kelly voted for Woggle and also Layla, because she thought that Layla looked down on her.

Jazz voted for Woggle and also Sally, because he found Sally's pious attitude to being a lesbian irritating.

Hamish voted for Woggle and also David, because he thought he'd have a better chance with the women with David out of the way.

Layla voted for Woggle and also David, because she thought David was an irritating and pretentious pseud.

Garry voted for Woggle and also Layla, because he thought she was a snob.

Moon voted for Woggle and also Garry, because she thought he was a fookin' sexist twat.

Sally voted for Woggle and also Moon, because of what Moon had said about the mentally ill.

Dervla voted for David and for Layla, because she was sick of their bickering. Dervla would have voted for Woggle. She certainly wanted Woggle out of the house – she was no more immune to him than anybody else was. But unlike the rest of the housemates, Dervla knew how popular Woggle was with the public. The mirror had told her.

It was a constant theme of the messages.

Woggle stood at number one, Kelly at number two and Dervla was stubbornly placed third.

'*Be nice to Woggle. People love him,*' the message-writer had said on the morning after Dervla had confronted Woggle over the hair on the soap. Since that time, Dervla had been careful to follow the advice.

When the nominations were announced on live television Woggle was acting very strangely. He was sitting in his usual corner but he had covered himself in a blanket and was swaying softly beneath it. He was humming to himself, almost keening. The other nine housemates sat on the couches.

'This is Chloe,' the announcement said. Chloe was the 'face' of *House Arrest*, the girl who worked the studio chats. 'The two housemates nominated for eviction this week are . . . in alphabetical order . . . Layla and Woggle.'

Everybody tried not to show it, but the relief was

palpable. Only four more days and Woggle would be gone. Even Layla was not unduly worried. Although hurt that she had been the other nominee, she knew that she would live to fight another day, because, like most of the others, she simply could not imagine the public not voting Woggle out. Surely they must find him as revolting as the housemates did.

Dervla, of course, knew better.

DAY THIRTY-FOUR. 4.15 p.m.

'The public did find Woggle revolting,' Bob Fogarty said, fishing a semi-melted square of chocolate out of his foaming plastic cup, 'but they just loved him for it, and by the time episode eleven was over, he'd become a national hero. It was so deceitful and unfair, I felt ashamed. I complained to that bitch Geraldine, but she said it came with the job and that cunts like me had forfeited our right to have principles.'

Once more Trisha had gone to the editing bunker in an effort to try to bridge the gap between what the public had seen and what had actually happened. It seemed just possible to her that the clue to solving the murder might lie in understanding how this trick was worked.

After all, everybody had *seen* the murder.

Fogarty sucked noisily on his chocolate. Trisha watched his mouth with growing distaste.

'That cow knew very well that she had been wickedly skewing public sympathy away from the main group and towards Woggle right from the start.'

'So when the attack on him came, shown in the context Geraldine had made you create, it looked absolutely damning?'

'It certainly did, and the nation went potty, as I'm sure you know. I told Geraldine that we were giving

113

Woggle too much of the running. I mean, quite apart from the fact that we were seriously demonizing nine relatively innocent people, we were also turning the show into a one-trick pony, which in my *humble* opinion was not good telly at all in the long term. Geraldine knew that, of course, but the footage was just irresistible. It made the other boys look like absolute *bastards*. Awful. Like something out of *Lord of the Flies*.'

DAY ELEVEN. 1.45 p.m.

The housemates had been called into the confession box to make their nominations in alphabetical order, therefore Woggle had gone in last.

'What's he doing in there?' Jazz said, after a minute or two had passed.

'I hope he's died and rotted,' David replied.

'He wouldn't have to die to rot, he's rotting already,' said Gazzer.

'We'll be doing him a favour,' Jazz concluded. 'Saving him from himself.'

To Jazz, the worst thing on earth would be to be filthy. He lived to preen.

When Woggle finally emerged from the little room, the boys were lying in wait.

'Afternoon, fellow humanoids,' said Woggle, wandering out into the garden. 'Happy summer solstice.'

Without a word, they jumped him. Hamish and Jazz held him down while Garry and David pulled off his ancient combat trousers.

'What's going on?' he shouted, but the boys were too intent on their mission to reply.

Woggle's skinny legs kicked about, glaring white in the bright sunlight. He was wearing filthy old Y-fronts with a hole in them where one of his balls had worn the cloth away. As he struggled with his attackers both balls fell through this hole. It didn't look funny, it looked sad and pathetic.

'No, no! What're you doing!' Woggle yelled, but still the boys ignored him. They had drunk the last of the house cider and were feeling righteous. This had to be done. Woggle had it coming to him. You could not just give people fleas and then expect them to do nothing about it.

'Get them pants off him, they'll be infested too!' Jazz shouted.

'I ain't touching them,' Garry replied.

'Nor me,' said Hamish.

'Fuck this,' said Jazz and, letting go of Woggle for a moment, he ran to the chicken coup and grabbed the gloves they used to clean out the birds. When he returned, Woggle had managed to twist himself round so that when Jazz pulled his underpants off him his bony white arse was on view to the cameras.

Next they pulled off his shirt, ripping the buttons as they did so, and finally they wrenched Woggle's filthy string vest up over his head. Now Woggle was naked. A struggling, shrieking, pale, bony little creature with a great mop of dreadlocks and his beard flying and flapping in the summer sun.

'This is assault! I am being defiled! Get off me!' he shouted.

'I'm being assaulted and defiled by your fleas!' Hamish cried, speaking for them all. 'My fucking armpits are bleeding.'

There was a barbecue at the back of the house and the boys had already cranked it up in preparation for the attack. Jazz threw Woggle's clothes and his sandals onto the fire. There was a strange fizzing sound. 'Fuck me!' he cried. 'I can hear the fleas popping!'

'Not popping, screaming!' Woggle shouted.

'Let's shave his head!' shouted David. 'He's bound to have lice.'

'No,' said Jazz firmly. 'You can't mess with a man's barnet, even Woggle's.'

'Fascists!' shouted Woggle, but his voice degenerated to a cough as Garry and Hamish began dousing him in flea powder. For a few moments they were all engulfed in a great cloud, and when they had finished Woggle was a luminous ghostly white from head to toe. Even his hair and beard were white as snow.

They left Woggle prostrate and naked in the middle of the lawn. As he turned briefly towards one of the garden cameras, flesh-coloured lines began to streak his death-white face as the tears sprang from his eyes.

DAY THIRTY-FOUR. 5.00 p.m.

'That was the image Geraldine made me close the show with,' Fogarty told Trisha. 'We didn't show any of this . . .' He tapped an assortment of the buttons on his editing console and there appeared on the bank of screens the coverage from inside the house recorded immediately following the attack.

The housemates were taking no pleasure from the incident. There was no whooping, no hollering. They were all genuinely sorry for Woggle. Dervla was already making him some herbal tea (which he accepted in silence), and Kelly was planning a tofu and molasses comfort cake. The mood was subdued but resolved. As one, they felt that the men had acted in order to counter a pressing social issue which threatened the wellbeing of the group.

In the editing suite Fogarty retreated to the little kitchenette area to get more of his chocolate from the fridge. Trisha wondered why he kept it cold when he was going to put it in his coffee.

'It's sad, isn't it?' Fogarty remarked. 'They actually deluded themselves that the nation would applaud their ability to police their own community.'

On the screens the self-justification continued.

'We could have gone on strike and asked for him to be ejected,' Hamish was saying, 'but what would we have looked like? A bunch of kids who couldn't handle their own problems.'

'Yes,' said Layla. 'The whole point of being here is to discover whether we can work together. If we had just gone running to Peeping Tom with our first group problem we'd basically have failed the test.'

Fogarty shook his head in disbelief. 'Incredible. That girl Layla is bright enough, and yet she actually believed all that bullshit about *House Arrest* being a genuine experiment in social engineering. It's a TV programme, for God's sake! How could she not realize that the single and only point of the whole bloody exercise is to attract advertisers?'

'Well, it certainly did that, didn't it?' said Trisha.

'Oh yes, our ratings shot up and with it Peeping Tom's revenue.' Fogarty turned his attention back to the screens. 'Watch this,' he said. 'There's more that we didn't broadcast.'

On the screens Woggle came in from the garden.

He refused Kelly's offer of cake without a word.

He also turned his back on the various offers of clothing and water.

Layla suggested that she read him one or two of her healing poems. 'Or else we could hold hands and hum together.'

Woggle did not even look at her. Instead he took up a blanket to cover his nakedness and retreated silently to his corner.

'This is it, coming up now,' said Fogarty. 'Dervla's confession.'

Sure enough, there was Dervla slipping into the confession box.

'Of course I understand the boys' frustration,' she said. 'We are after all suffering quite considerably here. But I did want to say that I feel enormous sorrow over Woggle's distress and wished that a better way could have been found to deal with his health issues. Deep down I think he is beautiful.'

Fogarty stopped the tape. 'Now I believed then and I believe now that Dervla is a lovely, lovely girl and that she was really upset about Woggle. But do you know what that shitty little cynic Geraldine made of it?'

'What?'

'She reckoned that Dervla had worked out that Woggle would be popular on the outside and was trying to curry favour with the public by supporting him.'

'Wow, you'd have to be pretty perceptive.'

'And pretty calculating, which I don't think she is.'

'On the other hand, she *was* the only person who didn't nominate him.'

'You're worse than Geraldine! She said exactly that! Said that if she didn't know better she'd think that Dervla had inside information.'

'But that's impossible, isn't it?'

'It certainly is. Let me tell you that if anyone was cheating I'd know. I see *everything*.'

'But if she *did* have a secret advantage, and one of the others found out about it . . .' Trisha stared into Dervla's deep-green eyes, trying to read the thoughts that Dervla had been thinking in the confession box. Before death had changed everything.

DAY THIRTY-FOUR. 8.00 p.m.

Trisha returned to the station without eating. Having watched Fogarty sucking chocolate for an hour, she

118

had lost her appetite, which she regretted now because it looked like it was going to be another long night.

'Let's get through Woggle this evening, shall we?' Coleridge suggested. I don't think I could face coming back to him tomorrow. What happened after the flea powder attack?'

'The public weren't happy, sir,' said Hooper. 'Within hours of show eleven going out there was a crowd outside the Peeping Tom compound calling for Garry, Hamish, David and Jazz to be arrested for assault. Geraldine Hennessy had to play music into the house to drown out the chants.'

Trisha put the tape Fogarty had given her into the VCR. 'People weren't happy inside the house either. Look at Woggle. He's devastated.'

'The rest of them don't look too good either.'

'They feel guilty about it.'

It was clear from the subdued conversation and unhappy faces that everybody was feeling very uncomfortable.

They took refuge in cleaning, frenzied cleaning. With Woggle, the carrier and principal breeding ground, de-flead, it was possible to begin cleansing the rest of the house, which the nine of them did with a vengeance. Every mattress and sheet was taken outside, washed, dried, powdered, then washed again. Every garment of clothing, every cushion and cloth. Everybody showered and applied more powder. They got through ten containers of it, all of which had had to come out of their weekly shopping budget. Not only had Woggle's fleas half eaten them alive, but they had also cost them the equivalent of eight precious bottles of wine or thirty cans of lager.

Throughout the whole of this day-long cleaning process Woggle remained beneath his blanket in his corner, swaying slowly and singing to himself. A traumatized troll, as one newspaper was to put it.

At the end of the day came the first eviction.

'They broadcast two episodes on eviction nights,' Hooper explained to Coleridge, 'which is very thoughtful, because it gives the nation just enough time to pop out for a beer and curry between the shows.'

'Don't talk about food,' said Trisha. 'I haven't eaten all day.'

'You can have half of my evening Mars Bar if you wish,' Coleridge suggested, but without enthusiasm.

'No, thank you, sir,' said Trisha. 'I'm a bit off chocolate at the moment.'

Coleridge struggled hard not to show his mighty relief.

'Anyway,' said Hooper, doggedly persevering with the matter at hand. 'The first broadcast on a Sunday is a live broadcast of the announcement of the person who's going to be evicted, and the second is live coverage of the departure.'

'Marvellous,' said Coleridge. 'An opportunity to spend an entire evening watching someone you don't know being asked to leave a house you've never been to by a group of people you've never met and whom you will never hear of again. It's difficult to imagine a more riveting scenario.'

'You have to be into it, sir, that's all. If you get into it it's brilliant.'

'Of course it is, Hooper. I wonder if when the ancient Greeks laid the foundation stones of western civilization they ever dreamt such brilliance possible?'

'Like I say, if you're not into it you won't get it.'

'From Homer to *House Arrest* in only twenty-five hundred years, a record to be proud of, don't you think?'

'Sir!' said Hooper. 'We're doing fourteen-hour days minimum to get through this! You have absolutely no right to extend them by constantly going off on one!'

There was an embarrassed silence, which lasted for

the time it took for Coleridge to unwrap his Mars Bar.
Hooper's face was red. He was tired, angry and
annoyed. Coleridge, who had had no idea he was being
so irritating, was slightly sad.

'Well,' he said finally. 'Let's get on.'

DAY FOURTEEN. 7.30 p.m.

'People under House Arrest, this is Chloe. Can you
hear me? The first person to leave the house will be,'
Chloe left a suitably dramatic pause, '. . . Layla.'

Layla looked like she had been hit in the face with a
cricket bat, but nevertheless managed to enact the
time-honoured ritual required from people in such situations.

'Yes!' she squeaked, punching the air as if she was
pleased. 'Now I can get back to my cat!'

'Layla, you have two hours to pack and say your
goodbyes,' Chloe shouted, 'when we will be back live
for *House Arrest*'s first eviction! See you then!'

Layla was stunned.

They were all stunned.

Even Woggle beneath his blanket was stunned. He
had presumed like everyone else in the house (except
Dervla) that his presence there had been evenly
reported and, although he considered his conduct to be
exemplary, he had not expected public sympathy.
Years of sneers and contempt from almost everybody
he met for almost everything he said and did had led
Woggle to presume that the viewing public's attitude to
him would be the same as that of the four fascists who
had stripped him in the garden and attacked him without *any* provocation.

But the public's attitude wasn't the same at all, they
loved their little goblin, the traumatized troll. He was
their pet, and although Woggle could have no idea of

121

the dizzy heights to which his popularity had risen, he was astonished and thrilled enough simply to have avoided eviction.

He poked his head out of his blanket briefly. 'Fuck you,' he said to the assembled inmates and then submerged himself once more beneath his cover.

Then Layla howled with anguish. She actually *howled*. The injustice of it all was clearly nearly unbearable. The tears streamed down her face as she rocked back and forth on the purple couch in an agony of self-pity. She could obviously not believe that the public had chosen Woggle over her! *Woggle!*

Layla went to the confession box to vent her spleen.

'You bastards!' she stormed. 'It's fucking obvious what you've done! Somehow you've made him the victim, haven't you? You've been having a laugh and we're the joke, aren't we? *I'm* the joke! You know what Woggle's like! What we've had to put up with! He doesn't clean up, he doesn't help out, he stinks like the rotting corpse of a dead dog's arse! *Everyone* wanted him out, but you haven't shown all that, have you? No! You can't have done or he'd be going, not me!'

DAY THIRTY-FOUR. 8.40 p.m.

'If she'd shown a bit more spirit like that before, she wouldn't have been nominated,' said Hooper, who had enjoyed watching Coleridge wincing at some of Layla's choice of phrases.

'But she's wrong about the eviction,' said Trisha. 'Certainly, Peeping Tom skewed the coverage in Woggle's favour, but everyone could still see what a slob he was. Layla would have been voted out whatever. The mistake the people who go on these shows make is to imagine that anybody actually *cares* about them. As far as we're concerned, they're just acts on the telly, to be laughed at.'

On screen Layla was beginning to break down. 'I think some of my flea bites will leave scars, you bastards! The ones around my bottom have gone septic!'

'Ugh!' said Trisha.

'Too much information!' Hooper protested.

'If I do get ill I shall sue you,' Layla fulminated. 'I swear I will! I'm going now, but one more thing: I know you won't broadcast this, Geraldine Hennessy, but I think you're a complete and utter shit and I will hate you for ever!'

'*Hate you for ever*,' Coleridge repeated. 'That's a long time, and it was only three weeks ago. I doubt she'd have got over it yet.'

On the screen Layla went into the girls' bedroom to get her bag. Kelly joined her. 'I'm really, really sorry, Layla,' Kelly said. 'It must feel rotten.'

'No, no, it's fine really . . .'

But then Layla broke down again, falling into Kelly's arms and sobbing.

'*Kelly is comforting Layla, but what Layla doesn't know is that Kelly nominated her for eviction*,' said the voice of Andy the narrator.

'They just *love* pointing it out when that happens,' Hooper remarked. 'It's the best bit of the show.'

'You have to be strong, right?' Kelly said, holding Layla close. 'Be a strong woman, which is what you are.'

'That's right, I am, I'm a strong, spiritual woman.'

'Go, girl. Love you.'

'Love you, Kelly,' said Layla. 'You're a mate.'

Then Layla went back into the living area and hugged everybody else, including, even, extremely briefly, Woggle.

Her hug with David lasted nearly a minute.

'The evictees always do that,' said Hooper. 'Have a great big hug. Pretending they're all big mates really.'

'I think while they're doing it they mean it,' Coleridge said. 'Young people live on the surface and for the moment. That's just how it is these days.'

'You are so right, sir,' put in Trisha. 'I'm twenty-five and I've never held a considered opinion or experienced a genuine emotion in my life.'

For a moment Coleridge was about to insist to Trisha that he was sure this was not the case, but then he realized she was being sarcastic.

'Layla, you have thirty seconds to leave the Peeping Tom house,' said Chloe's voice on the television.

DAY FOURTEEN. 9.30 p.m.

As she stepped out of the house Layla was bathed in almost impossibly bright light, which turned her and the house behind her bleach white. A huge bald security man in a padded bomber-jacket stepped forward and took her arm. He led her onto the platform of a firework-bedecked cherry picker which lifted her up and over the moat while the crowd cheered. Peeping Tom took great pride in its house exits; they turned them into what appeared to be huge parties. They bussed in crowds, let off fireworks and criss-crossed the air with search lights. As Layla was lifted high over the shrieking throng a rock band played live from the back of a lorry.

Then came the short limousine journey to the specially constructed studio and the live interview with Chloe, the beautiful, big-bosomed, ladette-style 'face' of Peeping Tom. Chloe was no mere pretty face, however, like the girls who presented the more mainstream shows. No, Chloe was a pretty face with a tattoo of a serpent on her tummy and another of a little devil on her shoulder, which was of course much, much more real.

Chloe met Layla at the door of the limo. She looked rock-chick stunning in black leather trousers and a black leather bra, while Layla looked hippie-chick stunning in a tie-dye silk sarong and cropped silk singlet. The women hugged and kissed as if they were long-lost sisters instead of complete strangers, one of whom was paid to talk to the other.

The crowd went berserk. Literally berserk. They whooped, they hollered, they screamed, they waved their home-made placards. There was absolutely no provocation for this madness beyond the presence of television cameras and the well-established convention that this was how up-for-it young people were supposed to behave in the presence of television cameras.

Finally the whooping died down, or at least died down enough for Chloe to make herself heard. It would continue, ebbing and flowing in volume, throughout the interview, but Chloe used her window of opportunity to express her own feelings of exuberance.

'Whooo!' she shouted. 'All right! Unreal! Wicked! Whooo!'

The audience concurred with these sentiments entirely and returned to their own whooping refreshed.

Chloe threw a proudly muscular arm around Layla. 'Do we love this chick or what? Is she not one strong, special lady?'

Further whoops and hollers indicated that the audience did indeed love Layla very much.

'We are soooooo proud of you, girl, you're brilliant.'

Once more the proceedings became mired in shouting and screaming. Chloe fought to make herself heard, or perhaps merely to make it clear that she was the most excited and up for it of them all.

'So how are you feeling, girl?' Chloe whooped.

The atmosphere was infectious. Layla smiled broadly. 'Wicked!' she said.

'All right!'

'Yeah, really amped up.'

'Go, girl!'

'But also quite spiritual.'

'I *so* know what you mean.'

'Yeah, like I've grown.'

'And you so have, girl. Respect to that!' Chloe turned to the mob and shouted, 'Do we love this ace lady or what!?'

And the mob whooped and hollered with renewed energy.

'So were you really, really shocked to be nominated?'

'Well, you know, all life is a season and seasons change. I really, really believe that.'

'That is so true.'

'You have to be positive in your own head space, the mind is a garden, it needs constant weeding.'

'Fantastic, and what about Jazz's cooking. Was that wicked or what?'

'Totally wicked.'

And so, with the in-depth psychological grilling over, Chloe turned to the big screen and showed Layla who had nominated her.

First came David. There he sat, on nomination day, looking beautiful and sincere as he addressed the confession box camera.

'And the second person I'm nominating is Layla, because although I think she's a very strong spiritual woman, she doesn't give a lot to the group as a whole.'

The nation watched Layla watching the screen. Her manic grin did not forsake her. 'David's great,' she said. 'I really love him totally, but you know when two strong, spiritual, loving, caring, strong people meet, sometimes their head spaces don't always connect, but that's OK, I really love him and I know he loves me.'

'And of course you nominated him,' said Chloe.

'Yeah, isn't that weird! It just shows what a connection we actually had.'

126

Dervla was a surprise. 'After David, I nominate Layla,' Dervla said, looking excruciatingly sincere, thoughtful and beautiful. 'She's a lovely, lovely girl, a very gentle, caring and beautiful spirit, but I feel that in the end her loveliness would be able to blossom more beautifully outside of the house.'

Which everybody, even Layla, knew translated as 'She's a pain in the arse.'

Then came Garry. 'Layles is a very, very tasty bird, and also I reckon she means well, but basically she's a bit snooty for my liking, you know what I mean? Reckons herself and all that.'

Layla smiled bravely at this, a smile which was meant to say, 'Yes, people often mistake my spirituality for conceit.'

And then finally there was Kelly. 'This is really, really difficult, but at the end of the day I have to choose someone, and I'm choosing Layla because I think she reckons she's better than me, and maybe she is, but it's still a bit hurtful.'

Chloe leant forward and squeezed Layla's hand, thereby offering comfort and showing off her lovely bosom simultaneously.

'You OK, girl?' said Chloe. 'Strong?'

'Yeah, strong.'

'You stay strong, girl,' Chloe insisted.

Layla rose to the challenge. 'I think David and Gazzer are brilliant,' she said, 'and Dervla and Kelly are great, really, really, strong ladies. The truth is that they all have to choose someone and sometimes my strength and my spirituality get misunderstood by people. But at the end of the day, right, I love those guys, they're my posse.'

'Big up to that! Respect!' Chloe shouted, and then abruptly got up and walked off into the crowd, leaving Layla sitting alone.

'So, one gone, only eight more rejects and we'll have

a winner!' Chloe shouted into the camera that was tracking backwards in front of her. 'Who's out next? Stinky man? Booby woman? David and his most irritating guitar-playing? Jazz with the top bod? Gazz who speaks for ENGERLAND!? Angry Sal? Dull Hamish? Bald lady? Or Dervla, our oh-so-sensitive little Irish Colleen. You are the executioners! You can crush their little dreams! YOU decide! The phone lines will be open after the next nominations! Respect! Love on ya.'

DAY THIRTY-FOUR. 10.20 p.m.

The three police officers watched as Layla disappeared behind the baying crowd, heading straight for obscurity.

'I think we should definitely talk to her,' Coleridge said. 'There's a lot of anger there and we need to know more about it.'

'Besides which,' observed Hooper, 'she knows them all better than we ever will. Perhaps she has a theory.'

'Everybody's got a theory,' Coleridge replied ruefully, 'except us.'

On the screens the remaining housemates still looked shell-shocked.

'Well, O hunters and killers,' Woggle said through a broken-toothed smile, 'the people sided with life over death and light over darkness. It appears that the revolution beginneth.'

David got to his feet.

'You're right there, Woggle. I'm going to have a word with Peeping Tom.'

DAY FOURTEEN. 10.45 p.m.

'I'm fookin' coming with yez,' said Moon.

David and Moon stormed into the confession box

together, where David made it clear that he had drawn the same conclusion that Layla had done earlier in the evening.

'You've betrayed us, Peeping Tom,' he said. 'You know we did our best with Woggle. But we saw the banners out there and the people all shouting for him. They think we're shits.'

'It's not a question of betrayal,' Peeping Tom replied, Peeping Tom being Geraldine, of course, who was frantically scribbling down her replies and handing them to her 'voice', a quiet, gentle, soothing lady named Sam, who normally did voiceovers for washing-up liquid commercials.

'The public have simply seen something in Woggle that they find attractive,' the soothing voice continued.

'They find him attractive because that's how you must have made him look!' David snarled. 'I'm a professional, I'm in the business, I know your tricks. Well, let me tell you I've had enough! I didn't come in here to be manipulated and made a fool of. I want out. You can get me a taxi because I'm leaving,' he said.

'Me fookin' too!' added Moon. 'And I reckon the rest'll go too, and then all you'll be left with is the plague pit with Woggle in it. It's fookin' obvious you're taking the piss.'

DAY THIRTY-FOUR. 10.25 p.m.

Hooper pressed pause. 'This is very interesting, sir. None of this stuff was ever broadcast. I had absolutely no idea that the inmates were so sussed out to what was going down.'

'Sussed out to what was going down?'

'It means . . .'

'I know what it means, sergeant. I'm not an imbecile.

I was just wondering if you'd given any thought at all to how ugly it sounds?'

'No, sir, actually I hadn't. Would you like me to hand in my warrant card for using inelegant sentences in the course of an investigation?'

DAY FOURTEEN. 10.46 p.m.

'Walking out would be very foolish. You would be sacrificing the chance of winning the half-million-pound prize,' Peeping Tom said, and Sam put every ounce of her ability to soothe into each syllable.

'I don't care,' David said. 'Like I said, I know this business. We're just a bunch of stooges to Woggle's funny man. I came in here to get the chance to show the world who I am, but you've turned it into a freak show, an endurance test, and I don't want to play any more.'

'Me fookin' neither,' said Moon.

There was another pause while Peeping Tom considered a reply. 'Give us two days,' the soothing voice said finally. 'He'll be out.'

'Two days?' David replied. 'Don't lie to me. There isn't another eviction for a week.'

'Give us two days,' Peeping Tom repeated.

DAY THIRTY-FOUR. 10.30 p.m.

'That's amazing,' said Trisha. 'Geraldine Hennessy must have known about Woggle all along. It's obvious she had it ready up her sleeve.'

'The sly bitch!' Hooper agreed. 'She said she got sent those clippings anonymously.'

'Kindly explain what you're talking about and please don't refer to our witnesses as bitches.'

'None of what we've just seen was broadcast, sir. We've only seen it because we impounded the tapes.'

'I'm amazed it wasn't wiped,' Hooper added.

'That'll be Fogarty. He *hates* Geraldine Hennessy.'

'What are you talking about?' Coleridge demanded once more.

'You must be the only person in the country who doesn't know, sir. Woggle was wanted by the police. But it only emerged on day fifteen. It's obvious now that Geraldine Hennessy knew all along; that's why she was able to promise to get him out.'

DAY FIFTEEN. 9.00 p.m.

'I simply cannot believe that they have just made the whole thing up about Woggle,' Layla told the assembled press on the morning after her departure. She had spent all of the preceding night looking at tapes of the show and press cuttings collected for her by her family. It had been a grim business. She discovered that what coverage there had been of her had made her look like a snooty, self-obsessed airhead. Much of that impression had been given in the first handful of shows, for increasingly during the second week Woggle appeared to be the only issue of any real interest in the house.

'It was so *not* all about Woggle,' Layla protested. 'There were nine other people in that house – interesting, strong, spiritual, beautiful people. It has fallen to me to speak up for all of us. We have spent our time under House Arrest interacting, talking, loving, hugging, being irritated and inspired by each other. Woggle, on the other hand, spent his time in the house being a dirty and unreasonable slob and spreading disease, and it is *so* not all about him.'

But as far as the public were concerned it *was*, and

131

that morning even more so, because that was the morning that Geraldine put her Woggle policy into drastic reverse.

The sensational news became public about halfway through Layla's press conference, and as it swept through the room Layla saw the interest in her and anything she might have to say diminish very rapidly to zero.

Geraldine had had to act, and act quickly. Woggle had been a colossal success, but he was now in danger of being an even more colossal failure. If the other inmates walked out now, as they were perfectly entitled to do, Peeping Tom would be left in default of seven more weeks of nightly television that it was contracted to deliver to the network. Peeping Tom would be bankrupted. Which was why Geraldine sent the old press clippings of the photo of Woggle kicking the girl to the police.

The incident had happened four years previously, and Woggle had looked quite different. He had been a little chunkier and had a pink Mohican haircut, but if you looked closely at the large nose and the bushy eyebrows and the spider's web tattooed on the man in the picture's neck, there was no doubting that it was Woggle. Actually Geraldine had been surprised that the papers had not dug it up themselves, but since Woggle had never been caught or identified it would have taken a good memory for faces to recall four years previously, when the photo had been splashed across all the front pages with the headline 'WHO ARE THE ANIMALS?'

It had been a hunt-saboteur operation that got out of hand. Woggle and a number of fellow sabs had invaded a kennels in Lincolnshire with the intention of freeing the dogs. The master of hounds and a number of stable hands had confronted them and an ugly row had developed. The sabs struck first, trying to force their way past the master, and when he refused to yield they had knocked him to the ground with an iron bar. A general fight then broke out, and Woggle had waded in with his boots and a bicycle chain. This was a side of Woggle of which the people in the house and indeed his fans the viewing population had no idea. There was much about Woggle of which the house-mates disapproved (everything, in fact) but it would never have occurred to them that a propensity for violence was one of his faults.

But, on occasion, it was. Although as Woggle and his old animal-liberationist colleagues sometimes pointed out, 'We're only ever violent to humans.' Like most zealots, Woggle had his dark, intolerant side, and while he valued the wellbeing of dumb creatures and even insects most highly, he was singularly unconcerned about his fellow man. Therefore when he had found himself confronted by a stable hand wielding a rake, he waded in and whacked her. The fact that she was only fifteen and weighed less than he did did not concern him. Chivalry was not an issue when it came to defending foxes. As far as Woggle was concerned, if you were a fox-murderer, or an associate of fox-murderers, you had sacrificed your right to any consideration. It did not matter if you were small and blonde and cute, you were fair game and deserved what you got. And this girl was small, blonde and cute, which was why, when the newspapers were choosing between the horrific images of violence taken by the master's wife from the upstairs window of her farmhouse, there had been no contest. It was an image that briefly shocked a nation: the jolly blonde ponytailed cutie in gumboots and a Barbour jacket spread out on the ancient cobbles of the stable yard with blood in her hair, while the ugly, crusty, pierced, punk thug lashed out at her with his great steel-capped boots. It had been a public relations disaster for the sabs, compounded by the fact that the fifteen-year-old in question was a dog-mad, fox-loving member of the RSPCA who regularly petitioned the local hunt to switch to the drag method.

Woggle had brought the press clipping to show Geraldine on the last night before he and the others were scheduled to go into the house. He had been delighted to have been chosen and had not told Peeping Tom about his past until this point, in case it counted against him. He was very much looking forward to going under House Arrest, not least because it guaranteed him full board and a dry roof, which was quite a tempting prospect after months spent in a tunnel. Now, however, he was worried that the subsequent notoriety might cause him to be identified as the man in the picture and possibly get him arrested.

'So why are you showing me all this now, Woggle?' Geraldine had asked.

'I don't know. I thought maybe if you knew about it then if anybody says anything you could say that you'd checked it out and it wasn't me but some other bloke with a spider tattoo.'

Woggle, like all the other house inmates, had been so taken in by Peeping Tom's protestations about the contestants' welfare being their first concern that he actually thought that Geraldine would be prepared to lie to the press and the police on his behalf. In fact her only concern on being confronted with Woggle's confession had been whether she could possibly get away with letting a person who was wanted for assault into a highly pressurized and confined social environment.

In the end she had decided to risk it. It had only been a scuffle at an animal-rights protest, and Woggle looked like such a peaceful old hippie. Besides which, there were only hours left before the game

134

started, and Woggle was potentially such very good telly that she simply could not face the idea of giving him up.

'We can always deny any knowledge of it if the cunt goes mad and bops someone for eating a ham sandwich,' Geraldine said to Bob Fogarty. 'I mean, the cops and the press never caught him at the time, so why should we have recognized him now?'

So Geraldine had hidden the old clippings in a drawer and thought no more about them. Until day fifteen, when she found Peeping Tom in a situation where, having made a hero out of Woggle, she needed, as she said at the emergency planning meeting held in the small hours of the morning, 'to get the cunt out sharpish'.

It did not take long for the photograph of Woggle kicking the teenage girl to find its way back to Peeping Tom Productions. Geraldine had sent it to the police at 9.15 a.m. with an accompanying letter explaining that she had received it at the office that morning from an anonymous source.

By 9.30 one of the press ringers at Scotland Yard had alerted the papers and by 9.45 they and the police had been beating a path to Peeping Tom's door. Inside the house, knowing nothing of these developments, the mood was very sombre.

Woggle had spent the night under his blanket in his usual corner. The others had been drinking out in the garden until the chill had forced them in at around four. They all felt very sorry for themselves, Woggle because he had been assaulted and defiled, the others because their lovely exciting adventure was being ruined by Woggle.

When it came, relief for the eight and disaster for the one struck like a thunderclap.

DAY FIFTEEN. 10.00 a.m.

'This is Chloe,' the tannoy announced. 'Woggle, would you please gather up your things. You are to leave the house in ten minutes.'

Garry, Kelly and Jazz cheered, the others, ever mindful of the game that they were playing, masked their inner delight beneath thoughtful, sensitive faces.

Woggle popped his head out from under his blanket. 'You can't chuck me out, I haven't been voted,' he said. 'I know my rights and I'm not fucking going.'

'Woggle, this is Chloe. We are not chucking you out. The police wish to interview you. Get your things.'

There was stunned silence.

'Fucking hell, Woggle, what you done?' Garry asked.

'Nothing, bollocks, I'm not going. They'll have to come and get me.'

And so they did, and that evening, in one of the television coups of the year, the nation watched as three uniformed police officers entered the Peeping Tom house and arrested Woggle for assault. Most of the other inmates were too stunned to react, but in what was without doubt a brilliant effort at audience manipulation Dervla suddenly cast herself in the roll of feisty, quick-thinking friend of the oppressed. She leapt up from the couch and gave Woggle the name of her solicitor.

'Insist on being allowed to look up the number in the book,' she said, allowing her Irish accent to ring out more strongly than usual, perhaps thinking it a fitting brogue in which to conduct a civil liberties protest. 'If you call directory inquiries they'll say you've used up your phone call. I know their tricks.'

David was not going to be upstaged. He stepped boldly in between the policemen and Woggle, who was still sitting on the floor.

'Be aware, officers, that I have committed all of your

faces and your numbers to memory. I am an actor and am trained in the art of mental retention. If anything happens to Mr Woggle you shall answer to me.'

It sounded great, and it would have sounded even better if the leading copper had not brought David down to earth by pointing out that since the arrest was being recorded by six separate video cameras he did not think that there would ever be a problem identifying the arresting officers. Then the policeman turned to Woggle.

'Get up, please, sir.'

'No. I ain't moving. I am the Peeping Tom One. Free the Peeping Tom One!'

'You can't arrest him for having fleas,' said Dervla.

'Why not?' Garry interjected. 'Should have done it weeks ago.'

Kelly stepped forward and put some apples and biscuits in Woggle's lap. 'In case they don't feed you.'

'Oh, for God's sake, Kelly,' David sneered. 'Like you give a toss.'

'He's a human being,' Kelly protested.

'That's debatable,' said Jazz, who was over at the kitchen area putting the kettle on and trying to look cool and unconcerned. 'I'm young, gifted and black,' his hip, easy stance was saying. 'Coppers come through my door every day.' In fact Jazz had never been arrested in his life, but the pose looked great and his standing with the public rocketed.

'We are bearing witness to this arrest,' Dervla said firmly.

'Yes, we are,' Moon added, rather weakly.

Hamish clearly decided that he couldn't compete and, following his plan that only the noticed get nominated, he got up and went into the boys' bedroom for a lie-down.

'Sir,' the lead policeman said, 'we do not know your name beyond the fact that you are known as Woggle.

However, we have strong photographic evidence to suggest that you are the person wanted by Lincolnshire Police in connection with the serious assault of one Lucy Brannigan, a girl of fifteen at the time of the attack.'

The other inmates stopped in their tracks, stunned.

'What? Sexual assault?' Garry asked.

'Come along, sir,' said the policeman.

'I can't believe it, Woggle,' said Jazz. 'I knew you were a dirty disgusting little toe-rag, but I never thought you were a nonce.'

Everybody drew back from the little figure squatting in the corner. Dervla disengaged herself and disappeared into the girls' bedroom.

Woggle wasn't having this. 'She was a fox-murderer!' he shouted. 'An animal-torturer! It was a fair fight and I kicked her in the head. She bloody deserved it, the fascist! If you live by the sword you die by the sword.'

And as if to prove this point the policemen picked Woggle up and carried him away. As they took him, struggling, through the door the blanket fell away to reveal Woggle's skinny body, still naked and covered in white flea powder.

He looked pathetic. It was the final indignity.

DAY THIRTY-FOUR. 11.50 p.m.

On the drive home Coleridge attempted to banish Woggle from his mind by listening to Radio 4. The thing about Radio 4 for Coleridge was that no matter what they were talking about he always got caught up in it. He had often found himself sitting in his car outside his house waiting to hear the end of some discussion about crop rotation in West Africa, or some other subject he had never heard of and would never think of again. Even the shipping forecasts made good listening, conjuring up as they did strange emotions and race memories of dark rocky coastlines, furious typhoons and the long lonely watches of the night.

The subject being discussed that night as Coleridge drove home was an economic slump in rural Ireland. The shift of money and young people to the cities, coupled with cuts in European agricultural grants, had left some villages in desperate financial straits. Negative loans and mortgages were forcing many households to the edge of despair. Coleridge's ears pricked up at the mention of one of the villages worst affected, Ballymagoon. Where had he heard that name recently? he wondered.

It wasn't until he was opening his second can of beer (and thinking about having a bit of ham with it) that Coleridge remembered. He had read the name on a suspect profile. Ballymagoon was the village in which Dervla was born.

DAY THIRTY-FIVE. 9.30 a.m.

'*It's day fifteen in the house, and after supper, in order to take their minds off Woggle's arrest, Peeping Tom sets the housemates a topic for discussion,*' Andy the narrator intoned portentously. '*The topic tonight is their deepest feelings.*'

Coleridge stirred his second mug of tea of the working day. Those he had at home did not count.

Trisha bustled in, pulling off her coat.

'You've arrived just in time, Patricia,' said Coleridge. 'Our suspects are about to discuss that most significant and sublime of all subject matters: themselves.'

'Suspects *and* victim, sir.'

It was early, and Trisha was not in the mood for Coleridge's superior tone, besides which, she felt that some respect at least was due to the dead. Coleridge merely smiled wearily.

On the screen Garry had taken the floor. 'I'm not going to mess you about,' he said. 'I've not always been a very nice person.'

'You still ain't,' Jazz chipped in, but nobody laughed. Instead they all hung on to the intense, caring expressions that they had had assumed when Garry had begun.

Coleridge pressed pause. 'You see how none of them share Jazz's joke? This is confession time. It's serious stuff. A matter of faith. Garry is worshipping at the altar of his own significance, and Jazz is laughing in church.'

'Sir, if we have to stop every time any of these people annoy you we'll never get through even this tape.'

'I can't help it, Patricia. They've ground me down.' But Coleridge knew he was being stupid and resolved to make an effort.

Garry began his story. 'Like I said, I was a bit of a geezer, you know what I mean? Little bit o' this, little bit o' that, dodgy stuff, done some rotten things that I don't mind admitting I'm not proud of, but at the end of the day, right, I done 'em and that's me and I can't change that. Truth is, I wanted it large and I wasn't too fussed about who I had a go at to get it. You know what I'm saying?'

There were murmurs of sympathy but not very enthusiastic ones.

'I think the truth of the matter was, right,' Garry continued, 'I didn't love myself.'

Now they all nodded earnestly. This they understood. Garry's other influences – the fighting, the boozing, the dodgy dealing – might have been different from their own, but when it came to that central subject of not quite loving oneself enough, they understood exactly what he meant.

140

'I know exactly what you fookin' mean,' Moon said.

'I don't think I was letting myself in,' Garry continued.

Coleridge's resolve to keep quiet had lasted less than a minute. 'Oh, for heaven's sake! Why do they all talk as if they're in therapy! Even *Garry*. Just *listen* to him! "I wasn't letting myself in." What on earth does *that* mean? He's a *yobbo*, for heaven's sake! Not a sociology graduate! Where do they *learn* all these ridiculous empty phrases?'

'Oprah, sir.'

'Who?'

Trisha could not tell whether Coleridge was joking. She let it go.

Back in the house, oblivious to how much they would one day annoy a senior police officer, the confessional continued.

'I just know *exactly* what you mean, I really do,' Moon was saying, 'and I think it's really dead strong of you that you can say it.'

Nourished by the support, Garry pressed on. Loving himself by pretending to hate himself. 'Anyway, I was getting into a lot of coke at the time, you know, quite a big habit, doing five hundred notes a week, bosh, straight up my hooter. Yes, please. Thank you very much. We like that. Blowing a grand was nothing to me. Nothing. I'm not proud of it, right, but that was me, right? I was having it large and what I wanted I fahking had, you know what I'm saying? I was a bad boy. I ain't proud of it.'

Coleridge thought about remarking that for a man who professed so much not to be proud of his behaviour, Gazzer was doing a pretty good job of showing the world just how proud of it he was. He decided against it, though. He could see that Patricia was getting sick of him.

On screen the rest of the group nodded earnestly at

Gazzer while clearly itching for the moment when they could take the floor themselves.

'But you know what saved me? You know what really worked me out?' Suddenly Garry was choking up. There were tears welling up in his eyes and his voice was cracking.

'Don't go on if you don't want to, mate,' said David, his voice awash with concentrated sincerity and sympathy. 'Take a break. Come back to it. Give yourself space. Now, when I—'

'No, no,' said Garry quickly. He wasn't losing hold of the conch that easily, not now he was on a roll. 'I'm all right, mate, thanks, but it helps to talk about it.'

David sank back onto the couch.

Garry took up the thread of his story. 'I'll tell you what changed me. My little lad, that's who, little Ricky. My kid. He means everything to me, everything. I'd fahkin' die for him, I would, I really would.'

There was much sincere and committed nodding at this. The body language of the group was highly supportive. Their eyes, on the other hand, told a different story. As the shot cut from one listener to another the message was clear: it said, 'I am bored out of my brains, I do not care about you and your little lad, and I wish you'd just *shut up and let me speak.*'

' 'Cos, like, I have Ricky most weekends, right, and he's just brilliant, I mean he's just so amazing, I'm so proud of him and like everything he says is just brilliant, right? You know what I mean? I'm not being funny or nothing, he's my little kiddie and he's like the best thing that ever happened to me.' Garry's voice was choking with emotion but he persevered.

'And one weekend I'd had it large the night before, you know what I'm saying? Did the lot, right, booze, coke, spliff, I ain't proud of it, and I was feeling well rough, and Ricky's mum brings him round and she says, "It's your day with him," and I'm thinking,

142

"Fahkin' hell! Oh no! This is all I need with a head like a sack full of broken glass." So I says, "I'll have him tomorrow," but she says, "You'll have him today," and she's gone, right? So I'm thinking, "Fahk, I'll take him round me mum's." But then, little Ricky says, "Don't you want to play with me, then, Daddy?" And you know what? He cured my hangover, there and then, just with his little smile and by saying that. So I stuck *Spot the Dog* on while I got myself together and then we went to the café for breakfast and after that we went down the park and had loads of ice cream and stuff. It was just brilliant, I mean really amazing, because I'm so proud of him and there's so much that I can learn from him, right? And at the end of the day, I know I have to treasure every moment with him and cherish him, because he's the most precious thing I've got.'

Gazzer wiped tears from his eyes. He had surprised himself. He didn't cry much in the usual run of things, but getting all that stuff about Ricky out had been brilliant. He felt genuinely moved.

The group paused for a nod. They were obviously anxious to leap straight in with stories of their own, but they held back, awarding Garry a moment of reflection and respect. None of them wanted to be portrayed on the television as taking somebody else's emotions lightly. Particularly when a little kiddie was involved.

It was into this pious pause that Kelly unwittingly slung her bucket of cold water. 'So what are you doing in here, then, Garry?' she asked.

'What?'

Kelly did not look as if she was trying to be horrid, but it certainly came across that way.

'I mean, if you have such a great time with him, and learn so much, what are you doing in here? You might be in here for nearly two and a half months. How old is he?'

'Nearly four.'

143

Garry was trying to work out what was going on. Was this woman *criticizing* his heartfelt confessional? Surely that was against the rules?

'Well, I think you're mad, then,' Kelly continued. 'I mean, at that age he'll be changing every day. You're going to miss it.'

'Yeah, I know that, Kelly, that's fahking obvious. I might even miss his birthday and I'm gonna be dead choked up—'

'So what are you doing in here, then?' Kelly repeated.

'Well, because . . . Because . . .'

Now Coleridge could contain his frustration no longer. He almost shouted at the screen, which was very unlike him. 'Well, come on, lad! Be honest, why don't you, for once in your life? Surely it's obvious! Because you have a *right* to be in that damned stupid house. You have a *right* to do *exactly* as you please. To lead an entirely selfish and irresponsible life while wallowing in the mawkish sentimentality of father-hood when you feel like it! Come on, lad! Be a man! Answer the girl.'

'Sir,' said Trisha. '*Shut up.*' She stopped, shocked at her audacity.

'I'm sorry, sir, I . . .'

'I did not hear anything, constable,' said Coleridge quietly, resolving once more to try to contain himself.

On the screen Garry was still lost for words.

'Don't get me wrong,' Kelly continued. 'I'm not knocking you for having a kid or nothing like that. My sister's got two by different blokes and they're brilliant. I just think, you know, if you do have a kid, shouldn't you be out there trying to look after it? Instead of sit-ting in here. That's all. I mean, only seeing as how you love him so much.'

Garry, normally so quick with a clever line and a put-down, was at a loss. 'Well, as it happens, Kelly,' he said finally, 'I'm doing this for him.'

'How's that work, then?' said Kelly.

'To make him proud of me.'

'Oh, I see.'

On the following evening's edition of *House Arrest* Dr Ranulf Aziz, the show's resident TV psychologist, gave his opinion for the benefit of the viewers.

'See Garry's body language now, his shoulders hunched, his jaw set, this is a classic quasi-confrontational stance, with overtones of semi-concealed malice and undertones of mental violence. We see it mirrored in the animal kingdom when a great beast is denied access to the best portion of the kill. Garry's arms are firmly folded, just as a lion or a tiger might shift its weight to its rear haunches, demonstrating current passivity but a willingness to attack violently and with extreme rage.'

Chloe, the sparkly, spunky, batty, booby *House Arrest* babe, put on her intelligent face. 'So you're saying Gazzer's a bit naffed off?'

'That is indeed what I'm saying, Chloe. Gazzer is a bit naffed off big-time.'

Gazzer was more than naffed off. He was speechless with rage, his heart and soul were a boiling, bubbling pit of hurt and anger.

He covered it well, in that he only looked furious. 'Yeah, well, whatever,' he said.

'I didn't mean to say anything, Gazz,' Kelly replied. 'You know, I'm just saying, that's all.'

'Yeah, right, whatever,' Garry said again. 'Who wants a cup of tea, then?' He turned away from the group but there was no escape from the cameras, and a hot-head followed him to where the kettle was. There were tears in Garry's eyes and he was biting his lip so hard that a thin line of blood could be seen emerging.

How dare she? It was incredible. It wasn't his fault

that him and the mother didn't get on any more. What was he supposed to do, camp outside their house twenty-four hours a day? He had to have a life, didn't he?

He *did* love his kid. She had no right. No right at all.

DAY SEVENTEEN. 10.00 a.m.

Layla had been back at work for only an hour when she left again.

Back at work? It was incredible. Terrible. Devastating.

During all the time she had been in the house, and indeed ever since she had received the thrilling news that she had been selected to join the *House Arrest* team, Layla had hardly dared to think of what she would be doing three days after leaving. Of course, she had allowed herself to dream a little and in her wildest fantasies had imagined herself juggling offers to model gorgeous clothes and to present exciting television programmes about beauty products and alternative culture. In her worst moments of fear and doubt she had feared being lampooned in the tabloids and having to go on radio chat shows to defend her dippy-hippie ways. What she never *ever* imagined, however, was that she would be going back to work.

The brutal fact was that nobody was interested in her. The story of Woggle's rise and spectacular fall had been *the* Peeping Tom story of the first fortnight, and now even that was becoming old news. The show had moved on. Layla had been useful to the press only in so much as she could talk about Woggle, and now that this one small nugget of notoriety had disappeared, she was just the beautiful but vain hippie one who got chucked out first.

The one who wrote shit poetry. The one who was

obviously entirely and completely absorbed in her own beauty and wonderfulness.

That was how Peeping Tom had presented her, when they presented her at all. As a snooty, stupid cow whose one redeeming feature was that she was highly shaggable. However, since the Woggle story had placed matters of the heart firmly on the Peeping Tom back-burner, even that tainted card had been totally underplayed.

Added to all of this was the fact that Layla's final act in the house had been to go into the confession box and to tell the world that she had clusters of septic flea bites around her anus. This had been the sole snippet of Layla's last rant that Geraldine had chosen to broadcast, and it considerably dampened her immediate sexual allure on the outside.

Layla had gone into the house with a chance of stardom and she had emerged just two weeks later as a desperate wannabe who had turned into a sad loser. Even her friends were looking at her differently.

'Couldn't you have stopped the others from being quite so mean to Woggle?' the more radical of them said. 'I mean, in a way he was right. What *is* the difference between a fox and a flea?'

'I think you should have let David read your poem for you when he offered,' her mother said. 'I'm afraid that refusing did look rather precious, dear.'

Layla felt that her life was ruined, and for what? Nothing. She was despised and, more pressingly, she was broke. Peeping Tom did not pay its contestants (except the winner). They were given a small stipend to maintain their rent or mortgages while they were in the house, but that was it. Ex-contestants were expected to fend for themselves, but the only offers of paid employment that Layla had received since leaving the house were to pose nude for men's magazines. In the end, with weekly shopping to be done and bills to be paid, she had no choice but to ask for her old job back, which had been as a shop girl in a designer clothes shop.

'What do you want to come back for?' the manager said, astonished at Layla's enquiry. 'You're famous, you've been on telly, you must be rolling in it.'

Nobody believed that Layla, who had been on telly every night for a fortnight, could possibly need a job in a shop.

But she did, and they were happy to take her back, thrilled to have a famous person working for them. Thrilled, that was, until they found themselves with a shop full of idiots with nothing better to do than snigger from behind the dress racks at somebody who had been on the television.

'I voted for you to leave,' said one mean-looking teenager. 'I rang twice.'

'I saw one of your nipples in the shower,' said another.

'Do you reckon Kelly's going to shag Hamish, then?'

They all called her Layla, or, worse still, Layles. They knew her name, they knew *her*, or at least they thought they did.

A middle-aged man brought her a small bottle of walnut oil, which for a moment Layla thought was nice, but then he asked her to go out with him and she realized that people thought that the sort of girl who went on *House Arrest* (and got chucked straight off) was the sort of girl who would shag you for half the ingredients of a salad dressing.

At shortly after ten a photographer from the local newspaper arrived. 'Must be the quickest "Where are they now?" feature in the history of showbiz,' he said, snapping away without asking.

The shop manager had called the paper. 'I thought you'd be pleased, Layles. I mean, after all, you must have done it for the publicity.'

Layla put down the jumper she had been trying to fold for some time, took £9.50 from the till, which was pay for one hour's work, and went home. Once there she picked up the phone and asked Directory Inquiries for the phone number of *Men Only* magazine.

They were delighted to get her call. 'What we wondered was would you do an erotic shoot with this beautiful girl who had her kitchen done up on *Changing Rooms*? We thought we could call it Celeblezzy, you know, just as a joke, like.'

Layla put down the phone. She was *so* angry. Angry with Peeping Tom Productions, of course, but particularly angry with the people who had nominated her for eviction. She tortured herself by watching the tape over and over again. There they were sitting in the box, so smug, so self-important. They had sealed her fate, they had doomed her to being the first out.

David. Dervla. Garry and *Kelly*.

Kelly was the real humiliation, that little ladette slapper had had the gall to nominate *her*.

Dervla she hated also. Those weasel words from the confession box burned into her soul. 'She's a lovely, lovely girl, a very gentle, caring and beautiful spirit, but I feel that in the end her loveliness would be able to blossom more beautifully outside of the house.' What a stuck-up, hypocritical Irish cow. The truth was she had wanted Layla out because she hadn't wanted someone better looking and more intelligent than her grabbing the sensitive male vote.

Dervla and Kelly. For some reason it was the women that hurt the most. Probably because Layla felt that she was so much better at *being* a woman than they were. They should have supported her, they should have made her their champion against pseuds like David and yobbos like Garry and Jazz. Their rejection of her was, she felt, almost *sexist*.

Dervla and Kelly. Those were the two she really

hated. But particularly Kelly. That same Kelly who had nominated her and then hugged her and kissed her when she was voted out, and said she loved her. Kelly, who had pretended to be upset, who had so compounded her humiliation for all the world to see.

DAY SEVENTEEN. 8.00 p.m.

It had been two days since Woggle's exit, and the *House Arrest* experience had returned to the basic formula of whining, back-biting and wondering who fancied whom.

'*It's day seventeen in the house,*' said Andy the narrator. '*After lunch, a meal of pasta and vegetable sauce, which Sally cooks, the group talk about first love.*'

'Well, it's gotta be Chelsea FC, hasn't it?' said Gazzer. 'You never forget the first time you see the Blues.'

'Because they're so shite,' Jazz opined.

'Even when they're shite they're beautiful.'

'We're talking about proper love, Gazzer,' said Moon. 'Not fookin' football.'

'So am I, gel. Let's face it, the love a bloke has for his team transcends all others. Think about it. I fancy loads of birds, *all* blokes fancy loads of birds, 'cept poofs, and they fancy loads of blokes. Gay or straight, men like to put it about a bit, full stop. But when it comes to football, you only ever support one team, don't you? You're *faithful*, Moon, it's true love.'

Watching from the depths of the monitoring bunker, Geraldine Hennessy could see that without Woggle life in the house was beginning to look dull. She needed to do something quickly to pep things up. Her solution was to give the housemates more to drink.

'What is the number-one interest people have in

watching these programmes?' she asked her production team at their morning meeting the next day. There was silence. Geraldine's minions all learned quickly that most of her questions were rhetorical.

'To see if any of the inmates shag, am I right? Of course I'm right. When you get down to it, that's what it's all about. But basically it *never* fucking happens, does it? Nobody ever actually does it! We all keep up the pretence that it's *going* to happen, us and the newspapers and the bleeding Broadcasting Standards Commission, we all *pretend* that it's all so bleeding titillating when it patently isn't. But nobody ever actually does the business. And why is that, I ask myself?'

She was indeed asking herself, for her cowed minions remained silent.

'Because nobody is ever *pissed* enough, that's why! Which, in a nutshell, is the problem with reality TV! Not enough booze! Oh, we can give them hot spas and massage rooms and nookie huts and all that bollocks, but in the long run no one is going to do the nasty, insert the portion, prise open the clam, heat up the sausage or cleave the bearded monster with the one-eyed lovesnake unless they are completely arseholed!'

Everybody shuffled their papers and looked embarrassed. They all knew that they were involved in a fairly tawdry exercise, but they fervently wished that Geraldine would not revel in it quite so much.

Then Geraldine announced that she was changing the rules. She was going to separate the food and alcohol budgets in order to remove the usual constraint of having to sacrifice a meal for a drink.

There were protests, of course, once it was announced, from the watchdogs and the bishops. Geraldine took the moral high ground, her usual defence for descending into the gutter. 'We believe that people should be treated as adults,' she sniffed. 'If you set up a valid experiment such as ours and then police it from the outside as if it was some fifth-form trip, you learn nothing about the people involved. Our intention is to facilitate and encourage genuine social interaction.'

Nobody was fooled, of course. The tabloids put it most succinctly with their leader comment: 'It's *House A'pissed*! Lets get 'em drunk and watch 'em shag.'

Of course even Geraldine had to draw a line somewhere. These people were locked in a house with no TV, no writing equipment, no sense of time and almost nothing to do except a few foolish tasks, for weeks on end. Given the chance, most people would start drinking the moment they got up in the morning and carry on until collapsing into unconsciousness at night. Peeping Tom could not allow that. There were, after all, strict broadcasting standards to observe. Therefore, Peeping Tom banned daytime drinking and also rationed it during weekday evenings. At weekends, however, it was party time, and the housemates could have as much to drink as they liked.

'And my rule in life has always been,' Geraldine told a press conference, 'that the weekend starts on Thursday.'

That afternoon, the Thursday following the drama of Layla's eviction and Woggle's arrest, found the store room where Peeping Tom left the house supplies filled with booze.

Under normal circumstances Thursday should have meant another round of eviction nominations, but because of Woggle's unexpected departure it was announced that the evictions for that week would be cancelled and that things would be picked up as normal on the following Thursday. If ever there was an excuse for a party, this surely had to be it.

DAY THIRTY-SIX. 1.00 p.m.

Coleridge had spent another fruitless morning out at Shepperton Studios wandering around the replica Peeping Tom house, foraging in his imagination for some stroke of insight that might lead on to a theory.

Something was forming in his mind, the beginnings of an idea, but it was just a theory. There was nothing much so far to back it up. Still, better to be chewing on something rather than nothing, even if it did prove to be a red herring in the end. He returned to the station to find a faxed letter from the Irish Garda waiting for him. It was in response to an inquiry he had made to them about Ballymagoon, the village which Coleridge had heard mentioned on the radio and which was at the centre of an economic slump in rural Ireland. Dervla's home village.

Suspect family still resident in village, the letter read. *Both parents and two younger sisters continue to live at family home. Family do not appear to have escaped effects of slump. Considerable financial hardship, car sold, negative equity on house and farm, mounting debts. Recent request for loans denied.*

Well, thought Coleridge, if ever a girl had a pressing reason for wanting to win half a million pounds it was Dervla. On the other hand, he knew from many years of experience that when it came to money most people did not need a pressing reason to covet half a million pounds.

Nonetheless, her parents *were* in danger of losing their farm. And volunteering to be on *House Arrest was* quite a strange choice for a girl like Dervla to make. Of all of the housemates, she was undoubtedly the most ... Coleridge struggled for the word ... 'beautiful' sprang into his mind, but he fought it out again. Finally he settled upon 'different.' Dervla was the most different.

There was no doubt about it that, as motives went, money was always a good one. Coupled with imminent family shame it was terrific . . . Except killing one housemate was scarcely going to guarantee her victory. It was only week four, there were seven other competitors, and it seemed unlikely that she had been planning to kill them all.

She could not even have known that she was a popular housemate. None of them knew anything about what the world was thinking.

Something to save for later was about all Coleridge could construe from his fax from the Irish police. He put it in the Dervla file and asked a constable to add a 'motive' note to her photograph on the wall map. Then he joined Trisha and Hooper at their habitual position in front of the video screen.

They were looking at day eighteen.

'Look at all that booze. Must be over a hundred quid's worth,' said Trisha.

'It was the only way to get things going,' Hooper replied. 'Geraldine Hennessy said as much to the press at the time.'

'Surely these people must have realized that they were being manipulated?' Coleridge observed. 'Getting them drunk is such a transparent ploy.'

'*Of course* they realized it, sir, but you have to try and understand that they're not like you. *They don't mind.* And frankly if I was stuck in a sealed house with David and his guitar for weeks on end and somebody stuck five crates of booze on the table, I'd get stuck in myself.'

'But have they no sense of personal privacy? Dignity?'

Hooper could disguise his exasperation no longer. 'Well, sir, being as how they've all volunteered to be on the programme and they've been wandering around in their knickers ever since, I would say that the answer to that would probably have to be no.'

154

'Don't take that tone with me, sergeant.'

'What tone, sir?'

'You know damn well what tone.'

'I do not know what tone.'

'Well, don't take it anyway.'

On the screen, while the other housemates began their evening's drinking, Moon got up and made her way to the confession box. 'I just wanted to say . . . that I've been thinking about the trick I played on Sally and the girls the other night, you know, when I said all that stuff about being abused and institutionalized . . .'

Moon then went into a lengthy ramble about herself and what a mad-for-it gangster she was, a straight-talker who just said what she felt like and at the end of the day people would have to take her as they found her. Finally, she got to the apology.

'What I'm saying is, I don't want people to think it was cruel and the like, especially 'cos I could hear her sobbing afterwards and all that, and I expect the public could too. Even though if you ask me it was a bit of an over-reaction . . . but what I'm saying is, if Sally's been abused or whatever and has got, you know, mental health stuff going on or whatever, then fair play to her, right, because at the end of the day I wouldn't like it myself if I thought someone was taking the piss out of me for being a nutter, particularly if I actually was a nutter, like Sally seems to be, although I'm not saying she is, if you know what I'm saying? So that's all I'm saying, right. If you know what I'm saying.'

All of this was news to Coleridge. Geraldine had never broadcast the original discussion that had taken place in the girls' bedroom; nor had she broadcast Moon's apology in the confession box.

'Sally has "mental health" stuff going on?' Coleridge asked.

'It seems so,' said Trish, ejecting the Moon confession tape.

'I talked to Fogarty the editor, and he told me that Sally pretty much said as much one night when the girls were chatting. They never broadcast it but Geri the Gaoler kept the tape for possible future use. That's why we didn't see it in our first trawl, it was still hidden on the edit suite hard disk. Fogarty sent it over. This is it.'

And so Coleridge, Hooper and Trish listened in on the conversation that had taken place in the girls' room on the eighth night when Moon had lied about her past and Sally had shown herself so sensitive about the subject of mental health. For all three of them watching, one phrase stood out above all the others. Something that Sally had said as she sat there in the dark, her voice shaking with emotion.

'. . . when once in a blue moon something happens, like some poor schizo who never should have been returned to the community gets stuck inside their own dark box and sticks a knife in someone's head or whatever, suddenly every mild depressive in the country is a murderer.'

Trisha had marked down the time code of the comment and now they rewound the tape and listened to it again.

'*Sticks a knife in someone's head.*'

'Sticks a *knife* in someone's head.'

With the knowledge of hindsight, it was certainly an unfortunate choice of words.

'Coincidence, do you think?' Coleridge said.

'Probably. I mean, if Sally was the murderer, how would she have known nearly four weeks beforehand how she was going to do it? We've already established that the murder was an improvisation.'

'We haven't established anything of the sort, constable,' Coleridge snapped. 'We have *supposed* such a thing because it seems difficult to see how it could have been planned. However, *if* someone in the house had an attraction for knives, *if* one of them was mentally predisposed towards stabbing, then we might *suppose* that this would make the murder method less a matter of chance and more one of inevitability.'

There was silence in the incident room for a moment before Coleridge added, 'And Sally is a very, very strong woman.'

'So Sally's the killer, then?' Trisha said with a hint of exasperation. 'That's an awfully big supposition to make from one little comment.'

'I am not supposing anything, constable. I'm ruminating.'

Ruminating? Did he speak like that for a joke? Who ruminated? People thought, they considered, they might even occasionally ponder, but nobody had *ruminated* for fifty years.

'Sally chose to use a phrase that exactly describes the murder. She said "stick a knife in someone's head". We have to consider the implications of that.'

'Well, how about considering this, sir . . .' Trisha fought down the feeling she had in her stomach that she might be being defensive on Sally's behalf out of some absurd sisterly and sexual solidarity. She truly believed that she would as happily convict a lesbian as any other person . . . On the other hand she did rather resent the fact that people were so eager to suspect Sally.

'She's very strong,' they kept saying. 'Very *very* strong.'

It wasn't Sally's fault that she was strong and muscular. Trisha herself would have loved to have been that strong. Although perhaps not quite as muscular.

'Go on, Patricia,' said Coleridge.

'Well, I was just wondering whether perhaps Moon *wanted* us to be reminded of what Sally had said. Perhaps she said all that stuff in the confession box because she wanted us to ruminate along the lines that you are ruminating along, sir.'

Coleridge raised a thoughtful eyebrow. 'That is also a possibility,' he conceded, 'and one upon which we must certainly ru— which we must certainly bear in mind.'

They turned their attention back to the screen.

DAY EIGHTEEN. 8.15 p.m.

Moon walked out of the confession box, having made her little speech about Sally, and announced her intention of getting immediately 'shitfaced'.

'I'm going to go large,' she said, pulling the ring on a can of Special Brew. 'I'm mad for it. I'm going to get shitfaced and rat-arsed!'

'Funny that, isn't it?' Jazz said. 'How we choose to describe having a good night.'

'You what?' said Moon.

'Funny way of describing a party, Moon,' he said.

'You what, Jazz?'

Jazz, ever watchful for opportunities whereby he could work on his patter and continue what he saw as his ongoing public audition for a career in comedy, had spotted what he thought was a fruitful opening. 'Well, the English language is the most extensive in the world, but that's the best you can do to describe having a good time. Tonight I'm going to have such a good time that it will be as if my face was covered in shit! My mood will resemble that of a rat's arse! What's all that about, then?'

'Eh?' said Moon.

Dervla tried to be supportive. 'Very amusing, Jazz,' she said, opening a bottle of wine. 'I'd laugh but I'm not yet sufficiently shitfaced.' And she smiled, hugging herself as if she had a special secret.

*

'*Kelly 1. Dervla 2.*' The secret hand had written in the condensation. '*Hang in there, Gorgeous. XXX.*'

The recipient of this little love note grinned broadly through the toothpaste foam.

So now she had risen to second place in the affections of the public. Not bad at all after only two and a half weeks. Only Kelly was ahead of her and Dervla felt far better equipped to stay the course than she believed Kelly was. After all, it was going to be a long, long game for those who survived, and Dervla was confident in her reserves of inner strength. Kelly, she felt, was not so well equipped for the struggle. She was too open, too sweet, too vulnerable, not so mentally attuned to stay the distance. Dervla felt that all she had to do was hang on. If she could just survive the process, she would win the game.

That was all she had to do.

Survive.

Jazz broke in on Dervla's reverie. 'So're you going to get shitfaced too, then, Dervo?' he said, throwing a friendly arm around her. 'Can I join you?'

'I'd be delighted, kind sir,' she replied.

Jazz's smooth, beautiful, scented face smelt sweet close to hers, his arm was strong.

'I never heard you swear before, Dervs,' he laughed. 'You're loosening up, my darling.'

'Ah, to be sure, even us nuns like to let our wimples down occasionally.'

Jazz had been working up a little idea and, encouraged by Dervla's friendly attitude, he decided to give it a trial run. 'You know what?' he said. 'You give so much away about yourself when you brush your teeth.'

Dervla almost leapt away from him. In fact, she jumped so suddenly that she caused them both to spill their drinks. Everybody turned in surprise.

'What the *fuck* do you know about me brushing my teeth?' she snapped angrily. It was rare that anybody heard Dervla say 'fuck'.

'Here, steady on, girl,' said Garry. 'Mind the language. I ain't as rough as you, you know.'

Dervla appeared shattered. She tried to collect herself. 'I mean, what do you mean, Jazz? What about me brushing my teeth?'

Jazz struggled for words, confused by her defensive reaction. 'Well, not just you, Dervs,' he said. 'I mean anybody, what I'm saying is people's toothbrushes give a lot away about them.'

'Oh, anybody,' Dervla said. 'So it's not like you've been watching me brush my teeth or anything?'

Now it was Jazz's turn to react. 'What you saying, girl? That I'm some sort of tooth pervert? I never seen none of you brushing your teeth, right? On account of the fact that when I ablute, girl, I ablute alone, it's a personal thing, OK? Because my body is a temple and I go there to worship.'

They all laughed and Dervla apologized. The moment passed, and Jazz pressed on with his comic material.

'What I'm saying, right, is that I ain't never seen none of you brush your teeth. But I bet I know who everybody's brush belongs to.'

This caused a moment of semi-drunken attention. From everyone, that is, except Hamish and Kelly. Kelly was already too far gone to take much interest in the conversation, and Hamish was too busy taking an interest in Kelly. Hamish had come into the house with the intention of having sex on television and in Kelly he was scenting a possible opportunity. He had put his hand on Kelly's knee and she was giggling.

Meanwhile, Jazz expanded on his theme. 'Like there was a time,' he continued, 'when a toothbrush was a functional item, they was all the same, man, there was different colours, but that was it. Now your toothbrush is a *fashion statement*, man! We are talking a *designer* commodity here!'

'Stop waffling and get on with it,' said David. 'Whose brush is whose?'

'Just setting the scene, guy, just setting the scene.'

'Whose brush is whose?

'Well, Gazzer's has gotta be the one like mine. It's hip, it's flash, it's well hard and it's the business! It's got shock absorbers, man! It's got a big soft round aero-dynamically palm-friendly handle, rear suspension and a detachable head. It's got a spring-loaded crumple zone at the front, it looks like a ray gun, and it's in Chelsea's away colours. Am I right, Gazz?'

'Fuck me, you're Sherlock fucking Holmes, Jazz.'

'Yes, I am, guy, because it is el-e-fucking-mentary. Now, Dervo, you got the one with the age-fading stripe, that's what I reckon.'

Dervla attempted to maintain a poker face. 'Why's that, Jazz?'

' 'Cos you are one fastidious lady, OK? You are sweet and clean and you don't want no dirty old worn-out thing stuck in your mouth.'

'Shame!' shouted Gazzer, at which Dervla blushed.

'Shut up, Gazz,' Jazz admonished. 'Dervo is a fuck-ing lady, so don't you go making no off-colour comments implying no blow jobs, all right? Anyway, the point is, am I right, girl? When you was in the chemist and you was buying a brush for your perfect pearly toothypegs, did you choose a basic bristle or did you choose the one what tells you when it's time to buy a new one?'

Dervla blushed again. 'All right, I did, you swine!' Dervla laughed, perhaps a little too loudly.

'All right then, Jason.' David still insisted on refer-ring to Jazz by his full name. 'Which one's mine?'

'Easy, man, piece of piss. You're the blue one, the

one without nothing on it at all, no spring-loaded bit in the middle, no go-faster stripe, just a plain basic brush.'

'Well, as it happens, you're right,' said David, slightly resentfully. 'I must say that I'm rather flattered that you understood that I was the sort of person who was unlikely to fall for all that marketing rubbish. I want a brush that gets the job done and shuts up about it. A toothbrush is a toothbrush, not a pair of trainers or a sports car.'

'But you're wrong, guy,' said Jazz. 'I didn't pick you for being no down-to-earth geezer, no way. I got you right because you're a bigger wanker than any of us.' Jazz was laughing, but David wasn't.

'Oh, and how is that, then?' he asked, attempting to maintain his rapidly evaporating air of superiority.

'Because you chose the *classic*, man! That's what they call that sort of brush these days. You ain't got no bog-standard brush in your toothmug, David, no way, guy, what you got's a Wisdom *classic*. And they're not easy to find these days either, not every chemist stocks them, and you got to search your way through all the pink spongy ones and the transparent bendy ones to find them. Because you see, David, it's the flash gimmicky brushes that are the *norm* these days. *They're* the bog-standard brushes, the ones ordinary people buy. What you got is the designer item, the retro classic, which you have to seek out, like you obviously did. Just like you must have looked high and low to get that retro-looking pair of old-style trainers you got on, and they're called "classics" too. Made just for that bit of the market that reckons it's got *style* and *class* and would never be a part of a *trend*, oh no, not them, they favour *classic* styles, or to put it another way, David, they're wankers.'

It was a good performance and everybody laughed loudly. David obviously felt he had better laugh along too, but he did not do a very convincing job of it. In fact he looked furious. Livid. And also astonished. Jazz had caught him out. David had obviously never expected any intellectual threat from Jazz's direction and yet this loudmouthed, conceited *trainee chef* had made him look a fool. What was more, it would probably be broadcast on national television.

In the back of his mind David kept a little book into which he would put the names of people with whom he intended to get even. Jazz had just reserved himself an entire page.

DAY EIGHTEEN. 10.00 p.m.

Kelly announced that it was time to go to bed. She had had a terrific night, she said, but now the room was really beginning to spin. As she got up she fell back down again, straight into Hamish's lap.

'Sorry,' said Kelly.

'Fine by me,' Hamish replied. 'You should do it more often.'

Kelly giggled and put her arms round Hamish's neck. 'I think I fell on something hard,' she said, laughing drunkenly. 'Give us a kiss.'

Hamish did not require any further encouragement and so they kissed. Kelly started with puckered lips but Hamish went in mouth open and for a moment or two Kelly responded, her jaw working against his.

In the monitoring bunker they cheered. This was the first proper kiss of *House Arrest Three*. They knew Geraldine would be thrilled.

'If he puts his hand up her top we win the magnum,' said Pru, Bob Fogarty's assistant, who was the duty editor that night.

Peeping Tom Productions had indeed promised a

163

magnum of vintage Dom Pérignon to the crew who were lucky enough to record the first grope.

Back in the house, sitting on the green couch, Moon was not impressed. 'Fookin' hell, Kelly, if you're not careful you'll suck his fookin' head off. What do his tonsils taste like?'

But Kelly was enjoying herself. She was drunk and feeling naughty, and Hamish was a lovely-looking boy.

'Very nice,' she said, getting up unsteadily, 'and now I'm going to bed.'

'I'll help you,' said Hamish, leaping up to great cheers from the rest of the group.

'Thank you, kind sir,' Kelly replied, giggling.

'Don't forget, Peeping Tom is peeping,' Dervla warned.

'I don't care,' Kelly replied, and she didn't. Quite suddenly she had decided that she was not ready for bed yet. Why not sneak off with Hamish for a little while? Who knows, she might even kiss him again. Why not, it was a party, wasn't it? And so together they staggered off towards the girls' bedroom, leaving the other six housemates to further boozing.

'Don't hurry back!' shouted Jazz.

'Yeah, not until we've drunk the rest of the booze, anyway,' Garry added.

In the monitoring bunker they were keeping their fingers crossed. This was certainly the most sexually promising development so far. Breathlessly, the editors, assistant editors and PAs watched as the drunken couple staggered from camera to camera, spinning across through each screen in turn.

Halfway to the bedroom they altered course. It was Kelly's idea. She grabbed Hamish's shirt and steered him out through the big sliding doors and out into the warm night. Together they staggered towards the pool and for a moment the watchers wondered whether they might luck out with a bit of skinny dipping.

'Camera four, under the pool, double quick!' Pru barked into her intercom, and down in the camera runs around the house a black draped dalek-like shape began to glide along the corridor, down the ramp and into the spying position under the pool's glass bottom.

But although the drunken couple teetered on the edge, kissing deep and laughing loud, they did not fall in.

'Oh my God! I think they're making for Copulation Cabin!' Pru could scarcely contain her excitement. 'Somebody ring Geraldine.'

Copulation Cabin was a wooden hut that had been placed beyond the swimming pool and filled with cushions and draped lamps. It looked like somebody had attempted to create an Arabian love tent in a garden shed, which was exactly what had happened. Peeping Tom had put it there in the transparent hope that if they supplied a place where people could get away from the prying eyes of the other housemates they might have sex. It was hoped that the existence of no fewer than *five* cameras covering this tiny space would not dampen the ardour.

Kelly led Hamish into the cabin and they collapsed together in a laughing boozy heap on the cushions.

Hamish had fancied Kelly from the start, and for him the cameras were a turn-on. Quite apart from the terrific thrill of the idea of bedding Kelly while millions of jealous men looked on, he felt that it would be a wonderful starting point towards presenting his own quasi-medical sex show on the television, which in his fantasies was called *Dr Nookie Talks*.

The kissing was becoming more intense: long, passionate, drunken kisses. Showy, chewy, gurgling kisses. Kisses that were in fact more about exhibitionism than passion, because if there was one thing that both Kelly and Hamish knew for sure, even in their drunken state, it was that this moment would make the cut of the following night's show and also that it would be in the papers the following morning.

What a wildly exciting thought that was! That simply by clamping their mouths together they were making themselves into stars!

Hamish boldly chanced a hand, spurred on by genuine lust and pure vainglorious exhibitionism. Gently he slipped it under the hem of the baggy vest that Kelly was wearing. It had been clear to him all evening and to the four million viewers who would later be watching on television that Kelly was not wearing a bra.

'Uh-oh, that's second base,' Kelly breathed, and removed his hand.

In the bunker they were on the edge of their seats.

'Did he touch a tit? Did we win the magnum?'

'I don't think so, she stopped him.'

'Cow! Let him have a squeeze, girl, go on. Think of England!'

'I think he might have touched it, I really do.'

'We'll have to wait for the replay.'

'Plenty of time yet, anyway. Look at them.'

In Copulation Cabin Hamish's disappointment over the failed grope was already forgotten. Kelly seemed to be turning hot again.

'I've got an idea,' she said. 'Let's sleep here tonight, eh? Then we can be really famous: Hamish and Kelly sleep together in poolside love nest! Ha ha!' Then she pulled off her jeans.

'Yes!' they cried in the monitoring bunker, punching the air with their fists as Kelly's gorgeous bottom, clad (if 'clad' could be considered the word) in a tiny G-string, was revealed.

'Oh, yes!' they shouted once more, their fingers positively quivering over their editing controls.

'Come on,' Kelly breathed, 'get your kecks off, you ain't sleeping in my love nest in dirty stinky boy trousers.'

Hamish did not need asking twice and immediately began pulling down his immaculate chinos. As he struggled to get them off over his shoes, which he had neglected to remove, the full erection struggling within his underpants was plain for all to see.

'Naughty,' said Kelly. 'Did you make that for me?' And with that she pulled the rugs up and over them.

'Damn,' they said in the bunker. 'We never should have given them anything to cover themselves with.'

In the darkness under the blankets Kelly put her hand over her microphone and whispered. 'That'll give 'em something to think about, eh?'

Kelly had reached her limit. Quickly, Hamish tried to push her on. 'Why don't we *really* give them something to think about, Kelly?'

'What sort of girl do you think I am?' Kelly giggled. She was already drifting off to sleep. 'I'm tired.' She whispered it so quietly that even Hamish had trouble hearing her. And her hand was over her microphone.

Nobody would have heard it but him.

The booze and the soft cushions were taking their toll. Kelly was losing consciousness. Inwardly Hamish cursed. Hamish kissed her. He kissed her again, whispering in her ear, trying to revive a mood, which had never really been the mood he thought it was anyway.

'No,' Kelly murmured. 'Don't be silly. Too tired, too drunk, too comfy.'

Or at least that's what it sounded like. She was so far away by this time that she wasn't speaking clearly.

Hamish held Kelly close. Her arms were still around him, exactly where she had placed them before she had fallen asleep. His body was pressing up against her, his whole bursting, desperate body. He slipped his hand back under Kelly's shirt, the hand that she had only recently removed. This time she did not remove it. She was asleep. Hamish held her breast.

In the bunker there were no celebrations. The crew did not realize that they had won their magnum. They could not see. They did not know.

'What are they doing under there?' Pru asked.

'Not very much, I'm afraid,' said the PA. 'Too bloody pissed. I know the feeling.'

*

Under the blankets Hamish gave Kelly's breast a little squeeze. Gently and then more boldly he allowed his fingertips to play with the glorious, sexy little nipple ring. He pulled at it a little. Kelly did not even stir.

Hamish was a doctor and he knew that Kelly was not asleep. She was unconscious. Hamish's head was swimming in the darkness.

The darkness! Hamish suddenly realized how dark it was. They were completely concealed. It was black as coal beneath the thick, heavy, musky blankets.

Slowly, being careful not to move the blanket that covered them, Hamish began to edge his hand down Kelly's body. Down across her ribs, which rose and fell so deeply, and so regularly, across her smooth, flat tummy, until finally slipping it beneath the tiny triangle of her G-string.

Hamish was blind with excitement. The prospect of touching such forbidden fruit had completely intoxicated his already drunken mind. Now Kelly let out a deep snore.

In the bunker they heard Kelly's snore and, noting that the blanket beneath which Hamish and Kelly lay was scarcely moving, they concluded ruefully that the excitement of the night was over.

But the excitement wasn't over: it was reaching fever pitch. Hamish had his hand between Kelly's legs now, he was touching her, discovering her, discovering to his surprise that Kelly had a little secret . . . her labia was pierced. This she had not revealed to the group; her nipple rings she had mentioned often, but this most private piece of jewellery she had kept to herself. Until now.

As Hamish gently explored, a phrase suddenly appeared in his fuddled consciousness, a phrase which he remembered from his class on forensic medicine. The phrase was *digital penetration*.

That's what he was doing now. That was what it would be called if anybody ever knew.

Suddenly Hamish became aware of the appalling risk that he was running. He was committing a *serious crime*. This crazy drunken improvisation, this *sex prank*, was assault. He could go to prison.

Hamish began to remove his hand, but reluctantly, very reluctantly. And as he did so, for a moment he pulled aside the thin, damp gusset of Kelly's G-string and in that moment, in that one blinding moment of lust, he seriously considered taking his straining, aching erection from inside his own underpants and with it entering Kelly's unconscious body.

The thought lasted only for a moment. Drunk as he was, the terrible, life-changing risks that he had already run were clear to him. In fact it was the momentary contemplation of this even greater abuse that truly brought home to Hamish the gravity of what he had already done.

Digital penetration. That was serious enough, for God's sake, leave it. Leave it. Quickly, gently, with the practised and steady hand of a doctor, Hamish rearranged Kelly's gusset in an impression of how he had found it, pushing the warm wet string into the crease of her vagina and then threading it up between her buttocks.

All the while he was deadly careful to avoid moving the heavy blankets and rugs that covered them. It was imperative that the people whom he knew were watching thought that he, like Kelly, had been asleep.

Having removed his hand, Hamish began to pretend to snore a little, not too much, just the occasional little noise to accompany Kelly's deep, drunken slumber.

Reaching down to feel himself, Hamish realized that his pants were wet. Unwittingly he must have ejaculated or at least leaked considerably during his excitement. Had he stained the cushions? Or, worse still, her knickers? If he had, could he pass it off as an embarrassing accident? Tense with fear, he felt about to discover if any evidence of his shame had escaped. It seemed not. He had been lucky.

Kelly was unconscious and he had left no sign.

The blankets were thick and they had scarcely moved.

He was safe. He truly believed that he was safe. But the risk. The *risk* he had run! It made him cold to even think of it.

Now Hamish let his body twitch a little, as if he had been sleeping and had startled himself awake. Kelly did not stir as he pulled back the rug, scratching his head, rubbing his eyes and looking around as if to say 'Where am I?'

Then he feigned a smile and winked at the camera. 'Nearly, eh?' he whispered up at the little red pin light. 'I can't believe it, and it was me that fell asleep first. For God's sake, don't show this on the telly. My mates will never ever let me live it down.'

170

With that he got up from the cushions, put his trousers back on, gently rearranged the rug over Kelly's unconscious form and returned to the party.

He was greeted with a chorus of leery cheers.

'Sorry to disappoint you people,' said Hamish, 'but we both nodded off. I think I went first, if you can believe that.' Hamish desperately hoped that they could.

Then he retreated to his bed and to a very troubled night, as over and over again he asked himself if there was any way that Peeping Tom could have known the terrible thing he had done.

Digital penetration.

Silently in the darkness he thanked God for stopping him before he had done something even worse.

DAY NINETEEN. 7.00 a.m.

Kelly groaned once and she was awake. 'What the f . . . ?' Then she remembered. She was in Copulation Cabin. The Shag Shack, Bonkham Towers, Haveitoff House. Even before the show had started, when Peeping Tom had announced this refinement to the house structure, the press had had about fifty names for it. And now she was in it, in front of the nation. What *must* she look like?

'Don't worry,' she said to the camera that hung directly overhead. 'Nothing happened.'

She reached out from under the rug for her jeans, grinning sheepishly. Like Hamish before her, she felt obliged to address the camera.

'Was I *arseholed* last night . . . ? Still you have it to do, eh?'

Kelly's shapely legs emerged now and she donned her jeans with considerable elegance considering her hangover. 'Bet Hamish feels rotten too.'

171

She smiled once more at the camera, but beneath the smile lay unease. Why did she feel so dirty? Why did she feel such a sad old slapper? Just the hangover, surely? After all, she knew that nothing had happened. *Had* anything happened? Had she let Hamish get further than he should have done?

Definitely not. She was sure about it. She remembered everything clearly, she had snogged him and then she had crashed out. Going exactly as far as she had intended to go.

So why this feeling? Why this unease?

There was something, something about herself that she could not quite define, except that she wondered . . . *Had* anything happened? How could it have? She remembered it all, she always remembered, that was one of her characteristics as a drinker, she *always remembered what she did. What she didn't do.*

And she remembered it now. She had kissed him, and crashed out. And yet . . . She had this feeling that she'd been . . .

Abused? Was that it? Did she feel abused? Surely not. Never.

It was an illusion. It had to be. The Peeping Tom house was the safest place on earth. There were cameras watching *all the time.* Nobody would take such a risk under those circumstances. Least of all Hamish. He was a good bloke. And a doctor.

Someone else? Later? No. It was absolute madness. Even as she sat there thinking, she knew that there were five cameras watching her. Five all-seeing chaperons there to look after her. She smiled up at them once more. 'Yeah, lucky nothing happened, eh? You're my protectors, aren't you, Peeping Tom? My dad don't have to worry, does he? Nothing's going to happen while you're watching.'

*

In the monitoring bunker Geraldine, who had arrived breathlessly in the small hours to be confronted with the night's disappointments, was livid.

'That's not the *idea*, you *stupid* cow!' she shouted at Kelly's face on the monitors. 'That's not the fucking idea at all!'

Kelly emerged from the hut and dived straight into the pool. She did not even take off her jeans. It was a spontaneous action, a sudden need to be *clean*. And another £500 microphone gone.

Behind the glass doors the house slept. Jazz, Moon and Sally had not even bothered to rise from the couch.

Even Hamish had finally fallen asleep, but his dreams were troubled and studded with guilt. And when he awoke it was worse. Did she know? Did anybody know? What had the camera seen? Nothing. If they had, then Peeping Tom would have intervened, otherwise they would have been compounding a felony. Surely, no. Hamish felt certain that from the outside nothing would have seemed amiss or, if it had, then nothing had been said. Discovery could only come from within. Did Kelly remember? How could she? She had been asleep. She had *definitely* been asleep.

DAY NINETEEN. 8.00 a.m.

Kelly did not go to bed. Having changed out of her wet clothes, she made herself a cup of tea and sat down on the green couch, trying to put from her mind the suspicions with which she had awoken.

It was here that Dervla found her an hour later as she made her way to the shower room. Dervla, like the rest of them, had been up late, but she did not want to sleep in, she never slept in, she always wanted to get to the shower room first. She wanted to look in the mirror.

'Good morning, Kelly,' Dervla said. 'Things got a bit close with Hamish there for a bit, didn't they?'

'What do you mean? We were only having a laugh.'

Kelly's defensive tone made Dervla smile. Perhaps something had gone on, after all.

'Well, you were both pretty drunk, weren't you? And he was drooling over you all evening, tongue fair hanging out, so it was. If the poor fella hadn't have nodded off first I think you'd have had to beat him off with a stick.'

'Nodded off first. Is that what he said happened?'

'That's what he said . . . Are you all right, Kelly?'

'Yes! Yes, absolutely fine,' Kelly replied, about twenty times too eagerly, and lapsed into silence.

Dervla headed for the shower room, left Kelly to it. She could hear the camera moving about beyond the glass.

'Morning, Mr Cameraman,' she said as she soaped herself beneath her T-shirt. 'I hope you feel better than I do.' She slid a slippery, sudsy hand inside her knickers.

Beyond the glass the camera's electric motor gave a little hum as it pulled focus. Dervla might have heard it had the shower not been running.

The message was already being written as Dervla approached the basin to brush her teeth. The writer's tone had changed.

'*K is your enemy,*' it said. '*Fucking slut is still ahead. She cockteases the boys to avoid nomination.*' And then the unseen finger underlined the first four words . . .

'*K is your enemy.*'

DAY THIRTY-SIX. 11.50 p.m.

Sergeant Hooper was thinking about ringing for a cab. He had had a long and fruitless day on the murder inquiry followed by a pretty monumental amount of beer and curry and it was time to pull the pin.

It had been a decent night out with the lads, but it was about to go boring on him. It wasn't that he particularly objected to pornography, although he was not a big consumer of it himself, it was just that he had never seen the point of watching it with your mates. As far as he was concerned, the purpose of porn was to stimulate sex, either sex with yourself or sex with a partner. That was what it was for. To be masturbated over or to be watched with a girlfriend as a way of expanding the horizons of your own nocturnal activities. What he was not into doing was sitting bleary-eyed on a friend's couch holding a kebab in one hand, a can of Stella in the other and drooling over it with a bunch of pissed-up off-duty coppers.

'You lot are sad,' he said. 'I'm going to finish me beer and leave you to it. Don't stain the sofa now.'

'You don't understand, Hoops,' said Thorpe, a detective constable from Vice. 'This isn't about sex, it's about quality. We're critics. Porn is an art form and we are aficionados. Do you know that at the blue movie Oscars in Cannes they have an award for best come shot?'

'I find that very hard to swallow,' said Hooper, unwittingly earning himself about five minutes of hysterical drunken laughter.

'Pornography is a legitimate film genre,' insisted Blair. 'Every bit as important as, for instance, the adventure movie or the romantic comedy.'

'Like I said, Blair, you're sad,' Hooper replied. 'Why can't you just be honest? You watch this stuff because it gives you a hard-on. Well, fair play to you, mate, I can understand that, I just don't see why you need company.'

'You're wrong, Hoop, you just don't understand at all. This is a social thing. We discuss the movies, the acting, the groaning, the relative success of a golden shower, whether the dick you see being slipped actually belongs to the bloke you see slipping it. What we have here is a critics' forum. You seem to be under the impression that all porn movies are the same.'

'Aren't they?'

'No more than horror movies are all the same, or westerns. Is *Butch Cassidy* the same as *A Fistful of Dollars*? Of course it isn't. Is *The Exorcist* the same as a Hammer Horror? I don't think so. Well, it's the same with porn. For instance, this one I'm putting on now. This is from the tacky end of the market, real hard-core humping. A proper down-and-dirty porn nasty.'

'Thanks for the warning, mate,' said Hooper, draining his beer. 'I think I'll give it a miss. I'll find a cab on the street.'

'You're mad. You're missing out on a classic of its type, a cultural icon. The *Fuck Orgy* series is a milestone of its genre.'

Hooper was already heading for the door when the little bell rang in his head. 'What series?' he said, turning back.

'*Fuck Orgy*. Legendary no-holds-barred, in-your-face porn. No stupid plot, no lengthy preamble, it does exactly what it says on the tin. *Fuck Orgy* is the name and fuck orgy is most definitely the game. This is number three, an early one, really only for the connoisseurs. The series hadn't found its feet yet. The recognized triumph of the collection is *Fuck Orgy Nine*, which won no less than—'

'Is there a *Fuck Orgy Eleven*?' Hooper enquired urgently.

'There certainly is. They've made fifteen so far. I can get you them all if you like . . . What are you looking so pleased with yourself about?'

Hooper was indeed smiling. He believed that he had

found out what Kelly had whispered to David in the hot tub. The thing that had made him look so concerned.

DAY THIRTY-EIGHT. 9.00 a.m.

As he removed his coat and hat in the cloakroom Chief Inspector Coleridge was surprised to hear cheering and shouting coming from the incident room. He walked in to see a group of his officers, both male and female, clustered round a video monitor from which strange moans and groans were emanating.

'She will *never* get that in her mouth!' a constable was saying.

'It can't be real!' shrieked one of the girls. 'It must be digitally enhanced.'

Now Coleridge realized what sort of video they were watching, and was about to begin the process of disciplining the lot of them when Hooper pressed the freeze-frame button and turned to his boss.

'Ah, sir,' he said. 'Sorry about the noise, but we're all a bit pleased with ourselves this morning. I think we know where Kelly had met David before.'

On the screen a young woman was frozen in the act of performing oral sex on a man who appeared to have been crossed with a donkey. The woman was most definitely not Kelly.

'That's not Kelly,' said Coleridge testily, 'and I don't see David either. What's your point?'

'Look behind the main lady, sir. Look at the two girls reaching round to feel her knock— breasts, the one on the right, she's partially obscured by the man's dick— penis, but it's Kelly all right.'

'Good heavens,' said Coleridge. 'So it is.'

'She said that she'd been a movie extra, sir. Now we know what sort of movie she was an extra in. No wonder she didn't rate it very highly. This film is Kelly's 'Far Corgi In Heaven', by the way.'

'Curious title.'

'Not when you know that what she actually said was *Fuck Orgy Eleven*.'

'Oh, I see. Well, I never . . . And the owner of that . . . um, appendage . . . Is that David?'

'No, sir, that's just one of the numerous disassociated penises that the movie features. This is David.' And Hooper fast-forwarded a little to reveal the entrance of the star of the film: an outrageous bisexual figure in a long purple wig and high-camp make-up, pink lips, glittery eye shadow and a fur and feather posing pouch, which he was in the process of removing.

'David, sir,' said Hooper, 'or Boris Pecker as he is known in the *Fuck Orgy* series. He also appears at times under the names of Olivia Newton Dong, Ivor Whopper and half of a mock Scottish gay-porn comedy double act known as Ben Doon and Phil McCavity.'

'Good heavens.'

'I talked to his agent this morning. He tried to hold out on me at first, but in the end he didn't fancy getting nicked for obstructing the police in their inquiries. Our David has a secret double life as a porn star. Apparently he's much in demand.'

'So that's how he manages to live so fat despite apparently not working.'

'Yes, sir, the high-and-mighty serious actor who would never take on extra work and believes it is better to be unemployed than prostitute your talent.'

'What a nasty little hypocrite our friend is.'

'Exactly. Remember the hard time he gave Kelly that day about getting a different dream because she'd already compromised any hope she had of being an actress?'

'I do indeed.'

'Well, look at him.'

The tape played on and David, or Boris Pecker, barely recognizable in his outrageous make-up, walked among the writhing copulating bodies. He was stark naked save for the purple fright wig and a pink bow on his penis.

'My name is Lord Shag!' he said. 'Bow before the power of my awesome schlong!' At which point all the naked extras stopped cavorting about and prostrated themselves before him.

'I'm amazed that none of the papers has picked up on this,' Coleridge remarked.

'Well, look at him, sir. All the make-up, the wig, the high-camp act. Would you have recognized him if you didn't know?'

'No, I suppose not.'

'And nor would anyone else. Unless of course they recognized some absolutely clear distinguishing feature. Watch Kelly.'

Kelly was very close to David, lying at his feet, her eyes barely two inches from his left ankle.

'To be or not to be, sir,' said Hooper smiling.

DAY THIRTY-EIGHT. 10.15 a.m.

While Hooper and Coleridge contemplated David's starring role in *Far Corgi in Heaven*, Trisha had once more made the trip out to the Peeping Tom complex in order to speak to Bob Fogarty.

'This business about Kelly and Hamish in the shag shack,' she had said to him on the phone before setting off. 'The day after it happened, Kelly went to the confession box, but we've only got the edited version of it here. Do you think you still have the original?'

'Nothing is ever actually wiped from a hard disk,' Fogarty told her, delighted to be able to talk about computers. 'Unless it's specifically recorded over, it just hangs around in the digital shadows for ever. Pressing delete or putting it in the trash simply hides it. If you know how to look you can get most things back on a computer. That's how porno people get caught.'

'Well, try to dig up Kelly's confession from day nineteen for me, then. I'll bring you a bar of chocolate.'

Fogarty had found the footage Trisha wanted and now they were sitting watching it together.

'*It's seven fifteen on day nineteen,*' said Andy the narrator, '*and Kelly comes to the confession box because she is worried about the events of the previous night.*'

'Hullo, Tom.'

'Hullo, Kelly,' said Sam, the soothing voice of Peeping Tom.

'Um, I just wanted to ask you about the party last night and . . . um . . . when I went off to the um . . . the little hut with Hamish.'

'Yes, Kelly,' said Peeping Tom.

'Well, I was a bit drunk, you see . . . Well, actually I was very drunk, and what I wanted to ask was . . . Did anything happen? I mean, I know nothing did, I'm sure nothing did, and I love Hamish, he's great, but, well . . . I can't really remember and, well, I just wanted to know.'

'Why don't you ask Hamish, Kelly?'

'Well, he was drunk too and . . . Well, it's a bit embarrassing, isn't it? Saying to some boy "Did we do anything last night?" '

'Peeping Tom reminds you of the rules, Kelly, that no outside influences or information are allowed to housemates. This includes retrospective discussion of an individual's behaviour. Peeping Tom expects you to *know* what you did.'

'I do know what *I* did, I just want to know what . . .'

Kelly stopped. She sat in silence for a moment, her eyes seeming to plead with the camera.

Trisha looked hard at Kelly. What had she been about to say? Could it have been 'what *he* did'?

'Please, Peeping Tom, I'm not asking for detail, all I'm asking is whether anything happened in the hut.'

There was a pause. 'Peeping Tom will get back to you on this, Kelly.'

'What!' Kelly gasped. 'Just tell me! Surely you don't have to think about it! I mean, you were watching. *Did anything happen?*'

Kelly's voice was shaking. 'Is this a gag? Are you having a laugh? Like when someone crashes out at a party and wakes up with their head shaved and tooth-paste smeared all over them? Come on, I can take a joke. Did I make a fool of myself? Did anyone make a fool of *me*?'

'I myself was not on duty last night, Kelly. We must consult with the relevant editors. You can wait in the box if you wish.'

And so Kelly sat and waited.

Trisha and Fogarty watched her waiting.

'She doesn't look very comfortable, does she?' Fogarty observed. 'She thinks that she got drunk and did the naughty, naughty. She didn't, of course. You've seen the footage. Very boring.'

Finally the voice of Peeping Tom returned. 'Peeping Tom has spoken to the editor concerned, Kelly, and we have decided that it is within order for us to assure you that you and Hamish kissed and cuddled, after which you both fell asleep under the blankets and no further movement was observed.'

Kelly looked relieved. She had just wanted to be reassured. 'Thanks, Peeping Tom,' she said. 'Please don't show this, will you? I mean, I was just being stupid and I wouldn't want to say anything about Hamish because he's great and I love him . . . You won't show it, will you?'

'Peeping Tom can make no promises, Kelly, but will bear your request in mind.'

'Thanks, Peeping Tom.'

'And of course as you've seen, we did show it,' said Fogarty, 'or at least an edited version. Geraldine *loved* it. She said it was *terrific* telly. "A sad, drunken old slapper pleading to be told she didn't make a twat of herself the night before," was how Geraldine put it. Said it happened to her all the time, that she was always bumping into blokes at parties who claimed to have shagged her rigid the previous Tuesday and who she didn't know from a bar of soap.'

'Quite a character, isn't she, your Geraldine?'

'She's a slag. That's all.'

'Strange how Kelly thought that she could say all that on camera and then ask you not to show it.'

'I know, they all do that. Amazing, really. They actually think we'd put their wishes before the prospect of a bit of good telly. They're always creeping into the box and saying, "Oh, please don't show that bit." I mean, if for one moment they stopped to think, they might ask themselves why we spent over two and a half million pounds setting up the house. I don't think it was to provide them with a nice shortcut into showbusiness, do you?'

'No, but then stopping to think isn't really what these people are about, is it? They're too busy stopping to feel.' Trisha realized that for a moment she had sounded exactly like Coleridge. She was twenty-five years old and had started to talk like a man in his fifties, going on seventies. She really would have to get out more.

'It's pathetic, really,' said Fogarty. 'They even thank us when we give them some little treat or other, usually designed to get them to take their clothes off. It's Stockholm Syndrome, you know.'

'When captives fall in love with their tormentors.'

'Exactly, and begin to rely on them, to *trust them*. I mean, how can that girl not have realized that as far as we're concerned she's a prop, an extra, to be used, abused and utterly misrepresented as we see fit?'

'I suppose it is pretty obvious, now you come to mention it. But I suppose it's not just the housemates who fall for it. The public believes in you too.'

'The public! The public, they're worse than us! At least we get paid to bully these people. The public do it for fun. They know they're watching ants getting burnt under a magnifying glass, but they don't care. They don't care what we do to them, how we prod them, as long we get a reaction.' Fogarty stared angrily at the screen upon which Kelly was still frozen. 'The people in that house think that they're in a cocoon. In fact it's a redoubt. They're surrounded by enemies.'

DAY TWENTY. 6.15 p.m.

'*It's two-fifteen,*' said Andy the narrator, '*and after a lunch of rice, chicken and vegetables cooked by Jazz, Sally asks Kelly to help her dye her hair.*'

Geraldine stared at the screen showing various camera angles of Kelly applying shampoo to Sally's mohican haircut prior to dyeing it.

'A new low,' mused Geraldine. 'I thought Layla's cheese was our nadir but I reckon watching some great lump of a bird getting her hair washed has got to plumb new and unique depths in fucking awful telly, don't you? Fuck me, in the early days of TV they used to stick a potter's wheel on between the programmes. Now the potter's wheel *is* the fucking programme.'

Fogarty gritted his teeth and continued with his tasks. 'What shot do you want, Geraldine?' he enquired. 'Kelly's hands on her head? Or a wide?'

'Put Sally up on the main monitor – the close-up of

her face, through the mirror. Run the whole sequence, right from where she bends down over the basin.'

Fogarty punched his buttons while Geraldine continued her reverie. 'Tough time for us, this. Eviction night tomorrow but no eviction. That cunt Woggle has deprived us of our weekly climax. We are in a lull. A low point, a stall. The wind is slipping out of our fucking sails, Bob. The Viagra pot is empty and our televisual dick is limp.'

Andy the narrator emerged from the voiceover recording booth to get a cup of herbal tea. 'Perhaps I could tell them what everyone had for pudding,' he suggested. 'David made a soufflé, but it didn't really rise. That's quite interesting, isn't it?'

'Get back in your box,' said Geraldine.

'But Gazzer didn't finish his, and I think David was a little bit offended.'

'I *said*, get back in your fucking box!'

Andy retreated with his camomile.

'Always trying to grab himself a few more lines, that bastard. I've told him, if he does one more beer ad voiceover he's fucking out. I'm going to get a bird to do it next time, anyway . . . Stop it there!'

Fogarty froze the image of Sally's face. Dribbles of shampoo foam ran down her temples; Kelly's fingertips could be made out at the top of the screen. Sally's hand was at her mouth, frozen in the moment of inserting a segment of tangerine into it.

'Run it on, but mute the sound,' Geraldine instructed.

They studied Sally's silent countenance for a few moments, as her jaw moved about, her lips pursed and her cheeks became slightly sucked in, then the lips parted a fraction and the tip of her tongue licked them.

'Very nice,' Geraldine observed. 'I love a bit of muted mastication, the editor's friend. Right, chop the tangerine off the front and run that sequence mute under Kelly's dialogue about finding head massage sensual.'

Fogarty gulped before replying. It really seemed as if this time he had had enough. 'But . . . but, Kelly made that comment to David while they were having the rice, chicken and vegetables that Jazz cooked. If we drop it over Sally's face it will look as if . . . as if . . .'

'Ye-es?' Geraldine enquired.

'As if she's getting a thrill out of massaging Sally's head!'

'While Sally,' Geraldine replied, 'with her grinding jaw and tense cheeks, sucky-sucky lips and little wet tongue tip, is positively creaming her gusset, and *we*, my darling, have got what can only be described as a half-decent lezzo moment.'

The silence in the monitoring bunker spoke loudly of the unease felt by Geraldine's employees. Geraldine just grinned, a huge, triumphant grin, like a happy snarl.

'We are in a ratings trough, you cunts!' she shouted. 'I'm paying your wages here!'

DAY TWENTY-TWO. 6.10 p.m.

'Such a shame there was no eviction last night,' the young woman was saying. 'The last one was terrific, although I was sorry to see Layla go. I mean I know she was pretty pretentious, but I respected the integrity of her vegetarianism.'

'Darling she was a *poseur*, a complete act, I *hated* her,' said the man, a rather fey individual of about thirty.

Chief Inspector Coleridge had been listening to them chat for about five minutes, and did not have the faintest idea who or what they were talking about. They seemed to be discussing a group of people that they knew well, friends perhaps, and yet they appeared to hold them in something approaching complete contempt.

'What do *you* think about Layla going, then?' said the man, whose name was Glyn, turning finally to Coleridge.

'I'm afraid I don't know her,' Coleridge answered. 'Is she a friend of yours?'

'My God,' said Glyn. 'You mean you don't know who Layla is? You don't watch *House Arrest*?'

'Guilty on both counts,' said Coleridge, attempting a little joke. He knew that they knew he was a policeman.

'You simply do not know what you're missing,' said Glyn.

'And long may that remain the case,' Coleridge replied.

It was an audition evening at Coleridge's local amateur dramatic society. Coleridge had been a member of the society for over twenty-five years and had attended thirty-three such evenings previous to this one, but he had never yet been offered a lead. The nearest he had got was Colonel Pickering in *My Fair Lady*, and that was only because the first choice had moved to Basingstoke and the second choice got adult chicken pox. The next production of the society was to be *Macbeth*, and Coleridge really and truly wanted to play the killer king.

Macbeth was his favourite play of all time, full of passion and murder and revenge, but one glance at Glyn's patronizing, supercilious expression told Coleridge he has as much chance of playing Macbeth as he had of presenting Britain's next entry for the Eurovision song contest. He would be lucky to score a Macduff.

'Yes, I am intending a very *young* production,' Glyn drawled. 'One that will bring *young people* back into the theatre. Have you seen Baz Luhrman's *Romeo and Juliet*?'

Coleridge had not.

'That is my inspiration. I want a contemporary, *sexy Macbeth*. Don't you agree?'

Well, of course Coleridge did not agree. Glyn's production would run for three nights at the village hall and would play principally to an audience that wanted armour and swords and big black cloaks.

'Shall I read, then?' he asked 'I've prepared a speech.'

'Heavens, no!' Glyn said. 'This isn't the audition, it's a *prelim chat*. A chance for *you* to influence *me*, give me your feedback.'

There was a long pause while Coleridge tried to think of something to say. The table that divided him from Glyn and Val was a chasm. 'So when is the actual audition?' he finally said.

'This time next week.'

'Right, well, I'll come back then, shall I?'

'Do,' said Glyn.

DAY TWENTY-THREE. 3.00 p.m.

Sally was not yet satisfied with her new bright-red mohican hair.

'I just want a tuft,' she said, 'like a shaving brush.'

'Well, just you leave it at that,' Moon said. '*I'm* the bald bird in this house. Can't have two of us, we'll look like a fookin' game of billiards.'

Sally did not reply. She rarely replied to anything Moon said, or even looked at her.

Dervla was relieved that Kelly elected to administer the haircut in the living area. It had been agony for her on the Saturday when Sally had done the dyeing in the bathroom. Dervla always rubbed out her messages, of course, and they were only condensation anyway, but seeing Sally with her face so close to the very place where they appeared had been most disconcerting. As

Kelly washed Sally's hair and the mirror steamed up, Dervla had been gripped with an irrational fear that a message might suddenly appear, there and then, right in front of Sally's eyes. She knew that this was unlikely, unless of course the man had decided to start writing to Sally.

'All done,' said Kelly.

'I like it,' Sally replied, having inspected the little red tuft which was all that remained of her hair. 'When I get out I'm going to have my head tattooed.'

'What will you get done, then?' Kelly asked.

'I thought perhaps my star sign. It's the ram, except obviously I'm not having a male animal on my head, so I'd have to have a ewe.'

'Well, that doesn't sound very empowering, Sally,' Dervla observed.

'Be a fucking lioness, Sal,' said Jazz. 'I mean, let's face it, them pictures they make out of the stars are just total bullshit anyway. Three bloody dots and they draw a bull round it, or a centaur. It's ridiculous. If you actually do join the dots all you get is a splodge, like an amoeba or a puddle. Born under the sign of the puddle.'

'Actually, Jazz,' said Moon, 'it's not just about the fookin' shapes, is it? It's about the personality, the characteristics of people born under certain signs.'

'It's bollocks,' Jazz insisted. 'People say ... Oh, Virgo, dead brave, or Capricorn, really clever and introspective. Where are the star signs for all the stupid boring people, eh? I mean, the world's full of them. Don't they get to be represented celestially? Taurus – we're really dull and don't get our rounds in ... I could tell you who was a Libra, they're very flatulent.'

'You know fook all, you do, Jazz,' said Moon. 'Do you know that?'

188

'So what's a sweatbox when it's at home?' asked Gazzer.

'It says here that it's an ancient Native American tradition,' Hamish replied.

'Native American?'

'Red Indian to you, I imagine,' said Dervla.

The housemates had been given their instructions for the weekly task, and so far Gazzer was not impressed.

'So what the fahk is it?'

'Exactly what it sounds like,' said Hamish, who was reading the instructions. 'A box in which you sweat. From what it says here it sounds pretty similar to a sauna, except a bit more friendly. It says this is a historical task because they were used by Native American fighting men.'

'And women,' Sally interjected. 'Native American fighting women.'

'Were there any?' asked Kelly. 'I thought they were just squaws.'

'That's because history is written by men,' Sally assured her. 'Women warriors have been denied their place in the chronicles of war, just like women artists and scientists never got credit for doing an amazing amount of art and science which their husbands took credit for.'

'Wow, I had no idea,' said Kelly, genuinely surprised.

'Well, think about it, Kelly. History . . . *his* story.'

'Oh, yeah.'

'Can we get back to this fahkin' sweatbox?' Gazzer protested. 'What are we supposed to do about it?'

Hamish applied himself once more to Peeping Tom's note. 'Well, we have to build one, for a start. They'll give us instructions and all the stuff we need, and when we've built it we have to use it.'

'Use it?' Dervla enquired.

'Well, apparently after these Native Americans had had a fight, or a sports day or whatever, they'd wait till it got dark and then get into a hot confined space all squeezed up tight together and sweat.'

'It sounds totally homoerotic,' said Sally. 'Most military rituals are, if you didn't know.'

DAY THIRTY-EIGHT. 4.45 p.m.

'Homoerotic, oh, for heaven's sake,' Coleridge snapped.

'Sounds reasonable to me,' Hooper replied.

'Yes, of course it does, sergeant! So easy to say, so impossible to contradict. Why is it that everybody these days insists on presuming a sexual motive for absolutely everything? Military rituals homoerotic? *Why*, for heaven's sake!'

Was Freud to blame? Coleridge rather thought that he might be, or else Jung, or perhaps some imbecile from the sixties like Andy Warhol.

'Whatever you say, sir,' said Hooper.

Coleridge let it go, as he let so much go that bothered him these days. At the end of the day, as the inmates of the house were so fond of saying, it wasn't worth it.

'I still cannot quite believe that these people actually agreed to do this task. I mean, four hours in that thing, naked.'

'Well, Dervla tried to object, didn't she?'

'Ah, yes,' Coleridge thought, Dervla objected, the one he secretly rather liked. For a moment he felt glad that she had objected. Then inwardly he cursed himself. He had absolutely no business liking any of them, or being glad about what they did or didn't do.

The sweatbox, which the housemates had been instructed to build in the boys' bedroom, was half finished. The false floor had been laid, underneath which the heating elements were to be installed; the support poles for the roof were in position and work had begun on stitching the thick plastic for the walls. The construction so far looked rather small and uninviting, with very little prospect of its looking any better when it was finished.

'I am so not sitting naked in that thing with a lot of nude boys,' Dervla said.

'For four hours, they say,' said Jazz.

'No way,' Dervla repeated.

'Why not? None of the rest of us fookin' object,' said Moon.

'What's that got to do with anything?' Dervla asked.

'Well, what's so special about you is what I'm saying? Anyway, don't you want to look sexy on the telly?'

Of course Dervla wanted to look sexy on the telly, or else she would never have applied to be on the telly in the first place, but she also understood that real allure depended on retaining a bit of mystery. She had a good body, but she knew that like all bodies it was even better when left to the imagination. Besides which, she had her misty green eyes and sparkling smile to rely on; she did not need to go flashing her knockers about the place.

Dervla went to the confession box and asked to be allowed to perform the task in her bathing suit. 'It's high cut on the thigh and a lovely pattern,' she said.

The answer when it came was broadcast to the whole house.

'This is Peeping Tom,' said a much sterner voice than usual, a voice that normally did ads for BMWs and aftershave. 'The traditional Native American sweatbox experience was undertaken naked, and this is the manner in which Peeping Tom requires the task to be performed. As with any of the group tasks, all housemates must comply with the rules and if any single housemate fails to do so then the whole group will be deemed to have failed and will therefore lose a percentage of their food and drink for the following week.'

It was jaw-dropping cynical and Geraldine knew it, which was why she had no intention of allowing this outrageous instruction to be aired publicly. Clearly she was blackmailing Dervla into stripping, but the public were to be given the illusion that the housemates one and all simply could not wait to get their clothes off.

'I cannot believe they're trying to get away with this,' Dervla fumed.

Then Sally spoke up. 'Actually, Dervla, I really think that we should do this, because I am worried that we might come across as racist if it looks like we think we're too good for a legitimate ethnic custom, particularly one with such obviously homoerotic overtones.'

Sally was pleased that Peeping Tom had provided her with an opportunity to hold forth on the one area about which she felt truly passionate.

'As a lesbian woman of mixed race I know what it's like to have my customs and rituals held in fear and contempt by the majority community. Peeping Tom is offering us the opportunity to experience the bonding rituals of an oppressed indigenous group. I think we should try to learn from it.'

DAY TWENTY-SIX. 9.15 a.m.

Bob Fogarty waited until the following morning's production meeting to make his complaint. He wanted his objections to be noted publicly. It was difficult for him to find his moment because Geraldine was roaring with laughter so much as she recalled Sally's unlikely take on the weekly task.

'All I'm trying to do is persuade them to feel each other up and it turns out I'm a champion of minority rights. Anyway, all ethnic and sexual bollocks aside, Dervla will have to get 'em out for the lads or nobody gets a drink next week.'

Fogarty had to stand up to get her attention. 'Geraldine, we are coercing this girl into taking her clothes off against her wishes.'

'Yes, Bob, we all know that. Why are you standing up?'

'Because I think it's morally corrupt.'

'Oh, do fuck off.'

Fogarty had finally had enough. 'Ms Hennessy, I cannot prevent you from using profanity to punctuate your sentences, but I am a grown man and a highly qualified employee and I am entitled to insist that you do not use such language towards me or those who work under me.'

'No, you're fucking not, you cunt. Now sit down or fuck off.'

Fogarty did neither. He just stood there, shaking.

'You think you can do me for constructive dismissal?' Geraldine asked. 'For swearing? Grow up, Bob. Even this cunt of a country isn't that pathetic yet. If you walk out it's a straight resignation and you get bugger-all. Now, are you staying or are you going?'

Fogarty sat down.

'Good. You may be an arsehole, but you're a talented arsehole and I don't want to lose you. And besides which,' Geraldine went on, 'Dervla is free to leave that house at any time. She could have walked out there and then, and she could walk out now. But she hasn't done, has she? And why? Because she wants to be on telly, that's why, and at the end of the day, if she has to take her clothes off to do it, then you can bet your last quid she'll allow herself to be persuaded.'

Bob stared down into his coffee. He looked like a man who needed a bar of chocoate. 'We're corrupting her,' he mumbled.

'What?' Geraldine barked.

'I said, we're corrupting her,' but this time Fogarty said it even more quietly.

'*Look!*' shouted Geraldine. 'I'm not asking the snooty stuck-up cow to show us her bits full on, am I? There are guidelines, you know. We *do* have a Broadcasting Standards Commission in this country. The polythene walls of that box are going to be translucent and the lights will be off. The idea is to make it so dark that the anonymity will persuade some of them to have it off, which I can assure you will be a lot more interesting than precious little Dervla's sacred little knockers. I want it to be literally dark as hell in that box.'

Eviction

DAY TWENTY-EIGHT. 6.00 p.m.

Coleridge pushed the record button on his audio tape-machine.

'Witness statement. Geraldine Hennessy,' he said before sliding the little microphone across the desk and setting it down in front of Geraldine.

'Bit of a reversal for you, eh, Miss Hennessy?'

'Ms.'

'I'm sorry, Ms Hennessy. Bit of a reversal, you being the one getting recorded, I mean.'

Geraldine merely smiled.

'So tell me about the night it happened.'

'You know as much as I do. The whole thing was recorded from start to finish. You've seen the tapes.'

'I want to hear it from you. From Peeping Tom herself. Let's start with the sweatbox. Why on earth did you ask them to do it?'

'It was a task,' Geraldine replied. 'Each week we set the inmates challenges to perform to keep them busy and see how they react when working together. They get to pledge a part of their weekly booze and food budgets against their chances of success. We gave them wood and tools and polythene, a couple of heating units and all the instructions, and as it happens they did a bloody good job.'

'You told them how to make it?'

'Of course we did, or how else would they have done it? If I gave you some wood and plastic and told you to construct a Native American sweatbox to seat eight, could you do it?'

'Probably not, I suppose.'

'Well, nor could this lot either. We gave them the designs and the materials and told them exactly where to put it to suit our hot-head camera. This they did and it took them three days. Then on the Saturday evening, as the sun went down, we gave them a shitload of booze and told them to get on with it.'

'Why did you let them get drunk?'

'Well, it's obvious, isn't it? To try to get them to have sex. The show had been going for three weeks and apart from a near miss with Kelly and Hamish in Bonkham Towers we'd had scarcely a hint of any nooky at all. I wanted to get them going a bit.'

'Well,' said Coleridge pointedly, 'you certainly did that.'

'It wasn't my fucking fault somebody got killed, inspector.'

'Wasn't it?'

'No, it fucking wasn't.'

Coleridge absolutely hated to hear a woman swear, but he knew he could not say anything about it.

'Look, I'm not a social worker, inspector. I make telly!' Geraldine continued. 'And I'm sorry if it offends you, but telly has to be sexy!'

She said it as if she was talking to a senile octogenarian. Coleridge was in fact only two years older than she was, but the gap between them was chasmic. She had embraced and joined each new generation as it rose up to greet her, remaining, in her own eyes at least, forever young. He, on the other hand, had been born old.

'Why did it have to be so dark?'

'I thought it would loosen up their inhibitions if

they couldn't see each other. I wanted them all completely anonymous.'

'Well, you certainly succeeded in that, Ms Hennessy, which is the principal factor inhibiting my investigation.'

'Look! I didn't know anybody was going to fuck off and murder someone, did I? Forgive me, but in my many years of making television it has never crossed my mind to arrange my work on the offchance that you coppers might want to look at it later in the light of a homicide investigation.'

It was a fair point. Coleridge shrugged and gestured Geraldine to continue.

DAY TWENTY-SEVEN. 8.00 p.m.

The sweatbox stood waiting in the boys' bedroom, but for the time being the housemates remained in the living area, trying to get drunk enough to take the plunge.

'Well, we gotta do four hours in there,' Gazzer said, 'and if we don't want to get caught all nudey when the sun comes up we'll have to get started by one at the latest.'

'I want to get it over with long before that,' said Dervla, gulping at her strong cider.

'Well, don't get too pissed, Dervo,' Jazz warned. 'I don't think the confines of a sweatbox are a very clever environment to honk up in.'

Peeping Tom had given them all the luxuries that they needed to get in an appropriately silly mood: plenty of booze, of course, also party hats, party food and sex toys.

'What are they, then?' Garry asked.

'Love balls,' Moon replied. 'You stick 'em up your twat.'

'Blimey.'

'I've got a pair at home. They're great, keep you permanently aroused, except they can be dead embarrassing. I don't wear knickers much, you see, and I were wearing me love balls to go shopping, right, and they fell out in the supermarket and went bouncing up the fookin' veggies isle. This old bloke picked 'em up for me, no fookin' idea at all. "Excuse me, dear, I think you dropped these." '

Jazz fished in the party box and brought out a sort of plastic tube. 'What's this, then?' he asked.

'Knob massager,' said Moon, who seemed to be something of an expert on the subject. 'You stick your knob in it and it whacks you off.'

'Ah well, you see, me, I'm a traditionalist,' said Jazz. 'Why get a machine to do something that is best done by hand?'

Everybody was getting quite deliberately drunk, slowly convincing themselves that they were at a party. That they were amongst friends instead of amongst rivals and competitors.

'Quite frankly,' said Moon, 'at the end of the day, ninety-five per cent of sex toys never get near a knob or a vag. People buy 'em for a laugh, to give as embarrassing birthday presents and whatever. It's like "What are we going to get Sue for her eighteenth?" "Oh, I know, let's get her a fookin' great big dildo with a swivel end. That'll be a laugh when she opens it in front of her gran." Nobody actually *uses* this shite. Quite frankly, I've got a pair of nipple clamps at home and I use them for keeping my bills together.'

Along with the sex toys, Peeping Tom had supplied a coolbox full of ice creams. The modern variety of expensive iced versions of well known chocolate bars. They all dipped in excitedly.

'I remember when there was ice creams and there was KitKats,' Jazz observed, 'and the idea of the two trespassing on each other's territory was simply not an issue, it just was *not* going to happen. Unimaginable. Kids today reckon it's the norm.'

'Mars Bars started the rot,' Dervla observed. 'I'm old enough to remember the excitement, it seemed such an incredible idea at the time, a *Mars Bar* made of ice cream. Stupid. Now they do ice cream Opal Fruits.'

'Starbursts, they're called now,' said Jazz with mock contempt. 'Get with the plot, girl. You probably still think a Snickers is a Marathon. It's fucking globalization gone mad, that is. We have to call our sweets the same as the Yanks do. There ought to be protests.'

'And what was wrong with Mivvis and Rockets anyway, I'd like to know?' Dervla added. 'We enjoyed them.'

'We are the last generation,' said Jazz solemnly, 'that will have known the joys of truly crap lollies. No kid will ever again be asked to suck the red and orange stuff out of a block of ice and be told that it's a treat.'

In the monitoring bunker Geraldine was already getting frustrated. When she had supplied them with ice cream it had been in the hope that they might eat it off each other's bodies, not talk about it.

'You're a philosopher, Jazz,' said Dervla.

'What's that, then? Irish for wanker?' asked Gazzer.

'It means,' said David, 'that there are more things in heaven and earth than you could ever dream of.'

'You don't have any idea what I dream about, Dave mate.'

'Naked women?'

'Fuck me! You're fucking clairvoyant, you are. You've got a gift.'

But Jazz was not being diverted so easily. He had struck on a subject which he knew his book on comedy would recognize as the stuff of top routines.

'It's like these days everything is pretending to be

something it's not, nothing is happy as it is. Take Smarties, not happy any more, now you have to have little mini Smarties and great big fuck-off Smarties.'

'And of course fookin' Smarties original,' Moon chipped in.

'Well, that is, of course, your Smarties Classic like with toothbrushes, *David*. Everything has to pretend it's something else, and it won't stop, you know, not now it's started. Everything we love will change, get repackaged and flogged back to us as an improvement . . . Fish-fingers. I'll bet you one day they start doing mini-fish-fingers, giant fish-fingers . . .'

'Ice cream fish-fingers,' said Dervla.

'That's coming, I swear that's coming,' Jazz replied.

Dervla was laughing now. 'It's salad dressing, but in a bar!'

'You got it, girl!'

'All your favourite breakfast cereals, in a series of bite-sized soups!'

'Yeah, all right, all right.'

Jazz was taken aback to have had the comic baton wrested from his hand so easily. He was supposed to be on the roll, not Dervla. She was a trauma therapist.

In the monitoring bunker Geraldine's impatience was growing. 'Come on!' she shouted. 'Get your kit off and get in the sweatbox, you cunts!'

Perhaps they heard her in the house, or else maybe they had got drunk enough by this time, but for whatever reason the conversation now turned to the forthcoming task.

'So how are we going to do it, then?' Sally asked. 'I'm not just getting undressed in here with all the lights on.'

'Do it in the bedroom, then,' said David. 'It's dark in there.'

'No way,' said Dervla. 'They have infrared cameras or whatever. We'd look like flipping porn stars, so we would.'

'Very nice,' Gazzer observed.

Kelly flicked a look across at David, just a look, and a little smile. If he noticed he did not return it.

'I don't give a fook, me,' said Moon pulling off her shoes.

'Well, I do,' said Sally. 'Just because the sweatbox represents a legitimate ethnic experience doesn't mean we have to do a striptease.'

'Why not?' said Moon. 'That's the only reason they're making us fookin' do it, ain't it?'

'I don't know, Moon,' said Hamish. 'They've given us sheets to cover up with if we have to go to the loo.'

'Ah, but that's just for show, a mask to hide their true agenda,' Dervla said.

'Exactly,' Moon concurred. 'Which is for us to show the lot and if possible have it off as well.'

'You can be so cynical, you,' said Hamish.

'Hamish,' Moon insisted. 'They've supplied us with fookin' chocolate-flavoured *condoms*, for God's sake.'

'I've got nothing to hide.' Garry laughed. 'If anybody wants to see my knob they only have to ask. Quite frankly, sometimes they don't even have to ask.'

'Yes, well, I do not have any desire to see your penis,' said David. 'We have to do this task or we get half-rations next week, but that's no reason for us to feel obliged to allow our bodies to be exploited.'

'Fookin' hell, David,' Moon sneered. 'You wander round the house in your little pose pouch the whole time exploiting what a great bod you've got, which I'll admit you have, but you still look a right ponce because you're obviously so fookin' pleased with it, and now you won't even get your kecks off for this week's task.'

'A man in his underwear, Moon,' David responded,

203

'is no more naked than a man in his swimming costume.'

Geraldine crushed her styrofoam cup in her hands. 'Oh, for fuck's *sake*, you precious bunch of *cunts*. Get your KIT OFF.'

Eventually the task had to be begun, and so they all made their way into the darkened bedroom and began to strip off with varying degrees of bravado. Dervla was easily the most cautious, keeping her undies on right up to the point of entering the sweatbox, before throwing them off in a flurry and scuttling inside.

Geraldine was fairly satisfied. 'I think we got one of her tits, didn't we?' she asked. 'Certainly her bum. We'll stick that in the trailers. The whole nation's been waiting to see a bit more of sweet pure little Dervo.'

Inside the sweatbox the darkness was absolute. Dark as the grave, as the newspapers were to remark the following morning.

And it was hot. Very, very hot.

Following the instructions given, Jazz and Gazzer had laid out a false floor made of scented pine wood, underneath which were electric heating units, which had been on all afternoon.

'Ooh, it smells dead lovely,' Moon remarked.

'Ow! This floor's burning my bum,' squealed Kelly.

'You'll get used to it,' Dervla assured her. 'Give yourself a minute to acclimatize.'

The floor was indeed hot on their bare flesh, but not unbearably so. In fact it was rather pleasant, exciting almost.

'Sweet Mother of Jesus,' Dervla's voice continued in the darkness. 'Now I know why they call it a sweatbox.' She had been inside for only a few moments, but already she could feel the perspiration streaming down her skin. Her forehead and armpits were instantly dripping wet.

'Well, it's giving *me* a sweaty box, that's for sure!' Moon shrieked, and they all laughed with her. 'Oh, my God! Who's arse was that!'

'Mine!' three or four voices answered simultaneously.

They could all feel their flesh gliding across each other's but the darkness was total. Nobody knew whose bottom belonged to whom.

'Four hours,' said Hamish. 'We need another drink.'

Somehow, and with much groping about, plastic bottles containing warm Bacardi and Coke (mainly Bacardi) were handed round.

'I could get to like this,' Garry remarked, and to varying degrees he spoke for them all.

In every sense, the party was warming up.

DAY TWENTY-NINE. 8.00 p.m.

Having spent the day reviewing the footage from the very first day in the house, Coleridge and Hooper turned once more to the tape of the night of the murder. The same images that Geraldine, the Peeping Tom production team and 47,000 Internet subscribers had watched live less than forty-eight hours before. Those same strange, fuzzy, bluish-grey pictures that the night-sight cameras had transmitted from the boys' bedroom. A bedroom that seemed innocent and empty, entirely normal, save for the weird-looking plastic box in the middle of the room, a box which they knew contained eight drunk, naked people, the only evidence of whom were the strange bulges that seemed to undulate against the polythene walls from time to time. It was an eerie and depressing sight for the two policemen, knowing as they did that one of those living bulges was shortly to die.

'He could have done it inside the box,' said Hooper thoughtfully. 'Why didn't he do it in the box?'

'Or she,' Coleridge reminded Hooper, 'or she. We refer to the murderer as a he for convenience's sake but we must never ever forget that it could be a woman.'

'Yes, all right, sir, I know. But what I'm saying is that nobody would have known, if he or she had done it inside the box, if a hand had reached out in the darkness holding a small knife, which the murderer could easily have sneaked in with him. It would have been relatively simple to just slit a throat in the dark and wait until people smelt blood, or felt it. By the time anybody realized that the warm stuff flowing all over them wasn't sweat they'd all have been drenched in it. Maybe that's what he planned.'

'There was no small knife in the box when we searched it, or in the room.'

'Well, sir, if he'd suddenly decided to follow the victim to the toilet instead, he could have put it back in the kitchen drawer when he got the bigger one.'

'I don't think so, sergeant. How could he have been sure of his kill in that darkness? Whether he'd stabbed the right person and whether he'd finished the job properly? Chances are it would have been a terrible mess. He would have just cut off a nose or something, or somebody else's nose, or his own fingers.'

'Well, he had to do it some time. How would he have known that a better chance was going to emerge?'

'He didn't know, but he was waiting. If the chance hadn't come, my guess is that he would have carried on waiting.'

'For how long? Until his prey got voted out and escaped him altogether?'

'Ah, but he or she knew that the prey hadn't been nominated that week, giving at least eight days' grace.'

'All I'm saying,' the sergeant insisted, 'is that if I was desperate to kill somebody in that house, I would have reckoned a crowded, darkened sweatbox, inside which everybody was drunk, to be about the best shot I was going to get.'

'Well, the drinking is a factor, surely. I suppose he knew that people would have to start going to the lavatory at some point.'

'He couldn't be certain.'

'No, he couldn't be certain of anything. However and whenever he chose to do it, this was always going to be a risky sort of murder.'

Coleridge looked at the time code on the video. They had pressed pause at 11.38. He knew that when he pressed play the code would tick over to 11.39 and Kelly Simpson would emerge from the sweatbox to take what would be the final brief walk of her life.

Kelly Simpson, so young, so excited, so certain of her splendid fun-filled destiny, gone into that stupid, pointless house to die. In Coleridge's mind there appeared the image of how she had been on that very first day in the house, jumping into the pool with excitement, shrieking about how 'wicked' it all was. And wicked was without doubt the word, because the time was now 11.38 on Kelly's last day in the house, and in a few more minutes she would be in a pool once more. A pool of her own blood.

'The point I'm making, sir,' Hooper pressed on, 'is that if he was planning to kill her, which we have presumed he was, then he must have been considering the possibility of doing her inside the sweatbox. He could not have known for certain that she would go to the loo, or that he would be able to conceal his identity when he followed her into it.'

Coleridge stared at the screen for a long time. Difficult to believe that there were eight people in that foolish little plastic construction. 'Unless the catalyst for the murder did not occur until after they had entered the box,' he mused. 'Unless whatever it was that made the killer want Kelly dead did not occur until moments before she ran to the toilet, and in fact he ran after her in an act of spontaneous fury.'

'Or fear,' Hooper added.

'Yes, that's right. Or fear. After all, since none of these people knew each other before they entered the house . . .'

'Or so we have been told, sir.' This remark came from Trisha, who had just returned with a round of teas.

'Yes, that's right, constable, so we have been told,' said Coleridge. 'We have been working on the theory that the catalyst that provoked the murder must have taken place at some point between the housemates entering the house and their entering the box. But of course something terrible might have happened *once they were inside* the box.'

'Well, it would certainly explain why the people at Peeping Tom have no idea about a motive,' Trisha conceded, sugaring Coleridge's tea for him.

'It would indeed. And this situation was after all developing into an orgy.'

Coleridge pronounced the word 'orgy' with a hard 'g'. Hooper wondered whether he did it deliberately and rather thought he must.

'Quite a volatile environment, I should imagine. An orgy,' Coleridge continued.

'Are you suggesting a rape, sir?' said Trisha. 'That someone forced themselves upon Kelly and then killed her in order to avoid the consequences?'

'It wouldn't be the first time a rape turned into a murder.'

'But the others? We've talked to them all. They didn't notice anything. I mean, you simply could not keep a thing like that quiet.'

'Couldn't you? In that environment? Besides, consider

the possibility that they were all conspirators. That they were all covering up for the one who actually did the dirty work.'

'You mean perhaps they *all* wanted Kelly dead?'

'Perhaps,' said Coleridge. 'It would certainly explain the startling lack of evidence in any of their statements.'

'You think that perhaps she had something on them, that she knew something about them all?'

Coleridge accepted his mug of tea from Trisha without looking at her. Instead he continued to stare at the box on the screen. He was imagining something very ugly. 'Or because they'd all done something to her,' he said finally.

'Some kind of group abuse?' Hooper said. 'A gangbang?'

Coleridge wanted to tell Hooper to use some other more suitable term, but he knew that there wasn't one. For the umpteenth time he pressed play and 11.38 ticked over to 11.39. Kelly emerged from the sweatbox.

DAY TWENTY-SEVEN. 11.39 p.m.

Geraldine was thrilled. Thrilled and very excited.

When asked to describe the scene later to the police, everyone who had been in the box with her that night commented on just how happy had been her mood. Almost hysterical, one or two of them had said.

And well Geraldine might have been happy. It was clear to them all as they watched the grey, translucent plastic box almost begin to *throb* that her plan was working and that real sex truly was on the cards. They had been in the box for just half the allotted four hours, and there had clearly already been some quite specific erotic activity, and it seemed certain that there would be more.

The shouts and shrieks and smart-alec comments of the first rush of embarrassed excitement had died down, and now only murmurs and whispers could be heard. The people inside the box were clearly very drunk and very disoriented after their two hours of sweating and writhing in the complete darkness of their little plastic hut.

Clearly anything might happen. And of course it did.

It was about ten minutes after Jazz's voice had been heard suggesting a touching game in which people were to attempt to identify each other in the darkness that the plastic flaps at the entrance to the sweatbox parted, and Kelly emerged.

'Aye aye,' said Geraldine. 'Piss break.'

Bob Fogarty winced and concentrated on his monitors.

On the screens Kelly straightened herself up. Her naked body was gleaming and dripping with sweat.

'Very nice,' whispered Geraldine, tense with excitement. 'Very, very, *very* nice.'

Kelly seemed to be in a hurry. She did not bother to take up one of the great long sheets that Peeping Tom had thoughtfully provided for such eventualities, but simply ran naked out of the boys' bedroom, across the living area and into the sole lavatory, which served the needs of the whole group.

'Beautiful!' Geraldine exclaimed. 'I never thought they'd use the cover-up sheets once they got amped up. Except maybe that snotty cow Dervla. Moon was right, I only put them there to make it look like I'm not a total perv, which of course I am, along with the rest of the population, I might add.'

Kelly's run had certainly been thrilling for the watchers in the monitoring bunker. The show's first moment of absolute, in-focus, full-frontal nudity.

'Minge and all,' as Geraldine delightedly put it. 'Now we won't have to keep running that same tired old shot of her tit coming out in the pool.'

'Superb image quality, too,' commented Fogarty.

'The body or the pictures?' Geraldine enquired.

'I'm a techy, I don't do aesthetics,' Fogarty replied with angry embarrassment.

He was right about the quality, though. This was no grainy-blue sneaky night-shot like the ones they occasionally caught in the bedrooms. Kelly had run right through the living area, which was permanently neon lit, and although the lights had been dimmed to avoid light intruding into the boys' bedroom when the door was open, it was still a glorious shot.

'Nice one, Larry,' Geraldine called into the microphone, addressing the one live cameraman on duty. 'Glad we decided to keep you on.'

Geraldine was referring to the fact that there had only the previous day been a debate about dispensing with night operators altogether, because so little ever actually happened in the house at night, and seeing as how the entire environment was covered by remotes anyway. Geraldine had, however, insisted on retaining at least one person in the camera runs at night for just such an eventuality as had occurred. A naked girl running right across the room needed the personal touch. The coverage from the hot-heads not only came from above but also encompassed three different arcs of vision, and would have had to be cut up accordingly. On the other hand Larry, the live cameraman, had got one long beautiful, tit-bouncing, thigh-wobbling, tummy-stretching, full-frontal shot with pubic hair in full and constant focus. A shot that would play absolutely beautifully in slow motion.

'Terrific work, out of the blue like that,' Geraldine continued, giving credit where it was due. 'Looks like there's still a role for you human beings in making television. Stick with her at the toilet door, Larry, and get her again when she comes out.'

Inside the toilet, of course, there was only remote coverage, a single camera mounted high in a corner above the door. This camera was looking down now on Kelly as she sat on the seat of the lavatory, her head in her hands.

In the monitoring box there was a slightly embarrassed silence. None of the production team had ever quite got used to this bit of their job. Listening to people pee and poop. In the daytime at least there were other things going on, something else to look at and listen to, but not at night. When any of the housemates went at night it was just them and the six people watching and listening from the box. This was always a strangely intense and rather degrading experience for the editing team. They felt like the most awful perverts.

On this occasion, of course, there should have been plenty of distraction coming from inside the translucent plastic box, but suddenly the party seemed to have arrived at something of a lull. The high hilarity, grunting and giggling of the touching game had rather abruptly died down into what sounded like something approaching a drunken stupor. Murmured conversations and giggles could be made out, but nothing very clear. Nothing distracting enough to take the team's minds off the girl on the toilet.

And so they sat there, grown-up, educated, professional people, waiting to watch a young woman empty her bladder and very possibly also her bowel. They all felt very stupid.

'Get on with it then, darling,' said Geraldine. 'You can't have stage fright after three weeks. We've all heard you piss before.'

'Maybe she's having a little cry or something,' said

212

Fogarty. 'She doesn't normally hang her head like that when she pees.'

'Somebody in the sweatbox pushed her a bit too far, do you think?' Geraldine replied eagerly. 'Well, we shall no doubt hear all about it in the confession box tomorrow.'

'She's just sitting like that 'cos she's drunk,' observed Pru, the assistant editor.

'Probably.'

Together they all continued to stare at the girl on the toilet. It was, after all, their job.

'That reminds me,' said Geraldine. 'I'm busting.' She had been in the bunker for many hours, drinking coffee almost continuously. 'Bet I'm back before she's been.' Geraldine rather prided herself on the efficiency of her physical functions.

'*And* I'm going to have a shit,' she remarked over her shoulder as she left. Geraldine knew how unpleasant her staff found her and she delighted in compounding it, surprising them by going further than even their grim expectations.

'Far, far too much information,' Fogarty said ruefully after Geraldine had left the room.

They waited in silence.

'I think she is upset,' said Pru.

'Who? Geraldine? I doubt it.'

'No, Kelly. She doesn't want a pee, she's just gone in there to get away, hasn't she?'

'Possibly, I suppose.'

'Well, she's not doing a wee, is she? She's just sitting there. She just wanted to get out of that sweatbox, but she knows if she does she'll forfeit the task and Geraldine will fine the group half their budget. The only way she can get a break is by pretending to have a pee.'

Shortly after this Geraldine returned and drew the same conclusion as Pru. 'She's skiving off,' Geraldine sneered. 'She's having a bunk. She's not *having* a piss, she's *taking* the piss, and I'm not putting up with that. I'm going to give her a Peeping Tom announcement to pee or get off the potty. Where's my voice? Where's Sam? I'm going to tell that young slapper to get her lovely body back in that sweatbox or pay the price.'

'Hang on,' said Pru. 'Something's happening.'

DAY TWENTY-NINE. 8.10 p.m.

The line of numbers at the bottom of the screen of the incident room television showed that it was 11.44. Eleven forty-four and twenty-one seconds, twenty-two seconds, twenty-three seconds.

Coleridge still found it difficult to watch, even after numerous viewings. He had heard that the whole sequence was already available on the Internet and had been downloaded many tens of thousands of times. As long as he lived Coleridge did not believe he would understand how a single race of beings could include both Jesus Christ and the sort of people who would download a video of a young woman being murdered. He rather supposed that had been the Messiah's point, but that didn't make it any easier to understand or accept.

He, Hooper and Trish watched as, while Kelly sat naked and unsuspecting on the toilet, at the other end of the house, in the boys' bedroom, the plastic flaps of the sweatbox moved. There was a sort of flurry of activity as a hidden figure swiftly gathered up one of the sheets that Peeping Tom had allowed for lavatory trips, spread it out to cover the entrance and on leaving the box enveloped his or her self in it. Try as they might, and using the best image-enhancement technology available, the police had been unable to gain any information whatsoever from that blurred bluish image. For

214

a moment a hand was visible, but it was not possible to even tell if it was male or female, or even to say whether it wore a ring.

Then, carefully, covered from head to toe in the sheet, the hunched figure made its way out of the boys' bedroom and into the glaring tube lighting of the living area. From there it went to the kitchen units, where it provided the police with another tantalizing glimpse of hand as it reached into one of the kitchen drawers and took out the largest kitchen knife available, a beautiful Sabatier. Then, as the murmuring and giggling that emanated from inside the sweatbox continued gently to waft into the microphones, the cloaked figure crossed the rest of the living room, went into the utility area and approached the toilet door.

DAY TWENTY-SEVEN. 11.44 p.m.

'Who the fuck is that, then?' said Geraldine, watching the sheeted figure emerge from the boys' bedroom.

'Don't know,' said Pru and Fogarty together.

'Someone's having a laugh,' opined Fogarty. 'Going to scare Kelly.'

Now the figure crossed to the kitchen units and picked up the knife from the kitchen drawer.

'That I do not like,' said Geraldine. 'That is not funny.'

The figure was making its way towards the toilet now.

'They're all far too pissed for this type of nonsense,' said Geraldine. 'We need to make an announcement. Tell whichever silly cunt is in that sheet to stop fucking around and put that fucking knife back in the drawer before he gets us censored by the bleeding Standards Commission. Sam's not here. You do it, Pru, quick, bang the intercom on.'

But there was no time.

The figure in the sheet suddenly threw open the toilet door and swept inside.

Kelly must have seen her killer's face, but she was the only person who did. Every housemate knew the location of all the cameras intimately and whoever burst into that toilet knew that the only camera covering him was the one above the door. As he entered, he raised the sheet high above his head with both hands, one of which also held the knife. Kelly must have looked up in surprise, but it was not possible to see her expression in that final moment because the sheet was billowing above and behind the killer, cutting them both off from the view of the camera.

Now, as Geraldine and her editing team watched, the sheet seemed to fall downwards onto Kelly. This, it was to transpire, was the first plunge of the knife. The one that skewered Kelly's neck.

In the monitoring box they still thought it was a wind-up. They had no reason to think anything else.

'What *is* that cunt doing?' Geraldine said, as the billowing sheet raised itself up again before plunging down once more.

DAY TWENTY-NINE. 8.30 p.m.

'I think he had been planning on making only one blow,' said Coleridge. 'After all, he couldn't afford to get any blood on him.'

'Tough call, that, if you happen to be knifing somebody.'

'Just one huge blow, straight into the brain. Instant death.'

'And no geyser of blood.'

'Exactly, but the girl must have moved her head and he hit the neck.'

'Fortunately for him not the jugular.'

'No, not the jugular. He got away without getting marked, just.'

'One lucky bastard.'

Coleridge was forced to agree: the killer had indeed been one lucky bastard.

'I still say it would take a man to deliver a blow like that, and a strong one,' Hooper continued.

'It doesn't. We proved that,' said Trisha with a touch of impatience. She herself had spent an unpleasant afternoon at a local butcher's shop plunging knives into pigs' skulls.

'I know that a woman *could* have done it, but at what risk?' Hooper insisted. 'If the knife had got stuck in the bone of the skull, for instance – that happened with the pigs, Trish, half the times you tried it. What's more, the force required is huge, and there's no guard on a kitchen knife. You were wearing gloves, but your hand slipped occasionally. What if hers had done? She'd have cut off her own fingers. Kelly would have grabbed the sheet. It would have been all up. The chances of a woman pulling off a blow like that are quite small.'

'Except for Sally,' Coleridge said. Big, beefy Sally. The Internet's murderer of choice.

'Why on earth would Sally murder Kelly?' said Trish, a little too quickly.

'Why would any of them?' Coleridge answered. 'The only thing we can say for sure is that any one of them *could* have done it. The killer was right-handed and so are all of the remaining housemates. However, I concede that it is more *probable* that one of the stronger ones did it. Probably a man.'

They all turned back to the screen. The figure had thrown open the door at 11.44 and twenty-nine seconds. The first blow had fallen two and a half seconds later, the next and final one two seconds after that. The

killer had been inside the lavatory for considerably
less than ten seconds in all.

'If it wasn't all so damned clinical,' Coleridge
observed, 'I would have said that the attack was frenzied.'

The tape played on. The killer had clearly taken two
sheets from the pile when he left the sweatbox, for now
as he raised himself up from making the second blow
he threw one over his victim. The other one continued
to cover him as he left the toilet.

'And you talked to the cameraman on duty, constable?' Coleridge enquired.

'Yes, I did, sir,' Trish replied, 'at length. His name
is Larry Carlisle. He saw the figure in the sheet enter
the lavatory and moments later he saw the figure
emerge.' Trisha gathered up her case notes and
quoted from the transcript of her interview with the
cameraman . . .

' "I saw the figure follow the victim into the toilet at
approximately twenty to midnight. He re-emerged
shortly thereafter and headed back across the living
area towards the boys' bedroom. I did not cover him
with my camera as I had been instructed to continue to
watch the toilet for Kelly in order to obtain more good
nude footage. I remained there, watching the door,
until the alarm was raised. I recall thinking that she
was having a long time in the loo. I had only twenty
minutes to go until my shift finished and I was beginning to think I'd have to leave her for the next bloke.
Anyway, about four or five minutes after the figure in
the sheet emerged, they all rushed down from the monitoring bunker, and you know the rest." '

'Four or five minutes?' said Coleridge when Trisha
had finished reading.

'That's what he said.'

'According to the people in the box and the time
codes it was no more than two.'

218

'I suppose if you're just standing staring at a door it would be easy to misjudge a period of time.'

'How long did he say elapsed between Kelly emerging from the bedroom and the killer following her?'

'He said two, but gets that wrong as well, because it was around five.'

Coleridge got out the big red ledger in which he kept his notes for the case and wrote down Carlisle's name and the discrepancies the man had made in his timings. Coleridge wrote in longhand, and it always seemed to take him about a week to complete a sentence.

DAY TWENTY-EIGHT. 7.00 p.m.

Geraldine's witness statement had arrived at the point of the murder. She told the same story as all the others. 'I saw the bloke in the sheet come out of the sweatbox, cross the living area, go into the toilet and kill Kelly.'

'How long would you say Kelly had been on the toilet before the killer emerged?' Coleridge asked.

'About four or five minutes, I think.'

'Did you actually see the murder?'

'Well, not actually, obviously, the sheet was in the way. We just saw the sheet billow up and down twice and wondered what was up. Then the bloke buggered off sharpish back to the sweatbox, leaving Kelly covered in his spare sheet.'

'You saw the sheeted figure return to the sweatbox and go inside it?'

'Yes, we all did.'

'What happened then?' Coleridge asked.

'We sat and watched. Kelly was still on the bog but covered in this sheet.'

'You didn't think that was strange?'

'Well, of course we thought it was fucking strange,

but the whole thing's fucking strange, isn't it? We didn't know what was happening. As far as we knew there'd been a bit of malarkey with the sheets, that was all. I mean, come on, inspector, we weren't *expecting* a murder, were we? I think we sort of presumed she'd fallen asleep. They were all completely pissed. It would have been strange if things *hadn't* been strange.'

'Then what?'

'Well, we saw the puddle, didn't we?'

'How long would that have been after the figure in the sheet had left the toilet?'

'I don't know. Five minutes, max.'

'Yes, that's what the operator in the camera run said.'

'Does it matter?'

'The editor and his assistants thought it was more like two.'

'Maybe it was, I don't know, it seemed like five minutes. Time drags a bit when you're sitting staring at a bird on a bog covered in a sheet. What's it say on the video time code?'

'Two minutes and eight seconds.'

'Well, you know, then. What are you asking me for?'

'So then you saw the puddle?'

'Yeah, suddenly we could see a wet sort of dark shiny glow spreading out from around the toilet.'

'Blood?'

'Well, we know that now, don't we?'

'It must have occurred to you then.'

'Well, of course it did, but it just seemed so impossible.'

'The sheet was already sodden with it. Why didn't you see that?'

'As you know, the sheet was dark blue. The stain didn't show up on the night camera. All the sheets in the house are dark colours. Our psychologist reckons it's more conducive to people having sex on them.'

'So what then?'

'Well, I'm embarrassed to say, inspector, that I screamed.'

DAY TWENTY-SEVEN. 10.00 p.m.

They had been inside the sweatbox for a few minutes now, waiting for their eyes to get used to the darkness. It was useless trying to see anything, however. The blackness was complete.

'Let's play truth or dare,' Moon's voice called out of the darkness.

'Dare?' said Dervla. 'Jesus, what more of a dare could we think of than this? We've already had to strip naked, for heaven's sake.'

'I can think of a few things,' Gazzer grunted.

'Well, keep them to yourself, Gaz,' Dervla replied, managing to make her voice sound almost prim, which was some achievement considering the situation they were all in. 'Because I'm not shaggin' any of yez.'

Dervla's voice and intonation were getting closer to Dublin with every syllable she spoke. She always took refuge in the comfort and protection of the tough, highly credible accent of her childhood when she felt vulnerable. 'Jesus, me mother'd kill me, so she would.'

'All right, then,' Moon conceded. 'Let's just play truth, then. Somebody ask a question.'

Now another voice rang out of the darkness, a voice that was jarring and bitter. 'What would be the fucking point of asking you to tell the truth, Moon?' It was Sally's voice, and it struck a disturbing note. Its hard, nasty edge cut through the drunken badinage.

'Hey, Sally,' Moon replied, angry and defensive. 'I were having a fookin' laugh, all right. Get over it, why don't you?'

'What's that, then?' Garry asked. 'What's been going on with you birds?'

'Ask Sally,' said Moon. 'She's the one who can't take a joke.'

But Sally remained silent. And would not get over it either. She had no intention of getting over it, ever. Moon had done a despicable thing. She had hijacked the terrible suffering of the abused and the mentally disturbed to score cheap points. One day Sally intended to make Moon aware of the offence that she had caused.

'Oh, fook it, then,' Moon continued, 'and fook you, Sally.'

There was a movement in the box. Somebody was leaving.

'Who's that?' Hamish asked.

'Who's got out?' said Jazz.

Sally was already outside the box. 'I'm going for a slash,' she said.

'Well, make sure you come back,' said Jazz. 'We all have to do this or we all fail.'

'I know,' Sally assured him.

In the monitoring box they watched as Sally came out of the boys' bedroom and crossed the living area to the toilet. Sally had not bothered to take up a sheet to cover herself, but Geraldine was less than thrilled.

'Well, not bad, I suppose, but she's hardly one of the lookers,' she moaned. 'And, anyway, we've seen her bloody great kajungas hundreds of times. What we need is Kelly or Dervo to give us a full frontal.'

Geraldine stared wearily at the screen. 'And I *do* wish she'd get that bikini line done. I mean, look at it. It's just not necessary. I've known lesbians with beautifully styled fur burgers.'

Bob Fogarty reached for a comforting pound or two of chocolate.

*

While Sally was away Moon resumed her theme. 'Come on, are we having a truth game or what? Let's have a juicy question.'

And of course Garry asked the inevitable one. 'All right. We all have to say who we'd shag in the house if we had to do it or die.'

'Dervla,' said Jazz, and as he said it he realized that he had responded rather embarrassingly quickly. He was rewarded with a chorus of 'Whoos'.

'Jazz fancies Dervo. Jazz fancies Dervo,' Kelly chanted drunkenly.

'Well, I'm very flattered, Jazz,' said Dervla, 'but as I said I'm not after looking for any nookie, so I'm not.'

'But if you were, Dervs,' Garry said, pressing his point. 'Who would it be?'

'You have to answer,' said Moon. 'We all have to answer.'

'Oh, all right, then,' Dervla replied. 'Jazz, I suppose, but only because he's been a gentleman and named me.'

'Me too, I'll have him after you've finished with him,' said Moon, ''cos I reckon you're dead fookin' lush, Jazz. I can say it in here because it's dark and I'm pissed and you can't see me going red, but at the end of the day I'd bang your fookin' brains out if I had a chance, so fair play to ya 'cos I think you're brilliant.'

'Bang his brains out? That'd take all of ten seconds!' shouted Garry.

'You're just jealous, Gazzer,' Jazz shouted back, 'because it's two nil to me! Two nil! Two nil! Two nil.' Jazz had turned his score into a chant.

Sally returned from the toilet. There was much groaning and giggling as she squeezed her way in among the naked bodies.

'I'll tell you one thing, Jazz,' she said. 'Listening to you and Gazzer I'm glad I'm a lesbian.'

'Yes, you'd better watch it, Jazz,' Dervla added. 'I'm thinking about changing my vote.'

'Well, I'll have Hamish, then,' Kelly shouted. 'Because he's a doctor and you've got to respect that, haven't you?'

Actually Kelly fancied Jazz, like all the other girls except Sally, but she nominated Hamish because she wanted to be nice to him. She had been feeling guilty about the strange half-formed suspicion that she had harboured after their drunken night together and in particular about the fact that she had spoken to Peeping Tom about the matter. Not in so many words, of course, but she had gone to the confession box to ask whether anything had happened, which was a pretty clear indication of what she was thinking. That had been really bad of her. It must have looked to everyone like she was worried that Hamish had attempted to take advantage of her drunken state. Kelly knew that was a pretty major thing to imply about anybody, particularly a doctor, and particularly since she had by now definitely decided in her mind that nothing untoward had occurred in Copulation Cabin that night. Kelly wanted to make amends, and she reckoned by naming him as her preferred partner she was making clear that she harboured no further suspicions.

Hamish was thrilled. He had noted Kelly's unscheduled trip to the confession box and had been horribly disturbed by it. Now, however, he knew that he was safe. Kelly had named him as her partner of choice, and if she had been harbouring any suspicions about his character or conduct she would scarcely have done that, would she?

'Besides which,' Kelly continued, 'doctors have such sensitive hands, and a girl does love a gentle touch.'

Garry and Jazz cheered drunkenly. Hamish gulped at the hot salty air. *'Sensitive hands'*? . . . *'gentle touch'*? Was it a coincidence? Did she know? Had she been conscious all along and enjoying his . . . his explorations, his . . . *digital penetration*? It was possible surely, after all Kelly was quite a wild one. Hamish smiled broadly, a big happy smile which nobody could see. It was all going to be all right, maybe even better than all right. Maybe he might even get another chance at her.

'Cheers, Kelly!' Hamish shouted out. 'I'm deeply flattered and most certainly reciprocate the nomination.'

'And I shall join you, my son,' Garry shouted. 'No offence to the other girls, but it's got to be Kelly, ain't it? I mean just for the knockers alone.'

'Forget it, Garry,' Hamish replied. 'Personally I'm not into threesomes.'

'Listen to these two!' Kelly shrieked. 'I'm being fought over, girls. I think it's dead romantic.' Which, considering she was sitting naked in a communal sweatbox, showed how drunk Kelly had become.

'What about you, then, Sally?' Jazz asked. 'Who'd you have if you had to have someone?'

'I'd have Dervla, thank you very much,' Sally replied quietly. 'I think we'd make a lovely couple at the next Pride Festival.'

'Well, I'm delighted and flattered,' said Dervla from somewhere in the darkness. 'I think that's a terribly sweet thing to say, Sally, and if I batted for your team I should take you up on the offer without further ado.'

'All *right*!' shouted Garry. 'Can I watch?'

'So you've got two nominations then, Dervo,' said Jazz. 'Impressive score, girl. Equal to the Jazz meister.'

'Do lezzo votes count, then?' asked Garry. 'I mean, I'm not being homo whatsit or nothing, but I'd have thought they'd be in a different category, wouldn't they?'

'What absolute rubbish, Garry,' snapped Dervla, 'and you are being homo whatsit.'

'No way,' Garry defended himself. 'I'm a big supporter of lesbian love. I could watch it all day. In fact

225

I've got some excellent videos if anyone's interested, for when we all get out.'

This comment put Kelly in mind of David and her little secret bit of knowledge about him. So Garry collected porn. She wondered whether he had any of the *Fuck Orgy* series. 'Who do you nominate, then, David?' she asked.

'To have sex with, out of our little group?' David replied, his voice being heard in the pitch-black sweatbox for the first time. 'Why, who else but myself? For me sex is nothing without love and commitment, and you all know that I love no one on this earth so much as I love *moi*.'

They all laughed, as David had hoped they would. He was perfectly well aware that he must have been coming across to the public as extremely vain. He always came across as extremely vain, and the reason for this was because he *was* extremely vain. But the funny thing about David's vanity was that it was both his most irritating and his most charming feature. There was something almost endearing or at least comical about how much David loved himself, and as people got to know him they began to see the fun in it. David hoped that this would work for him in the house. All his life he had progressed from being the one people simply hated, through being the one people loved to hate, until eventually ending up being a person people hated themselves for loving. It was a complex equation, but it was pretty much how things worked socially for David, and he thought he might have a similar relationship with the public. He imagined that his little joke about sex with himself (should it be broadcast) would do much to improve his standing with the voting public. David was an acquired taste, and he believed that once the penny dropped with people that he *knew* how vain he was, they would start to like him more.

'Not bad, not bad,' said Geraldine crouching over the monitoring controls. 'At least they're talking about sex. Got some lovely stuff to broadcast there. I loved David's wanking joke. He's really coming into his own. Might put a few quid on him to make the final three. Wouldn't that be a surprise?'

'I hope they continue to speak up,' the sound editor said. 'Don't forget they aren't wearing their radio mikes. We're relying on the ones dropping from the ceiling.'

'I know that, but what could we do? You can't fit bloody battery packs onto naked people. They'd get in the way. Besides, what would you hang the mikes off?'

'All right, come on, then,' said Moon. 'Another truth question. Who's got one, then? Here, I've got one. Has anybody ever paid for sex?'

'Fahkin' hell, Moon,' Gazzer laughed. 'I've paid for it the next day all right, when I told the girlfriend I'd just knocked off her sister or her best mate or whatever.'

'No, I mean paid money for gratification. Been with a tart or summat.'

The reason Moon was asking became clear with her next comment. 'All right, then. Who's ever *been* paid for sex, because I know I fookin' 'ave.'

This revelation definitely caused a flurry of interest.

'I'm not proud of it or anything, but at the end of the day I needed the money, right. I were doing arts and social studies at Preston uni, when it was the poly, and I hadn't got the fees, and I were fooked if I was going to stand behind a bar all night making the same money I could get in twenty minutes lying on my back.'

Everyone was enjoying themselves except Sally. She hated Moon so much, her endless boasting and story-telling. So what if she'd been a prostitute? Who cared? Besides, Sally didn't believe it. She didn't believe

227

anything that Moon said any more, and she never ever would again.

'I've been in a porn movie,' Kelly said. 'Does that count as being paid for sex?'

Silent in the darkness, David tensed. Where was she going with this?

'Well, it depends if you've actually done it for the camera or not,' Garry said. 'I've got this film, it's called *LA 100* and all it is, right, you'll never believe this, but it's true. All it is is this bird shagging *a hundred* blokes in a row. Can you believe that! I couldn't till I saw it. One after the other. In you go, my son, wallop, thank you very much, lovely jubbly, we like that! Next!'

'I don't believe it,' said Dervla. 'You couldn't shag a hundred times, it would be impossible.'

'No, no, honest. It was all kosher, they had authentic adjudicators with clipboards and everything. This bird really did do the ton. And at the end of the day, fair play to her, I say.'

'Yeah, well, I never actually had sex in the movie I did,' Kelly conceded. 'I wouldn't do that. You can forget it, they're all such sleazy bastards, those porn actors. You wouldn't risk it. I was just an extra, you know, a pair of knockers in the background. I had to kiss this other girl's nipples, but that was it and we just had a laugh about it, but there was plenty of them actually at it, let me tell you, and it was disgusting: shagging and sucking and slobbering and all. The star took it both ways at the same time. I could not believe it, *both ways*, bonking and being bonked. I mean, come on.'

'Not easy rhythmically, I would imagine,' Jazz opined. 'I should think you'd need a metronome, or there could be a nasty pile-up.'

'You wouldn't know whether you was coming or going!' Garry roared, and they all roared with him.

Except David. Where is she going with this? he was

228

thinking, his fists clenched with tension. *Where is she going with this?*

'He was called Boris Pecker, and he just stood there poking away at these girls in front of him while he got poked at by these blokes from behind him. Unbelievable, it was.'

David was already sweating profusely, but if it were possible he actually began to sweat a little more. Was she about to reveal all? Was this common, ignorant cow going to give him away? David longed to reach out into the darkness and shut that big fat mouth up before it could say any more. He longed to gag it, to ram it shut, to silence it for good.

It was obvious to David that Kelly was directing her remarks at him, and it was a bitter blow. He had almost begun to relax about that whispered moment of recognition that they had shared together in the hot tub. It had shocked him deeply at the time, but as the days wore on and she did not mention it again he had started to imagine that perhaps he had heard her wrong, or at the very least that his secret was safe with her.

And now . . .

Now she was teasing him, no, *taunting* him, with her knowledge of his secret, the secret that could destroy his dreams for ever.

Because there was only one thing in David's life that really mattered to him and that was his acting. All he had ever wanted, all he ever would want, was to be an actor, a celebrated actor, of course, a star. At one time in his life, just after he had left RADA, it had almost seemed as if this dream might come true. He had won prizes, got some decent first jobs, and his talent was spoken of highly amongst influential casting agents. But somehow it hadn't lasted. While others in his graduation class had found their way to the National Theatre, the RSC, and even Hollywood, his flame had sputtered and dimmed.

But David still believed from the depths of his soul that he had a fighting chance. He *was* a good actor, his was surely a talent too rare to go unnoticed for ever. What was more, he was handsome, achingly handsome. All he needed was a break, and that was why he had applied to join *House Arrest*. He knew, of course, that it was a pretty desperate final gambit, but he was a pretty desperate man, a *completely* desperate man, in fact.

After *House Arrest* David would be a telly name. He simply could not believe that this would not get him *somewhere*, a nice little Shakespearean lead at the Glasgow Citizen's, or perhaps the West Yorkshire Playhouse ... and then, if the notices were good, a short London transfer would follow ... and then ... then he would be back on track!

Back on track to catch up with all the bastards from his year who were doing so much better than he was. Back on track to be able to open the arts pages of the newspapers once more without having to curse every single fucking profile of some bastard ten years younger than him who had just redefined the art of playing Shakespeare in a promenade production in a garden shed on the Isle of Dogs.

But none of this would *ever* happen if people knew that David Dalgleish, actor, artist, man who took no job unworthy of his talent, was in fact none other than Boris Pecker! Olivia Newton Dong! *Ivor Biggun!*

Then he would be a laughing stock. 'Porn star' was not a label it was possible to shake off, particularly not the type of porn star that he had been, a fuck and suck man. Oh, certainly, a little bit of Polanski or Ken Russell early in one's career was fine. Without doubt one could bare one's youthful arse for a name director with impunity; it was actually considered rather classy. Even an early dabble in soft core classics was survivable, particularly if you were a girl. A daringly graphic *Lady Chatterley* rarely did any harm, nor did a corsets-off *Fanny Hill*.

But not *Fuck Orgy Eleven*.

Not *The Banging Man*.

Not . . . *Pussy Picnic*.

David wondered where Kelly was sitting. It was difficult to tell inside the hot, rank darkness. It crossed his mind that if he could reach her, he could strangle her where she sat and nobody would notice.

That would shut the bitch up.

But Kelly did not need shutting up, not immediately, anyway, because as time ticked on in the darkness of the sweatbox she made no further mention of David's secret. She had been having a laugh, teasing him. He certainly deserved a bit of winding-up. Kelly's inside knowledge did not have remotely the significance for her that it had for him. She had no idea of the emotional turmoil and hatred that she was causing, and soon the conversation moved on.

Now a series of fumbling, stumbling drinking games developed. Much booze was drunk and even more was spilt as the plastic bottles were passed about in the darkness. The alcohol hissed and steamed as it dripped between the hot wooden floorboards and onto the heating units beneath. It turned the sweatbox into a kind of sauna, using wine and spirits to create the steam instead of water.

David began to relax a little, but only a little. He believed that Kelly had been warning him, warning him to be nice to her and not to nominate her. Showing him that she held his future in her hands and that she could deploy her weapon whenever she chose. Well, if that was the case, David thought, she was playing a dangerous game. He was a proud man. He could not and would not put up with being blackmailed, particularly by a know-nothing nonentity like Kelly. But he would have to bide his time.

The drinking continued. There were songs and jokes, nice ones and dirty ones, some too dirty even for Geraldine to be able to broadcast.

And the atmosphere was slowing down. Slowing down and heating up. The heat, the booze and the housemates' utter disorientation in the darkness were beginning to take their toll. People were getting lazier and bolder, their defences were evaporating like the alcohol that was dripping onto the heaters.

'OK, then, let's see how well we *really* know each other, eh?' said Jazz in a hoarse, slurred voice. 'We're all mixed up and totally out of it, right? So everybody feel about with their left hand and when they touch someone, they have to identify them, right? But just by feel – no talking till you know.'

A mighty, boozy cheer greeted this suggestion, although, drunk as she was, Dervla was not too sure about it. However, everybody else seemed to be greeting the idea with such enthusiasm that she felt bound to go along with it. She did not want to end up on everybody's nomination list for being a killjoy and a prude.

'OK,' said Jazz. 'Everybody knows where I am 'cos I've been talking and I would like to be identified by my donga, not my voice, on account of the fact that I'm hung like a Derby winner, so I'm just going to slide around a bit, mix us all up good, right? Then let the feeling begin. Here I go, these are the last words I will say . . .'

There were drunken cheers, whoops and groans as the others felt Jazz's smooth, taut, sweating body moving about inside the tight, slippery little group of cramped and naked forms.

The observers in the monitoring bunker could scarcely contain their excitement. The translucent plastic walls of the sweatbox bulged and heaved. Even in the eerie blue light of the night cameras there were clearly discernible body parts constantly emerging and then disappearing in the shapes in the plastic. Elbows, heads, buttocks – sexy, exciting buttocks. There seemed to be a real possibility of an orgy developing.

'We should have made the plastic completely transparent,' Geraldine drooled. 'The sad cunts would have stood for it too, except Saint fucking Dervla, of course.'

'I don't agree,' Fogarty replied. 'Firstly, we couldn't have broadcast it if we'd done that. Secondly, it would have been all steamed up anyway, and thirdly, it wouldn't have been half as exciting even if we could see, because it's the anonymity that's so intoxicating. We don't know who's who and nor do they.'

'When I want your opinion, Bob, I'll ask for it.'

Inside the box the darkness was as intense as the excitement. Dervla felt Jazz slide across her. She felt his taut skin and beautiful rock-hard muscles against her own bare flesh.

'My God,' she thought. 'He doesn't know it's me he's sliding over.'

Jazz was pretending to be a snake, hissing and writhing. She could feel his muscular stomach in her lap as he giggled and wriggled across her and then . . . then she felt his penis dragging across her thighs, big and heavy, obviously already semi-hard. She could not resist it. Through the darkness she placed her hand in its path, palm upwards, deliberately letting him glide into it.

Then very gently she squeezed. It felt wonderful in that coal-black anonymity to be doing something so outrageous. She could feel herself sweating all the more as Jazz stopped his wriggling and slithering for a moment and allowed the object of her attentions to grow bigger and harder in her hand. In that moment, for Dervla, Jazz was no longer the beery-leery jack-the-lad fly-boy king of clubbing cool that she knew and was beginning to rather like, he was a Greek or a Roman God, a living, breathing version of all those wonderful works of art she saw on her summer holidays in Europe. He was a fantastical night-time love muse.

Then she heard his voice and of course it was only Jazz. 'Is that you, Kelly, you naughty, naughty slapper, you?'

'What?' said Kelly's voice from the vicinity of Jazz's feet.

'Ah,' said Jazz. 'So not Kelly, then.'

Dervla gave a tiny gasp and let go, shocked at her audacity!

She had been gripping Jazz's penis! That was terrible! Absolutely terrible! She would have to face him at breakfast in the morning! Her, the chief objector to crudity. The Lady High and Mighty. The good girl of the group. What if he knew it was her?

He did know.

Her tiny gasp had given her away. Even amongst the general grunting and giggling, Jazz had caught its tone.

'Who, then, I wonder,' he said, and then he sang a line of 'When Irish eyes are smiling.'

Dervla felt herself go crimson in the darkness. What if he told Peeping Tom? What if he went into the confession box and told the nation that she had grabbed his penis in the darkness and squeezed it until it was hard? Then her thoughts were interrupted, because Gazzer made them all roar with laughter.

'Fuck me, I'm glad Woggle ain't in here!'

Everybody shrieked. It was such a terrible, terrible, madly hilarious thought, to be stuck in a crowded sweatbox with Woggle. To have to feel him, smell him.

Dervla laughed too, and suddenly she didn't care about having touched Jazz. In fact she was proud of it. She hoped he did tell. She knew the other inmates thought her a prude, and it was certain that the public thought so too. It wouldn't do her chances of winning any harm at all to add a bit of generous, good-humoured ladette behaviour to the mix. Jazz thought that she was beautiful, he had made that clear often enough, and she *was* beautiful.Why shouldn't she touch his dick? He had loved it, it had made him hard. And the truth was she had loved it too, it had felt terrific. Having that big, strong, veiny piece of male flesh in her small soft hand had turned her on like a tap. As the waves of laughter that had greeted Gazzer's observation began to recede, Dervla topped them.

'Hey, Jazz,' she called out jubilantly into the darkness. 'I just felt your willy!'

'Any time, fine lady, any time!' Jazz shouted back and again they all roared.

In the camera corridor the one operator on duty recoiled as if he had been electrocuted.

Larry Carlisle had been covering the entrance to the sweatbox viewed across the living room and through the open door of the boys' bedroom, which had been left slightly ajar. Now, as he twitched involuntarily, the lens of his camera swung wildly upwards covering, for a moment, nothing more interesting than the ceiling. Fortunately for Carlisle nobody in the monitoring bunker was watching his camera feed at that moment because a much better picture of the shadowy box was being supplied by the remote hot-heads in the bedroom itself. Quickly Carlisle regained control of his camera and returned its focus to the proper place.

But he still had to struggle to stop his hand from shaking on the controls. Carlisle could scarcely contain his bitter anger. *His girl*, the gorgeous but prudish girl behind the mirror, the girl who was so careful to never show *him* anything, had just gripped the black one's cock! It was outrageous, it was disgusting. It was a betrayal of the purity of the relationship that they had established together.

They shrieked, they laughed, they whooped. Nobody could quite believe that Dervla had been the first to get so specifically raunchy. It emboldened them all, seeming to give the whole game genuine class.

The cleverer, more manipulative people in the box realized that Dervla's sudden sexiness was a pretty clever trick in terms of the public's perception of her. There was nothing that kept up audience interest better than surprises, particularly sexual ones, and Dervla's grabbing of Jazz had certainly been that. Moon, David, Hamish and Garry all realized that Dervla had raised the stakes and they would have to lift their game accordingly.

Moon decided then and there that she would later confess to Peeping Tom that she had had intercourse inside the box and had no idea with whom it had been. She resolved to admit to this whether it had happened or not, but actually she thought it probably would happen, because now the touching and feeling began with a vengeance.

'So are we going to play this identification game or what?' shouted Jazz.

'Yes!' came the reply.

'OK, then, go for it!' Jazz shouted. 'Everybody move around and nobody talk, OK? And when you've had a really good squirm, cop a feel and guess who you've got.'

Suddenly it was all shrieks and giggles and boozy lust as they slipped about together.

Hamish was almost beside himself with excitement. This was the reason he had come into the house. Like Moon, he wanted to have sex, and then he wanted everyone to know about it. With Kelly, preferably, but frankly any female partner would do. He felt a hand stroking his back, gently teasing his sweaty spine, gently running all the way down to the cleft of his buttocks. Was this the one? Should he turn about and try to make love to whoever was touching him?

He heard a whisper in his ear. 'Sally?' It was David's voice.

'You've been in this house too long, mate,' Hamish whispered back.

'Fuck!' David barked, snatching his hand away as if Hamish was a red-hot stove.

'Shhh!' whispered Jazz from nearby.

David was annoyed. His mistake made him feel vulnerable. He wondered if Kelly had heard. All his doubts flooded back once more. Was she laughing at him in the darkness? Was she thinking to herself that Boris Pecker would not have minded at all who he found himself feeling up? Would she tell? Would she suddenly blurt it out and tell? David wanted to leave the sweatbox there and then, he wanted to run. But perhaps that in itself might provoke Kelly.

'Funny how he couldn't take a bit of sex,' she would say. 'I would have thought it would have been right up his street.'

'Up his arse, more like,' Gazzer would say after Kelly had explained, and then David would be a laughing stock, a national joke. David decided he had better stay put. He reached for one of Geraldine's artfully placed plastic bottles of warm, strong booze and drank deep.

Hamish was not going to make the mistake that David had made. It was a woman's thigh he was holding, for sure. So soft and smooth and not too firm. Kelly? he thought. Possibly, but just as easily Dervla or even Moon. Not Sally, he was delighted to conclude, and probably not small enough for Dervla, but you couldn't be sure. Whoever it belonged to it was fun to touch and squeeze. Hamish was feeling much better about himself now. Kelly's kind gesture earlier in the game had truly put his mind at rest, and now he felt safe and powerful and ready for anything.

He let his hand slip around from the outside to the inside of the thigh that he was holding. The flesh was hot and slightly clammy, it seemed almost to tug gently at his fingertips as he slid them across it. Whoever's thigh it was, and he was sure now it wasn't Dervla's, she seemed quite happy to be touched. Her opposite leg was moving, her other inner thigh gently brushing against the back of Hamish's hand. Hamish's lips brushed against a soft shoulder. He kissed it.

There were hands on Hamish now. Someone was stroking his buttocks, but he ignored it. The girl he was holding was the one he wanted.

Kelly was now very drunk. As drunk as she had been the week before, when she had passed out. She had had to get drunk in order to get into the sweatbox, and she knew that if she didn't get into the sweatbox she would lose the game. Now that she was inside and this hand was touching her she no longer really felt a part of her body, it was as if she was hovering above it and some other Kelly was being touched and caressed. It was not an unpleasant feeling, just slightly detached and uninvolved. This was how Kelly always felt about sex, possibly because she was always drunk when she did it. She liked sex, she was pretty sure of that, but somehow she always ended up wishing that she liked it more. Secretly she was sure that the missing ingredient was love, and she knew that she would have to wait for that. You couldn't plan it.

The hand was being more daring now, working its way up to the very top of her thigh. Kelly didn't *think* she minded, although she knew that she would probably stop him quite soon, whoever he was. On the other hand, why not let him play? This was what you did, wasn't it? If you were a top bird, a mad-for-it, gagging-for-it personality like she was? You didn't bottle out.

That wasn't what it was about at all, was it? You went for it, you lived it large. One thing you weren't was a killjoy.

Now the hand was brushing at Kelly's most intimate self. Now she would stop him, move the hand away. But she didn't. She had become distracted. Something in her memory was stirring.

Hamish moved his hand and touched the little metal ring hidden within the folds of Kelly's private flesh. And now he knew who it was he was touching. He was thrilled: this was who he had hoped it would be: Kelly, the one he fancied most, the one who had named him as her choice if sex were on the agenda. Well, sex was on the agenda. This was his chance.

He found her ear and whispered into it and as he whispered he gave the little ring the gentlest of flicks with his finger.

'Kelly,' he said, with a big broad smile.

And at that moment, in that very instant, they both knew.

Kelly was certain that she had not told a soul about her pierced labia, not even the girls. She had been specifically holding the information back to use as a triumphant, sexy revelation at some strategic moment later in the game, when she felt the need to shine.

But the voice in her ear knew. The voice of Hamish. *Hamish* knew because the moment he had touched that tiny wire he had whispered her name. And now Kelly saw the truth. The bastard had touched her vagina before. The half-formed suspicions that had troubled her aching head the morning that she had woken up in that horrible little sex cabin were suddenly turned to cast-iron facts.

'My God!' Kelly breathed, momentarily more surprised than angered. 'You felt me up when I was passed out. You fingered me. You knew I was pierced.' Her voice was a whisper; the shock of the revelation

239

was still sinking in. All of the other people in the box were busy with their own affairs.

Nobody heard her. *Nobody heard.*

Like Kelly, Hamish had realized the moment that he said it, in the instant that he breathed those two give-away syllables 'Kell-y', that he had made a terrible, terrible mistake. But as yet it was still a secret. Only they knew; the others were all too busy with their own giggling, their own fumbling.

'Please,' Hamish pleaded into Kelly's ear. 'Don't tell them.'

But in the way her body recoiled from him he knew that she would. How could she not? Why *should* she not? She would tell the others, she would tell the world, and he would be finished. Of course, he would deny it, it was her word against his, but people liked Kelly, they would believe her. The minimum he could expect was national shame, and the worst . . . prosecution for sexual assault. For *digital penetration*. His career was over, that was for sure. Doctors could not afford that kind of scandal. What woman would trust him with her body now?

He almost laughed. Here they all were, pawing at each other like animals in muck, and he was in danger of being prosecuted for sexual assault! Hamish's blind black vision turned red with fury. The slag! The disgusting fucking slag! She had been happy enough to let him feel her up just then, to let him *finger* her. And yet now she would ruin him utterly for having done exactly the same thing before.

Hamish's rush of fear and fury were fully matched by what Kelly was feeling. She was outraged, disgusted. She wanted to be sick. This bastard had mauled her while she lay unconscious! Put his hand *inside her*. Had he raped her? He could have raped her. Probably not, Kelly's fevered brain was telling her. If he had raped her she would have known, for sure. But would she? Perhaps he was small, perhaps he had been very careful. She remembered the sensation with which she had woken up. That discomfort, the sudden over-whelming urge to dive into the pool. Had he *put it in her*? How would she ever know?

'Please, don't tell,' Hamish whispered once more, and suddenly his hand was at her mouth.

Now Kelly was struggling to get out of the sweatbox, pushing herself through the laughing, groping bodies that surrounded her, trying to find the exit flaps.

'She's getting out!' thought Hamish. 'What will the bitch do?'

David was also aware that it was Kelly who was rushing for the exit. Kelly, the woman who with her special knowledge of him held his fate in her hands . . . *The bitch*, the one who had been taunting him. 'What's on her mind?' he thought. 'What will the cow do?'

Kelly passed Dervla in her panting, sweating struggle to get out. Dervla knew it was Kelly, because she could hear her hurried breathing. To Dervla's mind she sounded excited, almost triumphant. What had she to be so excited about? Dervla thought about the message that she had read in the mirror that morning. '*The bitch Kelly still number one.*'

Did Kelly know that she was number one? That she was winning? Was that why she was so excited? Dervla felt a massive surge of irritation towards the silly young woman who was squirming across her. What was so special about Kelly? She wasn't particularly bright, her morals were not very impressive, her dress sense was questionable and yet there she was, seem-ingly unmovable in the lead. All the confidence that Dervla had felt before about playing a longer game than Kelly evaporated. Kelly was going to win.

She was going to grab all the fame and she was going to grab the half-million quid, too. The half-million quid, about which Dervla had privately been dreaming since the day her application had been accepted. The half-million quid that would save her family . . . her beloved mother and father, her darling little sisters, from disaster.

Dervla wondered why Kelly was running out so suddenly and so breathlessly. What was she up to?

Sally shrank back into the corner of the sweatbox in which she had been hiding since almost the moment she had entered it, pushing away any hands or limbs that intruded on her space. Sally pushed Kelly away as she passed, and as she did so Sally thought to herself, 'That girl's in a hurry to get out of the sweatbox.' And with that thought, despite the heat, Sally's blood ran cold. For a memory had come upon her and claimed her for its own. It was the memory of her mother, on the only occasion in her life when Sally had ever spoken to her, sitting behind a glass screen speaking through an intercom.

'I don't know why a person like me does the things she does,' Sally's mother's voice had crackled. 'You just get stuck in the dark box and then it happens.' Suddenly Sally believed she knew how her mother had felt. She too was stuck in the black box. The black box was real.

Gazzer was thinking the same thing that he always felt about Kelly. He kept it well hidden, but one day he intended to get even with that bitch. Inside the house or out he would pay her back for what she had implied about his little lad, his wonderful Ricky. Telling the whole nation that he was a selfish, scrounging, absent father who didn't give a fuck. That was basically what she had implied. Well, Gazzer would show her. Sooner, or later. Or sooner.

Kelly was past them all and out. She gulped down the fresher, cooler air that hit her as she emerged from the flaps of the sweatbox, and, with her bile still rising in her throat, she rushed out of the boys' room and headed for the toilet.

*

A few minutes later Geraldine and her editing team watching the monitoring screens saw somebody appear at the front of the sweatbox, swathe themself in a sheet and follow Kelly to the toilet, pausing only to pick up a knife.

And kill her.

DAY TWENTY-SEVEN. 11.46 p.m.

'Oh my God! Oh, please God, no!'

It was unlike Geraldine to ask assistance from anybody, least of all the Almighty, but these were, of course, very special circumstances. The puddle on the floor around Kelly had suddenly appeared and was spreading rapidly.

'Fogarty, you and Pru come with me. You too!' Geraldine barked at one of the runners. 'The rest of you stay here.'

Geraldine and her colleagues rushed out of the monitoring bunker and down the stairs into the tunnel which ran under the moat, connecting the production complex to the house. From the tunnel they were able to gain access to the camera runs and from these runs there were entrances to every room in the house.

Larry Carlisle, the duty cameraman, heard a noise behind him. Later he was to explain to the police that he had been expecting to see his relief clocking on early, and had been about to turn and tell the next man not to run and make such a clatter when Geraldine and half the editing team had rushed past.

'Through the store room!' Geraldine barked, and in a moment she and her colleagues found themselves blinking in the striplit glare of the house interior. Later they were all to recall how strange it felt, even in that moment of panic, to be there inside the house. None of them had entered the house since the inmates had taken it over and now they felt like scientists who had suddenly found themselves on a petri dish along with the bugs they had been studying.

Geraldine took a deep breath and opened the toilet door.

DAY TWENTY-EIGHT. 7.20 p.m.

'Why did you pull the sheet off?' Coleridge asked. 'You must know that it's wrong to disturb the scene of a crime.'

'It's also wrong to ignore an injured person in distress. I didn't know she was dead, did I? I didn't even know there'd been a crime, as a matter of fact. I didn't know anything. Except that there was blood everywhere, or something that looked like blood. If I really try to remember what I was thinking at the time, inspector, I honestly still think that I half hoped it was a joke, that somehow the inmates had managed to turn the tables on me for letting them down over Woggle.'

Coleridge pressed play. The cameras had recorded everything: the little group of editors standing outside the toilet, Geraldine reaching in and pulling at the sheet. Kelly being revealed still sitting on the toilet, slumped forward, her shoulders resting on her knees. A large dark pool, flowing from the wounds in her neck and skull, growing on the floor. Kelly's feet in the middle of the pool, a flesh-coloured island growing out of a lake of red.

And, worst of all, the handle of the Sabatier kitchen knife sticking directly out of the top of Kelly's head, the blade buried deep in her skull.

'It was all so weird, like a cartoon murder or something,' Geraldine said. 'I swear with that knife hilt sticking out of her head she looked like a fucking

244

Teletubby. For a quarter of a second I *still* wondered whether we were being had.'

DAY TWENTY-SEVEN. 11.47 p.m.

'Give me your mobile!' Geraldine barked at Fogarty, her voice shrill but steady.

'What ... What?' Bob Fogarty's eyes were fixed on the horrifying crimson vision before him, the knife. The knife in the *skull*.

'Give me your mobile phone, you dozy cunt!' Geraldine snatched Fogarty's little Nokia from the pouch at his belt.

But she could not turn it on; her hand was shaking too much. She looked up at the live hot-head that was still impassively recording the scene. 'Somebody in the edit suite call the fucking police! ... Somebody watching on the Internet! Do something useful for once in your crap lives! Call the fucking police!'

And so it was that the world was alerted to one of the most puzzling and spectacular murders in anybody's memory or experience: by thousands of Internet users jamming the emergency services switchboards and, failing to get through, calling the press.

At the same time, at the scene of the crime, Geraldine seemed unsure what to do next.

'Is she ... dead?' said Pru, who was peering over Fogarty's shoulder, trying to keep the bile from rising in her throat.

'Prudence,' said Geraldine, 'she's got a kitchen knife stuck through her fucking brain.'

'Yes, but we should check all the same,' stammered Pru.

'You fucking check,' said Geraldine.

But at this point Kelly saved them from further speculation about her state of health by keeling off the toilet seat and falling to the floor. She went head first, pulled forward over her knees by the weight of her own head. This resulted in her butting the floor with the handle of the knife, which buried the blade another inch or two into her head, as if it had been hit by a hammer. It made a sort of creaking sound which caused both Pru and Fogarty to be sick.

'Oh, great. Fucking brilliant,' Geraldine said. 'So let's just throw up all over the scene of the crime, shall we? The police are going to fucking love us.'

Perhaps it was the idea of what people might think of them that led Geraldine to turn once more to the watching cameras. 'You lot in the box. Switch off the Internet link. This isn't a freak show.'

But it was a freak show, of course, a freak show that had only just begun.

'What the fuck's going on?' It was Jazz, emerging from the boys' bedroom, a sheet stuck to his honed, toned and sweaty body. What with his sheet and his muscley physique, Jazz looked like Dervla's fantasy of him, a Greek God startled on Mount Olympus. He could not have looked more ridiculously out of place if he had tried.

Jazz stood on the threshold of the room staring, stunned by the bright lights and the extraordinary and unexpected presence of intruders in a house that he and his fellow inmates had had exclusive use of for weeks.

Dervla appeared behind him. She too had taken up a sheet and looked equally out of place staring at the casually dressed intruders, behind whom was the corpse. It was beginning to look as if a toga party had crashed into a road accident.

Geraldine realized that the situation was about to spiral out of control. She did not like situations that were out of control; she was a classic example of that tired old phrase, 'the control freak'. 'Jason!

Dervla!' she shouted. 'Both of you get back in the boys'
bedroom!'

'What's happening?' Dervla said. Fortunately for
them neither she nor Jazz could see into the lavatory.
The gruesome sight was blocked from them by the
cluster of people at its doorway.

'This is Peeping Tom!' Geraldine shouted. 'There has
been an accident. All house inmates are to remain in
the boys' bedroom until told otherwise. Get inside!
NOW!'

Astonishingly, such was the hostage mentality that
had developed amongst the housemates that Jazz and
Dervla did as they were told, returning to the darkness
of the boys' bedroom, where the others were emerging
from the sweatbox, hot, naked and confused.

'What's going on?' David asked.

'I don't know,' Dervla replied. 'We're to stay in here.'

Then somebody in the edit suite took it upon themselves to turn on all the lights in the house. The seven
inmates were caught almost literally in the headlights.
They stood around the redundant sweatbox blinking at
each other, naked, reaching for sheets, blankets,
towels, anything to cover their red-skinned, sweaty
embarrassment, memories of the previous two wild
hours turning their hot red faces still redder. It was as
if they were all fourteen years old and had been caught
in the process of a mass snog by their parents.

'Oh my God, we look *so* stupid,' said Dervla.

Outside, Geraldine was taking charge. Later on it
was generally agreed that, having got over her shock,
she had acted with remarkable cool-headedness.

Having confined the seven remaining inmates to one
room, she ordered everybody to retrace their steps and
do everything possible to avoid further altering the
scene of the crime.

'We'll stand in the camera run,' she said, 'and wait
for the cops.'

DAY TWENTY-EIGHT. 6.00 a.m.

Six hours later, as Coleridge left the scene of the crime, the light was beginning to break on an unseasonably grim and drizzly morning.

'Murder weather,' he thought. All of his homicide investigations seemed to have taken place in the rain. They hadn't, of course, just as his boyhood summer holidays had not all been bathed in endless cleansing sunshine. None the less, Coleridge did have a vague theory that atmospheric pressure played a tiny role in igniting a killer's spark. Premeditated murder was, in his experience, an indoor sport.

From beyond the police barriers hundreds of flash-bulbs exploded into life. For a moment Coleridge wondered who it might be that had caused such a flurry of interest. Then he realized that the photographs were being taken of him. Trying hard not to look like a man who knew he was being photographed, Coleridge walked through the silver mist of half-hearted rain and flickering strobe light towards his car.

Hooper was waiting for him with a bundle of morning papers. 'They're all basically the same,' he said.

Coleridge glanced at the eight faces splashed across every front page, one face set apart from the others. He had just met the owners of those faces. All but Kelly, of course. He had not met her, unless one could be said to have met a corpse. Looking at that poor young woman curled up on the toilet floor, actually stuck to it with her own congealed and blackened blood, a kitchen knife sticking out of the top of her head, Coleridge knew how much he wanted to catch this killer. He could not abide savagery. He had never got used to it; it scared him and made him question his faith. After all, why would any sane God possibly want to engineer such a thing? Because he moved in mysterious ways, of course; that was the whole point. Because he surpasseth all understanding. You weren't *meant* to understand. Still, in his job it was hard sometimes to find reasons to believe.

Sergeant Hooper hadn't enjoyed the scene much either, but it was not in his nature to ponder what purpose such horror might have in God's almighty plan. Instead he took refuge in silly bravado. He was thinking that later he would tell the women constables that Kelly had looked like a Teletubby with that knife coming out of the top of her head. It was the same thought that Geraldine had had. Fortunately for Hooper he never ventured such a remark within Coleridge's hearing. Had he done so he would not have lasted long on the old boy's team.

DAY TWENTY-EIGHT. 2.35 a.m.

They had received the call at one fifteen, and had arrived at the scene of the crime to take over the investigation by two thirty. By that time, probably the biggest mistake of the case had already been made.

'You let them *wash*?' Coleridge said, in what was for him nearly a shout.

'They'd been sweating in that box for over two hours, sir,' the officer who had been in charge thus far pleaded. 'I had a good look at them first and had one of my girls look at the ladies.'

'You *looked* at them?'

'Well, blood's blood, sir. I mean, it's red. I would have spotted it. There wasn't any. I assure you we had a very good look. Even under their fingernails and stuff. We've still got the sheet, of course. There's a few drops on that.'

'Yes, I'm sure there is, the blood of the victim. Sadly, though, we do not have a problem identifying the victim. She's glued to the lavatory floor! It's the killer we're looking for, and you let a group of naked suspects in a knife-attack wash!'

There was no point pursuing the matter further. The damage was done. In fact, at that point in the investigation Coleridge was not particularly worried. The murder had been taped, the suspects were being held, all of the evidence was entirely contained within a single environment. Coleridge did not imagine that it would be long before the truth emerged.

'This one's got to be a bit of a no-brainer,' Hooper had remarked as they drove towards the house.

'A what?' Coleridge enquired.

'A no-brainer, sir. It means easy.'

'Then why don't you say so?'

'Well, because .. Well, because it's less colourful, sir.'

'I prefer clarity to colour in language, sergeant.'

Hooper wasn't having this. Coleridge wasn't the only one who had been woken up at one in the morning. 'What about Shakespeare, then?' Hooper reached back in his mind to his English Literature GCSE for a quote. He retrieved a sonnet:

'What about "Shall I compare you to a summer's day? Thou art more lovely and more temperate." Perhaps he should have just said, "I fancy you"?'

'Shakespeare was not a policeman embarking on a murder inquiry. He was poet employing language in celebration of a beautiful woman.'

'Actually, sir, I read that it was a bloke he was talking about.'

Coleridge did not answer. Hooper smiled to himself. He knew that one would annoy the old bastard.

And Coleridge was annoyed once more, for, once they had arrived at the house, it became very quickly clear to him that this investigation was by no means straightforward at all.

The pathologist had no light to shed on the subject.

'What you see is what you get, chief inspector,' she said. 'At eleven forty-four last night somebody stabbed this girl in the neck with a kitchen knife and immediately thereafter plunged the same knife through her skull, where it remained. The exact time of the attack was recorded on the video cameras, which makes a large part of my job rather redundant.'

'But you concur with the evidence of the cameras?'

'Certainly. I would probably have told you between eleven thirty and eleven forty, but of course I could never be as accurate as a time code. Bit of luck for you, that.'

'The girl died instantly?' Coleridge asked.

'On the second blow, yes. The first would not have killed her had she gone on to receive treatment.'

'You've watched the tape.'

'Yes, I have.'

'Do you have any observations to offer?'

'Not really, I'm afraid. I suppose I was a little surprised at the speed with which the blood puddle formed. A corpse's blood doesn't flow from a wound, you see, because the heart is no longer pumping it. It merely leaks, and an awful lot leaked in two minutes.'

'Significant?'

'Not really,' the pathologist replied. 'Interesting to me, that's all. We're all different physiologically. The girl was leaning forward, so gravity will have increased the speed of blood loss. I suppose that accounts for it.'

Coleridge looked down at the dead girl kneeling on the floor in front of the toilet. A curious position to end up in, for all the world like a Muslim at prayer. Except that she was naked. And, of course, there was the knife.

'Who would have thought the old man to have had so much blood in him,' Coleridge murmured to himself.

'Excuse me?'

'*Macbeth*,' said Coleridge. 'Duncan's death. There was also a lot of blood on that occasion.'

Coleridge had gone to bed with the *Complete Works* the night before, preparing for the amateur dramatics audition that he knew he would fail.

'Well, there normally is a lot of blood when people get stabbed,' stated the pathologist matter of factly. 'So that's your lot for the moment,' she continued. 'We might find something on the knife handle. The killer wrapped the sheet round it for grip and also, one presumes, in order to avoid leaving prints. They'd all been in a sweatbox, secreting copiously, so some cellular matter might have soaked through. Could possibly get an ID from that.'

'Nobody's touched the knife, then?' After the washing incident Coleridge was ready to believe anything.

'No, but we'll obviously have to touch it to get it out of her head. We'll almost certainly have to cut the skull as well. Grim work, I'm afraid.'

'Yes.' Coleridge leaned over the body, trying to see as far as he could into the toilet cubicle without stepping in the pool of congealed blood. He put his hands against the walls to support himself. 'Hold my waist, please, sergeant. I don't want to fall onto the poor girl.'

Hooper did as he was told and Coleridge, thus suspended, took in the scene. Kelly's naked bottom stared up at him and, beyond that, the toilet bowl.

'Very clean,' he remarked.

'What, sir?' Hooper asked, surprised.

'The lavatory bowl, it's very clean.'

'Oh, I see, I thought you meant . . .'

'Be quiet, sergeant.'

'That was Kelly.' Geraldine spoke from behind him. 'Scrubbed the toilet twice a day. She can't stand dirty bogs . . .' Her voice trailed away as she reminded herself that Kelly was past caring about anything now. 'I mean, she couldn't stand it . . . She was a very neat and tidy girl.'

Coleridge continued his investigation. 'Hmmm, not a particularly thorough girl, though, I fear. She missed a few small splashes of what I think is vomit on the seat. Thank you, you can pull me back now.'

With Hooper's help and by walking his hands backwards along the walls, Coleridge rejoined the pathologist.

'What about the sheet worn by the killer?' he asked. 'The one he took back into the boys' bedroom?'

'You might be luckier with that. I mean, all that sweating must have loosened some skin. Some of it would certainly have stuck to the sheet.'

The original officer on the scene chipped in at this point. 'We think that the sheet the killer used was the same one as the black lad, Jason, put on when he emerged from the room after the event, sir.'

'Ah,' said Coleridge thoughtfully. 'So if by any chance Jason were our man, then he would have a convenient alibi for any residue of his DNA on the sheet.'

'Yes, I suppose he would.'

'It'll take a day or two at the lab,' said the pathologist. 'Shall I send it off?'

'Yes, of course. Not a lot of point in my looking at it,' Coleridge replied. 'I see that the lavatory door has a lock.'

'That's right,' said Geraldine. 'It's the only one in the house. It's electronic and they can open it from either side, in case one of them faints or decides to top themselves or whatever. We can also spring it from the control room.'

'But Kelly didn't use the lock?'

'No. None of them did.'

'Really?'

'Well, I suppose if you've got a camera staring at you while you do your thing privacy becomes sort of irrelevant. Besides, there's a light that says when the loo's occupied.'

'So the killer would not have expected to encounter a lock?'

'No, not since about the second day.'

Coleridge inspected the door and the lock mechanism for some moments.

'I only had it fitted as an afterthought,' said Geraldine. 'I thought we ought to give them at least the *impression* of privacy. If only she'd used it.'

'I'm not sure it would have helped,' said Coleridge. 'The killer was obviously very determined, and the restraining bar on this lock is only plywood. It would have taken very little force to kick it open.'

'I suppose so,' said Geraldine.

Coleridge summoned the police photographer to ensure that photographs of the door and its catch were taken, and then he and Sergeant Hooper retraced the killer's steps from the lavatory back to the boys' bedroom.

'Nothing to be got from the floor, I suppose.'

'Hardly, sir,' said Hooper. 'The same eight people have been back and forth over these tiles twenty-four seven for the last four weeks.'

'Twenty-four seven?'

Hooper gritted his teeth before replying. 'It's an expression, sir. It means twenty-four hours a day, seven days a week.'

'I see . . . Quite useful. Economic, to the point.'

'I think so, sir.'

'American, I presume?'

'Yes, sir.'

'I wonder if any item of colloquial English will ever again emanate from this country.'

'I wonder if anybody apart from you remotely cares, sir.' Hooper knew that he was safe to be as cheeky as he liked. Coleridge was no longer listening to him, nor was he really thinking about the changing nature of English slang. That was just his way of concentrating. Coleridge always turned into an even bigger bore than usual when his mind began to gnaw at a problem. Hooper knew that he was in for weeks of grim pedantry.

After another half-hour or so of searching, during which nothing of interest was discovered, Coleridge decided to leave the lab people to their work. 'Let's go and meet the suspects, shall we?'

DAY TWENTY-EIGHT. 3.40 a.m.

The housemates were being held in the Peeping Tom boardroom, situated on the upper floor of the production complex across the moat from the house. The seven tired, scared young people had been taken there after being questioned briefly at the scene and then allowed to shower and dress. Now they had all been sitting together for over an hour, and the truth of the night's terrible event had well and truly sunk in.

Kelly was dead. The girl with whom they had all lived and breathed for the previous four weeks, and with whom they had all been groping and laughing only a few hours before, was dead.

That was the *second* most shocking thing any of them had ever in their lives been forced to try to come to terms with.

The most shocking thing of all was the self-evident fact that one of them had killed her.

The penny had dropped slowly. At first there had been much weeping and hugging, expressions of astonishment, confusion, sadness and solidarity. They had felt as if they were the only seven people in the world, bonded by a glue that no outsider would ever understand. It was all so strange and confusing: the four

255

weeks of isolation and game-playing, then the mad, drunken excess of the sweatbox, the sudden onrush of raw sexual energy that had taken them all by surprise . . . and then the death of their comrade and the house suddenly *full of police*. That had almost been the strangest thing of all. To find their house, the place where nobody could enter and none could leave save by a formal and complex voting procedure, full of police officers! Of course, they had been intruded on before, when Woggle was arrested, but that had been different. The housemates had remained in the majority, in some way in control. This time they had been reduced to a huddled little ghetto in the boys' bedroom, pleading to be allowed to wash themselves.

All this common and unique experience had at first served to create a gang mentality for the seven surviving housemates . . . Jazz, Gazzer, Dervla, Moon, David, Hamish and Sally.

But as they sat together around the big table in the Peeping Tom boardroom, rapidly sobering up, that solidarity had begun to evaporate like the alcohol in their systems. To be replaced by fear, fear and suspicion. Suspicion of each other. Fear that they themselves might be suspected.

One by one Coleridge saw them, these people who were shortly to become so familiar to him. And with each brief interview the depressing truth became clearer. Either six of them genuinely knew nothing, or they were each protecting all the others, because none of them had anything to say to him that shed any light upon who had left the sweatbox in order to kill Kelly.

'To be honest, officer,' Jazz told Coleridge, 'I could not have told you what was up and what was down inside that box, let alone where the exit was. It was totally dark, man. I mean *totally*. That was the point of it. We'd been in there two hours, and we were just *so* pissed, I mean, *completely*—'

'How did you know it was two hours?' Coleridge interrupted.

'I didn't know, I heard since. Man, I would not have known if it was two hours, two minutes or two *years*. We was out to it, floating, zombied, brain-fucked to the double-max degree, and we was getting it on! I was getting it on! Do you understand? Four weeks without so much as a touch of a woman, and suddenly I was *getting it on*. Believe me, man, I wasn't thinking about where no exit was. I was happy where I was.'

This was the common theme of the majority of the interviews. Each of them had been utterly disoriented inside that box, losing all concept of space and time, and contentedly so, for they had been enjoying themselves.

'It was so fookin' hot in there, inspector,' Moon assured him, 'and dark, and we were drunk. It was like floating in space or summat.'

'Did you notice anybody leave?'

'Maybe Kelly?'

'Maybe?'

'Well, I didn't even know where the entrance was by then. At the end of the day, I don't think anybody knew fook all about anything, to be quite honest. But I did feel a girl suddenly moving, like, *amongst* us all . . . and quite quickly, which was a bit of a surprise because we were all so chilled.'

'You were chilled?' Coleridge thought he must have misheard. He wanted things to be clear for the tape.

'The witness means relaxed, sir,' Hooper interjected.

'Whatever the witness means, sergeant,' Coleridge snapped, 'she can mean it without your leading her to it. What did you mean, miss?'

'I meant relaxed.'

'Thank you. Please continue.'

'Well, I think that maybe after I felt the girl move there was like a little waft of cooler air. I think maybe

I realized that somebody was going for a piss or whatever, but quite frankly, at the end of the day, I weren't that bothered. I mean I were giving somebody – I *think* it were Gazzer – a blow-job at the time.'

Interview after interview told the same story: varying degrees of sexual activity plus the idea that someone, probably a girl, had scrambled over them shortly before the game was brought to an abrupt halt. They each remembered this moment because it had rather jarred the 'chilled' atmosphere that had developed.

'And this movement happened quite suddenly?' Coleridge asked each of them. They all agreed that it had, that there had been a sudden flurry of limbs and soft warm skin, followed by the faintest waft of cooler air. With hindsight it was clear that this must have been Kelly rushing off to the lavatory.

'Could anybody have sneaked off after her?' Coleridge asked them. Yes, was the reply, they all felt strongly that in the cramped, crowded darkness and confusion of it all, it would have been possible for a second person to follow Kelly out of the sweatbox unnoticed.

'But you yourself were unaware of it.'

'Inspector,' said Gazzer, and he might have been speaking for them all, 'I wasn't aware of anything.'

Sally's were the only recollections that differed substantially from the norm. When she appeared Coleridge had been taken aback. He had never seen a woman whose arms were completely covered in tattoos before and he knew that he would have to try not to let it prejudice his view of her.

'So you were not involved in the sexual activity?' Coleridge asked.

'No. I decided to try and use the exercise to improve my understanding of other cultures,' Sally replied. 'I found a corner of the box, ignored what the others were doing and concentrated on recreating the consciousness of a Native American fighting woman.'

Coleridge could not stop himself from reflecting that to the best of his knowledge all the Native American fighting had been done by men, but he decided to let it go. 'You didn't want to join in the, um, fun?' he asked.

'No, I'm a dyke, and all the other women who were in that box are straight, or at least they think they are. Besides, I had to concentrate on something other than them, you see. I *had to concentrate.*'

'Why?'

'I don't like dark, confined spaces. I don't like getting into black boxes.'

'Really? Is this something you have much experience of?'

'Not for real, no. But in my head I imagine it all the time.'

Coleridge noted that the cigarette Sally held in her hand was shaking. The column of smoke rising above it was jagged. Like the edge of a rough saw. 'Why do you imagine dark boxes?'

'To test myself. To see what happens to me when I go there.'

'So on being confronted by a real physical black box, you decided to use it as a test of your mental strength.'

'Yes, I did.'

'And did you pass the test?'

'I don't know. I don't remember anything about what happened in that box. It just totally weirded me out and so I went somewhere else in my head.'

And press her though he might, Coleridge could get nothing more out of Sally.

'I'm not holding out on you,' she protested, 'I swear. I liked Kelly. I'd tell you if I knew something, but I don't remember anything at all. I don't even remember *being* there.'

'Thank you, that'll be all for now,' Coleridge said.

As Sally was leaving she turned at the door. 'One thing, though. Anything Moon tells you is a lie, all right? That woman wouldn't know the truth if it stuck a knife in her head.' Then she left the room.

'Do you think she was trying to tell us Moon did it?' Hooper said.

'I have no idea,' Coleridge replied.

Both David and Hamish struck Coleridge as evasive. Their statements were much the same as Garry's, Jason's and Moon's had been, but they seemed less frank, more guarded.

'I couldn't tell you where Kelly was in the box,' said Hamish. 'I know I was feeling up one of the girls, but to be honest I couldn't tell you which.'

Something about his manner struck Coleridge as jarring. Later on, when discussing it with Hooper, the sergeant admitted that he had felt the same way. They had both interviewed enough liars to be able to spot the signs. The defensive body language, the folded arms and squared shoulders, the body pushed right back in the seat as if preparing for attack from any side. Hamish was probably lying, they thought, but whether it was a big lie or a little one they could not tell.

'You're a doctor, it says here,' Coleridge observed.

'I am,' said Hamish.

'I would have thought that a doctor might have been a little more aware. After all, there were only four women in that darkness. You'd known them all for a month. Are you seriously telling me that you were groping one of them and had no idea which?'

'I was very drunk.'

'Hmmm,' said Coleridge after a long pause. 'So much for doctors and their sensitive hands.'

Coleridge would have known that David was an actor without having to refer to Peeping Tom's notes. There was something mannered about his expressions of grief; not that this meant he wasn't sorry, but it did mean he was conscious of how he was presenting his sorrow. The pauses before he spoke were too long, the

260

frank manly eye contact a little too frank and manly. He smoked a number of cigarettes during his interview, but since he clearly did not inhale it struck Coleridge that the cigarettes were props. He held them between his thumb and forefinger, his hand cupped around the burning end which pointed towards his palm. Not a very practical way to hold a cigarette, Coleridge thought, but it certainly gave an impression of anguish. When David wasn't looking earnestly into Coleridge's eyes, he was staring intently at his cupped cigarette.

'I loved Kelly. We were mates,' he said. 'She was such a free and open spirit. I only wish I'd known her better. But I certainly was not aware of her in the box. To be honest, Dervla would be more my type if I'd been fishing, but I'm afraid I was too drunk and disoriented to take much interest in anyone.'

It was all so vague, so confused. Coleridge inwardly cursed these scared, bewildered young people. Or he cursed six of them, at any rate. The murderer he could only grudgingly respect. Six people had been present when the murderer left the box and also when he returned and yet they had all been too damned drunk and libidinous to notice.

Only Dervla, to whom he spoke last, was clearer in her recollection. This was of course Coleridge's first experience of Dervla, but immediately he liked her. She seemed to be the steadiest of the bunch, intelligent but also giving the impression of being frank and open. He found himself wondering what madness had moved a nice, clever girl like her to get involved with an exercise as utterly fatuous as *House Arrest* in the first place. He could not understand it at all, but then Coleridge felt that he no longer understood anything very much.

Dervla alone seemed to have been relatively aware of her surroundings during those last few minutes in the sweatbox. She recalled that when the agitated girl had made her hurried exit, she herself must have been close to the flaps, for she had definitely felt the waft of cooler air. She was also quite certain that the figure she felt slide across her and exit through the flaps had most definitely been Kelly.

'I felt her breasts slide across my legs, and they were big, but not as big as Sally's,' she said, reddening at the thought of the scene that she must be conjuring up in the minds of the detectives.

'Anything else about her?' Coleridge asked.

'Yes, she was shaking with emotion,' said Dervla. 'I know that I felt a real sense of tension, almost of panic.'

'So she was upset?' Coleridge asked.

'I'm trying to remember what I thought at the time,' Dervla said. 'Yes, I think I thought she was upset.'

'But you don't know why.'

'Well, a lot of strange things were happening inside that box, inspector, things that would be embarrassing enough to recall in the morning without having to relate them to police officers.'

'Strange things?' Coleridge asked. 'Be specific, please.'

'I can't see how it's relevant.'

'This is a murder investigation, miss, and it's not your place to decide what's relevant.'

'Well, OK, then. I don't know what Kelly was doing before she bolted, but I know she'd been feeling pretty wild earlier in the evening. We all had, and still were. I myself was getting close to the point of no return with Jason, or at least I think it was Jason. I *hope* it was Jason.' She glanced down, and her eyes rested on the little revolving cogs on the cassette tape recorder. She reddened.

'Go on,' said Coleridge.

'Well, after Kelly slid across me and went off, Jazz and I . . . carried on with our um . . . canoodling.'

Coleridge caught Hooper smiling at this choice of word and glared at him. There was nothing in his opinion remotely amusing about discussing the circumstances that led up to a girl's being murdered.

'And that was it, really,' Dervla concluded. 'Shortly after that we heard all the commotion, and Jazz went out to see what was going on and who was in the house. I remember that at that point I actually felt relieved at the interruption. It gave me a chance to collect myself and realize what I was doing, just how far I'd let myself get carried away. I was happy that something had occurred to stop the party.'

Dervla stopped herself, realizing how terrible this must sound. 'Of course, I felt differently when I realized what had actually happened.'

'Of course. And you don't know anything about what might have upset Kelly?'

'No, I don't, but I suppose somebody must have pushed their luck a bit with her, if you know what I mean. I always thought that Kelly was a bit of a tease on top but what my mother would call a "nice girl" underneath. I don't think she'd have gone all the way in that box.'

'Really?'

'Yes. The other night Hamish followed her out into the nookie hut, but I don't think he got anywhere . . . Not that I'm saying anything about Hamish, you understand.'

'Were you aware of anybody following Kelly out of the box last night?'

'No, I was not.'

'You've said yourself that you were situated near the entrance. You're sure you noticed nothing?'

'As I've told you, I was occupied at the time. The whole business was rather a giddy affair.'

Later, Coleridge was to ponder Dervla's choice of words and phrases: 'canoodling', 'giddy affair', as if she was talking about an innocent flirtation at a barn dance rather than an orgy.

After Dervla had completed her interview and returned to the conference room, Coleridge and Hooper discussed her evidence for some time.

'Very mysterious that she had no sensation of the second person leaving the box,' Hooper said.

'Yes,' Coleridge replied. 'Unless . . .'

Hooper finished his sentence for him. 'Unless she was the person who left.'

One Winner

DAY TWENTY-EIGHT. 7.30 p.m.

The door closed behind David. He picked up his guitar from the orange couch and began playing a mournful song. He was the last one in. They'd all come home.

There was never any real question in their minds that they would go on with it. Even as they were driven away from the house in seven separate police cars in the early morning following the murder, they were able to get some idea of the scale of interest that would henceforth be shown in them. The corpse was hardly cold, and yet already the word was out and the whole world was rushing to their door.

By the time they left the police station, without charge, eight hours later, there were over a thousand reporters waiting for them.

A thousand reporters. On a recent trip to Britain the President of the United States had rated only two hundred and fifty.

And once Peeping Tom announced that the seven remaining contestants intended to *continue with the game*, the media and the public went berserk with excitement. For these were no longer just seven contestants in a TV game show, as Geraldine continued publicly to maintain, they were seven suspects in a murder hunt. The only seven suspects.

All day and all night it seemed as if people could

talk about nothing else. Bishops and broadcasting watchdogs deplored the decision as a collapse of moral standards. Opportunistic politicians applauded it as evidence of a more open and relaxed society that was 'at ease with its traumas'. The prime minister was invited to comment on the matter during Parliamentary Question Time, and earnestly promised that he would 'listen to the people', attempting, if possible, to 'feel their pain' and get back to parliament the moment he had an idea about how they felt.

Many people expressed surprise that the seven contestants were legally free to go back into the house, but of course there was nothing to stop them. Even though it was clear that one of them had murdered Kelly, the police were unable to find evidence to detain any of them. They were all free to go for the time being, free to do what they wanted, and what they wanted, it soon turned out, was to go back into the house.

Efforts were made by concerned individuals to implement the law that states that people cannot profit from media exploitation of their crimes. But what profit? The inmates of the house were not being paid for their efforts. And what crime? Six of the people had not committed one, and the identity of the person who had done it remained a complete mystery. Once he or she was detected, it would of course be possible to prevent them from appearing on television, but until then there was nothing that could be done to restrain any of them.

DAY TWENTY-EIGHT. 6.50 p.m.

'I say we fahkin' go for it.'

Garry had been the first to speak. He was a geezer and a hard one at that, and he wasn't squeamish about using a toilet in which someone had been knifed.

'I've been in a lot of bogs with blood on the floor,' he said, thinking to himself that this comment would play rather well on the telly, before he remembered that he was outside the house and for the first time in a month there were no cameras being trained on him. 'So I say fahk it, let's have it large.'

Geraldine had managed to collect all seven of the tired, confused housemates as they left the police station and wrestle them onto a waiting minibus. It had not been easy: the offers of money had burst forth with a roar the moment the station door had opened. Any one of the remaining housemates could have got a hundred thousand for an exclusive interview there and then. Fortunately, Geraldine had brought a megaphone with her and she was entirely unembarrassed about using it. 'You'll do much better if you bargain collectively,' she shouted, 'so get on the bus!'

Finally, with the help of the ten huge security men she had brought with her, she managed to get her precious charges inside the vehicle and there they sat like obedient children while the police tried to clear a path for them to depart. Outside, hundreds of cameras were clicking and whirring, microphones were being banged against the windows; the noise of the shouted questions was cacophonous.

'Who do you think did it?' 'How do you feel?' 'Did she deserve it?' 'Was it a sex thing?'

Even inside the bus Geraldine had to use her megaphone to get their attention. She knew what she required of the housemates, and she got right down to telling them.

'Listen to me!' she shouted.

The seven shell-shocked people stared back at her.

'I know you're all sorry about Kelly, but we have to be practical. Look at what's going on outside! The entire world's press have turned up, and for what? Not for Kelly, she's gone, but for *you*, that's who. So think about that for a minute.'

While the seven housemates thought about it the minibus began to edge its way through the roaring sea of journalists.

'Why did you people get into this thing in the first place?' Geraldine continued. 'Why did you write to Peeping Tom?'

They were confused: there had been so many reasons given at the start of the whole business. 'To really stretch myself as a person . . .' 'To explore different aspects of who I am . . .' 'To discover new horizons and life adventures . . .' 'To provide a goal, and to be a role model.'

They had all known the codes, the things that they were *supposed* to say. The new language of pious self-justification. All rubbish, of course, and Geraldine knew it. She knew why they had applied to be on Peeping Tom, and no amount of pretentious New Age waffle could disguise it. They had done it to *get famous* and that was why Geraldine knew that they would all go back into the house.

The bus was finally pulling away from the mob at the police station, and the motorbike photographers were beginning their pursuit, weaving in and out of the traffic, oblivious to their own safety or anybody else's, intoxicated by the hunt.

'So,' Geraldine barked, 'let's leave aside for a moment the issue of who kill . . . of how poor Kelly died, and consider the opportunity that her sad demise has opened up for you people. I am talking about fame beyond frontiers, beyond your wildest dreams. This show will be broadcast worldwide, no question about that. By the time you come out of our house your faces will be recognizable in every town, village and *home* on the planet. Think about that. If you guys split up now the story's over in a week, you'll all make a few quid talking about Kelly to the papers and that'll be it. But if you stick together! If you go back into the house together! You'll be the biggest story on earth day after day after day.'

'You mean people will be watching to try to work out which one of us killed Kelly?' Dervla said.

'Well, that certainly,' Geraldine conceded. 'But the police are trying to work that out anyway, so you might as well make a profit out of it. Besides, there's so much more to this, the human angle of how you all cope with the tragedy, with each other. Believe me, this is a century-defining definition of what constitutes good telly.'

Geraldine could see that they were all still struggling with the terrifying and bewildering change in their circumstances.

Sally spoke up in a sad small voice, a voice no one had heard her use before. 'I thought that maybe it would be nice just to go home for a bit.'

'Exactly!' Geraldine exclaimed. 'That's what I'm saying.'

'No, I mean my real home.'

'Oh, I see . . . Fuck that. The house is your real home now.' Geraldine's own life was so entirely defined by her work that she simply could not understand the idea that somebody might be seriously considering putting toast and Marmite and a bit of a cry on the sofa with Mum before participating in the greatest tele-vision event in decades.

'All right, let's look at it this way,' Geraldine said, able to adopt a quieter, more conciliatory tone now that they had left the roaring crowd behind them. 'If one of you killed her, then that means six of you didn't, right? Six people who can either slink away having had your big chance ruined by a cruel psychopath, or six people who can have the guts to stand up for themselves. Don't forget that you have a *right* to pursue this journey of personal empowerment, you have a *right* to be stars.

Because, at the end of the day, you're all strong, fabulous, independent people, so I say just go for it! Crack on, because you're brilliant, you really are. And I really, really mean that.'

But still they wavered.

To go back into that house . . .

To sleep in those beds . . .

To use the toilet. The toilet where only hours before . . .

Having tried conciliation, Geraldine picked up her cosh once more and played her strongest card of all: the truth. 'All right, let's really get down to it, shall we? Yesterday you were all part of a crappy, unoriginal little cloned game show that we've all seen ten times before. You've all watched them and you all know that the people on them basically look like a bunch of arrogant self-absorbed arseholes. Do you think you looked any different? Think again. I'll show you the tapes if you like. Blimey, the public preferred *Woggle* to you lot. Stars? Fuck off. Disposable minor celebs is all you were. That's the truth. I'm levelling with you for your own good.'

'Now look here . . .' David began to protest.

'Shut up, David, this is my fucking bus and I'm fucking talking.'

David shut up.

'*Now*, however,' Geraldine continued, 'you can change all that. If you have the guts, you have the chance to be a part of the most fascinating television experiment of all time. A live whodunit! A nightly murder mystery with a *real live victim* . . .'

She realized what she'd said the moment she said it. 'Oh, all right, then, a real dead victim if you like. The point is that this will be the biggest show in history, and you are the stars of it! Kelly has given you the chance to be the thing *she* wanted most of all, to be a star! Do you hear me? Genuinely, properly famous, and to get it all you have to do is continue to play the game.'

Geraldine looked at their faces. She had won her argument. It had not taken long.

Together they quickly concocted a press release, which they issued through the bus window as they approached the house. 'We, the seven remaining housemates of *House Arrest Three*, have elected to continue with our sociological experiment as a tribute to Kelly and her dreams. We knew Kelly and know that she loved this show. It was a part of her, and she gave her life for it. We feel that for us to give up now and to jettison all that she worked for would be an insult to the memory of a beautiful strong woman and human being, whom we loved very, very much. *House Arrest* continues because it is what Kelly would have wanted. We are doing it for her. Crack on!'

'That's fookin' beautiful, that is,' Moon said.

Then Sally started to cry and in a moment they were all crying. Except Dervla. Dervla was thinking about something else.

'Just one thing,' she said, as the bus forced its way through the crowds who had gathered round the Peeping Tom compound.

'Yeah, what?' said Geraldine brusquely. Having secured their agreement, she wanted no further discussion, *particularly* from Princess fucking Dervla.

'Suppose the killer strikes again?'

Geraldine pondered this for a moment. 'Well, it's never going to happen, is it? I mean, come on, you'll all be on your guard, and we'd never do something like the sweatbox thing again. Obviously all anonymous environments and closed-in group activities are out. No more bunches of people, everything open and spread out. Really you should be sorry. I mean, imagine if it *were* possible for it to happen again. Just how fucking big would the remains of you be *then*?'

DAY TWENTY-EIGHT. 8.00 p.m.

They had been back inside for half an hour, but no one had spoken. Some lay on their beds, some sat on the couches. Nobody had yet used the toilet.

'This is Chloe,' the voice sounded through the house from the concealed speakers. 'In order to maintain the integrity of the game structure we have decided to treat Kelly's absence as an eviction from the house. Therefore there will be no further evictions this week. As a special treat, and in view of your long and tiring day, a takeaway meal for you has been placed in the store cupboard.'

Jazz went to get it. 'Chinese,' he said, returning with the bags.

It was the only word uttered in the house until long after they had finished the food.

Finally David broke the silence. 'So one of us killed Kelly?'

'So it would fookin' seem,' Moon replied.

There was silence again.

There was silence also in the monitoring bunker as the hours ticked by.

Late that night Inspector Coleridge slipped into the box and sat down beside Geraldine. He wanted to see for himself how the show was put together. When he spoke Geraldine actually jumped.

'You know that if I could have stopped you carrying on with this, I would.'

'I don't see why you would want to,' Geraldine replied. 'How many policemen get the chance to watch their suspects in the way you're doing? Normally when no charges are pressed the prey is gone, off covering its tracks and hiding its secrets. If this lot are holding onto any secrets, then they'd better keep them pretty close.'

'I would have liked to stop you on moral grounds. The whole country is watching your programme because they know that one of the people on it is a murderer.'

'Not just that, inspector, as if that wasn't good enough telly in itself,' Geraldine replied gleefully. 'They're also watching because there is always the chance that it might happen again.'

'That possibility had occurred to me.'

'And I can assure you that it's occurred to our little gang of wannabes. How good is that?'

'Murder is not a spectator sport.'

'Isn't it?' Geraldine asked. 'All right, then. If you didn't have to watch this because you're investigating it, would you still watch it? Come on, be honest, you would, wouldn't you?'

'No, I wouldn't.'

'Well, then, you're even more boring than I thought you were.'

Silence descended as they watched the housemates clearing away the debris of their meal.

'Why are they doing it, do you think?' Coleridge asked.

'Why do you think? To get famous.'

'Ah yes, of course,' said Coleridge. 'Fame.'

Fame, he thought, the holy grail of a secular age. The cruel and demanding deity that had replaced God. The one thing. The only thing, it seemed to Coleridge, that mattered any more. The great obsession, the all-encompassing national focus, which occupied 90 per cent of every newspaper and 100 per cent of every magazine. Not faith, but fame.

'Fame,' he murmured once more. 'I hope they enjoy it.'

'They won't,' Geraldine replied.

DAY TWENTY-NINE. 6.00 p.m.

Coleridge sat in the larger of the two halls in the village youth centre awaiting his turn among all the other hopefuls. He was very, very tired, having been up for most of the previous two nights investigating a real live 'murder most foul'.

Now he was in the realms of fiction, but the words of the great 'Tomorrow and tomorrow and tomorrow' speech, one of his favourites, seemed to be draining from his mind.

He tried to concentrate, but people kept asking him about the Peeping Tom murder. It was understandable, of course – the whole affair was colossal news, and they all knew that Coleridge was a senior policeman. He would not have dreamt of telling them about his direct association with the crime. 'I expect my colleagues will do their best,' he said, trying to fix his mind on being a poor player about to strut and fret his hour upon the stage.

To Coleridge's great relief his picture had not been shown on any of the news broadcasts during the day, and he did not expect it to be in the morning papers either. He simply did not look enough like a 'top cop' to warrant inclusion. When the press did print a photo it was of Patricia, there being nothing they liked more than a comely 'police girl'.

Finally, it was Coleridge's turn to audition, and he was called into the smaller room in order to perform before Glyn and Val's searching gaze. He gave it everything he had, even managing the ghost of a tear when he got to 'out, brief candle'. There was nothing like the murder of a twenty-one-year-old girl to remind a person that life truly was a 'walking shadow'.

When he had finished, Coleridge felt that he had acquitted himself well.

Glyn seemed to think so too. 'That was lovely. Absolutely lovely and very moving. You clearly have great depth.'

Coleridge's hopes soared, but only for a moment.

'I always think that *Macduff* is the key role in the final act,' said Glyn. 'It's a small part, but it needs a big actor. Would you like to play it?'

Trying not to let his disappointment show, Coleridge said that he would be delighted to play Macduff.

'And since you won't have many lines to learn,' Val chipped in chirpily, 'I presume I can put you down for scenery-painting and the car pool?'

DAY TWENTY-NINE. 9.30 p.m.

Episode twenty-eight of *House Arrest* went out in an extended ninety-minute special edition on the evening following the day after the murder. It should have been episode twenty-nine that night, but there had been no show on the previous evening, partly out of respect and partly because the inmates of the house had spent all day at the police station.

All except one inmate, who was in the morgue.

The special edition show included the lead-up to the murder and the murder itself. There was a tasteful ten-second edit for the actual moment when the sheet rose and fell, a pointless precaution, since it had been aired endlessly on the news anyway. Also included in the show was the return of the housemates into the house in order to bring the chronology up to date. The whole thing was generally considered to have been very good telly indeed. Straight after the broadcast, and by way of absolving themselves from all criticism and responsibility, the network aired a live discussion programme about the morality of their having continued to broadcast the show at all. Geraldine Hennessy appeared on the discussion, along with various representatives of the great and the good.

'I fear that what we have just watched was depressingly inevitable,' said a distinguished poet and broadcaster. Distinguished, as Geraldine would point out to him afterwards in hospitality, principally for appearing on discussion programmes.

'Reality television, as it is called,' drawled the distinguished broadcaster, 'is a return to the gladiatorial arenas of ancient Rome. What we are watching is conflict, conflict between trapped and desperate antagonists who compete for the approval of the baying crowd. Like the plebeians of old, we raise and lower our thumbs to applaud the victor and condemn the vanquished. The only difference is that these days we do it via a telephone poll.'

Geraldine shifted in her seat. She hated the way supposed intellectuals leeched off popular culture while loftily condemning it.

'Personally,' the distinguished broadcaster continued, 'I am astonished that it has taken so long for murder to become a tactic in these entertainments.'

'Yes, but does that justify its being broadcast?' the shadow minister for home affairs leapt in, angry that the discussion had been underway for over two minutes and that he had yet to speak. 'I say most definitely not. We have to ask ourselves what sort of country we wish to live in.'

'And I would agree with you,' said the distinguished poet, 'but will you have the courage to deny the mob? The public must have its bread and circuses.'

Geraldine swallowed an overwhelming desire to unleash a four-letter tirade and resolved to be reasonable. That was, after all, why she had come on the show. The last thing she needed at this crucial moment in her career was to be taken off the air. 'Look,' she said. 'I don't like what has happened here any more than you do.'

'Really?' sniffed the poet.

'But the truth of the matter is if we don't put it out one of the low-rent channels will. The moment the inmates decided to carry on with the show, we didn't have a choice in the matter. If we had refused to go on, some publicist or other would have packaged the lot of them up and sold them to the highest bidder. Cable or satellite, probably. A programme like this could finally bring those carriers into the heart of the mainstream.'

'You could have refused to let them use the house,' the programme's distinguished host interrupted.

'There are any number of similar houses currently empty overseas,' Geraldine said. 'I think I saw that the original Dutch one was being sold on the Internet, cameras and all. That would have been perfect. Besides which, the simple truth of the matter is that you could put these people in a garden shed and the public would watch them.'

'Because one of them is a murderer,' said the shadow minister. 'There is blood and gore to be enjoyed here. But let us not forget, Ms Hennessy, a girl has died.'

'Nobody is forgetting that fact, Gavin, but not everybody is attempting to make political capital out of it,' said Geraldine. 'There is a genuine public interest here in what is, after all is said and done, a major public event. The audience feel, I think legitimately, that they are a *part* of this murder. In many ways they feel some responsibility for it. They have been shocked and traumatized. They are grieving and they need to *heal*. They need to remain connected to what is happening in order to begin that healing process. We cannot suddenly cut them out of the loop. Kelly was much loved, an enormously popular contestant. She truly was the people's housemate, and in many ways this is the people's murder.'

It was a brilliant, jaw-droppingly audacious gambit, and totally unexpected. Everybody knew that the real reason Geraldine and the channel wanted to continue broadcasting was money, pure and simple. The stark truth was that Kelly's murder had turned *House Arrest* from a moderately successful programme into a television colossus. Episode twenty-six of the show, the last to be shown before the murder, had achieved a 17 per cent audience share. The episode that had just been broadcast, the one that included the murder, had been watched by almost 80 per cent of the viewing public. Almost half of the *entire* population. Thirty-second advert slots in one of the three commercial breaks had sold at fifteen times their normal price.

'To prevent further broadcasts would be entirely élitist,' Geraldine continued. 'What we would be saying is that *we* know what is good for the public. We, the high and the mighty, the great and the good, will decide what the proles can be trusted to watch. That is totally unacceptable in a modern democracy. Besides which, let me remind you that this event has already been seen live on the Internet. It's already part of the culture. It is already *out there*. Do you condone the social disenfranchisement of people who do not own a computer? Are they to be denied their chance to grieve? To come to terms with Kelly's death just because they are not on-line?'

Even the distinguished poet and broadcaster was caught off balance by such a breathtaking display. He was no slouch at pressing every argument into the service of self-promotion, but he was quickly realizing that with Geraldine Hennessy he was punching in a different league.

'Our responsibility to the public,' Geraldine concluded, 'is *not* to take responsibility for the public. Our duty is to enable them to take responsibility for *themselves*. Allow *them* to make a choice. We can only do that by continuing to broadcast. *That* is the responsible and moral thing to do.'

The last thing any of the other panellists wanted was to be seen to be élitist.

'We certainly must listen to what *the people* want,' said the shadow minister. 'Already Kelly Simpson has become part of their lives. They have seen her murdered, they have a right to view her legacy.'

'As I said,' Geraldine repeated. 'They have to be given the opportunity to grieve and to heal.'

The distinguished poet made a late attempt to give the impression that it was actually he who had led the argument to the place where Geraldine had taken it. 'As I believe I implied,' he said, 'in many ways this event crosses the Rubicon in the democratization of the human experience. Reality television has already shown us that privacy is a myth, an unwanted cloak which people eagerly discard like a heavy garment on a summer's day. Death was the last truly private event, but thanks to *House Arrest* it is private no longer. In our open, meritocratic age, no human experience need be seen as "better" or more "significant" than any other, and that includes the final one. If Kelly had the right to be seen living, then surely we must grant her the right to be seen dying.'

Geraldine had won her argument as she had fully expected to.

The simple truth was that people wanted to watch, and it would have been very difficult to deny them that opportunity. And not just in Britain either. Within thirty-six hours of the murder occurring it had been broadcast in *every single country on earth*. Even the rigidly controlled Chinese state broadcaster had been unable to resist the allure of such a very, very good bit of telly.

This worldwide exposure had been the cause of considerable frustration in the Peeping Tom office, which had been caught completely offguard by the sudden surge of international interest in *House Arrest*. When the flood of requests for tapes of the murder came in they had been handled like the ordinary clip requests that arrived in the office every day from morning TV and cable chat shows.

The clips had been *given away*!

Normally Peeping Tom was glad of the publicity. The nation was getting bored with reality television, and it was essential to give the impression that, when Jazz made an omelette or Layla got annoyed about the boys' flatulence, a national event was taking place. Therefore, Peeping Tom Productions actively sought out opportunities to air their show on other programmes. So when every news and current-affairs show on earth had suddenly requested a clip, the Peeping Tom Production secretaries had simply followed procedure and handed them over for nothing. In fact, running off the huge number of tapes requested had actually *cost* Peeping Tom thousands of pounds.

No one involved would ever forget Geraldine's reaction when she realized what had happened. There simply wasn't enough foul language in the vocabulary to encompass her rage. In private, however, she had to acknowledge that it was her fault. She should have thought more quickly. She should have recognized immediately how profitable this murder was going to become.

Geraldine soon made good her mistake, and, from that point on, broadcasters who wanted to show any further footage of *House Arrest* were asked to pay a very heavy price indeed. But no matter how high Geraldine pushed that price, it was paid without a murmur.

Within a week of the murder, Geraldine, the sole owner of Peeping Tom Productions, had become a millionaire many, many times over. Although, as she was to explain in numerous interviews, this fact was of course in no way her reason for wishing to continue to broadcast. Oh no, as she had already made abundantly clear, she did that because it was her *duty*. She did that in order to give the public an opportunity to *grieve*.

Geraldine also dropped heavy but vague hints about substantial charitable donations, the details of which had of course yet to be finalized.

DAY THIRTY. 10.30 a.m.

Some commentators had predicted that such unprecedented international interest in *House Arrest* could not be sustained, but they were wrong. Night after night viewers watched while the seven housemate suspects attempted to coexist in an atmosphere of shock, grief and deep, deep suspicion of each other.

Peeping Tom had announced that, until the police made an arrest, the game would continue as if nothing had happened. Nominations would take place as usual and the inmates would be given a task to learn and perform together in order to earn their weekly shopping budget. In the week following the murder, the task they were given was to present a synchronized water ballet in the swimming pool.

Geraldine had pinched the idea from the Australian version of the show, but in this new context it could not have been more perfect. Geraldine had also been acutely aware of the problem of maintaining the high level of excitement generated by the murder episode and its aftermath, and the idea of subjecting the seven housemates to a water ballet was hailed by many critics as a stroke of genius. The sight of these tired, nervous, desperate people, one of whom was a murderer, all rehearsing classical dance moves together while wearing high-cut Speedo swimwear, ensured that viewing figures for *House Arrest* went up. The sound of Mantovani's most soothing string selections wafting through the house lent an even more sinister and surreal note to the exercises and the bickering.

'You're supposed to raise your *right* fookin' leg, Gazzer!' Moon shouted as Garry attempted to execute a movement known as the Swan.

'Well, I've done my fahkin' groin in, haven't I? I'm not a fahkin' contortionist.'

'Point your toes, girl,' Jazz admonished Sally. 'It says we'll be judged on elegance and fucking grace.'

'I'm a bouncer, Jazz, I don't do fucking grace.'

Even an innocent comment like this caused many a worried look between the housemates and much discussion on the outside. Sally had only been replying to Jazz, but to be reminded that she had more than a casual acquaintance with violence ... Well, it did make you think.

Sometimes they confronted the ever-present agenda head on.

'This fahkin' swimming suit's riding right up my bum,' said Gazzer. 'If I could get hold of the bloke whose idea this was I'd stick a fahkin' knife in his head!' It was meant to be a joke, a dark and courageous joke, but nobody laughed when it was replayed *ad nauseam* in the *House Arrest* trailers, and Gazzer briefly climbed a notch or two in the 'whodunit' polls of the popular press.

DAY THIRTY-ONE. 11.20 a.m.

Coleridge was taking a break from reviewing the Peeping Tom archive when the pathologist's report came in.

'Well, the flecks of vomit on the toilet seat were Kelly's,' he remarked.

'Yuck,' said Trisha.

'Yuck indeed,' Coleridge agreed. 'And, yucker still,

284

there were traces of bile in her neck and in the back of her mouth. They think she'd been gagging. There's no doubt about it: when Kelly left that sweatbox she must have been extremely upset.'

'Poor girl. What a way to spend your last few minutes, trying not to puke up all over people in a tiny plastic tent. God, she must have been drunk.'

'She was. The report says eight times over the limit.'

'That's pretty seriously arsehole— legless. No wonder she was having trouble keeping it down.'

'The report also says that her tongue was bruised.'

'Bruised . . . You mean bitten?'

'No, bruised, reminiscent of someone forcing a thumb into her mouth.'

'Ugh . . . So somebody wanted to shut her up?'

'That would seem the obvious interpretation.'

'Perhaps that's why she was gagging, because someone had their thumb in her mouth. No wonder she wanted to get out of that sweatbox in such a hurry.'

'Yes, although if someone in that box had put a hand into Kelly's mouth sufficiently hard to bruise her tongue, you'd think that *someone* would have heard her complain, wouldn't you?'

DAY THIRTY-TWO. 7.30 p.m.

As the week went on the group began to get the hang of the ballet, and footage of them performing 'The Flight of the Swan' in unison, first out of the pool and then in it, became the most expensive four-minute item of video tape in the history of television.

Besides the ballet, there was of course the simple drama of the inmates' coexistence in the house for the viewing public to pore over and enjoy. Each of the inmates was forever looking at the others, eyeing them as potential murderers . . . as actual murderers. Every glance took on a sinister significance, sly, sideways looks, long piercing stares, hastily averted gazes. When properly edited, every twitch of every facial muscle on every housemate could be made to look like either a confession or an accusation of murder.

And then there were the knives. Flush with money, Geraldine now maintained six cameramen in the camera run corridors at all times, ten at mealtimes. And the sole brief of most of these camera operators was to watch out for knives. Every time a housemate picked one up, to spread some butter, chop a carrot, carve a slice of meat, the cameras were there. Zooming in as the fingers closed around the hilt, catching the bright flash as the overhead strip-lighting bounced off the blade.

The Peeping Tom psychologist stopped trawling the footage for flirtatious body language and started searching for the murderous variety. He was soon joined by a criminologist and an ex-chief constable, and together they discussed at length which of the seven suspects looked most at ease with a knife in their hand.

DAY THIRTY-TWO. 11.00 p.m.

The evenings were the worst times for the housemates. It was then, with nothing much to do, that they had time to think about their situation. When they spoke about it to each other, which was not often, they agreed that the worst aspect of it all was the not knowing. The rules of the game had not changed – they were allowed no contact with the outside world – and since their brief bewildering day in the eye of the storm they had heard and seen absolutely nothing.

The sound of madness had been abruptly and completely turned off. It was as if a door had been slammed, which of course it had. Collectively and alone they longed for information. *What was happening?*

Even Dervla with her secret source of information was in the dark. She had wondered whether her message-writer would stop after the murder, but he hadn't.

'*They all think you're beautiful, and so do I.*'

'*You look tired. Don't worry. I love you.*'

One day Dervla risked mentioning the murder, pretending that she was talking to herself in the mirror. 'Oh, God,' she said to her reflection. 'Who could have done this thing?'

The mirror did not tell her much. '*Police don't know*,' it said. '*Police are fools.*'

DAY THIRTY-THREE. 9.00 a.m.

The forensic technician brought the report on the sheet that had shrouded the killer to Coleridge personally.

'Glad of the opportunity of a break from the lab,' he said. 'We don't get out much and it's not often that anything involving celebrities comes our way. I don't suppose there's any way you could blag me a trip behind the scenes, is there? Just next time you're going. I'd love to see how they do it.'

'No, there isn't,' Coleridge replied shortly. 'Please tell me about the sheet.'

'Absolute mess. Tons of conflicting DNA. Dead skin, bit of saliva, other stuff. You know sheets.'

Coleridge nodded and the technician continued.

'I think they must have been sharing this one, or else they all slept together, because there's strong evidence of four different male individuals on it, one of whom is particularly well represented. There are also traces of a fifth man. I presume that the prominent DNA represents the four boys left in the house and the fifth is

287

Woggle. Let's face it, he'd leave a pretty strong trail, wouldn't he? Of course, I can't be sure without samples from them all to compare it with.'

'All of them? On that one sheet?'

'So it would seem.'

DAY THIRTY-THREE. 11.00 a.m.

'It's eleven o'clock on day thirty-three,' said Andy the narrator, *'and the housemates have been summoned to the confession box in order to give a sample of their DNA. The police request is voluntary but none of the housemates refuse.'*

'Charming,' Dervla observed drily. 'Today's task is to attempt to eliminate yourself from a murder investigation.'

Gazzer seemed disappointed. 'I thought I was going to have to have one off the wrist and give 'em a splash of bollock champagne,' he said, 'but they only wanted a scrape of skin.'

DAY THIRTY-FOUR. 8.00 p.m.

Layla stumbled away from the church, her eyes half blinded with tears. The priest had asked her what had made her feel the need of a faith that she had rejected when she was fifteen.

'Father, I have a death on my conscience.'

'What death? Who has died?'

'A girl, a beautiful girl, an innocent I despised. I hated her, Father. And now she's dead and I ought to be released. But it's worse, she's everywhere, and they're calling her a saint.'

'I don't understand. Who was this girl? Who's calling her a saint?'

'Everyone. Just because she's dead they print her picture and say she was a lovely girl and innocent and that she wouldn't hurt a fly. Well, she hurt me, Father! She hurt me! And now she's dead and she should be gone, but she isn't! She's still here. She's still everywhere, a star!'

The priest looked hard at Layla through the grille. He had never watched *House Arrest*, but he did occasionally see a newspaper.

'Hang on a minute,' he said. 'I know you, don't I? You're . . .'

Layla ran. Even in church she could not escape the shame of her poisonous notoriety as a nonentity. There was no sanctuary from her anti-fame. The fact that she was a failure, the first person to be thrown out of that house. And Kelly had nominated her and then *kissed her* in front of millions. The whole nation had seen Layla accept Kelly's sympathy. And now Kelly was dead and Layla did not feel any better at all.

DAY THIRTY-FIVE. 7.30 p.m.

It was the first eviction night following the murder.

An executive editorial decision had been taken that Chloe should remain upbeat and positive about events. This was, after all, the house style.

'We all *so* miss Kelly big time, because she was such a *top lady* and a sweet young life cruelly snuffed out, which just should *not* have happened, right? Kelly was a laugh, she was a gas, she was bigged up, amped up, loads of fun and just *lovely*. And no way did she deserve such a pants thing to happen to her, not that anybody does. Ooooooh, Kelly, we *miss you*! We all just want to give you a *big hug*! But the show goes on and as the other inmates have made it clear, this whole gig right now is a tribute to Kelly's gorgeous memory.

So you just amp it up in heaven, Kezzer babe, 'cos this one's for you. All right! Let's give it up large for another week *in the house*!'

This announcement was of course followed by the now famous credits.*One house. Ten contestants. Thirty cameras. Forty microphones. One survivor.* A sentence which now carried with it a highly provocative double meaning, but which, it was felt, it would be even more provocative to change. Either way, it was difficult to imagine better telly than this.

'House, can you hear me? This is the voice of Chloe.'

'Yes, we can hear you,' said the seven people assembled on the couches, and for a moment everything seemed back to normal. It was almost possible to imagine that nobody had died.

'The fourth person to leave the Peeping Tom house will be . . .'

A huge dramatic pause.

'David! David, it's time to go!'

'Yes!' said David, punching the air in triumph, following the necessary practice of appearing absolutely delighted to be going.

'David, pack your bags. You have one and a half hours to say your goodbyes, when we will be back live to see you leave the house!'

The nominees for that week had been David and Sally.

Everyone had nominated Sally, because she had become so depressed, and a majority had voted for David, because he was a pain in the arse.

By coincidence, the two people whom the inmates had nominated for eviction were also the nation's two biggest suspects for the murder. Outside the house the eviction vote had turned into a national referendum on who had murdered Kelly. David won by a shade, and when the results were announced it was for a moment almost as if the crime had been solved.

'It's David!' the press wires hummed. 'As we have suspected all along.'

'Yes! It's David!' they shouted on the radio and on the live TV news links. Some even added, 'We are expecting an arrest shortly,' as if while in the house David had been enjoying some kind of sanctuary from the law but now that the people had spoken he could expect no further reprieve.

Inside the house the 90 minutes of allotted departure time ticked by slowly. It did not take David long to pack, and there was only so much group hugging and swearing of undying loyalty that you could do to somebody whom you heartily disliked and whom you suspected might be a murderer. Under normal circumstances the correct etiquette at evictions would be for everybody to put up a hysterical pretence that, despite everything, they adored the person departing and were desperately sorry to see them go. But on this particular night, the tiniest whiff of real reality could not be prevented from intruding.

Not on the outside, though. Outside the house the rules of TV still applied.

David stepped out to the throbbing beat of 'Eye Of The Tiger' and into the white light of a thousand flash cameras. The crowd was enormous. David had been terrified moments before, but now he found himself uplifted by the noise of the crowd. For this one moment at least he was the star he so desperately wanted to be. The eyes of the entire world were upon him and to his credit he pulled off those few seconds with great aplomb. His beautiful shoulder-length hair was lent life by a light breeze, his big black coat billowed romantically. He gave a sardonic smile, threw wide his arms and gave a deep bow.

The crowd, who appreciated a bit of theatre, rewarded David with a redoubled cheer.

Then, smiling broadly, David swept a hand through

his beautiful hair and boarded the platform of the cherry picker to be lifted up over the moat. When he arrived at the other side he bowed deep once more and kissed Chloe's hand. The crowd whooped again while simultaneously observing that David was an even bigger arsehole than they had previously thought.

Together David and Chloe took the short limousine ride to the studio. The music throbbed, the lights bobbed and weaved and the crowd shouted and waved their placards. 'WE LOVE DERVLA!' and 'JAZZ IS LUSH!'

Finally David and Chloe managed to get to the couch, where only Layla had sat before, and begin their chat.

'Wow!' shouted Chloe. 'Amped up! All right! You OK, Dave?'

'Yes, Chloe, I'm fine.'

'*Wicked!*'

'Absolutely. Wicked indeed.'

'Look, fair play to you, David,' Chloe gushed. 'Respect and all that big-time. You've been through it, and we all haven't, and it must have been an incredibly weird experience and all that, but I've got to ask you this, you know that, don't you? Of course you do, you know what I'm going to ask, I can see it in your face, you do know, don't you? What I'm going to ask? Of course you do, so let's get it over with. The big question everybody wants to know is, "Did you kill Kelly?"'

'No, absolutely not. I loved Kelly.' David gave it his best shot – the short pause before answering to focus fully and assume the appropriate look of pained sincerity, the tiny catch in the voice, but it did him no good. The crowd wanted a result; they booed, they jeered; a chant developed: 'Killer. Killer. Killer.'

David was stunned. He hadn't expected this.

'Sorry, babe. They think you did it, babe,' said Chloe.

292

'Sorry and all that, but at the end of the day there it is, babe.'

'But I didn't do it, I promise.'

'*All right, then,*' said Chloe, perking up. 'Let's see if anybody thinks somebody *else* did it.'

There were substantial cheers for this proposition, some without doubt coming from the same people who had only moments before condemned David. The situation, like the police investigation, was confused.

'Well, fair play to you, Dave,' said Chloe. 'There are a lot of young ladies on your side, I can see that, and can you blame them? Wicked!'

And, of course, at this the cheering redoubled.

'So come on, then, David. If you didn't do it, who do you think did?'

'Well, I don't know. I'd have to say Garry, but it's just a guess. I really don't know.'

'Well, we'll just have to wait to the end of the series to find out, won't we? said Chloe, which was an outrageous and entirely unfounded statement, but it sounded convincing enough, such is the seductive power of television.

'In the meantime,' Chloe shouted, 'let's take a look at some of Dave's finest moments *in the house*!'

DAY THIRTY-FIVE. 10 p.m.

Coleridge's team had to deal with thousands of calls from cranks. Every second ring of the phone heralded yet another clairvoyant who had seen the culprit in a dream.

Hooper kept a little tally. 'Dervla appears in most of the male clairvoyants' dreams, and Jazz in the birds'. Funny that, isn't it?'

This call was different, though. It came just as the closing credits of the *House Arrest Eviction Special*

293

were rolling on the TV in the police incident room. When Hooper picked up the phone there was something about the caller's calm and steady tone that made him decide to listen.

'I am a Catholic priest,' said the rather formal, foreign-sounding voice. 'I recently heard a confession from a very distressed young woman. I cannot of course tell you any details, but I believe you should be looking not only at the people who remain in the house, but also those who have left it.'

'Have you been speaking to Layla, sir?' Hooper replied. 'Because we have so far been unable to locate her.'

'I can't say anything more, except that I believe that you should continue trying to find her.' At that the priest clearly felt that he had already said enough, because he abruptly concluded the conversation and rang off.

DAY THIRTY-SIX. 11.00 a.m.

The results of the house DNA tests took three days to arrive, which Coleridge thought was outrageous.

As expected, the individuals represented on the sheet were the male housemates. Jazz, most prominently, Gazzer, David and Hamish equally clearly, and Woggle the least. Woggle, of course, had not been available to supply a sample, having famously skipped bail and disappeared. However, when he left the house he had accidentally left his second pair of socks behind, which despite having since been buried in the garden by the other boys, yielded copious quantities of anarchist DNA.

'So the sheet points towards Jazz, then,' said Hooper.

'Well, perhaps, but we'd expect his presence to be detected more strongly, since he wore the sheet after Geraldine and her team had arrived.'

'Yes, convenient, that, wasn't it?' Hooper observed drily. 'Covers his tracks very nicely, except that if one of the others had worn it too we would expect their presence to show more strongly also. After all, the killer would have been sweating like a pig when he put it on.'

'But all the other three have come up equally.'

'Exactly, sir.'

'Which is a bit weird in itself, isn't it?' said Trish. 'Sort of supports the idea that they were all in it, and they had a pact, to divide suspicion.'

'Well, anyway, at least it rules the girls out,' said Hooper.

'You think so?' Coleridge enquired.

'Well, doesn't it?'

'Only if the sheet under discussion was the one the killer used to hide under, which it *probably* is, but we can't be certain. We know that it's the sheet Jazz grabbed after the Peeping Tom people had entered the house, but can we be sure it was the one that the killer dropped onto the pile when he returned to the sweatbox?'

'Well, it was on top.'

'Yes, but the pile was fairly jumbled, and all the sheets were the same dark colour. More than one sheet may have been on top, so to speak. The tape is not entirely clear.'

'So it doesn't help us at all, then?' said Trish.

'Well, I think it could strengthen a case; it just couldn't make one. If there was further evidence against Jazz, this sheet would help, that's all.'

DAY THIRTY-SEVEN. 9.30 p.m.

For six hours the house had been completely empty, the thirty cameras and forty microphones recording nothing but empty rooms and silence. Six hours of nothing, which had been diligently watched by millions of computer-owners all over the world.

It had begun at three o'clock that afternoon when the police arrived and collected all of the housemates, taking them away without explanation. Naturally this caused a sensation. The lunchtime news bulletins were filled with breathless stories of group conspiracies, and halfway round the world, down in the southern hemisphere, newspaper editors preparing their morning editions considered risking pre-emptive headlines announcing 'THEYALLDUNNIT!'

The reality made everybody look stupid, particularly the police.

'A tape measure!' said Gazzer as he and the others re-entered the house. 'A fahkin' tape measure! That's what Constable Plod's using to catch a killer!'

It had been Trisha's idea to take all of the housemates down to the Peeping Tom rehearsal house at Shepperton and ask them to walk the journey taken by the killer, thereby enabling a comparison to be made with the number of strides taken on the video. Coleridge had thought it was worth a try, but the results had been disappointing and inconclusive. A tall person might have scuttled, a short one might have stretched. The sheet made it impossible to work out clearly the nature of the killer's gait, and so the inmates were released without further comment.

Gazzer's frustration was echoed across the nation. 'The fahkin' FBI have got spy satellites and billion-dollar databases, and what have our lot got? A fahkin' tape measure!'

DAY THIRTY-EIGHT. 7.00 p.m.

Hooper had to ring David's doorbell for a long time before he could get him to answer it. While he waited on the steps of his apartment building the three or four reporters who were hanging about fired questions at him.

'Are you here to arrest him?'

'Was he in league with Sally?'

'Was it all of them that did it? Was it planned in the sweatbox?'

'Do you accept your incompetence in so far not making an arrest?'

Hooper remained silent until finally he was able to announce his credentials into David's intercom and gain admittance.

David greeted him at the lift dressed in a suit of beautiful silk pyjamas. He looked tired. He had been home for only three days but he was already heartily sick of the one thing he had gone into the house to get: fame.

'They don't want me,' he moaned when finally Hooper found himself inside the beautiful flat that David shared with his beautiful cat. 'They want the man that bitch Geraldine Hennessy created. A vain, nasty probable murderer. Vain and nasty I can handle, lots of stars are guilty of that, but probable murderer is something of a career no-no. If only that silly girl had not got herself killed. It's ruined everything for me.' He was entirely unabashed about his take on Kelly's death.

'You think I'm a right bastard, don't you?' he continued, making Hooper coffee from his beautiful shiny cappuccino machine. 'Because I don't pretend to forget my own interests and reasons for going into that house now that the girl is dead? Well, excuse me, but I do not intend to add hypocrisy to my many other faults, which seem now to have become a part of the national consciousness. She was a stranger to me, and if she hadn't been killed I might have had my chance to shine. To show people all the things I have to offer. To be the leading man. Instead it appears that I've been cast in the role of villain.'

'And are you a villain?'

'Oh, for Christ's sake, sergeant! You're worse than that silly bitch Chloe. If I had killed her do you think I'd be telling you? But, as it happens, I didn't. What possible motive could I have?'

'*Fuck Orgy Eleven.*'

David took it well. He clearly had not been expecting this, but he hardly let it show. 'Oh, so you know about that, then? Well, all right. I admit it, I'm a porn star. It's not a crime, but it's not very classy either, and by some appalling coincidence it turned out that the girl Kelly knew. Yes, of course I was hoping that she would keep quiet about it. But I can assure you, I didn't feel strongly enough about it to murder her.'

They talked for a little while longer, but David had very little to add to the statement he had made on the night of the murder. Except to expand on his reasons for suspecting Gazzer. 'He really truly hated her for what she said about his son, you know. He tried to cover it up a bit, but I know how to spot the signs. I'm an actor, you see . . .' David's voice trailed off. His handsome arrogance seemed to evaporate from him and he looked tired. Tired and sad.

Hooper got up to leave, but as he did so he asked one more question. 'If Kelly had not been killed,' he said, 'if the show had proceeded as they normally do, do you honestly believe that the sort of exposure you or anyone else could get on these things could ever lead to proper work – I mean, as a real actor or whatever?'

'Not really, no, sergeant,' David conceded. 'But, you see, I was desperate. Desperate to be a famous actor, certainly, but if I couldn't have that I was happy to settle for just being famous.'

'Well, you got your wish,' said Hooper. 'I hope you enjoy it.'

Outside the building the assembled press pack snapped and barked as he forced his way through to his car.

DAY THIRTY-NINE. 7.00 p.m.

'It's Thursday night,' said Andy the narrator, *'and time for the housemates to make their nominations for this week's eviction.'*

Again everybody nominated Sally.

'She's just got so strange,' Jazz said, when Peeping Tom asked him why he'd nominated her. 'I mean, she sleeps on her own out in the garden and she's so intense. It's a real strain having her around.'

The other four housemates who nominated her all had much the same reason. Moon put it most succinctly. 'I'm just sick to death of her being so fookin' moody . . .'

And then there was the little matter that they were all quite clearly scared of her.

Of course, besides these negative thoughts they all added that they loved Sally and that she was a top girl.

The other person nominated was Garry, his sick jokes having by this time begun to grate on the inmates.

'I mean, I love him, of course,' said Dervla, 'but if he does that screeching noise from *Psycho* one more time when I go to the toilet . . .'

'He's a diamond geezer,' Jazz assured the camera, 'but putting ketchup on Moon's neck while she was having a kip was totally out of order. I mean, he's brilliant, I love him, but you know what? At the end of the day I'm sick of him.'

When the nominations were announced Sally said nothing. She sat and stared into the distance for about half an hour before retreating to what had once been thought of as the nookie hut.

Garry assured everybody that he was happy to stay or go. 'At the end of the day I've got a top life out there. I've got my little lad, I'm looking forward to going to the pub. I'm happy to crack on and big it up. Long as none of you lot stick a knife in my head before I get a chance to snuggle up on that couch with Chloe.'

Later on that evening Sally returned to the living area, and when she spoke it was to nobody in particular. 'You all think I did it, don't you?' she said. 'And you know what? Maybe I did.'

In the monitoring bunker Geraldine did a little dance. 'Thank you, Sally, you gorgeous fat dyke, you! Out lines do not get any better than that. Stick it on the end, Bob, and bang to credits, then when the credits are over, play it again . . . "Maybe I did." Su-fucking-perb!'

DAY FORTY. 8.15 p.m.

Trisha had gone to see Sally's mother, a nervous, worried woman, who had been expecting her. 'I wondered how long it would take you people to get to me, and after what Sally said on the telly I knew you'd be here this morning.'

'Tell me about Sally,' Trisha said.

'Well, you obviously know that my late husband and I were not her birth parents.'

'Yes, we knew Sally was adopted.'

'Ever since the murder happened I haven't been able to sleep,' she said, staring down at her teacup. 'I know *exactly* what Sally will be thinking, I know it. She'll be worrying that people will think that it was her, because of . . . But you can't pass mental illness on, can you? Well, it isn't likely anyway. I've asked doctors, they've told me.'

'What was wrong with Sally's mother?'

'Paranoid schizophrenia, but I don't really know what that means. They seem to use these terms so often these days. Sally found out two years ago last Easter. I don't think adopted kids should be allowed to find out about where they came from. They never used to be. Adoption meant a completely new beginning, your new family *was* your family. These days they act as if adoptive parents are just caretakers. They're not *real*, they're not *birth*!'

'Is that what Sally said to you?' Trisha asked. 'That you weren't a real parent?'

'Well, she loved me, I know that, so she certainly never meant to hurt me. But she used to talk all the time about wanting to find her birth mother, her *blood*, as she put it. It broke my heart. I'm her real mother, aren't I? That was the deal.'

'So she found out that her mother had been a mental patient?'

'Well, I told her. I thought better coming from me than from some bloody librarian at the Public Records Office.'

'Is that why Sally was adopted? Because of her mother's mental instability?'

'You really don't know, do you? You actually don't know.' Mrs Copple was surprised.

'We don't know much at all, Mrs Copple. That's why we've come to you.'

'Oh dear. I don't want to tell you. If I do you'll suspect her, but you can't inherit what that woman had, at least it's not likely. I've talked to doctors. I've looked it up on the net.'

'Please, Mrs Copple, I'd much rather talk about this here with you now, at your home.' It was a gentle threat, heavily veiled but effective.

'Her mother was in prison. She killed someone . . . with a knife. That's why Sally was put up for adoption.'

'What about the father? Couldn't he have had her?'
'It was Sally's father who her mother killed.'

DAY FORTY-ONE. 2.15 p.m.

Trisha did everything she could to keep Sally's sad past a secret. She knew that if it came out Sally would be crucified in the press. Being aware of what leaky places police stations are, she asked to see Coleridge privately to explain her findings.

'There's no suggestion of abuse or provocation,' Trisha said. 'By all accounts Sally's father was a decent sort of man, if rather weak. Her mother was just pathologically unbalanced, and one night she just flipped.'

'Why did she get prison?' Coleridge asked. 'It seems obvious that the woman was ill.'

'Senile judge? Incompetent defence? Who knows, but the prosecution managed to get her tried as a sane defendant. Maybe it was because she was black. This was twenty years ago, remember. Anyway, she got life for murder in the first degree.'

'But appealed, of course.'

'Of course, and won, but sadly not before she'd stabbed two other inmates in Holloway with a sharpened canteen spoon. After that she went to a hospital for the criminally insane, where she still lives. Sally had been born shortly before her father was killed, and I imagine that these days they might have established some link with postnatal depression or whatever, but then they just banged her up and left her. She's thoroughly institutionalized now, apparently. Sally found out a couple of years ago and went to see her. Shook her up quite a bit.'

'Well, it would do. Does Sally have any mental problems?'

'Yes, depression and plenty of it, right back to

puberty. Been on numerous prescriptions and hospitalized once. The adoptive mother thinks it must have all been bound up with working out that she was gay, but I don't know about that, it certainly never . . .'

Trisha was about to say that it had never bothered her, that at the age of fourteen when she had finally worked out that she was a lesbian it had in fact been an enormous relief, explaining as it did the abject confusion that she had been experiencing in her relationships with both boys and girls. But she decided to leave the sentence hanging. Now was not the time.

'Whatever the reason, Sally has definitely had problems with depression, and of course ever since she found out about her mother she's been worrying that she's going the same way.'

'And what's the likelihood of that? I mean in medical terms?'

'Well, she's more likely to flip than, say, you or I, but the chances only become truly significant if both parents were sufferers. Then some doctors say it rises to nearly forty per cent.'

'What on earth were these appalling Peeping Tom people doing letting a serial depressive with a family history of mental illness into their grotesque exercise in the first place?'

'They claim that they didn't know, sir, and I believe them. Sally didn't tell them, and they would have had to dig pretty deep to find out, what with medical confidentiality and all that. It's not as if Sally's considered dangerous at all. I only found out because her mother told me.'

Coleridge leaned back in his chair and sipped at his little paper cup of water. It had been Hooper who had led the movement to get a water cooler installed in the incident room. Coleridge had resisted it fiercely, believing the whole business to be just another example of everybody these days wanting to look like Americans. However, now that the thing had been installed, he rather liked to be able to sip at clear cold water while he ruminated, and it had helped him to cut down on tea.

'So, tell me, Patricia,' he said. 'What are your thoughts? Do you think this information about Sally is significant – I mean, to our murder inquiry?'

'Well, sir, it certainly explains Sally's touchiness about mental health. But on the whole I'm tempted to say that this puts her more *out* of the frame than into it. I mean, now we know why she said what she said the night she quarrelled with Moon.'

'Yes, I'm inclined to agree with you, constable, although it must be admitted that the similarity between Sally's mother's crime and the crime committed in the house is a pretty nasty coincidence. Anyway, whatever we might think, I doubt that the press will consider Sally exonerated if they ever get hold of this.'

DAY FORTY-TWO. 7.00 a.m.

Mrs Copple was awoken by the ringing of the telephone. Almost at the same time her doorbell began to sound. By seven thirty there were forty reporters in her front garden and her life was ruined.

'SALLY'S THE ONE. JUST ASK HER MUM' was the most pithy of the headlines.

'The press always find out everything,' Coleridge said sadly when Trisha told him what had happened. 'They're much better than us. Nothing can ever be kept from them. They don't always publish, but they always know. They're prepared to pay, you see, and if you're prepared to pay for information, somebody will always be found to give it to you in the end.'

'Housemates, this is Chloe, can you hear me?'

Yes, they could hear her.

'The fifth person to leave the Peeping Tom house will be . . .'

The traditional pause . . .

'Sally!'

In that moment Sally made a little bit of TV history by becoming the first evictee from a programme of the *House Arrest* type not to shout 'Yes!' and punch the air in triumph as if delighted to be going.

Instead she said, 'So everybody out there thinks I did it too.'

'Sally,' Chloe continued, 'you have ninety minutes to say your goodbyes and pack your bags and then we'll be back to take you to your appointment with live TV!'

Sally went over to the kitchen area and made herself a cup of tea.

'I don't think you did it, Sally,' said Dervla, but Sally only smiled.

Then she went into the confession box. 'Hallo, Peeping Tom,' she said.

'Hallo, Sally,' said Sam, the soothing voice of Peeping Tom.

In the monitoring bunker Geraldine crouched close to the monitor, pen and pad in hand, ready to give Sam her lines. She knew she must play this one very carefully. Dangling before her was the prospect of some very good telly indeed. The result turned out to be even better than she had hoped.

'I expect by now the press have found out about my mum,' said Sally. 'How she's been held at Ringford Hospital for the last twenty years.'

'Horrible place,' whispered Geraldine, 'the worst loony bin of the lot.'

'Ever since Kelly died I've been wondering,' said

305

Sally. 'Could I have done it? Is there some way I could have gone into a sort of trance? Got into the sweatbox and turned into my mother? I know that my mum told me she couldn't remember a thing about when she did it, and when the police talked to me I couldn't really remember even being in the sweatbox. So perhaps I did it and can't remember that either? Was I in a box *inside* a box? My own black box? To be honest, I don't know. I don't *think* it was me. Paranoid schizophrenics don't cover their tracks, wear sheets and avoid getting even one drop of blood on themselves. I think it was too good to have been me. I don't think I could commit the perfect murder. I know my mother didn't when she killed my father . . . but it *could* have been me. I have to accept that. I just can't remember.'

'Fu-u-u-ucking hell,' Geraldine breathed. 'This is fa-a-a-a-abulous.'

'One thing I do know,' said Sally, 'is that everybody will think it was me and that I'll never escape that as long as I live. It's obvious that the police haven't got a clue. They'll probably never arrest anyone, so for the rest of my life I'll be seen as the black dyke nutter who murdered Kelly. Therefore, I've decided to make the rest of my life as short as possible.'

And with that Sally produced a kitchen knife from within the sleeve of her shirt. She had palmed it when she had made herself a cup of tea.

DAY FORTY-TWO. 9.00 p.m.

When Chloe went back on air she was able to announce yet another dramatic exit from the house. Not live as planned, because Sally had departed an hour earlier in an ambulance, her attempted suicide having been watched live on the Internet all over the world. She had managed to stab herself twice in the chest before Jazz burst into the confession box, having been alerted to do so by Peeping Tom.

Nobody yet knew whether she would survive her wounds or not.

Chloe explained all of this to the viewers, and promised a regular update throughout the show. 'I'm afraid that we cannot show you the footage of Sally's final, brilliant, heartfelt, totally honest and spiritual visit to the confession box, because apparently suicide is a crime and our legal people are worried that some authoritarian government office or other might attack us for showing you the *truth*. Right! I mean how fascist is that? Apparently you're not *grown up* enough to see what's actually *going on* in this world, which is *so* all about mind control and Brave New 1984-type stuff, which is not what Sally wanted at all!'

It was not a vintage performance, but Chloe's autocue had been hastily assembled. The message was clear enough. Any attempt to stop Peeping Tom from exploiting the anguish of a deeply disturbed young woman was an *outrageous* infringement of the civil liberties of the viewer.

Chloe was able to show the public the footage of Jazz's heroic and dramatic entrance into the confession box, when he managed to grab Sally's hand and wrest the knife from her grasp. After that she introduced a compilation of footage of Sally's brilliant weeks in the house.

Peeping Tom would of course have liked to cut live to the house to show the reactions of the other house-mates to Sally's horrifying act, but sadly they couldn't, because Geraldine was currently in the house conducting a crisis negotiation with the remaining inmates. Trying to persuade them to carry on with the show.

'We can't, we just can't,' Dervla was saying. 'Not now. People will think we're absolute ghouls.'

Even as the Peeping Tom nurse had been rushing

along the corridor under the moat in order to help Sally, the other inmates had been clamouring to leave. This would be financially disastrous for Peeping Tom, of course, particularly after such a dramatic crowd-pleaser as Sally's attempted suicide. They stood to lose tens, possibly hundreds of millions of pounds.

'You're wrong, Dervla, you're wrong,' Geraldine said. 'They love you out there, they admire your courage, they respect you, and if you have the guts to see this through they'll respect you even more. Nobody thinks any of you five killed Kelly, they all think it was Sally, and it probably was. She just about confessed to it before she stabbed herself. In a way that's kind of an end to the whole murder thing, isn't it? Now all you lot have to do is sit out the rest of the game.'

'No way,' said Dervla. 'I want out.'

'Me too,' said Jazz, still shaking violently from his encounter with Sally.

The others agreed. They had had enough.

In the end Geraldine offered the inducement that she had been expecting to have to use much earlier. 'I'll tell you what I'll do. I'm doing pretty well out of all this, I won't deny it. There's no reason why you lot shouldn't profit too. How about this? The prize is currently half a million. What if we double it *and* guarantee the other four a lump too ... let's say a hundred grand for the next one out, two hundred for the one after that, three hundred for whoever comes third, and four hund ... No, half a mill for the runner-up? How about that? Not bad moolah for sitting on your arses for another few weeks, eh? If you agree now, the *minimum* all of you will make is a hundred grand.'

This offer pretty much clinched it, the prospect of being rich *and* famous being enough inducement for anyone.

'Just one extra thing,' said Dervla. 'If the police make an arrest on the outside – you know, David or whoever

308

– you have to tell us, OK? We can't be the only people in the country who don't know.'

'Fine, whatever, I promise, absolutely,' said Geraldine, thinking to herself that she would have to give that one some thought.

DAY FORTY-THREE. 9.00 a.m.

The morning after Sally's attempted suicide Coleridge was forced for the first time to allow a public statement to be issued, something which he believed to be no part of the police's responsibilities. But Sally was out of danger, and the world press wanted to know whether the police intended to arrest her.

'No,' Coleridge said, reading laboriously from prepared notes, 'there are no plans to arrest Miss Sally Copple for the murder of Miss Kelly Simpson, for the obvious reason that there is absolutely no evidence against her. Her own statements regarding a hereditary disposition towards murder and the fear that she might have done it while in a trance do not constitute grounds for an arrest. The investigation continues. Thank you and good day.'

After he had retreated into the building, Hooper and Trisha joined him.

'So what do you think, then, sir?' Hooper asked. 'I mean, I know we have no proof, but do you think Sally did it?'

'I don't,' Trisha said quickly, causing both Hooper and Coleridge to look at her curiously.

'I don't think she did it either, Patricia,' said Coleridge. 'And I don't *think* she did not do it either.'

Coleridge was of course a show-off in his small way, and he enjoyed the confused looks that this little paradox engendered. 'I *know* she did not do it,' he said. 'The killer is without doubt still in place.'

DAY FORTY-THREE. 4.40 p.m.

Dervla's little secret finally began to unravel when Coleridge started to view Geraldine's 'bathroom tapes', the hoarded compilation of flesh-revealing shots that she was saving for an X-rated Christmas video.

'She just seems to love brushing her teeth,' Coleridge observed.

Geraldine had retained quite a lot of footage of Dervla's dental hygiene routine, because this was the point of the day when quiet and reserved Dervla was at her most sexy and coquettish. Not just because she was either in her underwear or a wet T-shirt or a towel, having just had her shower, but also because standing at the mirror, particularly in the early weeks, she seemed so jolly and full of fun, smiling and winking at her reflection in the glass. It was almost as if she was *flirting* with herself.

'She's not like that when she does her teeth in the evening,' Coleridge remarked.

'Well, maybe she's a morning type of person,' said Hooper. 'So what? She's not the first girl to smile at her reflection.'

Coleridge flipped the switch on a second VCR machine, a rather complicated new one that he had only partly mastered. He had been able to convince the bureaucrats who administered his budget that the nature of the evidence he had at his disposal justified the hiring of a great deal of video and TV equipment. His only problem now was that it was so very complicated. Hooper could work it all, of course, and made no secret of displaying his superiority.

'What I could to for you, sir, is upload the tapes from the VCR onto digital format in my camcorder, bung it across a flywire into the new iBook they gave us, chop up the relevant bits and crunch it down via the movie-making software, export it to a Jpeg file and email it straight to you. You could watch it on your mobile phone when you're stuck at traffic lights if we get you a WAP.'

Coleridge had only just learned how to use the text message service on his phone. 'I do not have my phone on when I am in my car, sergeant. And I hope that you don't either. You'll be aware, of course, that using one when driving is illegal.'

'Yes, sir, absolutely.'

They returned to the job in hand. Coleridge had lined up a moment of tape from a discussion that the group had had on day three about nominations.

'I'm at my most vulnerable to nomination in the mornings,' Dervla was saying, 'because that's when I'm going to snap at people and hurt their feelings. I'm crap at mornings, I just don't want to talk to anyone.'

Coleridge turned off his second machine and returned to the tape showing Dervla brushing her teeth.

'She may not like talking to anyone,' Coleridge observed, 'but she certainly likes talking to herself.'

On screen Dervla winked again into the mirror and said, 'Hallo, mirror, top of the morning to you.'

'Now watch her eyes,' Coleridge said, still staring intently at the scene. Sure enough, on the screen Dervla's sparkling green eyes flicked downwards and remained on what must have been the reflection of her belly button for perhaps thirty seconds.

'Maybe she's contemplating her navel, sir. It's a very cute one.'

'I'm not interested in observations of that kind, sergeant.'

Now Dervla's eyes came up again, smiling, happy eyes. 'Oh, I love these people!' she laughed.

'This tape is from day twelve, the morning after the first round of nominations,' Coleridge said. 'You'll

311

recall that nobody nominated Dervla, although, of course, she's not supposed to have any idea about that.'

Hooper wondered whether Coleridge was onto something. Everybody knew that Dervla was in the habit of laughing and talking to herself before the bathroom mirror. It had always been seen as rather an attractive, fun habit. Could there be more to it than that?

'Look, I've had some of the technical boffins make up a toothbrushing compilation,' said Coleridge.

Hooper smiled. Only Coleridge thought you needed 'boffins' to edit a video compilation. He himself made little home movies on his PowerBook all the time.

Coleridge put in his compilation tape and together they watched as time and again Dervla dropped cryptic little comments at her reflection in the mirror before brushing her teeth.

'Oh God, I wonder how they see me out there,' she said. 'Don't kid yourself, Dervla girl, they'll all love Kelly, she's a lovely girl.'

Coleridge switched off the video. 'What were Dervla's chances of winning the game at the point when Kelly was killed?'

'The running popularity poll on the Internet had her at number two,' Hooper replied, 'as did the bookies, but it was pretty irrelevant, because Kelly was number one by miles.'

'So Kelly was Dervla's principal rival in terms of public popularity?'

'Yes, but of course she couldn't have known that. Or at least she's certainly not supposed to.'

'No, of course not.'

Once more Coleridge pressed play on the video machine that held his toothbrushing compilation.

'I wonder who the public loves most?' Dervla mused archly to herself. Moments later her eyes flicked downwards.

DAY FORTY-FOUR. 12.00 p.m.

Coleridge picked up the phone. It was Hooper, calling from the Peeping Tom production office. He sounded pleased.

'I've got the duty log here, sir. You remember Larry Carlisle?'

'Yes, the operator who was working in the camera runs on the night of the murder?'

'That's the one. Well, he's been a busy boy, seems to have taken advantage of the fact that a number of people stopped working on the show out of boredom. He's done twice as many shifts as anyone else, often eight hours on, eight hours off. Loves the show, can't seem to get enough of it. And, what's more, he's covered the bathroom on almost every morning so far. If Dervla's chatting through the mirror to anyone, she's chatting to Larry Carlisle.'

'The operator who was working on the night of the murder,' Coleridge repeated.

DAY FORTY-FIVE. 7.58 a.m.

Coleridge had been in the dark hot corridor for only a few minutes and already he loathed it. He felt like a pervert, it was disgusting.

The east–west camera run of the Peeping Tom house was known as 'Soapy' to the teams who serviced it, on account of the fact that part of the run covered the mirrored shower wall and the mirrors above the basins, which often became splashed with suds and foam. The north–south run was known as 'Dry'.

Soapy and Dry had smooth, highly polished black floors, and were entirely cloaked in thick black blankets. Any light came from inside the house and shone through the long line of two-way mirrors that ran along

313

the inside wall of the corridor. The camera operators were covered completely in black blankets and slid about silently like great coal-dark ghosts.

Coleridge had already seen Jazz walk out of the boys' bedroom and across the living space to use the toilet. That same toilet that had been Kelly's last port of call upon this earth. The only part of the house that was not visible through the two-way mirrors. Coleridge gritted his teeth as he was forced to listen to what seemed to him to be the longest urination in history. Coleridge could find no words to describe the horror and contempt he felt for the whole tawdry business. Was there ever a better example of humankind's utter lack of nobility and grace? Here, where with such care, such immense ingenuity, such untold resources, the comings and goings of a communal bathroom were recorded for posterity.

It was eight o'clock and time for a change of shift in Soapy corridor. Coleridge heard the faintest swish as a heavily padded door was opened and Larry Carlisle crept in, dressed from head to foot in black. He even wore a ski mask, which further increased the grim and chilling atmosphere of the corridor. Without a word Carlisle disappeared under the blanket that covered the camera and its dolly while the previous operator emerged from the other side and crept away.

Coleridge slunk back into the darkness, drawing his black cowled cassock close about him. Carlisle had not been informed of Coleridge's presence, and imagined himself alone in the corridor as usual.

At the other end of the house Dervla emerged from the girls' bedroom and wandered into the living area. She entered the bathroom and approached the shower, where she took off her shirt to reveal her usual shower attire of cropped vest and knickers.

Coleridge turned away, a natural instinct for him in

314

the circumstances. There was a lady in a state of undress and he had no business looking at her.

Carlisle also followed his natural instincts, those of a reality TV cameraman, in that he slid along the darkened corridor to get as close as he could to the flesh.

Dervla stepped into the shower and began to wash herself, her hands running all over her body with soap. Coleridge forced himself to look again. It was not that he found the sight of Dervla soaping her near-naked body unattractive; quite the opposite. Coleridge bowed to no man in his appreciation of the female form, and Dervla's in particular with its youthful, athletic grace was just his type. It was *because* he was attracted that Coleridge wanted to look away. He was a deeply Christian man; he believed in God and he knew that God would be extremely unimpressed if Coleridge started getting hot and bothered while looking at unsuspecting young women in their underwear. Particularly when he was on duty. Coleridge, that is, not God. God, in Coleridge's opinion, was always on duty.

Making absolutely certain in his own mind that his mind was on the job and nothing else, Coleridge turned back from the darkened wall and looked once more on the girl showering herself and the black-cloaked cameraman recording it.

Then he saw something that almost made him cry out. It was as much as he could do to stop himself from leaping forward and arresting the dirty little swine there and then.

Carlisle had a second camera. The man had emerged from beneath the thick black cape, having left his professional camera locked in position on its dolly, covering the young woman in the shower in a wide shot. Now he was using a small, palm-held digital camcorder, and was clearly making his own private video.

Coleridge watched in furious disgust as Carlisle

placed his little lens within millimetres of the soapy glass, clearly desperate to get as close to the unsuspecting woman as possible. Shamelessly he explored Dervla's body, zooming in on her navel, her cleavage, the faint darkened outline of her nipples showing through the material of her top. Then Carlisle crouched down to the level of Dervla's groin and began recording a long continuous close-up of her crutch area. Dervla's legs were slightly apart, the knickers thin and lacy. There was the faintest hint of soft wet hair escaping onto the uppermost part of her thighs. Water cascaded from her gusset in a sparkling stream.

When Dervla had finished showering she turned off the taps, knotted a towel across her breasts, removed her sodden undergarments from beneath it and crossed to the basin to brush her teeth.

Carlisle quickly turned off his personal camera and disappeared back under the black cape in order to push his professional camera over to cover the two-way mirror above the basin.

Beyond the mirror Dervla looked briefly at her own reflection and shook her head.

Coleridge had never been behind a two-way mirror before, and it was almost possible to believe that the girl was shaking her head not at herself but at the camera lens that hovered immediately in front of her nose. She did not speak, but she sang a snatch of an old Rod Stewart song, her voice faint beyond the glass but audible. 'I don't wanna talk about it,' she sang.

And then: 'Hey, boy, don't bother me.' After that she was silent and avoided engaging directly with her reflection.

Now Coleridge saw Carlisle's hand reach out beyond the front of his camera. He was holding something – a small white pouch which he took by a corner and shook. There was a tiny rattling sound in the deathly silence of the dark tunnel, and Coleridge realized with surprise what the pouch was: he had shaken one like it himself only a few weeks before during a hill walk in Snowdonia. It was a walker's instant heat pack, an envelope full of chemicals and iron filings designed to produce a great heat in moments of need. He watched, amazed, as Carlisle crunched the pouch in his fist to form a blunt point, and began to trace letters on the glass. Clearly the heat was intended to warm the condensation on the other side.

Carlisle wrote slowly, partly no doubt in order to give the heat time to conduct through the glass, but also, it seemed to Coleridge, because Carlisle was enjoying himself. His forefinger was gently stroking the glass, following the line traced by the heat pack, almost as if, by touching the two-way mirror, Carlisle felt he was in some way touching Dervla. Coleridge strained to see what Carlisle was writing. The letters were inscribed backwards, of course, but they were not difficult to follow.

On the other side of the glass Dervla was watching too, her eyes darting downwards as the message appeared.

'*Don't worry. People still care about you,*' emerged though the condensation.

Dervla's expression did not change. She kept her eyes fixed on the letters.

Behind the glass in the dark corridor, unaware that he was being observed by a police inspector, Carlisle stretched out his arm and wrote a few more words.

'*Nobody out here thinks you did it.*'

Three separate pairs of eyes watched as the words were slowly spelled out: '*But you're number one now. The people love you . . . and so do I.*'

Coleridge was an accomplished watcher of faces, and he knew Dervla's well from many hours of study. As he looked he saw clearly the distaste that flickered across her face.

'La de da,' she said, with a shrug of indifference, and began to brush her teeth.

Coleridge could sense Carlisle's tension as the cameraman fumbled to lock focus on his machine and get sight of Dervla through his own little camcorder. Clearly Carlisle coveted every image of his secret love, and once more he pushed his little lens as close to the glass as he dared without tapping it. First he stole himself a close-up of the dark tuft of hair in Dervla's armpit, revealed to him because her arm was raised to brush her teeth. Then he panned across a little in order to capture the faint jiggling of her breasts beneath the towel caused by the movement of her arm. Finally, with the practised timing brought by experience, he swung his sights upwards just in time to capture the unwitting girl spitting the toothpaste from between her lips. Coleridge could hear the tiny motor of the camcorder hum as Carlisle zoomed into extreme close-up on Dervla's wet, white, foaming mouth.

When she had finished, Dervla went out of the bathroom and back to the girls' bedroom. The house was silent once more. All of the inmates were in the two bedrooms on the opposite side of the house from Soapy corridor. Coleridge pressed the button on the little communicator that the Peeping Tom sound department had given him, which alerted Geraldine in the control room to the fact that he had seen enough.

A moment or two later Carlisle left his camera, having been recalled by Geraldine under some professional pretext, as she had promised to do.

Coleridge followed Carlisle out as he left the corridor. Once outside, blinking in the striplight of the communication tunnel that linked the house with the control complex, Coleridge laid his hand on Carlisle's collar in time-honoured fashion, and asked him to accompany him to the station.

318

DAY FORTY-FIVE. 12.00 noon

'Oh my God, I think I'm going to be sick. I really do think I'm going to be sick.'

Coleridge was showing Dervla some of the contents of the camcorder that he had taken from Larry Carlisle. Stacked up beside the VCR were seventeen similar mini-cassettes, retrieved by the police from Carlisle's home.

'You seem to have become something of an addiction for this man,' Coleridge said. 'Viewing his tape collection, it looks like he simply could not get enough of you.'

'Please don't. It's horrible, horrible.'

There was so much of it. Hours and hours of tape. Close-ups of Dervla's lips when she talked, when she ate, her eyes, her ears, her fingers, but most of all, of course, her body. Carlisle had recorded virtually every single moment that she had spent in the bathroom from day three onwards, becoming ever more practised at gaining close-ups of any intimate area that had been carelessly revealed to him.

Often in the shower the weight of the water had pulled at Dervla's sodden knickers, revealing the top of her pubic hair and, when she turned round, an inch or so of the cleft of her bottom. Carlisle had clearly lived for these moments, and he zoomed in to extreme close-up whenever the opportunity arose.

'I can't believe I've been so stupid,' Dervla said, her voice choking with disgust and embarrassment. 'Of course, I should have guessed why he was being so encouraging towards me, but I had no idea . . . I . . .'

Dervla, normally so strong, so self-assured, contemplated the creepily silent dislocated images of her own body on the screen, a body rarely viewed whole but broken up into intrusive, intimate close-ups, and she wept. The tears ran down her face as the soapy water on the screen ran down her stomach and her thighs.

'Did you get messages in the mirror every day?'

'Not every day, but most days.'

'What did they say?'

'Oh, nothing very startling. "*How are you?*" That kind of thing. "*You're doing great*".'

'So he talked about the game.'

'Well, not in any great detail. He was writing backwards in condensed steam, after all.'

'Did he ever mention Kelly?'

'No.'

It was a fool's lie.

'Actually, yes, I think he did mention her,' Dervla said quickly.

'Yes or no, Miss Nolan?'

'I just said yes, didn't I? Sometimes . . . a little . . . he mentioned them all.'

Half a lie. Was that any better? Or worse?

'I don't know why he sent me messages,' she added. 'I never asked him to.'

'He's in love with you, Miss Nolan.'

'Please don't say that.'

'He loves you, Dervla, and that is something that you are going to have to deal with, because I doubt that what he has done is going to get him any kind of prison sentence. When you come out of the house he'll be waiting for you.'

'You really think so?'

'That's my experience of obsessives. They can't just turn it off. You see, he thinks you love him back. After all, you've been flirting with him for weeks.'

'I haven't . . .' But even as she said it Dervla knew that denial was pointless. 'I . . . just sort of fell into it,' she continued. 'It was a laugh, a game. It's so *boring* in that house. The same dull stupid people that you can't

320

even really get to like because you're in competition with them. You've no idea . . . And then there was this jokey thing going on, just for me. I had a secret friend on the outside who wished me luck and told me I was doing all right. You can't imagine how weird and insecure it is in that house, how vulnerable you feel. It was nice to have a secret friend.'

Dervla looked at the screen on which Larry Carlisle's tape was still playing. She was in the shower again, her hand inside the cups of her sodden bra, soaping her breasts, the shape of her nipples clearly visible. 'Can we turn that off, please?'

'I want you to see this next bit.'

The image on the screen flickered and changed to the girls' bedroom. It was night and all the girls appeared to be asleep.

'My God, he had a nightsight on his camcorder!' Dervla gasped.

'I'm afraid to say, my dear, that this man did not miss anything.'

On the screen Dervla was lying in bed. It had clearly been a hot night, as she was covered by only a single sheet. She was asleep, or so it seemed until her eyes opened for a moment and flickered about the room. Now the camera panned down from her face to her body. It was possible to make out Dervla's hand gently moving beneath the sheet, moving downwards to below her waist, the outline of her knuckles standing out against the cotton as her fingers moved gently beneath it. The camera returned to focus once more on Dervla's face: her eyes were closed but her mouth was open. She was sighing with pleasure.

Sitting in Coleridge's office, Dervla turned deep crimson with angry embarrassment. 'Please!' she snapped. 'This isn't fair.'

Coleridge switched off the tape. 'I wanted you to see

and to know just how little respect this man has had for you. You and he have been partners of sorts. You are partners no longer.'

Dervla felt scared. 'Surely, inspector, you can't really be thinking that there's any connection between this silly lark and . . . and . . . Kelly's death?'

Coleridge waited for a moment before replying. 'You said his messages mentioned Kelly?'

'Well, yes, they did but . . .'

'What did they say?'

'They said . . . they said that people liked her and that they liked me. They liked us both.'

'I see. And did he ever tell you who they liked more? Your ranking, so to speak.'

Dervla looked the chief inspector in the eye. 'No. Not specifically.'

'So you did not know that prior to Kelly's death you were in second place after her.'

'No, I did not.'

'Just remind me once more, Miss Nolan. How much is the prize worth for the winner of this game?'

'Well, it's gone up since, but at the time of the murder it was half a million pounds, chief inspector.'

'How are things at your parents' farm in Ballymagoon?'

'I beg your pardon?'

'I believe your parents are in danger of losing their farm and family home. I was wondering how all that was going. How they were taking it, so to speak.'

Dervla's face turned cold and hard. 'I don't know of late, inspector. I've been inside the house. But I imagine they'll survive. We're tough people in our family.'

'Thank you. That will be all, Miss Nolan,' Coleridge said. 'For the moment.'

DAY FORTY-FIVE. 1.30 p.m.

At first Geraldine had not wanted Dervla back in the house. 'Fuck her, the cheating little cow. I'll teach her for cock-teasing my cameramen and giving the show a bad name.'

Geraldine was angry and embarrassed that such a thing could have been going on under her nose without her having any idea about it. Her professional pride was deeply wounded, and she wanted to have her revenge on Dervla, of whom she was jealous anyway. Soon, however, wiser counsel prevailed. To eject Dervla would almost certainly mean admitting the reason for it, which would only compound Geraldine's embarrassment. Dervla was now the most popular and most fancied housemate, added to which was the fact that she had been removed by the police for further questioning, which massively increased her fascination.

Her photograph was all over the morning's papers, looking pale and beautiful as she was led from the house. The press had been forced to rethink their conviction that Sally was the killer, and their banner headlines read 'POLICE DETAIN DERVLA', 'DERVLA ARRESTED'. Soon she would be all over the evening news with reporters standing outside the house breathlessly announcing that the police had failed to lay charges against her. This was exactly the kind of incident that Geraldine needed to keep the whole story at the top of the nation's, and indeed the world's, agenda.

All in all, Dervla was too important to the show to let go.

'It'll mean keeping that disgusting pervert Carlisle,' Geraldine complained. 'If we sack him but leave her alone the cunt will blackmail us. At least I know I would.'

DAY TWENTY. 12.40 p.m.

William Wooster, or Woggle as he was more generally known, was released on bail of £5000, which was stood by his parents. The police had appealed against bail being granted on the grounds that Woggle, being a member of the itinerant, alternative community and a known tunneller, might easily abscond. The judge took one look at Dr and Mrs Wooster, him in tweeds, her in pearls, and decided that it would be an insult to two such obvious pillars of the community to deny them the company of their wayward son.

Woggle absconded within two hundred yards of the court.

After his brief appearance before the majesty of the law he and his parents had fought their way through the crowd of reporters who were waiting outside the courtroom, got into the waiting minicab and had driven off together. That, however, was as far as Woggle was prepared to go in this return to family life. Woggle waited for the first red traffic light and, when the cab pulled up to stop, simply got out and ran. His parents let him go. They had been through this so many times before and were just too old for the chase. They sat together in the car, contemplating the fact that the company of their son had this time cost them over £1000 a minute.

'Next time we won't do this,' said Woggle's dad.

Woggle ran for about a mile or so, dodging this way and that, fondly imagining that his dear old father was tearing after him waving his umbrella. When he finally believed himself safe, he decided to stop in a pub for a pint and a pickled egg. It was here that he was forced for the first time to come to terms with the extent of the blow that Peeping Tom had dealt him. For it was not just the police and the press who knew him now. Everybody knew him, and they did not like him, not one little bit.

A group of men surrounded him at the bar as he waited to be served. 'You're that cunt, aren't you?' said the nastiest looking of the gang.

'If you mean am I beautiful, warm, welcoming and hairy, yes, then you could say I was a cunt.'

It was a piece of bravado that Woggle had cause to regret as the man instantly decked him.

'I offer up the hand of peace,' Woggle said from the floor.

The man took it and dragged him outside by it, where the whole gang comprehensively beat Woggle up.

'Not so easy when you ain't kicking little girls, is it?' said the thugs, as if by attacking him with odds at six to one they were doing something brave. They left him lying in the proverbial pool of blood with broken teeth filling his mouth and hatred filling his soul. Hatred not for the thugs, who as an anarchist he considered merely unenlightened comrades, but for Peeping Tom Productions.

He skulked away from the pub, dressed his wounds as best he could in a nearby public toilet and then went underground. Literally. He returned to the tunnels whence he had come. There better to nurse his colossal sense of grievance. To dig it deeper into his angry heart with every stone and ounce of earth that he moved.

They had brought him low. All of them. The people on the inside of the house and the ones across the moat in the bunker.

Dig, dig, dig.

Geraldine Hennessy. That witch. He had thought that he could trust her, but he had been mad.

Dig, dig, dig.

You could not trust anyone. Not straights, not muggles, not fascist television people, and certainly not those *bastards* in the house. Particularly the ones who had pretended to be his friend. He hated them most. Not Dervla, of course, not the Celtic Queen of the Runes and Rhymes. Dervla was all right, she was a beautiful summer pixie. Woggle had seen the tapes and she had not nominated him. But the other one, the one who had made the tofu and molasses comfort cake! What a hypocritical *slag* that bitch had been! He'd eaten it, too. Late at night when she wasn't looking. Well, he'd show her.

Dig, dig, dig.

He hadn't wanted to kick that girl. She'd come at him with her dogs and now the whole country loathed him and he was facing a prison sentence. Woggle was scared of prison. He knew that the people in prisons were even straighter than the ones on the outside. They didn't like people like Woggle. Especially people like Woggle who kicked fifteen-year-old girls.

That was why he had gone back underground. To hide and to plan. Woggle decided as he scraped away at the earth that if he was going down, he was not going down alone. He would have his revenge on them all.

Dig, dig, dig.

DAY FORTY-FIVE. 3.00 p.m.

Trisha and Hooper checked the lab report for the final time, took deep breaths, and walked into Coleridge's office.

The police had had the two-way mirror glass through which Carlisle had been sending his messages to Dervla removed and sent to the forensic lab for analysis. The conclusions had come back within a few hours, and it seemed to Trisha and Hooper that they rather changed everything.

'We think this builds a pretty strong case against the cameraman, Larry Carlisle, sir.'

Coleridge looked up from the notes he had been reading.

'Look at this.' Hooper produced the summary of the evidence found by the forensic technicians. 'Carlisle wrote his messages with his instant heat pack, but he also traced them with his finger. The heat from the pack warmed the condensation on the other side.'

'I know that, sergeant. I told you.'

'Well, because Dervla wiped away the steam on her side it looked as if the messages were gone for ever. But the residue his finger left on the glass on his side remained. There are stains, sir. Stains and smears.'

'Stains and smears?'

'Semen, I'm afraid.'

'Ye gods.'

'I've spoken to Carlisle. He admits that he regularly masturbated during his duty shifts. He claims they all did.'

'Oh no, surely not!' Coleridge protested.

'Carlisle seemed to think it was hardly surprising, sir. As he said, once Geraldine cut the shifts down to one man, the operator was all alone in a darkened corridor for eight hours, covered in a big blanket. They're all men and they're staring at beautiful young women undressing and taking showers.'

Hooper almost added, 'What would you do?' but he valued his job and restrained himself.

'Carlisle says they sometimes called the corridors the peep booths,' Trisha added.

Coleridge stared out of the window for a moment. Three years. That was all he had left, then he could retire and go away for ever and listen to music and reread Dickens and tend the garden with his wife, give more time to amateur dramatics and never have to consider a world of secretly masturbating cameramen ever again. 'You're saying he wrote his messages in semen?'

'Well, there weren't puddles of it. I think it was more a case of traces of the stuff being left on his fingers.'

Trisha noticed that during this part of the conversation Coleridge addressed himself exclusively to Hooper. He absolutely did not look at her. Coleridge was a man who still believed that there were some things which were better off not discussed in mixed company. Not for the first time Trisha found herself wondering how it was that Coleridge ever came to be a police officer at all. But on the other hand, he was incorruptible, believed passionately in the rule of law and was acknowledged as a superb detective, so perhaps it was not necessary that he also live in the same century as everybody else.

'All right,' Coleridge said angrily. 'What did the lab say?'

'Well, sir, it's all pretty jumbled up and overlaid, but when dusted, four messages can be made out and some of others are partly there. They all give Dervla the current popularity score. Two of the clear ones are pre Woggle's eviction and put Dervla in third place behind him and Kelly, then with Woggle gone the two girls both move up one. Dervla knew the score from the start. Carlisle told her.'

'But she denied it when we asked her. What a foolish young woman.'

'Well, she could obviously see that her knowing her position relative to Kelly would give her a motive for murder. Half a million pounds is a lot of money, particularly if your mum and dad are broke.'

'And she *was* closest to the exit in the sweatbox,' Trisha added.

'The least that she's been guilty of is withholding evidence, and I intend to make sure that she regrets it,' said Coleridge.

'Well, of course, sir, but we think Carlisle is the issue,' said Trisha. 'Dervla was his motive. He wanted desperately to be the one who helped her to win, and he was convinced that Kelly stood in the way.'

'You think his desire for her to win could be a strong enough motive for murder?'

'Well, he's pathologically obsessed with her, sir, we know that. And you only have to look at the tapes he made to see how weird and warped that love is. Surely it's possible that this aching, gnawing proximity to the object of his affections totally unbalanced him.'

'Love is usually the principal motive in crimes of passion,' Hooper chipped in, quoting Coleridge himself, 'and this was clearly a crime of passion.'

'Do you remember what happened to Monica Seles, sir, the tennis player?' said Trisha eagerly. 'Exactly what we're suggesting happened here. A sad, besotted psycho fan of her rival Steffi Graf stabbed Seles in the insane belief that such an action would advance Graf's career, and that Graf would thank him for it.'

'Yes,' conceded Coleridge. 'I think the example is relevant.'

'But consider this, sir,' Hooper jumped in. 'Not only did Larry Carlisle have the motive, he had the *opportunity*.'

'You think so?' said Coleridge.

'Well . . . *almost* the opportunity.'

'In my experience opportunities for murder are never "almost".'

'Well, there's one bit we can't work out, sir.'

'I look forward to hearing you admit that to a defence lawyer,' Coleridge observed drily, 'but carry on.'

'Until now we've all been working on the assumption that the murderer was one of the people in the sweatbox.'

'For understandable reasons, I think.'

'Yes, sir, but consider the case against Carlisle, who was even *closer* to the victim. First of all he sees Kelly emerging from the boys' bedroom and sweeping naked across the living area towards the toilet. Carlisle captures this moment beautifully and gets complimented

329

from the monitoring box for his efforts. Now Kelly disappears into the toilet and Carlisle is instructed to cover the door in the expectation of getting more good nude material when she emerges.'

'But she doesn't emerge.'

'No, because he kills her, sir. It could so easily have been him. Put yourself in his shoes, the shoes of a besotted man, a man who from the very beginning has been risking his job, his future in the industry, his marriage – don't forget, sir, Carlisle is married with children. He's been risking *everything* for the love of Dervla—'

'A love that's mirrored by his hatred of Kelly,' Trisha chipped in. 'Look at this, sir.' She had brought a large folder into the room with her, the sort of folder that an artist or graphic designer might use to keep their portfolio of work in. Inside it were a series of photographs that the people at Forensic had taken of their work on the tunnel side of the two-way mirror.

In the first photo it was impossible to make anything out. All that could be seen was a streaky, dusted surface where a finger had clearly traced numerous letters on top of one another. Then Trisha produced a second copy of the photograph, and then a third, on which the relevant experts had struggled to make sense of the mess; here in different-coloured translucent pastel shades they had followed different sentences, sometimes getting a clear reading, sometimes making informed guesses.

'Look at that one, sir,' said Trisha, pointing to a sentence that was traced out in red. 'Not very nice, is it?'

DAY TWENTY-SIX. 8.00 a.m.

'The bitch Kelly still number one. Don't worry my darling. I will protect you from the cocksucking whore.'

Dervla reached forward to the mirror and angrily rubbed out the words. She had come to dread brushing her teeth in the morning. The messages had been getting steadily angrier and uglier, but she could say nothing about it for fear of revealing her own complicity in the communication. Of course, she no longer encouraged him, she no longer spoke to the mirror, and had wracked her brains to think of a way of telling the man on the other side to stop. The only idea that she had had was singing songs with vaguely relevant lyrics.

'I don't wanna to talk about it'. 'Return to sender.' 'Please release me, let me go.'

But the messages kept coming. Each one uglier than the last.

'*I swear to you my precious, I'd kill her for you if I could.*'

DAY FORTY-FIVE. 3.10 p.m.

' "I'd kill her for you if I could," ' Coleridge read out. 'Well, that's pretty damning, isn't it?'

'So there he is,' Hooper pressed on eagerly. 'The man who wrote that message, standing with his camera pointing at the toilet door, knowing that the object of his hatred is inside. What does he do? He locks his camera in the position he has been told to maintain, creeps back along Soapy corridor, up Dry, through the wall hatch into the boys' bedroom, picks up a sheet from outside the sweatbox, emerges from the bedroom covered in it, and the rest we know. It's Carlisle we see cross the living area to pick up the knife from the kitchen drawer, Carlisle who bursts in on Kelly, and Carlisle who murders her.'

'Well . . .' said Coleridge warily.

'I know what you're going to say, sir. I know, I know.

What about the bedroom? It's covered by cameras too . . .'

'It had occurred to me, yes,' Coleridge answered.

'If he'd entered the room from Dry and gone and picked up a sheet at the sweatbox we would have seen it and we didn't.'

'Yes, and not only did we not see it, but what we *did* see was a person emerge from the sweatbox and pick up the sheet.'

'Yes, sir, but only on video. No one who was in the sweatbox recalls a second person leaving it. Therefore either one, some or all of them are lying.'

'I agree.'

'*Unless* the video is lying. Carlisle is a trained camera operator. We know from his extraneous activities that his interest in the tools of television is not merely professional. Is there some way that he could have corrupted the evidence of the hot-head camera in the bedroom? The imaging of the figure emerging into the sheet is pretty unclear. Trisha and I have been wondering if he could have somehow *frozen* the picture being broadcast for a few moments—'

'After all, the image had remained unchanged for hours already,' Trisha interrupted. 'Is it possible that he somehow looped a few seconds or simply paused it for long enough to cross the room to the sweatbox?'

'After which it would all happen in real time as we saw it,' Hooper concluded.

'He would have had to pull the same trick on the way back,' said Coleridge. 'We saw the murderer return to the sweatbox, don't forget.'

'I know. There are a lot of problems with the theory,' pressed Hooper, 'but don't forget, sir, that Carlisle was very hazy about the timings of when the events happened. Do you remember that he claimed that only two minutes had passed from when Kelly went to the toilet to when the killer emerged from the bedroom, while everybody in the monitoring bunker said it was five, which was proved on the time code. And he claimed that as much as five minutes passed after the killer had re-emerged until the murder was discovered, whereas in fact it was only two. Again the people in the box and the actual time code all concurred. Those are big discrepancies, sir, but understandable ones, of course, if it was actually Carlisle who committed the murder. Anybody might imagine that two minutes was five and that five was two if they had spent those minutes killing someone with a kitchen knife.'

'Yes,' conceded Coleridge. 'I think they might. I suggest you speak to the relevant boffins in order to see how these remote cameras might be interfered with. And of course we'd better have another word with *Miss Nolan*.'

DAY FORTY-SIX. 2.30 p.m.

The sight of Dervla being escorted from the house by the police for the second time in one day caused a sensation both outside and in. Surely this must mean that she was now the number-one suspect?

Geraldine could scarcely contain her delight. 'The fucking cops are flogging our show for us,' she crowed. 'Just when everybody thought 'Loopy Sal' done it, they nick the virgin princess *twice*! Fuck me sideways, it's brilliant. But we have to make plans. A lot of moolah's riding on this. If they don't give us Dervla back we'll cancel this week's eviction, all right? Can't lose two of the cunts in one week, just can't afford it. A week of this show is worth more money than I can count!'

Hamish and Moon were up for eviction this week, but if Dervla went it seemed that they would get a reprieve. The nominations had been the most relaxed since the relatively calmer days of Woggle and Layla.

333

With Sally gone there had been a general lifting of the gloom, besides which Sally was a prime suspect for having committed the murder, so her absence had made the house feel safer.

It felt safer no longer, of course. There had been shock and fear at Dervla's second removal by the police.

'Fookin' 'ell, I thought I were all right with her,' said Moon. 'We've been sharing a fookin' bedroom! I lent her a jumper.'

'I don't believe it,' said Jazz. 'The cops are fishing, that's all.'

'Just because you fancy her don't mean she ain't a mad knife-woman, Jazz,' Garry said.

Jazz didn't reply.

DAY FORTY-SIX. 4.00 p.m.

Dervla's lip quivered. She was trying not to cry. 'I thought if I told you I knew the scores you'd suspect me.'

'You stupid stupid girl!' Coleridge barked. 'Don't you think that lying to us is probably the best way to engender our suspicion?'

Dervla did not reply. She knew that if she did she really would cry.

'Lying to the police is a criminal offence, Miss Nolan,' Coleridge continued.

'I'm sorry. I didn't think it would matter.'

'Oh, for God's sake!'

'It was only between him and me, and he was on the outside! I didn't think it would matter.' Now Dervla *was* crying.

'Right, well, you can start telling the truth now, young lady. You were, I take it, aware at all times of your standing with the public, and of Kelly's?'

'Yes, I was.'

'What would you say was Larry Carlisle's attitude towards Kelly?'

'He hated her,' Dervla replied. 'He wanted her dead. That was why I tried to stop him sending me messages. His tone changed so completely. It was vile. He called her some terrible things. But he was on the outside. He couldn't have . . .'

'Never you mind what he could and couldn't do. What we're concerned about here, my girl, is what *you* did.'

'I didn't do anything!'

Coleridge stared at Dervla. He thought of his own daughter, who was not much older than the frightened girl sitting opposite him.

'Are you going to charge me?' Dervla asked in a very small voice.

'No, I don't think there'd be much point,' said Coleridge. Dervla had not been under oath when she had given her statement and she *had* been under stress. Coleridge knew that any half-decent brief could make a convincing case that she had simply been confused when she gave her evidence. Besides, he had no wish to charge her. He knew the truth now and that was all he was interested in.

And so Dervla went back into the house.

DAY FORTY-SEVEN. 11.00 a.m.

The days dragged by in the house and the tension remained unrelenting. Every moment they expected either word of an arrest from the outside, as Geraldine had promised, or another visit from the police to take one of the remaining housemates into custody. But nothing happened.

They cooked their meals and did their little tasks,

always watching, always wondering, waiting for the next development. Occasionally a genuine conversation would bubble up out of the desultory chats and interminable silences that now characterized most of the house interaction, but these moments never lasted long.

'So who believes in God, then?' Jazz asked as they all sat round the dining table, pushing their Bolognese around their plates. Jazz had been thinking about Kelly, and about heaven and hell, and so he asked his question.

'Not me,' said Hamish, 'I believe in science.'

'Yeah,' Garry agreed, 'although religion is good for kiddies, I think. I mean, you've got to tell them something, haven't you?'

'I'm quite interested in Eastern religions,' said Moon. 'For instance, I reckon that Dalai Lama is a fookin' ace bloke, because with him it's all about peace and serenity, ain't it? And at the end of the day, fair play to him because I really really respect that.'

'What sort of science do you believe in, then, Hamish?' Dervla asked.

'The Big Bang Theory, of course, what else?' Hamish replied pompously. 'They have telescopes so powerful nowadays that they can see to the very edges of the universe, to the beginning of time. They know to within a few seconds when it all began.'

'And what was there *before* it all began, then?' asked Moon.

'Ah,' said Hamish. 'You see, everybody asks that.'

'I wonder why.'

'Yeah, Hamish,' Jazz taunted. 'What was there before?'

'There was nothing there before,' said Hamish loftily. 'Not *even* nothing. There was no space and no time.'

'Sounds like in here,' Jazz replied.

'Fook all that, Hamish, it's bollocks.'

336

'It's *science*, Moon. They have evidence.'

'I don't see what you're arguing about,' said Dervla. 'It seems to me that accepting the Big Bang theory or any other idea doesn't preclude the existence of God.'

'So do you believe in him, then?'

'Well, not *him*. Not an old man with a big beard sitting in a cloud chucking thunderbolts about the place. I suppose I believe in *something*, but I don't hold with any organized religion. I don't need some rigid set of rules and regulations to commune with the God of my choice. God should be there for you whether you've read his book or not.'

Coleridge and Trisha had caught this conversation on the net. The *House Arrest* webcast played constantly in the incident room now.

'I should have arrested that girl for obstruction,' he said. 'There's one young lady who could do with a few *more* rules and regulations.'

'What's she done now?' said Trisha. 'I thought you liked her.'

'For heaven's sake, Patricia, did you hear her? "The God of my choice." What kind of flabby nonsense is that?'

'I agreed with her, actually.'

'Well, then, you're as silly and as lazy as she is! You don't *choose* a god, Patricia. The Almighty is not a matter of whim! God is not required to *be there for you*! You should *be there for him*!'

'Well, that's what you think, sir, but—'

'It is also what every single philosopher and seeker after truth in every culture has believed since the dawn of time, constable! It has always been commonly supposed that faith requires some element of humility on the part of the worshipper. Some sense of awe in the smallness of oneself and the vastness of creation! But not any more! Yours is a generation that sees God as some kind of vague counsellor! There to tell you what you want to hear, when you want to hear it, and to be entirely forgotten about inbetween times! You have invented a junk faith and you ask it to justify your junk culture!'

'Do you know what, sir? I think if you'd been around four hundred years ago you'd have been a witch-burner.'

Coleridge was taken aback. 'I think that's unfair, constable, and also unkind,' he said.

The brief conversation around the dinner table had died out as perfunctorily as it had begun, and the housemates had returned to the uncomfortable contemplation of their own thoughts.

What could possibly be going on out there?

They speculated endlessly, but they did not *know*. They were cut off, at the centre of this mighty drama and yet playing no part in it. Not surprisingly, they had begun to turn detective, conjuring up endless theories in their own minds. Occasionally they took their thoughts to the confession box.

'Look, Peeping Tom,' said Jazz on one such occasion. 'This is probably really stupid. I never even thought to say anything about it till now, I just think maybe I ought to say it so you can tell the police, and then it's done, right? Because I reckon it ain't nothing anyway. It's just I was in the hot tub with Kelly and David. I think it was about the beginning of the second week and Kelly whispered something in David's ear that freaked him out. I think she said, 'I know you,' and he didn't like it at all. It did his head in big time. Then she said the weirdest thing. I don't know what, but I think she said, pardon my French, "Fuck Orgy Eleven", and he was pole-axed, man. That, he *did not* like.'

'Great,' said Hooper, who had now joined Trisha at the computer. 'Two weeks staring at those bloody tapes.

We wrestle one piss-poor clue out of the whole thing, and now it turns out this bastard knew about it all along anyway.'

'Well, at least he left it till now to tell us,' said Trisha, 'and gave you the satisfaction of working it out for yourself.'

'I'm thrilled.'

Hooper may not have been thrilled, but everybody else was, because it took the press, who were also monitoring the Internet, all of five minutes to find out what *Fuck Orgy Eleven* was, and of course who Boris Pecker was. The news of this juicy development hit the papers the following morning, to the delight of the legions of *House Arrest* fans. David's downfall was complete.

DAY FORTY-NINE. 10.00 a.m.

It was eviction day, but many long hours would have to pass before the excitement of the evening. As usual the Peeping Tom production team had been racking their brains trying to think of things for the housemates to do. It wasn't that interest in the show was waning, far from it. *House Arrest* remained the single most watched show on the planet. Geraldine had just brokered a worldwide distribution deal for the following week's footage of US$45 million. It was more a matter of professional pride. Peeping Tom knew that it was running a freak show, but, freak show or not, it was still a television programme and they were responsible for it. The general feeling at the production meetings was that some artistic effort was required, if only for form's sake.

The week's task had been a success. Geraldine had challenged the housemates to create sculptures of each other, and this inspired thought, with all its possibilities for psychological analysis, had provoked an incident of genuine spontaneous drama. An incident that once more confounded the sceptics who thought that *House Arrest* had run out of shocks.

The trouble started when Dervla returned from her second visit to the police station. She was tired and upset after her grilling from Coleridge. Then there had been all the gawpers and reporters outside the house, screaming at her, asking if she had killed Kelly, and if it had been a sex thing. And finally there had been the looks of doubt and suspicion on the faces of her fellow housemates when she re-entered the house. Even Jazz looked worried.

All in all, she was in no mood for jokes, so when she noticed that Garry had placed a kitchen knife in the hand of his half-finished representation of her, she flipped.

'You bastard!' Dervla screamed, white with fury. 'You utter, utter bastard.'

'It was a fahking joke, girl!' said Garry, laughing. 'Joke? Remember them? After all, you are the coppers' favourite, love!'

At which point Dervla slapped him across the face with such force that Garry toppled backwards over the orange couch.

'Fahk that!' said Garry, leaping up, tears of pain and anger in his eyes. 'Nobody slaps the Gaz, not even a bird, all right? I intend to give your arse a right proper spanking, you nasty little Paddy bitch!'

'Oi,' said Jazz, and leaped forward with the intention of intervening, but this act of chivalry turned out to be unnecessary. Dervla did not need any help, for as Garry advanced upon her, fists clenched, intent upon mayhem, she spun round upon one foot and in a single smooth movement planted the other one firmly into Garry's face.

He fell to the ground instantly, blood gushing from his nose.

'Blimey,' said Geraldine in the monitoring bunker.

Dervla had been practising kickboxing since she was eleven and was by now a master at it, but she never told anybody if she could help it. She had discovered early on that once people knew, it was all they ever wanted to talk about. People were always asking for demonstrations and asking earnest questions: 'OK, say if three, no, *four* blokes, *with* baseball bats, jumped you *from behind*, could you take them out?'

On the whole Dervla had kept her special skill private. Now, however, the world knew and frankly she didn't care. She realized that she had a score to settle, and that it had nothing to do with Garry.

Suddenly weeks of pent-up fear and rage exploded within her. Dervla knew that lurking not ten feet from her was almost certainly the message-writer, Larry Carlisle, the agent of her recent distress. Ignoring Garry, who was crumpled up on the floor howling in pain, Dervla turned to face the mirrors on the wall. 'And if you're out there, Carlisle, you disgusting little pervert, that's *exactly* what you'll get if you come within a hundred miles of me when I get out of this house. You made the police suspect me, you bastard! So you just leave me alone or I'll kick your fucking head off and pull your balls out through your neck!'

'Wow,' said Geraldine in the monitoring bunker. 'Is *he* going to have some explaining to do when he gets home.'

Thus it was that the affair of the perving cameraman unexpectedly entered the public domain, giving Peeping Tom yet another day of high drama. Carlisle was sacked, of course, but Dervla, who should by rights have also been kicked off the show for conniving with him, was allowed to stay.

'Dervla did not solicit these messages, nor did she welcome them,' said Geraldine piously, which was complete rubbish, of course, but the press did not care because nobody wanted to remove Dervla from the mix, particularly now that she had suddenly become so interesting. Particularly after Geraldine broadcast a selection of Carlisle's private footage of Dervla in the shower.

All of that excitement, however, had been some days before, and the voracious public appetite for surprises now needed feeding again. The hours until eviction would have to be filled. Geraldine decided to dig out the predictions package.

'*Peeping Tom has instructed the housemates to open the "predictions" package, which they had all been a part of preparing at the end of week one,*' said Andy the narrator. '*The package has lain untouched at the back of the kitchen cupboard since the day it was produced.*'

'Uh'd fugodden all abah did,' said Garry, who was still nursing a swollen nose. Garry had decided to accept his surprise beating at Dervla's hands in good part and let it be known both to her and in the confession box that there were no hard feelings on his side. 'At the end of the day,' he said through his bloody sinuses, 'if you get bopped you got bopped. No point crying about it. In fact, getting hit by a bird is good for me and has made me more of a feminist.'

Garry was not stupid. There was a big difference between the hundred grand that the next person out would get and the million that would go to the winner. He wanted to stay in the game while the money grew, and he guessed that sour grapes would not help his cause at all. Therefore, once the doctor had treated his nose, which had been neatly broken, he shook Dervla's hand and said, 'Fair play to you, girl,' and the nation applauded him for it.

Inside, of course, Garry was seething. To have been duffed up by a bird, a *small* bird, on live TV. It was his worst nightmare. He'd never be able to show his face down the pub again.

Watching Garry's efforts to make up with Dervla on the police computer, Hooper did not believe a word of it. 'He hates her. She's number one on our Garry's hate list,' he said.

'The place that Kelly used to occupy,' Trisha mused. 'And Kelly, of course, got killed.'

They had all forgotten about the predictions envelope, and there was eager anticipation as Jazz solemnly opened it and they all dipped in. The whole thing reminded them of a happier, more innocent time in the house.

Peeping Tom had supplied some wine and there was much laughter as all the wrong predictions made six weeks earlier were read out.

'Woggle reckoned he'd be the only one left,' said Jazz.

'Fook me, Layla picked herself to win the whole thing!' laughed Moon.

'Listen to David!' shrieked Dervla. ' "I believe that by week seven I will have emerged as a healing force within the group." '

'In your dreams, Dave!' Jazz shouted.

The laughter died somewhat when they came to Kelly's prediction. Moon read it out, and it was a moment of pure pathos.

' "I think that all the others are great people. I love them all big time and I shall be made up if I am still around by week seven. My guess is I'll be out on week three or four." '

There was silence as they all realized how right Kelly had been.

'What's that one, then?' Moon asked, pointing at a piece of paper that had not yet been read out.

Hamish turned it over. It was written in the same blue pencil that Peeping Tom had provided for everybody but the handwriting was a scrawled mess, as if somebody had been writing without looking and also with their left hand. This, the police handwriting expert was later to confirm, was indeed how the message had been written.

'What does it say?' asked Moon.

Hamish read it out. ' "By the time you read this Kelly will be dead." '

It took a moment for it to dawn on them just what had been said.

'Oh, my fook,' said Moon.

Somebody had known for certain that Kelly would die. Somebody had actually written out the prediction. It was too horrible to imagine.

'There's more. Shall I read it?' Hamish asked after a moment.

They all nodded silently.

' "I shall kill her on the night of the twenty-seventh day." '

'Oh my God! He knew!' Dervla gasped.

Still Hamish had not finished. There was one final prediction in the note. ' "One of the final three will also die." '

'Oh, my God,' Moon gasped. 'No one's touched that envelope in six fookin' weeks. It could have been any of us wrote that.'

DAY FORTY-NINE. 12.05 a.m.

Woggle had taken to sleeping in his tunnel. He felt safe there. Safe from all the people who did not understand

344

him. Safe to dig away at his hate. Planting it deeper with every blow of his pick. Watering it with his sweat.

Occasionally at night he would emerge to get water and to steal food. But more and more he existed entirely underground. In his tunnel.

The tunnel that he had dug to take his revenge.

Dig, dig, dig.

He would show them. He would show them all.

One evening, when the time had nearly come for what he had to do, Woggle took his empty sack and crept from his tunnel once more, but this time his mission was not for food. This time he made his way to a squat in London where he had once lived, a squat occupied by anarchists even stranger and more stern in their resolve than he was. These anarchists Woggle knew had the wherewithal to make a bomb.

When Woggle crept back to his tunnel just before the morning light the sack he carried was full.

DAY FORTY-NINE. 7.30 p.m.

Hamish was evicted in the usual manner, but nobody noticed very much. Try as Chloe might to drum up some interest in his departure, all anybody wanted to talk about was the sensational news that another murder was to take place.

The whole world buzzed with the news that one of the final three would die.

'It's curious, isn't it?' Coleridge said, inspecting the ugly scrawled note that lay in Geraldine's office in a plastic evidence bag.

'It's fucking chilling, if you ask me,' said Geraldine. 'I mean, how the hell would he have known he was going to be in a position to do Kelly on day twenty-seven? I hadn't even had the idea for the sweatbox then. Besides, he might have been evicted by then. I mean, he couldn't get back into the house, could he? And what about this stuff about killing one of the last three? I mean, nobody knows who the last three will be. It's up to the public.'

'Yes,' said Coleridge. 'It is all very strange, isn't it? Do you think there'll be another murder, Ms Hennessy?'

'Well, I don't really see how there can be . . . On the other hand, he was right about Kelly, wasn't he? I mean, the predictions envelope was put in the cupboard at the end of week one. There've been cameras trained on that cupboard ever since. There is no way it could have been interfered with. Somehow the killer *knew*.'

'It would certainly seem so.'

At that point Geraldine's PA entered the office. 'Two things,' said the PA. 'First, I don't know how you did it, Geraldine, but you did. The Americans have agreed to your price of two million dollars *a minute* for the worldwide rights to the final show, the *Financial Times* are calling you a genius . . .'

'And the second thing?' asked Geraldine.

'Not such good news. Did you see Moon in the confession box? They want a million each, right now, up front, to stay in the house for another moment.'

'Where's my cheque book?' said Geraldine.

'Isn't that against the rules?' Coleridge asked.

'Chief inspector, this is a *television* show. The rules are whatever we want them to be.'

'Oh yes, I was forgetting. I suppose that's true.'

'And this show,' Geraldine crowed triumphantly, 'goes right down to the wire.'

DAY FIFTY-THREE. 6.00 p.m.

Over the next few days the police did everything they could to gain some information from the note that had been found in the predictions envelope. They re-entered the house and took samples of everybody's handwriting, both right and left. They fingerprinted the kitchen cupboard. They pored for hours over the surviving footage from week one when the predictions had been written.

'Nothing. We've learnt nothing at all,' said Hooper.

'I didn't expect that we would,' Coleridge replied.

'Oh well, that's a comfort, sir,' said Hooper as testily as he dared. 'I just don't see how it could have happened.'

'And there,' said Coleridge, 'is the best clue you're going to get. For it seems to me that it *couldn't* have happened.'

Trisha had been on the phone. Now she put the receiver down with a gloomy face. 'Bad news, I'm afraid, sir. The boss wants you.'

'It is always a pleasure to see the chief constable,' Coleridge said. 'It makes me feel so much better about retiring.'

DAY FIFTY-THREE. 8.00 p.m.

The chief constable of the East Sussex Police was sick to death of the Peeping Tom murder. 'Murder is not what we here in New Sussex are all about, inspector. Here I am, trying to build a modern police service' – the chief constable did not allow the term police *force* – 'a service that is at ease with itself and comfortably achieving its goal targets in the key area of law uphold-ment, and *all* anybody wants to talk about is *your* failure to arrest the Peeping Tom murderer.'

'I'm sorry, sir, but these investigations take time.'

'New Sussex is a modern, thrusting, dynamic com-munity, inspector. I do not like having our customer service profile marred by young women falling off lavatories with knives in their heads.'

'Well, I don't think any of us do, sir.'

'It's an image-tarnisher.'

'Yes, sir.'

'Quite apart, of course, from the human dimensions of the tragedy *vis-à-vis* that a customer is dead.'

'That's right.'

'And now we have this appalling new development of further threats being made. We are a modern community, a dynamic community and, I *had hoped*, a community where groups of sexually and ethnically diverse young people could take part in televised social experiments without being threatened with illegal life termination.'

'By which you mean murder, sir.'

'Yes, I do, chief inspector, if you wish to so put it, yes I do! This new threat is making us look like fools! We must be seen to be taking it very seriously indeed.'

'By all means, sir, let us *be seen* to take it seriously, but I am of the opinion that we do not need to *actually* take it seriously.'

'Good heavens, chief inspector! A murder has been announced! If the law upholdment service doesn't take it seriously then who will?'

'Everyone else, no doubt, sir, particularly the media,' said Coleridge calmly. 'But as I say, I do not think that *we* need to. I do not think that there will *be* another murder.'

'Oh yes, and what grounds do you have for this confidence?'

'I don't think that the killer *needs* a second death. One was enough, you see.'

The chief constable did not see, and he did not think much of Coleridge's enigmatic tone. 'One was too bloody many, Coleridge! Do you know that when this story broke I was about to make public my new policy document style initiative entitled *Policing The Rainbow*?'

'No, sir, I was not aware.'

'Yes, well, you weren't the only one who was not aware. *No one* was aware. The damn thing sank without trace. *Weeks* of work, ignored, absolutely ignored because of this ridiculous murder. It's not easy catching the eye of the Home Secretary these days, you know.'

DAY FIFTY-SIX. 7.30 p.m.

'Moon,' said Chloe 'you have been evicted from the house.'

'Yes!' Moon shouted, punching the air, and for once an evictee actually meant what she said. Moon had her million pounds plus the two hundred thousand Geraldine had promised for the next one out, and she was ecstatic to be free. She had no desire to be one of the last three, not now one of them was under sentence of death.

The three remaining inmates looked at each other. Gazzer, Jazz and Dervla. One more week. Another million to the winner. Half a million to the runner-up. Three hundred thousand even for the one who came third.

If all three survived, of course.

Worth the risk, certainly. Gazzer would use it to pursue a life of luxury. Jazz would start his own TV production company. Dervla would save her family from ruin ten times over. Definitely worth the risk.

Nobody spoke. They did not speak much at all any more, and they had all taken to sleeping in separate parts of the house. Even Jazz and Dervla, who had become close, could no longer trust each other. After all, it was they who had been closest to the exit on the night Kelly was killed. And now there was this new threat. The whole process was nothing more than a long, grim waiting game.

Gazzer, Jazz, Dervla and the whole world, all waiting for the final day.

DAY SIXTY. 1.30 a.m.

Woggle was digging for as much as sixteen hours a day now. Not consecutively: he would dig for a few hours then sleep a while and, on waking, begin again immediately. Days did not matter to Woggle. It was hours that counted. Woggle had one hundred and fifteen of them left until the final episode of *House Arrest* began. He would have to hurry.

DAY SIXTY-TWO. 9.00 a.m.

Coleridge decided that it was time to take Hooper and Patricia into his confidence and admit to them that he knew who had killed Kelly.

He had had his suspicions from the start. Ever since he had seen the vomit on the seat of that pristine-clean toilet bowl. But it was the note that convinced him he was right, the note predicting the second murder. The murder he did not believe would happen because it did not need to.

What Coleridge lacked was proof and the more he thought about it, the more he knew that he never would have proof, because no proof existed, and therefore the killer was going to get away with the crime. Unless . . .

The plan to trap the killer came to Coleridge in the middle of the night. He had been unable to sleep and in order to avoid disturbing his wife with his shifting about and sighing he had gone downstairs to sit and think. He had poured himself a medium-sized Scotch and added the same amount again of water from the little jug shaped like a Scottish terrier. He sat down with his drink in the darkened sitting room of his house, the room he and his wife referred to as the drawing room, and considered for a moment how strange all the familiar objects in the room looked in the darkness of the middle of the night. Then his mind turned to the killer of Kelly Simpson, and how it might be that Coleridge could arrange to bring that foul and bloody individual to justice. Perhaps it was the words 'foul' and 'bloody' falling into his head that turned his thoughts from Kelly to *Macbeth* and the rehearsals that would commence a fortnight hence and thereafter take place every Tuesday and Thursday evening throughout the autumn. Coleridge would have to attend these rehearsals because Glyn had asked Coleridge if, given that he was in only the last act, he would be prepared to take on various messenger roles and attendant lords. 'Lots of nice little lines,' Glyn had said. 'Juicy little cameos.'

Oh, how Coleridge would have loved to play the bloody, guilty king, but of course it was not to be. He had never been given a lead.

Coleridge's mind strayed back in time to the first production that had stirred him as a boy: the Guinness *Macbeth*. How Coleridge had gasped when Banquo's ghost had appeared at the feast, shocking the guilty king into virtually giving the game away. They had done it quite brilliantly: Coleridge had been nearly as shocked as Macbeth was. These days, of course, the ghost would probably be on video screens or represented by a fax machine. Coleridge had already heard Glyn remark that his ghosts were going to be *virtual*, but way back then people weren't embarrassed by a bit of honest theatre. They liked to see the blood.

'Never shake your gory locks at me,' Coleridge

murmured under his breath. And it was then that it occurred to him that what was required to trap his murderer was a bit of honest theatre. Coleridge resolved that, if he could not find any genuine proof, natural justice required that he make his own. It was a desperate idea, he could see that, and there was scarcely time to put it into action. But it offered a chance, a small chance. A chance to avenge poor, silly Kelly.

The following morning Coleridge spoke to Hooper and Trisha. 'Banquo's ghost,' he said. 'He pointed a finger, all right?'

'Eh?' said Hooper.

Trisha knew who Banquo's ghost was. She had studied English literature at A-level, and had actually done three months' teacher training before deciding that if she was going to spend her life dealing with juvenile delinquents she would rather do it with full powers of arrest. 'What's Banquo's ghost got to do with anything, sir?' she asked.

But Coleridge would say no more and instead gave her a shopping list. 'Kindly go and make these purchases,' he said.

Trisha scanned the list. 'Wigs, sir?'

'Yes, of the description that I've noted. I imagine the best thing would be to look up a theatrical costume dresser in *Yellow Pages*. I doubt that the civilians in Procurements will view my requests with much favour, so for the time being I shall have to finance them myself. Can you be trusted with a blank cheque?'

DAY SIXTY-THREE. 6.30 p.m.

If Woggle's calculations were correct, he was directly under the house. He had the location right, he had the time right and he had the heavy canvas bag that he had been dragging along behind him in the latter stages of his tunnelling.

Woggle knew, as he crouched in the blackness of his tunnel, that a few feet above him the three remaining housemates, whoever they were, would be preparing for the final eviction. Well, he'd give them and Peeping Tom a send-off they would not forget.

DAY SIXTY-THREE. 9.30 p.m.

And so it came to the end game.

The killer's last chance to kill, and Coleridge's last chance to catch the killer before the whole edifice of *House Arrest* was broken up and scattered. Every instinct he possessed informed Coleridge that if he did not make an arrest that evening the killer would escape him for ever.

Yet how could he make an arrest? He had no evidence. Not yet, anyway.

Coleridge was not the only one feeling frustrated. The viewing public felt the same way; the final eviction show was almost over and so far nothing much had happened. The largest television audience ever assembled were watching what was proving to be the biggest non-event in the history of broadcasting.

It was not as if Peeping Tom had not put in the effort. All the ingredients were in place for a television spectacular. There were fireworks, weaving searchlights, rock bands, three separate cherry pickers for three separate trips across the moat. The world's press was there, the baying crowds were there. Chloe the presenter's wonderful breasts were there, almost entirely on display as they struggled to burst free from the confines of her pink leather bra.

Perhaps most intriguingly of all, five out of the six

353

previous evictees were also there. All of the suspects had returned to the scene of the crime.

In fact the ex-housemates were obliged to come back for the final party under the terms of their contracts, but they would probably have come anyway. The lure of fame remained as strong as ever, and with the exception of Woggle, who had jumped bail, Peeping Tom had assembled them all. Even Layla had made the effort and spruced herself up, as had David, Hamish, Sally (who got a huge cheer when she entered, walking slowly but on the way to recovery), and Moon.

After the opening credit music, played live on this special occasion by the month's number-one boy band, who performed on an airship floating overhead, the cameras cut live to the last three people in the house. The sense of expectation in the audience was huge. They had been assured by the mystery killer that one of the three people that they could see on the huge screen was going to die.

But it didn't happen. The bands played, people cheered, Kelly's old school choir sang John Lennon's 'Imagine' in her honour, and one by one the final three were voted out of the house, but *nobody was killed at all.*

First came Garry. 'Yeah, all right! Fair play! Big it up! Respect!'

Then Dervla. 'I'm just glad it's over and I'm not dead.'

And finally Jazz. 'Wicked.'

Jazz had been the favourite to win ever since his dramatic intervention to save Sally's life in the confession box. Dervla's kickboxing attack on Garry had closed the gap considerably, but it could not make up for the fact that people knew she had been cheating, and so Jazz emerged a clear and popular winner. Garry was nowhere, having been losing ground all week.

And that was it. They were all out of the house, safe

and sound, and no matter how much the viewing public might wish it, it seemed unlikely that any of the three finalists, grinning with happy relief and holding onto their cheques, was going to leap on to one of the others and murder them.

The whole thing was rapidly coming to a close. A deeply sugary tribute to Kelly in words and music had been played, giving the impression that she had been a sort of cross between Mother Teresa and Princess Diana. Elton John had provided the music which further increased this impression. And now Chloe was doing her wind-up speech, making appropriate comments about how awesome and wicked it all was, and trying not to look too disappointed that nothing more exciting had happened.

Inspector Coleridge stood beside Geraldine in the studio. He was trying to look indulgent and relaxed, but he kept looking over his shoulder to glance at the big door at the back of the studio. He was waiting for Hooper and Patricia to appear, but so far there had been no sign of them. He knew that if they did not come in the next few moments and provide him with the proof he needed, the killer would escape.

'Well, you were right,' said Geraldine grudgingly. 'Nobody did get killed. You know, I really thought the bastard might pull it off. I suppose it was stupid, but he did do such an extraordinary job the first time round. Either way, it makes no difference to me. The show was pre-sold.' She looked at her watch. 'Fifty-three minutes so far, that's a hundred and six million dollars. Very nice, very nice indeed.'

Geraldine addressed Bob Fogarty in the control box via her intercom: 'Bob, give Bimbo Chloe a message to wind it up as slow as she dares, words of one syllable, please. When she's finished, replay the Kelly tribute and then stick on the long credits, every second is money.'

Coleridge looked at the door once more: still no sign of his colleagues. It was all about to slip away from him. He knew that somehow he must delay the end of the show. Banquo's ghost would only work on air. There had to be a feast. Macbeth's confusion would mean nothing if it happened in private.

'Hold on a minute, Ms Hennessy,' he said quietly. 'I think I can earn you a few more million dollars.'

Geraldine knew a sincere tone of voice when she heard one. 'Keep the cameras rolling!' she barked into her intercom, 'and tell my driver to wait. What's on your mind, inspector?'

'I'm going to catch the Peeping Tom killer for you.'

'Fuck me.'

Even Geraldine was surprised when Inspector Stanley Spencer Coleridge asked if it would be possible for him to be given a mike.

A hand-held microphone was quickly thrust into his hand, and then to everyone's complete surprise Coleridge stepped up onto the stage and joined Chloe. All over the world and in every language under the sun, the same question was asked: 'Who the hell is that old guy?'

'Please forgive me, Chloe . . . I'm afraid I don't know your surname,' Coleridge said, 'and I hope that the public will forgive me also if I trespass for a moment on their time.'

Chloe stared about her wildly, wondering where the security men were, seeing as a senior citizen appeared to be making a stage invasion.

'Run with it, Chloe,' the floor manager whispered at her through her earpiece. 'Geraldine says he's kosher.'

'Oh, right. Wicked,' said Chloe in an unconvinced voice.

Everybody stared at Coleridge. He had never felt such a fool, but he was desperate. There was still no sign of Hooper and Patricia. He knew that he would have to stall. He looked out at the sea of expectant, slightly hostile faces. He tried not to think of the hundreds of millions more that he could not see but who he knew were watching. He fought down his fear.

'Ladies and gentlemen, my name is Chief Inspector Stanley Coleridge of the East Sussex Police, and I am here to arrest the murderer of Kelly Simpson, spinster of the parish of Stoke Newington, London Town.' He had no idea where the 'spinster' bit had come from except that he knew he must spin it out, *spin it out at all costs*. He had absolutely no idea how long he would have to stall.

Once the sensation caused by his opening remark had died down, Coleridge turned and addressed the eight ex-housemates, who had been assembled by Chloe on the podium. The eight people whose faces he had stared at for so long. The suspects.

'This has not been an easy case. Everyone in the world has had a theory, and motives there have been aplenty. A fact that has caused my officers and myself some considerable confusion over the last few weeks. But the identity of this cruel killer, that despicable individual who saw fit to plunge a knife into the skull of a beautiful, innocent young girl, has remained a mystery.'

Something rather strange was happening to Coleridge. He could feel it deep in the pit of his stomach. It was a new sensation for him, but not an unpleasant one. Could it be that he was *enjoying himself*? Perhaps not quite that. The tension was too great and the possibility of failure too immediate for enjoyment, but he certainly felt . . . exhilarated. If he had had a moment to think, he might have reflected that circumstance had granted him that thing which he most craved and which his local amateur dramatic society had so long denied him: an audience and a leading role.

'So,' said Coleridge, addressing the camera with the red light on top, presuming correctly that this was the live one. 'Who killed Kelly Simpson? Well, in view of the wealth of suspicion that has been visited upon various innocents, I think it fair to begin by clearing up who definitely did *not* kill Kelly Simpson.'

'This bloke's a natural,' Geraldine whispered to the floor manager. She was deeply impressed with this new side of Coleridge's character, and well she might have been, for every minute that he spoke was earning her an extra two million dollars.

Spin it out. Spin it out, Coleridge thought to himself, a sentiment which Geraldine would have applauded wholeheartedly.

'Sally!' Coleridge said, turning dramatically to face the eight suspects. 'You were the victim of a terrible coincidence. Your poor mother's suffering, which you had hoped would remain a private matter, has become public knowledge. You have anguished over your fears that the curse that blighted your mother's life might also have blighted yours. You've tortured yourself with the question Did I Kill Kelly? Was your true personality revealed in the darkness of that black box?'

Sally did not answer. Her eyes were far away. She was thinking of her mother sitting in the terrible little room where she had sat for most of the last twenty years.

'Let me assure you, Sally, that never for *one moment* did I imagine that the killer was you. You had not the ghost of a motive save family history, and the coincidence of that history repeating itself in so exact a manner is so unlikely as to be virtually impossible. Many families have some mental disorder in their line ... Why, the producer of this very show could say as much, couldn't you, Ms Hennessy?'

'Eh?' said Geraldine. She was enjoying Coleridge's

performance hugely, but had not expected to be drawn into it.

'I gather from interviews my officers have held with your staff that on the two occasions when both Sally and Moon spoke about life inside mental hospitals you remarked quite clearly that it was not like that at all. You in fact explained clearly what it *was* like. I can only presume that you yourself have some experience?' Coleridge glanced once more at the studio door. No sign. *Spin it out.*

'Well, as it happens you're right.' Geraldine spoke into the boom mike, which had hastily descended above her head, the studio crew having reacted according to their instincts. 'My mum was a bit of a fruitcake herself, Sally, and my dad, as it happens, so believe me, I sympathize with the outrageous prejudice you have had to put up with.'

'A sentiment that does you great credit,' Coleridge said. 'Particularly since medical opinion informs me that when *both* a person's parents suffer serious mental instability, their offspring has a thirty-six per cent chance of inheriting their challenges.'

Geraldine did not much like having her family's linen so publicly washed, but at two million dollars a minute she felt she could put up with it.

Coleridge turned once more to the suspects. 'So, Sally, I hope that you can learn from this terrible experience that you need not fear the burden of your past. You did not kill Kelly Simpson, but you were very nearly killed yourself, as I intend to show.'

This comment was greeted with gasps from the audience, which Coleridge did his best to milk.

'Now, what about the rest of you? Did Moon kill Kelly? Well, did you, Moon? You're a wicked liar, we know that from the tapes. The public never saw you make up a history of abuse in order to score cheap points against Sally, but I did, and it occurred to me that a woman who could invent such grotesque and insensitive deceits might lie about pretty much anything, even murder.'

The cameras turned on Moon.

'Extreme close up!' shouted Bob Fogarty from the control box.

Moon was sweating. 'Now just a fookin' . . .'

'Please, if we could try to moderate our language,' Coleridge chided. 'We are on live television, after all. Don't upset yourself, Moon. If there were as many murderers as there are liars in this world we should all be dead by now. You did not kill Kelly.'

'Well, I know that,' said Moon.

'Nobody has really known anything during this investigation, Moon. Heavens, even Layla has come under suspicion.'

The cameras swung to face a shocked Layla.

'What?'

'Oh yes, such was the apparent impossibility of the murder that at times it seemed possible to imagine that you had wafted in through an airvent on that grim night. After all, everybody saw Kelly nominate you in that first week and then hug and kiss you goodbye. That must have hurt a proud woman like you.'

'It did,' said Layla, 'and I'm ashamed to say that, when I heard about the murder, for a moment I was glad Kelly died. Isn't that terrible? I've sought counselling now though, which is helping a lot.'

'Good for you,' said Coleridge. 'For let us be quite clear: there is no circumstance or situation in our world today that cannot benefit from counselling. You were simply being selfish, Layla, that was all, but I'm sure that somewhere you can find somebody to tell you that you had a right to be.' Coleridge was being deeply sarcastic, but the crowd did not get it and applauded him, assuming, as did Layla, that Coleridge's comment was a love-filled Oprah moment of support.

'Layla was long gone by the time Kelly died,' Coleridge continued, 'but Garry wasn't, were you, Gazzer? So how about you? Did *you* kill Kelly? You certainly *wanted* to kill her. After the whole country saw her teach you a few home truths about the responsibilities of fatherhood there was no doubt you had a motive. Wounded pride has been a cause for murder many times in the past, but on the whole I suspect that you don't care quite enough about *anything* to take the sort of risk this killer took. But what about you, Hamish? Only you know what passed between Kelly and yourself the night you reeled drunkenly together into that little cabin. Perhaps Kelly had a story to tell, but, if she did, fortunately for you we'll never hear it. Did you wish her silenced as you sat together in that awful sweatbox? Did you reach out a hand to stop her mouth?'

Hamish did not answer, but just glared at Coleridge fiercely, biting his lip.

'Perhaps you did, but you didn't kill her. Now then, what about David?' Coleridge turned his gaze to the handsome actor, whose face was still proud and haughty despite all that he'd been through. 'You and Kelly also shared a secret. A secret you hoped to keep hidden, and with Kelly's death you thought it safe.'

'For heaven's sake, I didn't . . .'

'No, I know you didn't, David. Sadly for you, though, because of her death and the subsequent investigation, the world has discovered your secret anyway and, like her, I doubt now that you will ever achieve your dream.'

'Actually, I've had some very interesting offers,' said David defiantly.

'Still acting, David? I recommend you try facing up to the truth. In the long run life is easier.'

As David glared at him Coleridge looked once more at the door at the back of the studio. There was still no sign of Hooper and Patricia. How long could he keep on stalling? He was running out of suspects.

'Dervla Nolan, I have always had my doubts about you,' said Coleridge, turning to her and pointing his finger dramatically.

Once more the focus of the cameras shifted.

'Have you now, chief inspector?' Dervla replied, her green eyes flashing angry defiance. 'And why would that be, I wonder.'

'Because you played the game so hard. Because you have a rogue's courage and risked it all by communicating with the cameraman Larry Carlisle through the mirror. Because you were closest to the entrance of the sweatbox and could have left it without anybody else's knowing. Because you needed money desperately. Because you had been told that, with Kelly dead, you would win. Not a bad circumstantial case, Ms Nolan. I think perhaps a good prosecuting lawyer could make it stick!'

'This is just madness,' said Dervla. 'I loved Kelly, I really . . .'

'But you didn't win, did you, Dervla?' Coleridge said firmly. '*Jazz* won. In the end, good old Jazz was the winner. Everybody's friend, the comedian, the man who was *also* in the key position in the sweatbox and could have left it without being noticed! The man whose DNA was so prominent on the sheet that the murderer used. The man who so conveniently covered his tracks by putting the sheet back on after the murder. Tell me, Jazz, do you honestly think that you would have won if Kelly had not died?'

'Hey, just a minute,' Jazz protested. 'You ain't trying to say that . . .'

'Answer my question, Jason. If Kelly had survived that night, the night she brushed past you in the sweatbox and someone followed her out in order to kill her, would you have won? Would that cheque you are now holding not have had her name on it?'

'I don't know ... Maybe, but that doesn't mean I killed her.'

'No, Jazz, you're right. It doesn't mean that you killed her, and of course you didn't. *Because none of you did.*'

The sensation that this statement caused was highly gratifying. Coleridge's emotions were torn. Part of him, the main part, was in absolute torment, desperately awaiting the arrival of his colleagues. An arrival which if put off much longer would be useless anyway. But there was another part of Coleridge, and that was Coleridge the frustrated performer: this part was loving every minute of his great day.

'You are all innocent,' he repeated, 'for it is a fact that no one who shared the sweatbox with Kelly on the night she died killed her!'

'It was Woggle, wasn't it?' Dervla shouted. 'I should have guessed! He hated us all! He took revenge on the show!'

'Ah ha!' shouted Coleridge. 'Woggle the tunneller! Of course! Everybody's mistake in this investigation – *my* mistake – was to presume that the murder was committed by a person who was a housemate at the time. But what of the *ex-housemates* – not Layla, but Woggle! How simple for a committed anarchist like him, a saboteur, an expert underground tunneller, to break into the house and take his revenge on the show, and in particular on the girl who nominated him and then insulted him with a tofu and molasses comfort cake!'

The studio erupted. All around the world the press lines jammed. So Woggle had done it after all, the evil kicker of teenage girls had surpassed even his previous levels of brutality.

'Of course it wasn't Woggle!' said Coleridge impatiently. 'Good heavens, if that highly distinctive fellow had popped up through the carpet I think we would have noticed, don't you? No, let's stop looking for opportunity and start to consider *motive*. What are the common motives for murder? I suggest that hate is one. Hatred drives people to kill, and my investigations have discovered that there was one truly hate-filled relationship souring the Peeping Tom experience, and it did not fester inside the house. It was the hatred that Bob Fogarty, the senior series editor, felt for Geraldine Hennessy, the producer!'

Coleridge pointed above the heads of the audience to the darkened window situated high in the wall at the back of the studio. 'Behind that window sits the Peeping Tom editing team,' Coleridge continued, 'and they are led by a man who believes that his boss, Geraldine Hennessy, is a television whore! He said as much to one of my officers. Bob Fogarty claimed that Hennessy's work represented a new low in broadcasting, she had ruined the industry he loved and that he longed for her downfall! But! He did *not* kill Kelly.'

Coleridge could detect a tiny edge of impatience in the crowd. He knew that he could not play the trick he was playing for much longer. The spin was running out. But it no longer mattered. Coleridge was smiling, for at the back of the studio he saw the big door open and Hooper steal through it. Hooper gave Coleridge the briefest of thumbs-up signals.

Geraldine did not see the smile spreading across Coleridge's face. She was too busy smiling herself because, glancing down at her watch, she worked out that the mad policeman had been on the stage for five and a half minutes and had therefore earned her an extra eleven million dollars, and clearly the idiot had not finished yet.

The smile was about to be wiped from Geraldine's face.

'So!' said Coleridge dramatically. 'We know now who did *not* kill Kelly Simpson. Let us come to the real business at hand and establish who *did* kill her. Nothing happened in that dreadful house without first being arranged, manipulated and packaged by the producer. Nothing, ladies and gentleman, not even murder most foul. Therefore let us be quite clear about this. The murderer was ... *you*, Geraldine Hennessy!' Coleridge pointed his finger and the cameras swung around to follow its direction.

For once Geraldine found herself at the wrong end of the lens.

'You're out of your mind!' Geraldine gasped.

'Am I? Well, I think you'd know something about that, Ms Hennessy.'

Trisha entered the editing box carrying a plastic bag filled with video tapes. She went up to Bob Fogarty and whispered in his ear.

'I can't leave now,' Fogarty protested.

'I can cover it,' said his assistant, Pru, eagerly. All her life she had longed for just such a chance.

'I'm afraid I must insist, sir,' said Trisha, whispering once more into Fogarty's ear.

Fogarty rose from his seat, took up his family-sized bar of milk chocolate, and left the editing box.

Pru took over the controls. 'Camera four,' she said. 'Slow creep in on Coleridge.'

Down on the stage the object of this command was in full flow.

'Perhaps you will allow me to explain,' Coleridge said. 'First let us consider motive.' Coleridge was standing tall now, strong and commanding. This was not just because his performance muscles, which had for so long lain dormant, were flexing themselves, but also because he knew that success could only come with confidence. She had to believe that the game was up.

'Well, a motive is simple enough, it's the oldest one of the lot. Not hate, not love, but greed. Greed, pure and simple. Kelly Simpson died to make you rich, Ms Hennessy. The whole media establishment expected series three of *House Arrest* to be a failure. The Woggle affair drew attention to you, certainly, but it was Kelly's death that turned your show into the biggest television success story in history, *as you knew it would!* Can you deny it?'

'No, of course not,' Geraldine said. 'That doesn't mean I killed her.'

Geraldine was alone now on the studio floor. The happy throng of excited young audience members and studio staff had drawn back to form a large circle. Geraldine stood in the middle of this, like a lioness at bay, the focus of that vast room, three big studio cameras hovering around her, for all the world like great hunting animals of prey.

Beyond them, still standing on the stage with Chloe and the eight housemates, was Coleridge, returning Geraldine's defiant stare. 'You have been clever, Ms Hennessy, brutally, fiendishly clever. I do believe your finest hour, perhaps, was allowing the early profits from the worldwide interest that Kelly's murder produced to be given away. Oh yes, that certainly made me wonder, when your editor, Bob Fogarty, told us of your fury at the missed opportunity, a million lost? Perhaps two? And then, I thought, what a small price to avoid suspicion falling immediately upon your shoulders, as since then you have milked *hundreds of millions* of dollars from your ghoulish crime.'

'Now you be careful, chief inspector,' Geraldine said. 'You're on live television here. The whole world is watching while you make a fool of yourself.' The mention of money had put the spirit back into Geraldine. Coleridge's accusation had certainly been a shock, but she could not imagine on what grounds he was going to base it, let alone prove it. Meanwhile, the *House Arrest* drama continued and the profits kept on mounting.

'You may bluster all you wish, Ms Hennessy,' Coleridge replied, 'but I intend to prove that you are the murderer and then I intend to see you punished under the full majesty of the law. Let me say now that I knew even on the night of the crime that things were not as they appeared. Despite your impressive efforts, there was *just so much* that was wrong. Why was it that cameraman Larry Carlisle, the only person to witness the cloaked murderer follow Kelly to the lavatory, thought that the killer had emerged only two minutes after Kelly left the sweatbox, while the people watching *on video* could see very well from their machines that it had been more like five?'

'Larry Carlisle has been proved to—'

'Not a very reliable witness, I accept that, but on this occasion I suggest reliable enough. Otherwise, why was it that the blood which flowed from Kelly's wounds seemed to accumulate so very quickly? The doctor was surprised, and so was I. *Who would have thought the young girl to have so much blood in her*, to paraphrase the Bard. A great deal of blood to flow in the *two minutes* that was supposed to have passed between the murder and your arriving on the scene, Ms Hennessy, but not so much if you reckon on the *five minutes* that Carlisle thought had passed.'

'Not all blood flows at the same speed, for fuck's sake!' Geraldine barked, forgetting for a moment that she was on live television.

'Then there was the vomit,' said Coleridge. 'Kelly had been drinking heavily, and she rushed to the lavatory in a mighty hurry, didn't she? But according to what we saw, when she arrived she simply sat down. More curious still, even though the lavatory bowl had clearly been scrubbed clean, the lavatory *seat* had a few flecks of vomit on it. Vomit which has been confirmed as having emanated from Kelly. How could this be? I asked myself. Watching the tape again I can see that Kelly does not throw up, she merely sits . . . and yet *I know that she was sick*. I have vomit from her mouth, I have her vomit from the lavatory seat. Without doubt this is a girl who ran into the lavatory, knelt before it and was sick. Yet when I watch the tape, *she just sits down.*'

Up in the studio editing box, Pru was having the gig of her life. She had taken over the controls of the edit box and, working live and entirely off-script, she had first managed to ensure perfect camera coverage of the scene unfolding down in the studio, barking cool clear instructions to the shocked team of operators. And now she excelled herself by managing to dial up footage of the murder tape and drop it into the broadcast mix as Coleridge spoke. Once more viewers around the world watched the familiar footage of Kelly entering the toilet and sitting down, this time seeing it in an entirely new and mystifying context.

Down on the studio floor the thrilling confrontation continued.

'Next I come to the matter of the *sound* on the tapes that were recorded during the murder. In the earlier part of the evening much of what was said inside that grim plastic box was clearly audible, and, I might add, little of it did any of the people you see standing on this stage much credit.'

Coleridge turned to the eight ex-housemates. 'Really, you all ought to be ashamed of yourselves. You're not animals, you know.'

'It wasn't me!' Layla protested like an anxious school child. 'I'd been evicted, I wasn't there!'

Such was the authority of Coleridge's performance that, instead of telling him to mind his own business, the other seven housemates, even Gazzer, blushed and stared unhappily at their feet.

'But I'm straying from the point,' Coleridge admitted, 'which is that while Kelly remained in the sweatbox we could hear what was being said, but from the moment that Kelly entered the lavatory the sound becomes vague, a mere cacophony of murmuring. Why? Why could we no longer make out any of the voices?'

'Because they were all too pissed, of course, you stupid—' Geraldine bit her lip. She knew he had no proof. She had no need to lose her cool.

'I don't think so, Ms Hennessy. Seven people do not simultaneously begin to mumble in unison. What had happened? Why had the sound changed? Was it because the sound that I could hear on the tape of the murder was *not* the sound that was being generated in the sweatbox? Could it be that the person who made that tape did not wish for any discernible voices to be heard from the box during the murder because *she did not know who it was who was going to be killed*? Strange it would be indeed if the voice of the victim could still be heard in the sweatbox after her death. Was this the reason that the sound on the murder tape was so revealingly anonymous?'

Geraldine remained silent.

'Let us leap forward for a moment in time, to when the note predicting the second murder was discovered. Oh, what a fine sensation that made. But for me, Ms Hennessy, that note was the absolute proof I needed to convince me that the murder was *not* committed by a housemate.'

'Why, babe?'

Coleridge almost jumped. He had forgotten that Chloe was standing beside him. Throughout his speech she had been attempting, not very subtly, to remain in shot, and she now made a play to really get involved.

Chloe felt she had a right, she was the presenter of the show, after all.

'Why, Chloe? Because it was utterly ridiculous, that's why. Impossible, a transparent piece of *theatre*. None of the contestants could *possibly* have known at the end of week one when and how Kelly Simpson would die. Even if they had been planning to kill her it is quite absurd to think that they would have been able to see into the future in such detail and be assured that an opportunity would arise on the twenty-seventh day. So how did that note come to be among the predictions in the envelope? An envelope which we had seen the housemates fill and seal on day eight? Clearly someone from the outside had put that prediction note there, put it there at the *time that they killed Kelly*. That note was a little extra piece of drama that you could not resist, Ms Hennessy. You were desperate to maximize your price for footage of the final week, and yet you knew that with each passing day the murder grew colder and with each eviction the chances of the killer still being in the house lessened. Hence your absurd, ridiculous note, a note which fooled the world but which served only to convince me that there definitely would *not* be another murder.'

'Excuse me, sorry to interrupt, babe.' It was Chloe again, delighted to have another chance to get into the action. 'They've asked me from the box to ask you to tell us how she did it. I mean we've got as much time as you like, but the problem is that we're live and at some point we have to cut to an ad break, but we do all *really really* want to know.'

'Justice has its own pace, miss,' said Coleridge grandly. He was grimly aware that he had no proof. If he was to gain a conviction then he needed a confession, and only Banquo's ghost, only a set of shaking gory locks, could get him that. The time had to be right, the killer had to *sweat*.

'Fine, babe,' said Chloe. 'They say it's cool. Respect. Whatever.'

'Surely you must all have guessed how she did it anyway?' said Coleridge. 'I mean, isn't it obvious?'

The sea of blank faces in the audience was most gratifying.

'Ah, but of course, I was forgetting. You have not had the privilege as I have of visiting Shepperton Studios, a place where *an exact replica* of the house exists. A place where Geraldine Hennessy made a video recording. A recording of a murder that *was yet to happen.*' Coleridge had abandoned all pretence at quiet reserve. He was an actor now, an actor in a smash hit.

'One dark night shortly before the *House Arrest* game began, Geraldine Hennessy crept onto the set of her replica house. With a crank and a clang she turned on the studio lights and activated the remote cameras that would shortly thereafter be installed in the real house. She also pushed one manual camera into position in front of the lavatory door, where she locked it off, just as a month or so later she would instruct Larry Carlisle to do. Then Ms Hennessy stripped naked and put on a dark wig, a wig that was the colour of Kelly Simpson's hair. She then entered the replica lavatory, where she was recorded by the only camera in the room, high above and behind her. Swiftly she sat down and put her head into her hands, not a difficult deception to pull off – the foreshortening quality of an overhead camera angle would make any differences in height and figure an irrelevance, and, when looked at from almost directly above, one hunched figure on a lavatory looks much the same as another. So, a month or so before it actually happened, Kelly's final trip to the lavatory had been ... I can't say *re*constructed – I'd therefore better say *pre*constructed.'

Coleridge was having a wonderful time. Banquo's ghost was waiting in the wings, Macbeth (perhaps he should say Lady Macbeth) stood before him in all her arrogance; all he had to do now was bring her to the point where her spirit collapsed, and he truly believed he could do it. In thirty-five years of dedicated and usually successful police work, Coleridge could never have been said to have shone. But on this night, as he neared the end of his long career, he was sparkling.

'So,' he continued, 'Hennessy playing Kelly sits on the lavatory and now, across the replica living area, in the boys' bedroom, where a small sweatbox has been constructed – a sweatbox built to exactly the same specifications for construction and positioning that were later given to the housemates – a cloaked figure emerges. Your accomplice in the drama, Ms Hennessy. The figure crosses the living area, picks up a knife and bursts into the lavatory, raising his sheet behind him to block the camera's view. He then makes two plunging movements. A clever bit of deception that, Ms Hennessy: *two* blows, the first a miss hit, giving the impression that what occurred was a desperate improvisation rather than a cold and cunning decep- tion. One single death blow might have appeared just *too* pat. Then, having left a sheet over you, hunched up on the lavatory, your accomplice goes back across the little stage at Shepperton and gets back into the replica sweatbox.'

'Who? Who was the accomplice?' gasped Chloe.

'Why, Bob Fogarty, of course. It could *only* be Bob Fogarty, the man who made such a heavy-handed point of hating Ms Hennessy, a man with video-editing skills equal to your own, Ms Hennessy. Because I put it to you, Geraldine Hennessy, that the world never saw Kelly murdered! That dark event remains unrecorded. It is the tape that you and Fogarty made at Shepperton that was played that night and which has so absorbed the interest of the public ever since! Your *construction* of a murder that had yet to happen and which you and he dropped into edit mix at the point at which the *real* Kelly entered the lavatory. I have taken some advice on this matter and have been told that the opening of the door would be a good point at which to switch the tapes. From that moment on, you and all the people in the monitoring bunker were watching the tape you had made and *not the actual feed from the cameras*. You yourself have boasted that computer time codes can easily be falsified, and with you and Fogarty working together it was a simple matter to switch your television monitors over to playing the tape.'

Geraldine tried to speak, but no sound came. The floor manager did what all floor managers do and brought her a plastic cup of water.

'Now that Kelly was in the lavatory, although you of course could no longer see her, you used the remote-controlled lock that you yourself had insisted on having installed and sealed the lavatory door, trapping poor Kelly and thus insuring yourself against the possibility of her completing her lavatorial functions before you could get to her. You then excused yourself from the monitoring bunker, saying that like the girl on the screen you too needed to spend a penny, and you rushed off to do your terrible deed!'

There was sensation in the studio and, of course, across the globe. Seldom can any television performer have had so attentive an audience. All over the world pans boiled dry, dinners burned and babies' cries went unheeded. There was no talk of cutting to an ad break now.

'Go on,' sneered Geraldine. 'What am I supposed to have done then?'

'You ran under the moat, along the connecting tunnel, I imagine having first grabbed for yourself a strategically placed smock. I feel certain that somewhere there is an incinerator in London that could tell a tale of a blood-stained coverall. You ran into the corridor and from there you made your way into the boys' bedroom. Once inside the house you grabbed a sheet from the top of the pile that you had instructed the housemates to place outside the sweatbox. That polythene construction in which the people you see standing here tonight were sweating with drunken lust—'

'Not me, I'd been evicted,' Layla piped up, but Coleridge swept on.

'You covered yourself with the sheet, emerged into the living area and went to get the knife, pausing briefly at the kitchen cupboard to take out the predictions envelope, tear it open and put its contents inside a new but identical envelope. It was then, of course, that you added your extra note, predicting a second murder. No one saw any of this, of course, because the editors were watching the video that you and Fogarty had made a month before, a video on which Kelly Simpson was sitting peacefully on the lavatory, and for the time being no other figures were to be seen. There was the live cameraman to consider, of course, but Larry Carlisle had been instructed to cover the lavatory door and wait for Kelly. *This* is why Carlisle claimed a much shorter time had elapsed after Kelly went to the lavatory before the killer emerged, because the figure he saw rush past him in a sheet was you, *the real killer*. Meanwhile, in the monitoring bunker, your accomplice Fogarty and the editing team were still watching a peaceful house in which a lone girl was sitting on the lavatory. You, Ms Hennessy, would be *back in the monitoring bunker* before your tape revealed a besheeted figure entering the lavatory.'

There were gasps and applause from the audience.

'Unreal,' said Chloe. 'Mental. Absolutely mental. Just totally wicked.'

Geraldine remained aloof and silent, seemingly held at bay by the three cameras pointing at her.

'But I'm getting ahead of myself,' said Coleridge. 'Poor Kelly Simpson is still alive . . . Although only for a few more moments. The door to the lavatory springs open, unlocked at the appointed time by your colleague in the bunker, you burst in on the unsuspecting girl, but you do not find her as you had hoped, sitting on the lavatory as per your impersonation on the video you had made. No, she is kneeling *in front* of the lavatory, being sick. This is no good – everything must be as it is on the tape: the girl must die sitting and, most importantly, she cannot have been sick because she is not seen being sick on your tape. You grab her, you spin her round, she no doubt thinks that someone has come to help her, but no, you've come to kill her. With admirable coolness you stab her first in the neck and then, deploying the full force of your passion, your strength and your *greed*, you bury the blade in her skull, working quickly, knowing that seconds count. You flush the toilet and clean the vomit from the bowl. You do a good job, Ms Hennessy, but not quite good enough. A few tiny flecks are left on the seat. Then, and at this point I can only gasp at your icy cool, you *clean out the dead girl's mouth*. Did you have a cloth? Toilet paper would have stuck to her teeth. Your shirt cuff, perhaps? I don't know, but crucially I do know that in doing what you did you marked the dead girl's tongue! Kelly was only seconds dead and so could still bruise, unfortunately for you, Ms Hennessy. You could not, of course, clear the vomit from the back of her mouth and her throat, but you had done your best, a best which was very nearly good enough. But time is short, Kelly is bleeding. If she bleeds too much on you, you're done for. Quickly you place the corpse in the same sitting position that you yourself took on your tape. You put a second sheet on top of the dead girl and, covering yourself once more in your own sheet, you leave the lavatory. Again, Larry Carlisle sees the besheeted figure exit the lavatory minutes before the editors do, because on their screens still *nothing has happened yet*; on their screens Kelly Simpson is still alive! I applaud you, Ms Hennessy, you designed the process so that Larry Carlisle's story concurred exactly with what was seen in the monitoring bunker. It was only the timings that you could not fix.'

Once more there were murmurs of appreciation in the studio.

'Now you run, back through the living area and into the boys' bedroom,' Coleridge said, his voice rising, 'pausing only to take the sheet you have been using to cover yourself and quickly wipe it round all of the boys' beds in order that a confusion of skin cells and other DNA matter will be present on it. Perhaps you wore gloves and a hair scarf? I don't know, since at the time I was too stupid to consider the possibility of testing for anyone other than the people who had been in the sweatbox.'

There were cries of 'No!' at this. Coleridge was the hero of the hour and the audience would not hear a word said against him, even by himself.

'You go back into the corridor,' Coleridge continued, 'you run through the tunnel, hide your coverall and arrive back in the monitoring bunker just in time to see *your identical* version of the murder take place on screen. You have created the perfect alibi: you're sitting safely and prominently with your editors when the murder takes place, so nobody could suspect you. The murder, like everything that happens on these so-called "reality" programmes, was built in the edit, it was nothing more than television "reality".' Coleridge paused momentarily for breath. He knew that shortly he must bring on his ghost.

'All that remained for you to do then, Ms Hennessy, was to switch your viewing monitors back from showing your video to the genuine reality of the live camera feed. This, I imagine, was a big test. Was Fogarty ready with his altered time codes? Had you placed the sheet on Kelly's body *exactly* as it was in your Shepperton video? If you had, then the switchover would be smooth. If you hadn't, there would be a jump of position. Once more I congratulate you, Ms Hennessy. I've watched the tape many times and even now I'm only half sure I can tell where you make the switch, and of course you never imagined that anybody would be looking for such a thing.'

'That's because there's nothing to look for. There was no switch, you *utter cunt*! I didn't kill her and you know it. You've made this up because you're too fucking thick to work out which one of those sad bastards standing beside you actually did it!'

Editors worldwide taking live sound and vision from Peeping Tom struggled to activate their bleeper machines.They all missed it; they had been too absorbed in what Coleridge was saying. Geraldine's string of obscenities went out to the world, a genuine moment of reality TV.

Coleridge did not look at Geraldine. He looked past her to the back of the studio, where once more Hooper silently gave him the thumbs-up. He knew that the time had come to introduce Banquo's ghost to the feast.

'Ah, but Ms Hennessy,' Coleridge said, 'I do not make these accusations lightly. I have proof, you see, because I have the evidence of your *other murders*.'

'What!'

'Let them shake their gory locks at you, Ms Hennessy! Let them point their bloody fingers.'

'What the *fuck* are you talking about, you silly old cunt!' said Geraldine.

A slightly bashful look flickered across Coleridge's face. 'Perhaps I have been slightly indulgent in my language. I should of course say your other murder *preconstructions*! Because you see, Ms Hennessy, it occurred to me that you could not possibly have known who it was who would leave the sweatbox in order to go to the toilet that night. It was a virtual certainty that *somebody* would, of course, and it was on that assumption that your whole murder plan was based. But you could not know *who*. I reasoned therefore that for your plan to work you would need to have recorded your scenario featuring not just poor Kelly but at the very least all of the other girls, so that when a girl, *any* of the girls, emerged and headed for the lavatory, you could activate the appropriate tape and go and kill her. That is perhaps the saddest aspect of this investigation. I have found many possible motives for killing Kelly, but not one of them is remotely relevant, because she died by *pure chance*. She was murdered simply because she was the *second* girl to go to the toilet. Ah! I hear you say. Second? Why second? Surely Sally went to the lavatory at the very beginning of the evening? Why was she not murdered? I shall tell you why: because since entering the house Sally had *dyed and cut her hair*! Sally's dark mohican had become no more than a red tuft, a fact which definitely saved her life, for had you not altered your looks, Sally, then *you*, not Kelly, would have died, and your murder would have looked like this!'

And with a nod and a wave which quite frankly he enjoyed, Coleridge gestured to the technicians in the editing box that he was ready.

Pru, who had been acting under instructions from Trisha, pressed the cue button which she had hastily marked 'Sally'. And to the astonishment of the entire world the naked figure of Sally, but Sally with her old mohican haircut, could be seen entering the toilet, or at least it easily *could* be Sally. Being a high, overhead shot, all that could really be seen were flashes of bare female limb, in this case tattooed, and of course the distinctive top of the head. The girl who could be Sally then sat on the toilet, put her head in her hands and was murdered by the same person in the sheet in exactly the same way that Kelly had been.

'Oh my God,' the real Sally murmured, suddenly aware of how close she had come to death.

Now the screen flickered and a second video was shown. This time it was the bald pate of Moon that was viewed from overhead entering the toilet. Again the sheeted figure stole across the living area, took up the knife and acted out the murder.

'Fookin' hell!' Moon shrieked. 'Are you saying that if I'd gone for a piss . . . ?'

'Indeed I am, miss,' Coleridge replied. 'Indeed I am. Interesting, isn't it, how Geraldine Hennessy selected women with such particular heads of hair, or in your case, Moon, lack of it.'

Now the distinctive raven hair of Dervla was seen entering the toilet and, of course, the story was the same.

Finally, to everybody's surprise, the beaded ringlets of Layla appeared, and once more the murder was enacted.

'Oh yes, Layla was there too,' said Coleridge, 'Layla with her blond beaded braids. For how could Geraldine Hennessy have known before the series began who it was that would be evicted?'

Again there was applause.

'All those girls were played by *you*, Ms Hennessy,' Coleridge shouted, pointing his finger at Geraldine, who was now beginning to look rather worried, 'as I have no doubt the digital enhancement of the tapes will prove!'

'I told that fucking swine Fogarty to burn those tapes!' Geraldine shrieked.

Banquo's ghost had done its work.

Geraldine knew that the game was up. Further deception was pointless. Coleridge had her tapes.

Except, of course, he didn't have them, because he had tricked her.

Fogarty had burnt the tapes, as he was currently trying to tell her, shouting at the soundproofed walls of the little viewing gallery into which Trisha had taken him, from where he had watched the whole thing on a monitor.

'I did burn the tapes! I did, you silly cow!' he shouted at the screen, tears of terror welling up in his eyes. 'He's tricked you. He made those tapes himself.'

'I made them, actually,' Trisha told Fogarty rather proudly. 'Me and Sergeant Hooper out at Shepperton this afternoon. Hell of a rush to get back . . . I hated wearing that bald wig – it really pulls at your hair when you take it off.'

Trisha had had a good day. It had meant being naked in front of Sergeant Hooper, of course, but in fact this had brought about a happy and unexpected result. Hooper had been much taken with Trisha naked and had instantly asked her to go out with him.

'Sorry, sarge. I'm gay,' she replied and so finally she said it and she had felt much better ever since.

Down on the studio floor Coleridge arrested Geraldine in front of hundreds of millions of people. Finest hours rarely get any finer.

'So what if I did kill her?' Geraldine shrieked. 'She got what she wanted, didn't she? She got her fame! That's all any of them wanted. They're desperate, all of them. They probably would have gone through with it even if they'd known what I was planning, the *pathetic cunts*! Ten to one chance of dying, nine to ten chance of worldwide fame? They'd have grabbed it! That was my only mistake! I should have got their fucking permission.'

380

DAY SIXTY-THREE. 10.30 p.m.

Because of Coleridge's moment of theatre, the final eviction show overran by half an hour, and half an hour after that, exactly one hour late, owing to his forgetting that the clocks had gone forward, Woggle blew up the house.

'Ha ha, you witches and you warlocks, how about that?' Woggle shouted, emerging from his escape tunnel as the last bits of brick and wood descended. Woggle had planned for this to be the crowning moment of the eviction show, the moment when he, Woggle, showed his contempt for the lot of them and upstaged all their petty egos by destroying the house at the very apex of Peeping Tom's party. However, because of his error, most of his hoped-for audience were making their way to their cars when the bomb went off.

Geraldine, the principal target of his revenge, did not see it at all because she was in the back of a sealed police van on her way into custody.

Coleridge saw it, though, and judged it a good effort and, on the whole, justified. However, this did not stop him from arresting Woggle for jumping bail.

DAY SIXTY-THREE. 11.00 p.m.

When Coleridge got home he was delighted to find that his wife had watched it all.

'Very theatrical, dear, not like you at all.'

'I had to do something, didn't I? I had no proof. I needed to trick her into a public confession and to do it tonight. That was all.'

'Yes, well, you did very well. Very very well indeed, and I'm just glad we don't have to watch any more of that appalling programme. Oh, by the way, someone

381

called Glyn phoned, from the am-dram society. He said he'd been meaning to phone for ages. He was terribly complimentary about your audition, said that you had done a brilliant reading, which apparently blew him away, and that on reflection he wants you to play the lead after all.'

Coleridge felt a thrill of eager anticipation. The lead! He was to give the world his Macbeth after all. Of course Coleridge wasn't stupid. He knew that he had only got the part because he had been on television. But why not? If everybody else could play the game, why couldn't he? Fame, it seemed, *did* have its uses.

THE END

BLAST FROM THE PAST
Ben Elton

It's 2.15 a.m., you're in bed alone and the phone wakes you. As you wake, in the tiny moment between sleep and consciousness, you know already that something is wrong. Only someone bad would ring at such an hour. Or someone good with bad news, which would probably be worse. You lie in the darkness and wait for the answer machine to kick in. And then you hear the one voice in the world you least expect . . . your very own Blast from the Past.

'ONLY BEN ELTON COULD COMBINE UNCOMFORTABLE QUESTIONS ABOUT GENDER POLITICS WITH A GRIPPING, PAGE-TURNING NARRATIVE AND JOKES THAT MAKE YOU LAUGH OUT LOUD'
Tony Parsons

0 552 99833 8

INCONCEIVABLE
Ben Elton

Lucy desperately wants a baby. Sam wants to write a hit movie. The problem is that both efforts seem to be unfruitful. And given that the average IVF cycle has about a one in five chance of going into full production, Lucy's chances of getting what she wants are considerably better than Sam's. What Sam and Lucy are about to go through is absolutely inconceivable. The question is, can their love survive?

'THIS IS ELTON AT HIS BEST – MATURE, HUMANE, AND STILL A LAUGH A MINUTE. AT LEAST'
Daily Telegraph

0 552 14698 6

BLACK SWAN

The war on drugs has been lost. The simple fact is that
the whole world is rapidly becoming one vast criminal
network. From pop stars and royal princes to crack whores
and street kids, from the Groucho Club toilets to the poppy
fields of Afghanistan, we are all partners in crime.

High Society is a story about Britain today, a criminal
nation in which everybody is either breaking the law or
knows people who do. It takes the reader on a hilarious,
heartbreaking and terrifying journey through the
kaleidoscope world that the law has created and from
which the law offers no protection.

PUBLISHED IN NOVEMBER 2002 BY BANTAM PRESS